PRAISE FOR *MAN ON THE RUN*

"One part heist movie, one part psychological thriller, three parts great character and blend. Salzberg's superb *Man on the Run* will keep your head spinning from the first page to the last."

—Reed Farrel Coleman

"Smart, sly and compelling, with a fascinating main character—the very definition of intelligent suspense."

—Lee Child

"*Man on the Run* grips you from the opening page and doesn't let go. The plot will leave you breathless with anticipation as a master burglar and a crime podcaster try to outwit and outmaneuver each other before an outrageous heist. There's nothing better than smart characters, with smart dialogue, going head-to-head. You won't want to miss a twist or turn."

—Michael Wiley, Shamus Award-winning author
of the Sam Kelson mysteries

"Francis Hoyt, Charles Salzberg's brilliant burglar anti-hero from *Second Story Man*, is back on the prowl in *Man on the Run*. Old-school crime meets the podcast age as Hoyt tangles with a true-crime reporter as well as fellow felons and the law. Like his hero, Salzberg is a total pro who always brings it home."

—Wallace Stroby, author of *Heaven's a Lie*

"Charles Salzberg is a genius at not only crafting a helluva page-turner of a heist novel, but he also manages to make the reader care about Francis Hoyt, master burglar and pathological narcissist. Hoyt is the man on the run, and the story of how he eludes the law, the mob, and a retired cop who has become his personal nemesis packs a solid punch and leaves you rooting for the guy who'd steal your family jewels without breaking a sweat."

—James R. Benn, author of
the Billy Boyle World War II mystery series

"When it comes to Charles Salzberg's work, you can expect a hard-edged story, crisp dialogue, and memorable characters. This is certainly true—and then some!—in his latest, *Man on the Run*. Featuring master burglar Francis Hoyt, a tough and intelligent criminal who can't seem to turn down tempting criminal scores, despite the inherent danger, *Man on the Run* features a true-crime podcast host, a criminal fence, and an investigator hot on the trail of Francis Hoyt as his most challenging and dangerous burglary comes into play. Very much recommended."

—Brendan DuBois, award-winning and
New York Times bestselling author

"It's a battle of wits and nerves as a cop, a robber, and a journalist dance around one another, weaving a tapestry of deceit and suspense. Salzberg's dialogue flows like water until it finds truth in this most entertaining read."

—Matt Goldman, *New York Times* bestselling author

MAN ON THE RUN

BOOKS BY CHARLES SALZBERG

Henry Swann Mystery Series
Swann's Last Song
Swann Dives In
Swann's Lake of Despair
Swann's Way Out
Swann's Down

Stand Alone Novels
Devil in the Hole
Second Story Man
Canary in the Coal Mine
Man on the Run

Novella
Triple Shot (Twist of Fate)
Three Strikes (The Maybrick Affair)
Third Degree (The Fifth Column)

Non-Fiction
On a Clear Day They Could See
Seventh Place: Baseball's Worst Teams
From Set Shot to Slam Dunk: The Glory Days
of Basketball in the Words of Those Who Played It

CHARLES SALZBERG

MAN ON THE RUN

Down & Out Books
3959 Van Dyke Road, Suite 265
Lutz, FL 33558
DownAndOutBooks.com

Cover design by Margo Nauert

ISBN: 1-64396-307-4
ISBN-13: 978-1-64396-307-5

"Don't look back. Something might be gaining on you."
—Satchel Paige

"I do perceive here a dividing duty."
—William Shakespeare, *Othello*

Now

"The desire to make off with the substance of others is the foremost—the most legitimate—passion nature has bred into us and, without doubt, the most agreeable one."
—Marquis de Sade

1

Francis

I ambush her as she's coming out of Starbucks, a mega-size coffee cup in one hand, her phone in the other.

"Know who I am?" I say.

She's confused. Or embarrassed. Like when you have no idea who someone is but you don't admit it because you think you should.

"Noooo. I don't think so," she says, wrinkling her brow and cocking her head, like she's giving it serious thought. "Should I? Have we met before?" she adds, shifting her weight to her back foot in an unconscious move to put a little distance between us.

This chick doesn't know me yet, but she will.

It's early Sunday morning. A typical late spring day in L.A. West Hollywood. The temp's hovering in the mid-seventies. This won't hold for long. We're in the middle of a heatwave and they're predicting the low nineties by mid-afternoon. Above us, there's that familiar low-hanging ceiling of grey cloud-cover they say will burn off by noon. They swear it always does. They even have a name for it. The June Gloom. Maybe all months should come with a warning label. I mean, life's already full of enough surprises, right?

Other than a few people out for an early run, or picking up breakfast, the sidewalk is empty. Except for the two of us.

She looks like she's in her mid to late twenties. But I know she's older than that. Closer to thirty-five. She isn't as pretty as I'd imagined. It's probably the voice that throws me off. Soft. Sweet. Seductive. A sexy, midnight radio voice. Or one of those sex-line phone voices. The kind of voice that makes promises without actually promising anything. And any promises made she has no intention of keeping. Not that she's a dog. Not by a long shot. It's just that she isn't going to win any beauty contests. Not here. Not in L.A., where good-looking chicks fall from palm trees like coconuts. Third, fourth runner-up, maybe. First place? Not a chance. Her looks don't quite fit with her voice. Still, there's something very sexy about her. Not hard-on sexy. But sexy enough so you can't help but wonder what she looks like on the beach in a bikini.

But it's more than just the voice. Maybe it's the short, blonde hair, which gives her a pixie look. Maybe it's the face. A mishmash of sharp angles. A nose that looks like it's been broken—if she were a guy you might guess in a barroom brawl—tilting slightly to one side. Like that Ellen Barkin chick. Her skin is lightly tanned and smooth. She has a slight overbite. High cheekbones. Makes me think of those Picasso paintings. But in a good way. Maybe it's the tight, faded black jeans, stylishly frayed just below the knees. Or the sky-blue Rolling Stones T-shirt with the image of a giant red tongue unfurled. Maybe it's because she isn't wearing a bra. Maybe it's because she's confident enough to wear no make-up to cover up the freckles scattered haphazardly across her cheeks and nose. Do not, under any circumstances, underestimate confidence. It's a definite turn-on.

Whatever it is, it works.

This isn't a pick-up. Or a stick-up. This is business. More than business, actually. Curiosity. No. More than that. Self-preservation. But there's always that promise, like her voice, that it might turn into something else.

She doesn't recognize me because we've never met. But recently our lives have unexpectedly intertwined. Her doing, not mine.

"Trust me. If you'd have met me, you wouldn't forget me."

"Really? Why's that?" she asks, cocking her head to the other side, as she slowly turns her coffee cup away from me. I know why she's doing it and I'm impressed. She's got a quick mind. The barista has scribbled her name on it in black magic marker. This is the kind of information, assuming I don't already have it, she would not want me to have.

I'm starting to make her nervous. I can see it in her eyes. They swivel wildly in their sockets like she's some kind of whacky cartoon figure. She's a couple, three inches taller than I, but that doesn't give her the kind of advantage height sometimes offers. I should know. I'm small of stature. I claim five-four, but I might be lying. Or exaggerating. Take your pick. It's not a handicap. Never has been. It works for me. Always has. It's been a long time since anyone's tried to take advantage of me because of my size. A long, fucking time.

"Maybe it's the baseball cap. It kinda hides your face," she says, straining to figure me out. Am I harmless? Is she in danger? Should she dial 9-1-1? Should she turn tail and head back into the relative safety of Starbucks?

I take off the hat in one swift, flowing motion and wave it across my body. The only thing missing is my bending forward in a bow. Like the Japs do.

"Better?"

She shakes her head. I put the hat back on.

"Maybe the sunglasses?" she says.

"Let's see," I say, as I slip them off.

I know what she's doing. Making sure she gets a good look at me. Taking a mental snapshot of my face. Just in case later she has to describe me to the cops. It should make me feel like a specimen under glass, but it doesn't. Actually, I'm enjoying the attention. Besides, by the time we're finished she'll know who I am and then she won't have to describe me to anyone.

Even after all this she's still baffled. I put my sunglasses back on and adjust my cap so it angles down slightly over my forehead.

It's almost imperceptible, but she's slowly inching away from me. Like she's getting ready to bolt. She has that thin, athletic build of a runner. We have that in common. Maybe, if we get to know each other, we'll run together. But no matter how fast she might be, I'll leave her in the dust. Maybe it's because you might say I run for a living. Maybe it's because I'm always in excellent shape. Especially for someone flirting with his mid-forties. But it's not just that. It's more like I don't take losing very well. I never hold back. That's the real reason I never lose. Ever.

Her eyes dart back and forth as she slowly dips her right hand, the one holding her cell, into the black leather satchel dangling from her shoulder. Maybe she thinks I can't see what she's doing. She'd be wrong. I've trained myself to note every detail, every nuance. When I walk into a room, any room, I immediately know two things: where the exit is and exactly where everyone is standing. I'm a fucking living, breathing motion detector. It's one of the things that makes me as good as I am at what I do. I doubt she has a serious weapon in there. Maybe pepper spray. Maybe a set of keys she's been taught to use as a weapon in one of those self-defense classes for women. The key chain held tight in your fist. The keys poking out between your index and forefinger. A sudden thrust to an eye. If your aim is good, you can do some serious damage.

But neither of these things will do her any good. I'm much too quick. I'll have hold of her wrist before she gets her hand out of her bag.

I smile, hoping this will lighten the mood. I don't want her to think I'm a predator and she's the prey.

Maybe she is. Maybe I am. But I don't want her to think so. Not yet.

"I'm a memorable guy," I say, smiling. I've been told I've got a killer smile. They say it makes me look very approachable. This can be a good thing. A very good thing. I inject a dramatic pause. "What's that expression? The Most Unforgettable Character

You've Ever Met? That would be me."

"You're starting to frighten me a little," she says, glancing over my left shoulder, then my right. Looking to see if anyone else is around. In case she needs help. She even looks back into Starbucks to see if anyone might be coming out. Someone who might rescue her. Though she can't possibly know from what. Not yet.

Her right hand is frozen inside her purse. She isn't quite ready to commit herself. There's still time to defuse the situation.

"I'm not going to hurt you, if that's what you're afraid of," I say, raising my hands, palms out, midway to my chest.

"I'm not afraid," she says. Not very convincingly.

"Good. Because you haven't seen my scary face yet."

She starts to laugh, then realizes maybe I'm not trying to be funny. Hollywood is the land of weirdos and crackpots. She has no way of knowing I am not one of them.

"Then why are you acting so creepy?"

I shrug. "This is me, darlin'. It's just the way I am. But I swear, I really am harmless. You sure you don't know me?"

"Pretty sure," she says, hesitatingly, like she thinks maybe she should know me but still can't quite figure out why.

"Don't worry," I say with a wink. "You will."

2
Dakota

He looks nothing like I thought he would. I'm not sure what I expect, but this isn't it. First off, I'm surprised how tiny he is. It's like you have this urge to pick him up, dust him off and put him on the mantle above your fireplace. But when you look closer you see there's nothing dainty or frail about him. He's in perfect proportion. Dressed in a form-fitting black T-shirt and tight black jeans, just like mine. I can see he works out. No one gets a physique like that without putting in a lot of gym time. But he doesn't look like one of those greased-up dudes obsessed with bulking up, the ones I see when I work out, the ones who look like they live in the weight room, the ones who hang out on the Venice beach, the ones who can't pass a mirror or a window without checking their reflection and flexing a muscle. These are the guys who don't care if you see them admiring themselves. They want us to see them, envy them, and feel bad about ourselves because they care about their appearance and we obviously don't. And then there's their counterparts, the women clad in neon-colored Spandex, who never leave the house without makeup.

Later, when I give it some thought, after I realize who he is, it dawns on me he's built exactly how he should be to do what he does. He reminds me of those photographs I've seen of a bare-chested Houdini, wrapped in chains, just before he's going to be thrown into a trunk or a giant glass container of water. Short, well-muscled and handsome. In fact, after our encounter on my way home, it occurs to me that maybe I should start referring to him as the *Houdini of Housebreaking*. The man who can get in and out of anything, no matter how impossible it seems.

At first, I can't see his face because he's got a Dodger cap pulled down low and he's wearing a pair of those silver mirrored sunglasses. I'm not sure if he's presenting this way because he doesn't want to be recognized or because it's actually protection against the sun which, by the way, is still hidden behind the early morning, low-hanging cloud cover. He's fair-skinned, so maybe that's it. But I also wouldn't be surprised if it's all just part of the package. Man of Mystery, and all that jazz.

He's the kind of guy you look at twice if he passes you on the street. And not just because of his size. He's a handsome man. His chiseled face reminds me of Clint Eastwood—when you live in L.A. all your references are to actors and actresses. There's something very charismatic about him. I think it's probably because of how he holds himself. Very self-assured. Very confident. Cocky even. But not the self-absorbed, look-at-me-aren't-I-great kind of cocky. There's plenty of that here. L.A. is chockablock with puffed up, narcissistic actors who think they're God's gift. He's the kind of cocky who doesn't think he's better than you are. He knows it. There's a difference. A big difference. It's the difference between sexy and pathetic.

He's also got this palpable sense of danger thing about him. And it's not because I know who he is and what he's done. He's just like, like dangerous looking. And there's something else. It's his eyes. Intelligence. I'm not so sure about that thing they say about the eyes being the window to the soul, if there even is such a thing as a soul. But I do think they're a window to the brain. There's something going on behind those eyes, something that only adds to this sense of danger that surrounds him.

It's the kind of dangerous that attracts rather than repels.

Because, let's face it, we all know how we women feel about dangerous guys. My mom, in one of our few mother-daughter exchanges that didn't end in a screaming match, once said to me, "Dakota, I know when you're young you'll get involved with plenty of those 'bad boys,' and me warning you off them won't do a bit of good. I only hope by the time you're ready to settle down you've moved through that phase and wind up with one of the good ones."

I'm well over thirty now, but it appears I'm still not through that phase. I mean, if I sat down and listed the last three guys I was with they'd probably have one thing in common. And it wouldn't be a good thing. But there is progress. At least now I know one when I see one. Unfortunately, that doesn't mean I avoid them. It just means I recognize them when they're heading in my direction. The only difference now is I don't just *think* it might end badly, I *know* it will.

Maybe that's why I do what I'm doing now. Trying to build a new career. So, I don't have time to date. I don't have time for a relationship. That's why I'm still single. At least that's what I tell myself. What I tell my mother is something completely different. Every so often she'll let some passive-aggressive comment drop, wondering if she'll ever be a grandmother. That *every so often* has become more often lately. She doesn't even have to say it anymore. I can hear her voice in my head, especially when she calls when my birthday rolls around: "You know, Dakota, you're not getting any younger." I know. Believe me, I know. And when she launches into what seems to be her mantra, rather than get into a lengthy discussion with her that will only end with one of us hanging up the phone—that would be me—I just let it pass. Or I change the subject. It seems to work so far.

Maybe I'm doing what I'm doing now as a way to avoid commitment. I mean, what kind of guy am I going to meet in my new, chosen line of work. I'll have to bring this up with Angela at our next appointment. Of course, I say that, but our next scheduled session isn't until Thursday, and that's four days away, which is plenty of time for me to come up with other issues to discuss.

I've been doing my true crime podcast, *Prime Crime all the Time*, for almost a year now, and I have learned some life lessons. Maybe that's why I don't turn around and duck right back into *Starbucks* as soon as he approaches me. So long as I stand my ground and don't go anywhere with him, like I definitely wouldn't get into a car with him, I know I'll be fine. But I'll tell you this. If I thought he was just another Hollywood wannabe asshole trying to pick me up, I would have been out of there in a flash.

But without even knowing who he is—photos of him are scarce, and the ones I've found are old booking photos that make him look like one of those sleazy porn stars—I don't do that. Now, seeing who he is, I'm glad I didn't.

3
Dakota

He keeps me dangling. Like he's playing head games with me. I can see he's enjoying himself and I see a hint of something in his eyes I don't like. It's the same look I used to see in Johnny Murtaugh's eyes when he followed me around in fourth grade and teased me during recess. My mother made excuses for him. "He likes you, that's why he teases you, Dakota. That's how boys are. They don't know how to express their real feelings, so they tease. When I was a little girl, the boys would throw rocks at us. Well, not really rocks. More like pebbles, although they sure stung and left a nasty bruise if they hit you. It wasn't because they wanted to hurt us. It was because they wanted to get our attention and they didn't know how else to do it. It's their way of flirting, because they don't have the emotional vocabulary yet to tell us how they really feel, that they like us and they want us to like them."

At the time, I have no idea what "emotional vocabulary" means, nor do I think Johnny Murtaugh is flirting with me. My mother doesn't know Johnny the way I do. He is a fucking sadist. He smiles, all right, but behind that smile there is evil. Pure evil. He is just a rotten kid who likes being mean to girls. When I start planning this podcast of mine, it occurs to me I might come across Johnny one day while I'm looking for stories to do for the show. Maybe I'll find he's in prison for assault and battery. Or worse. Like a serial killer. Sure. I could see Johnny Murtaugh as a serial killer. I haven't come across him yet. But I won't be surprised if I do.

It's been a long time, but I think I see in his eyes the same thing I saw in Johnny's. He's not exactly pulling wings off flies or torturing cats, but he is enjoying this a little too much. At least that's the way it seems to me.

He smiles when he finally tells me his name. Like he's delivering the hilarious punchline to some elaborate joke. The next thing he says shocks me enough to send a chill down my spine. "I understand you're using me as a subject for one of your upcoming podcasts."

Ho-ly shit!

For a moment, I'm speechless. I mean, what am I supposed to say? This guy, his name's Francis Hoyt, would be a shoo-in for the Burglar's Hall of Fame, if there is one. He's the Babe Ruth of thieves. And in terms of notoriety, he's right up there with Jack "Murf the Surf" Murphy and Alan Kuhn, who broke into New York's American Museum of Natural History and waltzed away with a couple dozen precious gems, including the Star of India, the Eagle Diamond and the DeLong Star Ruby. The big difference is they didn't get away with their burglary, while Hoyt does. So far. It might seem like hyperbole, comparing him to legends like Ruth and Houdini, but from what I'm finding out from reading and from the few people I've interviewed so far—people who've crossed paths with him for some reason or another—it's no exaggeration. He really is *that* good.

After he drops this bombshell, he stands there with this shit-eating grin plastered across his face, like a kid who's just gotten away with eating all the Halloween candy in one sitting. All I can think of are the words from that Rolling Stones song, "Sympathy for the Devil." *Please allow me to introduce myself/I'm a man of wealth and taste/I've been around for a long, long year/Stole many a man's soul to waste.*

The first thought that goes through my head is, *Oh, what a coincidence.* But I quickly realize, *Girl, this is no coincidence. He knows exactly who you are and what you do.* He's stalking me, for God's sake. Who knows for how long? It's creepy, but I can't decide if I should be frightened or flattered. I'm sure I'll have the answer pretty soon.

At this point, after getting over my initial surprise and vague sense of danger, my reporter's instinct kicks in. There's a good chance I'll never get another opportunity like this, so why am I bantering back and forth with him? Why not take advantage of the situation? I'll admit, I'm confused. I don't think he's here to threaten me, to make me cease and desist. But if he isn't, why has he sought me out? Is it that maybe he wants to make sure his story is told his way? If that's it, it wouldn't surprise me. Early on in my research I learned he's a control freak. But maybe I can make this work for me. Maybe I can persuade him to talk to me. On-air would be great. What a coup! Even off the record for background would be good. Besides, once I get him to talk to me, letting him think he's in charge, I might be able to persuade him to be an active part of the project. So, I decide to take a shot. After all, what do I have to lose?

At first, I'm real nervous. My stomach is doing flip-flops. But after the initial shock wears off, after I realize he's not here to harm me, I'm surprisingly relaxed. Any fear I might have had has disappeared. I'm not surprised. I'm pretty tough. Why shouldn't I be? I grew up with three older brothers, all of them bigger than I. All of them jockeying for the alpha position. At some point, I had to figure out a way to defend myself. To let them know they couldn't push me around. At first, I did what came naturally. I tried being physical with them. But it didn't take long to realize that was never going to work. They didn't seem to have a problem hitting or wrestling with a girl half their size. So, I chose the verbal route—calling them every name in the book. Then the more passive-aggressive options presented themselves. Like screaming bloody murder until my mom came in, pried them off me, and then pronounced punishment while I stood there with a big, fat smile on my face.

Finally—enough with the games—I come right out and ask, "why are you here?"

"You want an existential answer?"

Obviously, from the look on my face, he knows I'm surprised he uses the word. And that he uses it properly. I hate that about me. Why should I automatically think someone like him is ignorant?

"I see," he says, with a smile on his face. "You think I'm some kind of uneducated idiot."

"It's not…"

"Sure, it is. You obviously know I barely made it out of high school."

"Technically, you didn't make it out of high school."

If he's surprised that I know that little factoid, he's not letting on.

He shrugs. "A technicality."

"What's that supposed to mean?"

"It means technically I didn't have enough credits to graduate. But that's because I didn't show up the last four or five months. Even if I had, they wouldn't have let me graduate."

"Why not?"

He smiles. "Because I didn't return a fucking textbook."

I laugh. I can't help it. I don't know if he's making this up, but the idea of someone like Francis Hoyt, a master burglar, not graduating high school because of a missing textbook is kind of ridiculous.

"A textbook? Did you steal it?"

He laughs. "You gotta be kidding. What the fuck reason would I have to steal a fucking textbook?"

"Defiance."

"You think that's the way I'd show defiance?" He shakes his head back and forth. "Lady, you don't know jack shit about me."

I'm hoping this will change, so I continue this ridiculous line of questioning, figuring the longer I keep him talking, the better the chance he'll sit for a proper interview.

"Why didn't you show up the last semester?"

He shrugs his shoulders and I see the muscles in his neck tighten. "I didn't see the point."

"The point, for most people, would be to graduate, get that certificate, and then maybe go on to college."

"You think everyone is college material?"

"Of course not. But..."

"I wasn't. I guess you could argue I wasn't high-school material, either. But let me give you a little tip, Dakota." He leans into me, real close, disturbingly close, like he's going to kiss me. One of those awkward first kisses where you don't know whether to turn your head or hope his aim is true. Of course, a kiss is not what he has in mind. He just wants to make a point. "Underestimate me at your peril," he whispers.

"That's the last thing I'd do, Francis," I say, using his first name for the first time. It feels both awkward and right. It's an old reporter's trick. Bond with the subject, so they'll think of you more as a friend than an interrogator. "But let's get back to my first question. What do you want from me?"

As soon as the words tumble from my mouth, I straighten up, hoping my body language doesn't reflect fear or uncertainty. I've been around bad guys long enough to know they can sense weakness a mile away. And once they sense it, they take advantage of it. That's not going to happen to me.

"It's more like what you want with me, isn't it?" he says. I know what he's trying to do. While I'm making a feeble attempt to bond, he's making sure I know he's in charge. The only way he can do this is to keep me off-balance, and he can do this by not giving me what I want.

"Are you going to keep being incredibly annoying by turning everything back on me as a question?"

"I don't know. Am I?" he says, with a smile.

I can't help myself. I'm smiling along with him. He's got a

sense of humor. That helps humanize him. Only time will tell if he deserves that description. Make no mistake, Francis Hoyt is a dangerous man. I know he doesn't have a history of violence, at least from anything I've managed to uncover so far, but I also know, just by looking into his eyes, that he's capable of it.

Usually, when I'm taken by surprise, when I'm off-balance, unsure of what's happening, I want to extricate myself from the situation as quickly as possible. Right now I'm not so anxious to end this, whatever it is. Meeting? Confrontation? Maybe, if I can somehow win Holt's confidence, I can get him to cooperate. Wouldn't that be incredible? I mean, an on-air interview with Francis Hoyt, notorious outlaw, wanted man, man on the run. Holy shit! That would really be something, wouldn't it? I can only dream how much publicity this will generate. The audience for the podcast will be over the moon. And when that happens, advertising will follow, and the podcast will not only be self-supporting, it'll finally allow me the freedom to do what I want when I want. And so, I try everything I can to keep him on the hook.

When I was a kid, before my parents divorced, my father, who obviously wanted a son rather than what he got, used to take me fishing with him. It was the one place he was patient with me, teaching me the ins and outs of becoming a successful fisherman. Not that I cared. I remember his advice for when I get a fish on the line: "Don't pull or yank it, Dakota. Just the opposite. Give the fish more line. Let him run with it, until he gets tuckered out, and then, just when he thinks he's free, that's when you start reeling him in."

I hated fishing. Maybe it's a guy thing. I never quite understood its allure. And yet I have to admit there are lessons to be learned.

Francis Hoyt is the fish and I'm the fisherman. Now that he's got my hook in his mouth, I'm not about to lose him by pulling back too early.

I put one hand on my hips, spread my feet apart, like I'm

anchoring myself to the sidewalk and say, as firmly as I can, "I'm not letting you leave until you tell me why you're stalking me."

He smiles, a crooked, cynical smile. I'm not quite sure how to interpret it other than at that moment it's indicating anything and everything but happiness. Mine or his.

"You won't let me?" he asks, raising an eyebrow. "How do you intend on stopping me? Oh, wait, maybe you think you can cry damsel in distress and someone will call the cops. And that I'll just stand here and wait patiently for them to arrive? Or maybe you know one of those martial arts. Karate? Judo? Kung fu? Krav maga? Or maybe you think if you turn on the tears, I'll give you what you want?"

"I have no intention of 'turning on the tears' as you put it, and I have no intention of trying to defend myself or calling the cops. I just want to know why you've gone out of your way to...meet me?"

"You think you know a lot about me, Dakota, so I figured I'd introduce myself and get to know you. And maybe, if we get along...?"

"How's it going so far?"

"Not bad. Let's cut to the chase. I understand you're doing a podcast on me."

"I'm *considering* doing a podcast on you."

I'm lying, of course. I'm not considering it, I've already committed to doing a six-part series focusing on the exploits of Francis Hoyt, also known as the Suppertime Bandit. But how does he know what I'm up to?

Suddenly, before I embarrass myself by asking, the light bulb goes on. Duh? Of course, he knows. I have an old friend who works for the entertainment section of the *L.A. Times* and a couple weeks ago she did a piece on the best true crime podcasts, and included mine, noting not only past episodes but also those we're planning in the future. Or maybe he got wind of it because of the digging I've been doing. Today, in the Age of Social Media there's no such thing as a secret.

It doesn't matter how he found out. The fact is, he knows. Now I'm wondering what he plans to do about it? About me? Will he try to shut me down? Will he cooperate? The only way I'll find out is to keep him talking.

"I'm guessing by now you think you're the world's best authority on me," he says, so casually I can't tell whether he's kidding.

"I wouldn't say that. I'm just beginning the process. Of course, if you'd like to help me out…"

"Whatever you think you know about me probably isn't true," he says, waving his hand in front of him like he's shooing away the truth.

"Fake news?"

He smiles. But this time it's different. This time, he doesn't look anywhere near as menacing as he did a few minutes ago. In fact, he's actually kind of cute when he smiles. I have to watch out for that. Whenever a guy smiles at me like that, it's trouble. Sometimes, I walk away. Sometimes I should, but I don't.

"You mean you've been misunderstood?" I say, realizing I'm being a little, well maybe more than a little, condescending.

"How long you been seeing a shrink?" he asks.

Good comeback, though I can't quite tell if he's serious or joking.

Whatever I'm doing appears to be working. He's engaged. But how long can I keep it up? Is it time to reel this fish in? Maybe I need to go to another trick in my bag. A trick that worked with the Albany cops when I was a beat reporter. I'd turn all girly on them. I decide to call on my paltry feminine wiles and see if they'll work on Francis Hoyt.

First, I relax my stance. I position my hands on my hips, which I thrust slightly forward. I move my legs closer together and lean forward. Not a lot. Just enough to show I'm not frightened of him. "Oh, that's just downright mean. And uncalled for," I say, with a sing-songy flirtatious lilt in my voice. "You know, I'd really love to sit down with you and get the real story."

"What makes you think I want you or anyone else to have the *real* story?"

I look into his eyes and I could swear they've turned a darker color.

"Maybe there isn't a 'real' story," he says.

"Oh, Francis," I say as casually as possible. As if we're two old friends who've accidently met on the street. "You know that old saw about three sides to every story."

"So, you think you've got my story and yours and now you're looking for the truth?"

I smile. Yet another attempt at disarming him. "Of course. That's my job."

"And you think I want to talk to *you* about the truth?

"Oh, come on. You took the trouble to track me down. I know there's a reason. Here we are in broad daylight, well, almost broad daylight as soon as the morning fog burns off, and you're taking the time to chat with me."

"Fog or smog?" he says, glancing up at the sky.

"They used to call it smog when I was growing up, but now that we've become environmentally enlightened, it's fog. It's a tomato, tuh-mah-toh, potato, puh-tah-toh kind of thing, I think."

"And you think me being here means *what*?"

"It means you're dying to tell me your story. If not, why else would you be here?"

He glares at me, but doesn't say anything. I don't know if he's angry with me for asking or he's considering it. Whatever it is, he doesn't make a move to walk away. Nor does he threaten me to drop the podcast.

Conversation abhors a vacuum, at least when I'm around, so I dive back in.

"Under normal circumstances, someone like you might be trying to persuade someone like me not to do your story. First, you'd ask nicely. And then, if I didn't agree, you'd ask not-so-nicely. Maybe you'd even threaten me."

"And what would that sound like? The threat, not the nice part."

I drop my voice, so it's deep. "Drop the damn story or else?"

He laughs. "Or else what?"

"I guess that would be up to you."

"I don't threaten women."

"You mean you treat them bad without warning them?"

Yes. I know. I might be pushing the envelope a little. But something tells me this guy appreciates a little sass. Suddenly, the idea of his cooperating with me doesn't seem so far-fetched.

"What do you *think* you know about how I treat women?"

I smile, using another weapon in my vast arsenal. My mother used to hate when she'd criticize me about something and I'd just stand there and smile back at her. "Dakota," she'd say, "I just hate it when you smile like that. It's soooo *sinister*. It's like that girl in the *Bad Seed* movie." I loved that movie. I discovered it on Turner Classics when I was fourteen and I kept watching it over and over again. I'm glad my mom didn't find out because if she had, I'm sure she would have immediately shipped me out to a funny farm or, even worse, one of those wilderness "scared straight" operations.

"Like what?" I'd say, knowing exactly what she means but relishing the opportunity to get under her skin. I know. I know. Like mother like daughter. It's inevitable. We become the thing we hate most.

"I never know what you're thinking when you smile like that, but I know it's nothing good."

Only much later, when I'm an adult, do I realize this is the very definition of passive-aggressive behavior. Men show their aggression openly and aggressively, while we have to settle for showing it passively. Men do, women think.

"You think you're tough, don't you?" he says.

I thrust a hip forward, striking what I think is an especially feminine pose. But I'm probably spoiling the effect when I realize I'm also clenching my fists by my sides. "Little, old me?

Tough? Why no, I'm not tough at all. I'm a cream puff."

"You're salivating, aren't you, Dakota? What a coup for your little podcast if you get yourself an interview with the one and only Francis Hoyt."

"You're saying you'd go on my show?"

"Did you hear me say that?"

"Not in those exact words, but you intimated…"

"When you hear those exact words, let me know. In the meantime, let's just say this is an exploratory meeting."

"Meaning?"

"Meaning, I meet you and if I like you then maybe I sit down with you, find out what you're all about. Find out what you expect of me."

Oh, my God! He's going to do it!

"I've got a proposition for you," he says.

"What kind of proposition?" I ask tentatively, suddenly remembering he's not one of my brothers. I'm standing here out on the sidewalk in front of Starbucks talking to a very dangerous man. I don't know exactly how dangerous, but I know someone who's lived the life he has is no choirboy. He's probably a regular on those Crime Stopper shows.

"You might try getting your mind out of the gutter. It's not the kind of proposition you're thinking about."

He grins. He knows now he's the one who has *me* on the line.

"You have no idea what I'm thinking about. But okay, I'm all ears. What's this offer?"

"Not yet."

"'Not yet?' What's that supposed to mean?"

"It means I'm not going to discuss it with you out here on the street. We're going to meet in more quiet surroundings and then we'll talk about it."

I don't mean to, but I laugh in his face. "You really think I'm going to meet you somewhere private? Like maybe out in the desert? Or up in the hills? The old Spahn Ranch, perhaps? No, thanks. I don't think I want to become one of those bleached-out skeletons some kid finds in a ravine."

"I'm not Jack the Ripper, Dakota," he says.

I don't know that. The man standing in front of me could be anyone. Most guys aren't that complicated. You can pretty much figure them out from the get-go. But Hoyt is different. He's complicated. There are layers upon layers. He can be charming. He can be threatening. He can be mysterious. He can be obvious. He can be inscrutable. He can be maddening. He can be those things and I'll bet more. Right now, he's leaning toward charming. He is whatever he has to be at any particular moment.

"I was thinking something more along the lines of a restaurant. In the middle of the day. Outside, if you like. In plain view. And I'll even let you pat me down before we're seated."

I know that won't be necessary. In all my research, I've never come across anything that would make me think he's ever used a weapon or is armed. Of course, there are other ways of eliminating someone. Besides, things can change. People can change. Especially, if you're on the run as Hoyt has been for over a year now.

"Well, I guess we could do that... And then you'd let me interview you on-air?"

"You know what they say."

"What's that?"

"Miracles can happen."

A chill runs up my spine and settles in my neck. It's not what he says, it's the way he says it. Suddenly, I realize this is no game for him. This man in front of me is dangerous. He's a master manipulator who loves playing mind games. If this goes any further, and it looks like it might, (yay!), I'm going to have to be very careful. There is this incredibly scary, super-strong gravitational pull toward him. I can see why he's so successful as a thief. It's not only because he's smart and he's physically fit. Sure, there's that. But there's more. This little guy knows how to play the game. He knows how to get what he wants. At this point, I have no idea what that is, which is even more reason to admit to myself just how dangerous he is.

"After we meet, if I like you enough, maybe I'll cooperate with you and go on your little podcast. You'd like that, wouldn't you? I mean, how many of the people you've profiled or crimes you've told your listeners about—that is, if you actually have any listeners…"

I don't let myself be offended. That's exactly what he wants. He wants to get a rise out of me. Not this time, Buster.

He gives me the name of this place in Venice Beach. The Rose Café. It's not far off the boardwalk. Very upscale but very casual. They've got a nice outdoor space. I've been there before, but not with a wanted man.

"Tomorrow at one," he says.

He doesn't wait for my answer. He doesn't need one. He just turns and walks away and as he disappears around a corner, I wonder, what the heck have I got myself into?

Then

"What's past is prologue."
—William Shakespeare, *The Tempest*

1

Francis

Nothing is planned. It just happens.

When opportunity knocks, you answer. Otherwise, it's an opportunity squandered. An opportunity lost. An opportunity that will most likely never come again.

In my line of work, you have to be ready for anything and everything. Instinct. Reflex. Call it what you want. It's not something you learn. It's not something you turn on and off. You don't control it. It controls you.

Maybe it comes from when you're a kid and your old man comes home in the middle of the night and he's fucking loaded. And when he's like that, you can never be sure what to expect. You know odds are pretty good he's gonna come home plastered—because why should this night be different from any other night? But you don't know what kind of drunk. Is it the passing-out-on-the-couch drunk? Is it the puking-onto-the-carpet drunk? Is it the mean-mother-fucker drunk where he's looking to beat the shit out of someone, anyone, because he's goddamn mad at the world? If it's that kind of drunk, the worst kind, then all you can do is try to stay the hell out of his way. If you're forewarned, you try to make yourself scarce. Blend into the woodwork. But if he's really pissed, he'll find you. And when he does, it'll be worse. He'll punch the hell out of you until his arms get tired or he loses interest. When he's like that all you can hope for is he finds someone that isn't you. Someone else to punch. Or kick. Or slap around. But as you get older, and bigger and stronger, he knows you're gonna make him work for it. Only he doesn't like to work. For anything. Ever. Even though he's got a wife and two kids to feed. So, he goes through the motions. He picks up any kind of work he can find. But it's never enough. What little money he makes he blows on cheap rot-gut and non-filtered Camels, which offers the only hope you have: that he'll fucking get cancer and die. And when he doesn't have enough dough for booze and cancer sticks, that doesn't stop him. You know you'd better hide the mouthwash or anything else with alcohol in it. And if you got any money, make sure you hide it well.

Sometimes, when he's too fucking drunk to beat the crap out of you, he'll find other ways to make you pay. Like calling you a "fucking, no-good little bastard." Or "a worthless piece of shit." It's all white noise, except that the damage is already done because you can't help believing that's exactly who and what you are. You don't know it then, but later you realize you spend most of your life trying to prove he's wrong. That's why you work so hard to be the best at something.

Then, just like one of those passing summer storms, it's over. Like it never happened. Only it did. And you know, just like you know the sun's gonna come up every morning from the same direction, it's gonna happen again. You just don't know when. The tide rolls in, the tide rolls out. It's not like it misses a day every now and then. All you can hope is you're not around when it happens again.

That's why you get the hell out of Dodge the first time you can. And it's why you never come back.

With my arraignment coming up in a week, I have Angie bring me a suit. I tell her money's no object. Because I'm small, maybe she has to shop in the boy's department, or maybe there's a special shop for the well-dressed jockey. Maybe it's called *The Well-Dressed Jockey Shop*. I have to hand it to her, she's got good taste. Dark blue Brioni suit. Powder blue button-down Brooks Brothers shirt. Red tie, because Angie claims that's the power color. Only she's wrong. The real power color is black. Black like the night. So black, you become invisible. As black as your heart, if you have one.

An hour before my court appearance, I put on the Brioni. Everything fits perfect. Suddenly, I'm not me anymore. I'm someone else. Because I'm dressed like the *other,* I am the *other.* For that brief moment in time, I blend in. I am fucking invisible. No wonder no one gives me a second look. Why should they? I look and act like I belong. I am them and they are me.

I look like I belong in a courthouse. Not a defendant, but someone else. A lawyer. A court reporter. A witness. A judge. Dress the part, and you are the part.

I tell my court-appointed chaperone I gotta use the can. He leads me there, then sticks his head in. No windows. The only way in or out is the door we're standing in front of. He takes the cuffs off. He steps outside. I finish my business and come out that door.

Only the cop who's supposed to be escorting me isn't waiting for me in front. Instead, he's twenty-five feet down the hall, bending over the water fountain.

Suddenly, the world stands still. Everyone is frozen in place. Except me. All it takes is a split second and I'm on the move. I don't think about it. I see an opportunity. I take it. But I don't run. I walk slowly, like I have all the time in the world. I walk in the opposite direction from the water fountain. Toward the front entrance of the courthouse. I walk like no one can see me. Like I'm invisible. Because, for that one glorious moment in time, that's exactly what I am. Invisible.

I keep waiting to hear a booming voice coming from behind me. "Stop! Hands in the air. Turn the fuck around!"

When that voice comes, will I run? Or will I stop in my

tracks, throw up my hands and wait for him to put his hand on my shoulder and snap the cuffs back on?

I won't find out because that moment never comes. And so, I keep walking. At a normal pace. I look straight ahead. I smile at anyone who passes me. I walk until I get to the revolving door. I step into it. I push it forward until I'm outside. I walk down the steps. I walk out onto the sidewalk. The heat from the mid-day July sun, almost directly above me, beats down. It's a feeling I haven't had in almost a week. It's the feeling of freedom.

I make a quick decision to turn left. I don't know why. I just do it. Instinct? Divine inspiration? Whatever it is, it turns out to be the right choice. It's lunchtime and soon I'm on a sidewalk crowded with pedestrians going to or coming back from lunch. This is the crowd I'm part of, the lunchtime crowd. I'm not sure where I'm going. But wherever it is, I know it's not here.

Here is somewhere I'll never be again.

This happens more than a year ago. I am different now. Everything is different now. Since that day, I am a man on the run.

2

Francis

Kenny Staples reminds me of that dude hanging from the clock in one of those old-timey, silent movies. He's the guy desperately clinging to the edge of the cliff. You know it's just a matter of time before he tumbles into the abyss. You just don't know when.

Kenny's a leech. A bug smashed against my windshield. A barnacle that attaches itself to an idle ship. You don't know where he came from. You don't know how he got here. You don't know where he's going. You don't even know why he's here. He just *is*. Guys like Staples have no reason to exist other than to serve my needs. He's someone I can't trust. Someone I shouldn't trust. And yet, at some point when you least expect it, guys like Kenny Staples come in handy.

I meet Staples when I'm doing time upstate. As soon as he finds out who I am, he gloms onto me, and I can't shake him. Like he's my fucking shadow. Anywhere I go, he goes. He follows me around like he's one of those baby ducks and I'm his mama. And there's nothing I can do to get that fucking piece of gum off my shoe. Every time I fucking turn around there's Kenny Staples in my face, his tongue hanging out, panting like a dog, waiting for me to toss him a fucking bone. He might seem harmless, but if you don't keep an eye on the Kenny Staples of the world, they can fuck you good. If he was a package, you'd slap a *Handle with Care* sticker on his ass. Because Staples is a hand-grenade with the pin sticking half-way out. And when that fucker explodes, no matter where you are, you're bound to take a couple chunks of shrapnel. So, the last thing you wanna do is get too close or turn your back on the Kenny Staples of the world.

When I meet him, Kenny's in for armed robbery. Second offense. One more and he'll be a three-timer and never see the light of day. Like most guys in the joint, Staples isn't smart enough to get away with shit. The first time he's pinched it's for holding up a gas station. The damn fool doesn't bother to hide his face. So, when they catch him looking straight into the fucking camera, like he's auditioning for some crappy reality show, they don't have any trouble tracking him down. Might as well leave a fucking calling card, Kenny. Why the fuck doesn't he just grab the fucking purse and run? Does he really have to smack her, which adds assault and battery to the ticket? It's why I never carry a weapon or anything that could even be mistaken for a weapon. Kenny's second offense is for mugging an old lady. Why's he fucking around with two-bit shit like that in the first place? The answer's easy: it's because he's Kenny Staples. I mean, how much cash could the old bitch have? When he tells me about it, he claims he was dead broke and when he sees her withdraw a fistful of cash from the ATM he panics and lets his instincts take over. "She didn't need it; I did," he says, like this makes a difference. Problem with instinct is that when it comes to losers like Kenny Staples, it's always bad. You wanna mug an old lady, just about the lowest of street crimes, at least be smart enough not to carry a weapon. You don't need to be in fucking MENSA to know there are half a dozen cameras on every fucking block, recording everything in sight. And when they pinch him a couple blocks from the scene after some good citizen 9-1-1s him, they search him and find a blackjack and a Boy Scout knife. Hear that ding? That's the sound of petty theft moving up to a felony.

Guys like Staples are a crucial part of the food chain. He'll do anything for a buck, which means he's easily manipulated.

Kenny does have a particular talent. He's a scrounger. He can get you just about anything you need and if he can't get it himself, he can connect you to someone who can. He's a human Rolodex.

We meet at a Burger King way the fuck out on Long Island, where there's little chance we'll be recognized. When I get him on the phone, I tell him to make sure no one follows him. And I warn, "Stay the fuck out of trouble till then, Kenny."

When I arrive, he's already seated at a table, scrolling through his phone. As soon as he sees me, he jumps up and rushes toward me. Instinctively, I back away, but that doesn't stop him from getting in my space.

"Francis, Man, it's fucking great to hear from you," he says, pumping my hand like he hopes to strike oil. He's a skinny little fucker, just a couple inches taller than I. He's got a head of straggly, dirty blond hair and it looks like he hasn't shaved in maybe a week. He's wearing a raggedly pair of blue jeans and, even though it's gotta be seventy-five degrees, a heavy, blue plaid flannel shirt at least two sizes too big with the shirttail hanging out. The only thing that's changed since I last saw him, maybe half a dozen years ago, is that he's got fewer teeth. I'm guessing the result of too much meth. Right away, I begin to second-guess myself, but it's too late now.

"What can I get you, Francis?" he asks, hovering over me as I slide into a booth in the back of the joint.

"I'm good, Kenny."

"No. Really, man. It's on me. How about one of them Whoppers? With cheese. Without cheese. I'll get it your way," he says, grinning at the cleverness of his little joke.

"I don't eat this crap, Kenny."

He slaps his forehead, like he's some kind of cartoon cliché. "Oh, yeah. I remember now. You're some kind of vegetarian, right?"

"Some kind," I say, wondering just how long I'm gonna have to sit here listening to his bullshit before I get what I've come for.

"How's about a salad, Francis? They got salads here."

"Nothing, Kenny. I'm not here to eat. But get yourself something, if you want and then we'll get down to business."

"A cuppa joe? How 'bout that?"

If I don't say yes, we'll be here all fucking day.

"Sure. Black. No milk, no sugar. Can you remember that, Kenny?"

"Gotcha," he says. He doesn't walk to the counter, he dances over, doing some kind of funky-ass salsa, complete with arm movements that make him look like he's been possessed by the ghost of Jerry Lewis.

When he gets back, he plops down a cup of coffee in front of me. He pulls a Whopper and large order of fries from the bag and puts it on the table. He stuffs his hand back into the bag and comes out with a second order of fries. He pushes the fries across the table toward me.

"I know you didn't want anything to eat, Francis. But I don't like eating alone. But these fries are somethin' special. And they're a vegetable, right?" He stuffs a handful into his mouth.

All I want to do is punch him in the face. But I have to play nice with Kenny because I need something from him. Something my grandma said all the time pops up in my head. "You'll catch more flies with honey than you will with vinegar, Francis."

That'd be fine, grandma, only what the fuck am I gonna do with flies? Or fries?

Working hard to make sure there's a little of that non-existent honey in my voice, I say, "That's right, Kenny. Potatoes are a vegetable."

He smiles. Like he just got the right answer to Final Jeopardy.

Once again, there's that urge to punch him in the fucking face and drive those disgusting half-chewed fries down his throat. But instead, I turn up the charm.

"You're a good man, Kenny. How's about we get down to business?"

"Ab-so-fucking-lutely, Francis. So, what do you need, my friend? You want it, you got it. Kenny Staples" —he pounds his chest like a gorilla—"can get you anything you need. So, what is it I can do for you, my friend?"

"I need papers."

He looks confused. Although with Kenny, it's sometimes hard to tell. I stare at him until it finally sinks in.

"You mean like I-D, right? Shouldn't be no problem but," he stuffs another fistful of fries into his mouth. "But a passport, well, what with all the shit that's going down, Homeland Security is breathin' down everyone's neck. That's gonna be a tough one."

"I don't need a passport, Kenny."

"You mean you ain't gonna blow town? With all the heat on you, Francis? I mean maybe you're better off somewhere else…I don't know, Francis…"

"I like it here, Kenny. It's the land of the free and home of the brave."

"So, you're sticking around?" he says.

"You want my new address, Kenny?"

He looks at me like I'm speaking a different language.

Finally, the light goes on. "You're fucking amazing, Francis. It was me, I'd be on the next fucking train, plane or donkey cart outa the country. I mean, don't lyin' on some beach in the Caribbean sound nice? That's what I'd do."

I pull out my phone, click on the photo icon, switch it to selfie mode, and aim it, like it's a .45, at Kenny's face.

"Look at this, Kenny."

"Huh?"

"Look at the fucking phone. What the fuck do you see?"

"Huh?"

"What. Do. You. See?"

"Um, I see me?"

"That's right, Kenny. You see *you*, not me."

He goes quiet. Like he's in deep thought. Only I know Kenny's not capable of that.

Suddenly, the light bulb goes on. "Oh, man! I see. You mean what I'd do ain't necessarily what you'd do."

"Bingo."

"So? What you need?"

"Driver's license, a few fake utility bills, any kind of shit you'd find in a wallet. Think you can handle it?"

"No problem. All's I need is a name and address."

I'm a control freak. Of course, I've got a name and an address. Two of them, in fact.

I pull out my wallet and hand him a two-sided business card I've had made up with two phony names and two phony addresses on it. "Here," I say, handing it to him, as I twist my hand, flipping it over so he can see both sides. "Two separate sets, and make sure your man gets the spelling right."

He looks at it, then slides it into his shirt pocket.

"I gotta warn you, Francis, this ain't gonna come cheap. 'Specially if you need it quick."

"How much?"

I reach across the table, put my hand on his shoulder and squeeze. Just hard enough to remind him who he's dealing with. "And remember, Kenny, you aren't the only ship in the harbor."

"I know, Francis. And believe me, I'm honored you came to me. There ain't no one I'd wanna help more than you. You coulda gone to anyone, man, so I appreciate you chose me."

I tap my watch. "I haven't got all day, Kenny."

"Yeah. Right. So, um, how much you think it's worth?" he asks, his fingers nervously drumming on the table.

"You tell *me* what you think it's worth."

"Uh, I'm thinking maybe like five grand? That sound like it's in the ballpark? I'd hardly be making anything, but it's all about helping you out. But I know you don't wanna do this on the cheap. You want the best, right?"

"Tell you what, Kenny. I'm in a generous mood, so I'm gonna give you twice that. But understand this. I'm no sixteen-year-old punk looking for fake I-D to get him into the local bar. Understand? Don't waste my time with crap. And if you fuck me over, Kenny, there isn't a rock big enough for you to hide under. Understand?"

"Yeah, Francis. I absolutely do. And that's very generous of you. Very generous. And for that kind of dough, no shit, I can get you top of the line."

I'm not being generous because I like Kenny. It's purely a business decision. The more you pay, the better service you get. The less you pay, the more you'll regret you didn't pay top dollar.

"I'm counting on it, Kenny. And like I said, if you fuck me over, trust me, I will find you and you will fucking live to regret it. I will hunt you down like a dog. Understood?"

He shakes his head vigorously. "Yes, Francis. I absolutely do."

"And if I don't think it's up to snuff..."

"No chance of that, Francis. I swear," he says, crossing his heart with his index finger.

"One more thing, Kenny. If anyone finds out I'm the buyer, well, I don't have to finish the rest of this sentence, do I?"

"Absolutely not, Francis." He raises his right hand and puts his left hand forward, like he's swearing on a nonexistent bible. "You've got my word on that."

Not that I'd want to stake my life on Kenny Staples's word.

3

Francis

I put in a call to Artie, my Florida fence. We haven't been in touch for almost a year, but I know he hasn't forgotten me. That's because the sound he hears when he picks up the phone when I call isn't "Hello," it's "ka-ching."

As fences go, this fat fuck is relatively honest. He doesn't nickel-and-dime me. Not because he doesn't want to, like he's got some kind of fairness gene. But because he knows what'll happen if he tries to jew me down or rip me off. But I'll give him this: he's damn good at what he does. He gets me top dollar. Even if that means he has to shop out of the country to find a buyer who'll pay for quality, which is what I deliver.

I've known Artie a long time, but that doesn't mean I trust him. If the stakes were high enough and he thought he could give me up with no consequences, he'd do it in a New-York minute. There's no statute of limitations on rewards. Cops and insurance companies never give up. How long was it Whitey Bulger was on the lam? Close to twenty years, right? But they eventually nailed his ass. Living in that little hidey-hole not far from where I am now, near the beach, shacked up with his long-time girlfriend, trying to stay on the down-low. Turns out, it doesn't help him. They nailed him because he was careless and because they never fucking give up. Especially those pricks Floyd and Perez. They'll go to the fucking ends of the world to nail me again. That's one reason I'm putting three thousand miles between us.

Poor Artie. He doesn't know it yet, but the Hoyt gravy train won't be stopping in Miami anymore.

I have a dozen burners. I buy them in different places, different times, and always pay cash. I'm careful not to leave a paper trail because there's a pretty hefty reward out on me. Not enough, if you ask me. I've cost insurance companies plenty over the years and they don't like having their bottom-line fucked with. There'll always be some asshole who wants to pick up an easy buck. No matter what you've heard, there's no such thing as honor among thieves. The only reason Artie wouldn't drop a dime on me is because a) he makes money off me and b) if word gets out he's a rat, not only is his business done for but so is he. Still, I'm not stupid. Everyone's got their price.

I power down the burners when I'm not using them. Leave those fuckers on and you might as well paint a big, fat arrow in front of where you are, or where you've been. I use 'em a week or two, then smash them and deposit the parts in different trash bins around town. I've seen enough *Dateline* to know walking around with a live phone is like walking around with a GPS device shoved up my ass.

I can tell Artie's surprised to hear from me because all he can manage is a weak, "Francis?" Like he's hearing a voice from the dead.

"Don't fucking use my name, Artie," I hiss. My phone isn't tapped but his could be.

He's talking to me from his favorite spot, poolside at the Fountainbleu Hotel in Miami Beach. I can hear kids splashing around in the water. Every so often I catch the sound of Artie chewing, which results in a quick mental picture of him demolishing one of those disgusting pastrami sandwiches he loves. Some of it actually gets in his mouth. The rest winds up on his shirt. He loves those fucking sandwiches. I tell him they'll give him a heart attack one day, but he doesn't listen. "Hey, you only live once, right? So, might as well enjoy it."

"So, what's shaking?" he asks.

Suddenly, Artie's in the mood to shoot the breeze. I shut that down real quick. "Listen. I want you to hang up, then get your fat ass into the hotel lobby and find a public phone. Call this number. You got something to write it down on?"

"Yeah."

I hear him fumbling around. I'm losing patience.

"Shoot," he says. I give him my burner number. "Got it!" he says.

Five minutes later, he calls back. He sounds out of breath.

"It's me, Francis…"

"What the fuck, Artie? Did you just run the fuckin' marathon? For Chrissakes, you gotta get in shape, man. Try laying off those fucking pastrami sandwiches."

"I… I'm okay. I didn't wanna keep you waiting and I got these fuckin' allergies."

"Hold the medical reports for someone who fuckin' cares. Listen, I need someone out on the West Coast."

"That where you're holed up now, Francis?"

"You really think I'm gonna tell you so's you can shoot your big fat mouth off? Maybe you want my fuckin' address?"

The line goes dead for a moment. Poor Artie. I've hurt his feelings. Who knew he even had any?

"Francis. I'm hurt. We've known each other for what, close to twenty years. You really think I'd do something like that? I mean, come on, man. We're friends for Chrissakes."

I laugh. "Friends, Artie? Is that what we are?"

"Well, strictly speaking I guess we're business associates. But I like to think we've gotten past that. I like to think we're friends."

Friends? Does he think we're gonna sit around a fucking table playing poker once a month? Dinner and a movie? What the hell's his address in Fantasyland?

"Think whatever the fuck you want, Artie. How about that connection?"

"You mean like another fence?"

If we were in the same room, I'd be wringing the fat fuck's neck. I know no one's tuned into our conversation, but you never know who's listening, like someone standing close by. Even if there's no one, bad habits turn into lethal habits. If someone hears him talking about fences they might put two and two together. Besides, it's not out of the question he's being watched. I'm sure the cops know what he does for a living and that I've used him in the past. But rather than ream Artie out, I decide to play nice. It's not something I'm practiced at, but I can do it if I have to. If it gets me where I need to go.

"You might want to be careful of your word choice, Artie," I scold as gently as I can.

"Word choice?"

I don't say anything, hoping he'll get my point.

"I don't..." Suddenly, the clouds begin to part. Blades of sunlight shine through. "Oh, yeah. Right. Sorry about that. Oh, sure. I can help you out. There are a couple good ones out there," he says.

"Only the best, Artie. I need someone I can trust. Someone who isn't gonna fuckin' rip me off. Someone can keep his mouth shut..." I swallow hard and miraculously the words tumble out. "Like you, Artie."

I don't have to see the smile on the fat fuck's face. I can hear it in his voice.

"I appreciate that. I really do. I got just the right guy for you."

"Who's that?"

"He handles your kind of stuff and he'll turn it around pretty quick. For a decent price, too."

"You know me, Artie. I don't want some tweaker off the street."

"No. Really, Francis. He's the best out there. The guy even handles fine art, and you know how tough that shit is to..." He catches himself. "...to appreciate. Especially if it's one of the biggies. Picasso. Matisse."

"I got it, Artie. I got it."

"He's originally from back East. Long Island. Chances are you and he probably know some of the same people."

"He as good as you, Artie?"

A laugh quickly turns into a coughing spell. I just hope he doesn't get a fuckin' heart attack before he gives me a name.

When he finally recovers, he says, "No one's as good as me, Francis. You know that."

Artie is on a roll now and I don't know how to shut him up. Even though I'm fifteen hundred miles away, living on the down-low in Jersey, I can imagine Artie puffing up his hairy chest in pride. He's just been complimented by Francis Hoyt.

"I've always tried to do right by you, Francis. Whoops! Sorry 'bout that. Anyway, I know the kind of pressure you're under, so's I can understand you sometimes got a short fuse."

I've wasted enough time.

"The name, Artie?"

"Vince Capowitz. Five fuckin' stars, man. He's honest and discreet."

An honest fence? Will wonders never cease?

"He's a kike?"

"Uh, yeah. But only half. The other half's Italian. Best of both worlds, right?"

"You got his number, Artie?"

"Sure. Sure. Just give me a sec."

The line goes dead. A moment later he's back.

"Got a pen, Francis?"

"Yeah, sure." I don't have one because I don't need one. I've got a photographic memory, both for the spoken and the written word. Comes in handy, especially since I have a healthy aversion to writing stuff down. I've known cops who'll dig through your fuckin' garbage looking for something to help bring you down.

He recites the number. Twice, to make sure I get it, even though I had it the first time.

"Thanks, Artie."

"No problem. And Francis, if you're ever back down this way, I hope you'll let me take you out for a nice meal. No pastrami." He laughs. "I promise. And, man, it goes without saying I'd really love to do some business with you again. I understand the heat's on and all right now, but eventually it's gonna die down. And when it does, I'm expecting you'll be back down here. The sheep down here are lining up to get sheared."

"Sure, Artie. And when I do, you'll be the first to know."

As soon as I hang up on Artie, I call Capowitz. It's eight a.m. his time. He picks up on the third ring. I introduce myself. I don't get much past giving my name before he breaks in.

"Well, well. The one and only Mr. Francis Hoyt. I've heard about you for years, sir. It's an honor…"

I don't trust anyone who kisses my ass, but I let him get it out of his system.

"Fucking genius, the way you just waltzed out the front door of that courthouse, Mr. Hoyt. I know how easy it is for you to get into places, but I had no idea how easy it is for you to get out," he says in an obvious Long Island accent. "So let me guess. You're looking to do some business."

"That's a possibility," I say. "At some point in the future."

"I'd be honored to work with you. But perhaps we shouldn't be talking about this on the phone. How about we put a face-to-face on the calendar," he says.

So far, I'm liking what I hear.

"Not possible."

"Excuse me?"

"I'm not out there yet."

"I see. Then an in-person encounter is not in the cards right now, is it? But I suppose there are other ways to do business. Everything's remote today anyway…"

"That's not the way I work, Vince. I don't do business with anyone I haven't met. I need to look you in the eye. You don't have a problem with that, do you?"

"Not at all. When do you plan to relocate?"

"Haven't decided yet."

"Well, why not give me a call when we're in the same time zone."

"Life is short, Vince. I'm not a patient man. Too much can happen between now and then."

There's a moment of silence.

"What did you have in mind?" he asks.

"How about you come out here? On my dime, of course."

"I'd have to ask myself, are you worth it?"

"What do you think?"

"I like the idea of working with a legend, Mr. Hoyt. I think it would be profitable for both of us. When would you suggest this happens?"

"If I were you, Vince, I'd want it to happen as soon as possible. You don't want me shopping around for someone else. Look at it this way, Vince. I'm the worm and you're the bird. The question is, are you up early enough to get that worm?"

He laughs. "You can get a second opinion about me if you so desire. But I guarantee you won't find anyone better than me. On either coast. Never been pinched. No complaints. And in case you're worried, I am very discreet. My own family has no idea what I do for a living. Nor will they. Ever. I'm scrupulously careful. I write nothing down. Nothing."

I like the way he talks. Maybe Capowitz is the real deal.

"I gotta look you in the eye, Vince. Gotta shake your hand. Gotta look into your soul. Gotta see your aura," I add, a little jab at L.A.

"I've been told I have a very firm handshake and an impeccable aura, Mr. Hoyt. But let me make myself perfectly clear. I do not *need* your business. I'd appreciate your business, of course. But I do not *need* it. Another thing I do not need is attitude. It's a waste of my time and yours. Guys like Artie need the business, so they might put up with it. Not me. This isn't New

York and it isn't Miami. Out here, we don't impress easily. I walk outside, I see Brad Pitt or Chris Hemsworth or Jennifer Aniston or Jennifer Lawrence walking down the street, or sitting in a restaurant. They do not impress me and neither do you. And to be perfectly honest, things are quite busy right now. As much as I'd like to have you as a client, I have to make sure my time is well spent…"

"You're saying you don't want to meet me, Vince?"

"I'm saying I don't want to be wasting my time or yours. Either I have your business or I don't. Either way, the sun will rise from the east in the morning and set in the west."

"I guess I've got the wrong guy, Vince. Have a good life…"

"Please, don't hang up yet, Mr. Hoyt. I'm a careful man. A prideful man. But I'm not a stupid man. I know whatever trouble might come in the long run with you will probably be worth it. And as it happens, I believe I may have some wiggle room in my schedule."

"How quick can you wiggle out here?"

"Depends on where here is."

"Jersey."

"I suppose I could get out there sometime this weekend."

"That's acceptable. And Vince, because I know this is an imposition, I'll be picking up your expenses. Make a reservation to fly in Friday night. Take the redeye. We won't need more than an hour. You can fly right back, unless you have other business back here."

"I believe a few hours in Jersey fills my required time in hell."

"The redeye gets into Newark around six-thirty. Reserve a rental car. When you land, I'll text you where we'll meet. Does this work for you?"

"It does, Mr. Hoyt."

His flight arrives a few minutes early. He texts me as he's heading toward his rental. I text back, instructing him to meet me in the parking lot of the Mills Mall at New Jersey Garden.

He texts me the make and color of the car he'll be driving. I tell him to park as close to the exit of the mall as possible.

I park behind a mini-van a good forty, fifty yards away from the main entrance, giving me an unobstructed view of everyone coming and going into the mall parking area. A few minutes past seven, I see him pull into the lot. He maneuvers the car into a spot adjacent to the lot's exit. He sits there for several minutes before he finally gets out. He stands by the door, puts his hand, palm down, above his eyes and scans the horizon. When he doesn't see me, he shrugs and gets back into the car.

To make sure he hasn't been followed, I let him sit there for several minutes. Once I'm convinced he's alone, I exit the car and walk slowly toward the rear end of his car. He doesn't see me because he's staring down at his phone and I'm coming up on his blindside.

I rap on the passenger-side window. Startled, his head snaps up. It takes a split second for him to realize it's me. I motion him to roll down the window.

"Mr. Hoyt, I presume," he says as he sets his phone down on the dashboard. "You kinda sneaked up on me."

"Maybe you should pay better attention."

I open the door and slide into the passenger seat.

Capowitz looks like he's in his mid-to-late forties. Even though he's just come off a flight of close to five hours, he looks surprisingly fresh. He's wearing a suit and tie, like he's going to a board meeting. I catch the slight scent of aftershave. His dark hair, graying near the temples, is slicked back. Even though he's sitting, I can tell by how far the seat is back that he's tall, over six feet, and slim. He has a prominent nose and thin, hawkish face, with a faint scar running down the right side of his cheek.

I gesture toward the dashboard. "Do me a favor, Vince, turn off the phone."

"Excuse me?"

"Shut down the fucking phone, Vince."

He hesitates, gives me a funny look, then does what I ask.

"You've got some heavy-duty trust issues, don't you, Mr. Hoyt?"

"Give it to me," I say, holding out my hand.

He shakes his head in exasperation, but hands it to me. I open the back, and remove the battery and toss it onto the backseat. I hand back the phone, then thrust my hand out again.

"What now?" he snaps.

"Give me your wallet."

"I understand caution, Mr. Hoyt, but isn't this taking things a little too far?"

I snap my fingers three times. "The wallet, Vince."

He digs into his back pocket, pulls it out and hands it to me.

I look through it. The usual junk. Credit cards, driver's license, a few photos of kids, and a woman I assume is his wife. I make a mental note of his home address. I hand it back to him.

"Satisfied?" he says, as he bends forward and tucks the wallet into his back pocket, then wiggles in his seat, trying to get comfortable.

"You carrying?" I ask.

"You gotta be kidding. I just got off a fucking plane."

"You coulda checked it through."

"What you see in the backseat is what I traveled with," he says.

I look over my shoulder and see a brown briefcase.

"What's in it?"

"Newspaper, magazines, a book, a change of underwear, in case I have to stay over."

I reach back, grab the briefcase and hand it to him.

"Open it."

He shakes his head, clicks it open, then turns it toward me. "Be my guest."

It holds just what he says. "Okay," I say, handing it back to him. "Open your jacket and raise your arms above your head."

"This is getting ridiculous."

"Just do it, Vince. Otherwise, we'll be here all fucking day."

He does what I ask. I pat him down, including both legs. "Lean forward," I say.

I run my hand down his back.

"Okay, we're done."

"How would you feel about me doing the same? Maybe I'm the one being set up."

"Go ahead, Vince." I raised my hands over my head. "Enjoy yourself."

"Not my thing," he says. "Now that that's over, why don't we go somewhere we can sit and talk?"

"This works fine."

He shrugs, then reaches forward to adjust the rearview mirror.

"Looking for someone, Vince?"

"I've got as much at stake as you do, Mr. Hoyt. I'm not all that comfortable in unfamiliar surroundings. Especially with someone else calling the shots."

He pulls a pack of smokes from his top pocket, taps the bottom a couple times till one pops out. He offers the pack to me.

"Those fucking things are gonna kill you, Vince."

"I'm pretty sure something else'll get me first. I suppose I should give it up some day. Only today's not the day."

"Gimme the pack, Vince."

"Excuse me?"

"Just give me the fucking cigarettes."

"You think maybe I got a tiny camera in there?" he says, as he hands it over.

I take out the half dozen or so left in the pack, crush them in my fist, stuff the mixture of paper and tobacco back into the package, crumple the whole thing up, power down the window, and toss it out.

"What the fuck...?"

"You can thank me later, Vince. Look at it this way. I just added twenty fucking minutes to your life."

His expression hardens. Defiantly, he inserts the one cigarette left between his lips, then pulls a pack of matches out of his breast pocket. Before he can light up, I grab the cigarette out of his mouth, crush it between my fingers, then toss it out the window.

He glares at me. I've pushed him about as far as I can, and the look of fury on his face tells me everything I need to know about him. He's no pushover who's gonna fold the first time things get rough. He knows how to swallow his anger when he has to, which to me is a sign of strength, not weakness.

We stare each other down till I finally break the tension with a smile. He throws his head back and laughs.

"You're some piece of work, Hoyt."

"I do my best."

"Well, I guess I gotta stop sometime. Might as well be now."

4
Dakota

I'm one of those rare birds who was born and bred in Los Angeles. Well, not really L.A. proper. South of here, on the coast, not far from Capistrano, where the birds come back every year. There's one big difference between me and those birds: once I left Capistrano, I never went back.

My mom still lives there. My father left when I was eleven. I'm not even sure they bothered to get divorced. Whenever I ask my mom, she gets this weird smile on her face and, depending on the time of day or week or month, gives me a different answer. Her favorite, my least favorite, is when she says, "What does it matter, Dakota? It's not like I'm ever going to tie myself to another man."

I remember asking her once about the circumstances, how he left, why he left and she deadpanned, "He went out for a pack of cigarettes and never came back."

"I didn't know Dad smoked," I answered, showing her two can play that game.

There's that smile and then, after a pregnant pause if there ever was one, she replied, "He doesn't."

Today, he lives somewhere else. If that sounds vague, it's because that "somewhere else" changes frequently. I never know quite where he'll pop up next. On those rare occasions when I speak to him, and I ask him where he's living, he'll say, "I'd tell you, Dakota, but then I'd have to kill you."

I'm pretty sure he's kidding.

Another thing about him is that I've never been quite sure what he does for a living. For all I know he works for the CIA. Or he's a Mafia hitman. Occasionally, just for fun, because I know I'm not going to get an honest answer, I'll ask him, "Dad, exactly what is it you do for a living?" He usually makes a joke out of it. He starts to sing that Sinatra song, "That's Life." *"I've been a puppet, a pauper, a pirate, a poet, a pawn and a king…"*

Funny thing is, he doesn't have a bad voice, though I'll never tell him that. With my father, you give him an inch, he takes a mile.

Naturally, that answer shuts down all conversation. Once, only once, I made the mistake of asking my mom what dad does for a living and she replied, "He's a jack-of-all-trades, Honey," and then she lowered her voice, as if not wanting to be held responsible for what she was about to say, and added, "And master of none…"

Is it any wonder I'm as screwed up as I am?

I attended college back East. I don't tell people where because then they think they know who I am and judge me. I hate being judged, but if I'm going to be judged I don't want it to be because of where, when I was eighteen years old, I went to college. Let it be for something I did or didn't do. That's fine, because I judge other people all the time. Ask any of my former boyfriends. So, let's just say it was one of the Ivy League schools, and leave it at that.

I always knew what I wanted to be when I grew up. A writer. I didn't discriminate. Fiction. Nonfiction. It didn't matter. In fact, I'm not even sure back then I knew the difference. And today, sometimes I'm not sure there is a difference. It didn't take long to find out that no matter what kind of writing I chose, it would be tough to make a living. So, I settled on one that would allow me to sell my skills on the open market. That's what led me to journalism. It wasn't an overwhelming desire to follow in the footsteps of Woodward and Bernstein, but sheer practicality.

After I graduated from that unnamed Ivy League school (I'll give you a hint—it was not the one that starts with the letter H), I realized I had to decide what to do with the rest of my life.

I was accepted into the graduate program at the S.I. Newhouse School of Communications. I'm a Californian, so when I applied, I had no idea what "lake effect" snow was. I learned soon enough. Translation for all you Californians: because of cold air passing over large bodies of water, it can snow eight months of the year. And when it does, we're talking serious snowfall, measured not in inches, but feet. When someone asked me where I lived, I couldn't help answering, "The North Pole."

By the time I get out of Syracuse, aka the Salt City (I'm sure you can figure out what that refers to) I have a profession but no job. Newspapers are going out of business. Magazines are folding. But the Internet had not yet completely devastated the print business, and I'm fortunate enough to find a job as a reporter on the *Albany Times*. Fortunate, not lucky, because I can't seem to break out of the Snow Belt. I only manage to inch a bit closer to the coast and New York City, which is my dream destination. But I don't want to be Pete Hamill or Jimmy Breslin. I want to be Joan Didion or Margaret Atwood. Albany is cold and snowy, but nowhere near as cold or snowy as Syracuse. Evidently, the full lake-effect snow does not reach quite as far as Albany.

As the newbie on staff, I get the beat no one else wants. Crime. And the shift no one else wants—eight p.m. to four a.m. But that's when most crime happens—during the witching hours and the drinking hours. I quickly learn that no story is too small to be covered. I meet people I would never meet if I hadn't been writing about them. Most of all, I learn that lives of quiet desperation are not limited to small California coastal towns.

None of this bothers me. In fact, I embrace the crime beat and even come to love it. Burglary. Assault. Murder. Hit-and-run. Mugging. Arson. Domestic violence. Abuse. I quickly learn that crime takes no holidays, nor does it ever sleep. It is exciting and I don't have to cover boring city council meetings or write about late or non-existent garbage pickups and snow removal. I am out of the office much more than I'm in, and I get to love tooling around the greater Albany area in my beat-up, blue Toyota, one ear glued to my police scanner, eyes scanning the streets, looking for any kind of disturbance, anything out of the ordinary, which means there isn't much difference between me and the cops I'm covering. After a while, I develop a new dream. Not to win a Pulitzer but to stumble upon a serious crime in progress, call it in, then be the only reporter on the scene.

Being a fairly attractive California blonde surfer-type girl doesn't hurt (that I've only surfed once in my life, and couldn't stay on the board, doesn't matter). Cops love talking to me. They think it's cute that someone who looks like me is asking questions like, "What condition was the body in when you arrived on the scene?" Or, "How many stab wounds were there?" Or, "How long has he been dead?" In the beginning that bugs me. But after a while I let it work to my advantage. I even begin to dress the part, shunning my usual jeans and replacing them with "modest" girlie mini-skirts and high heels. Some might consider this flagrant flirting. I think of it as another tool to help me in my job. Besides, my male colleagues are using that really annoying macho male bonding thing, like talking sports or rating "chicks," so why is my method any worse? Use what you got, Baby. That's the advice from the managing editor when I complain to him one day.

I spend three years at the *Times* before the weather and the soul-deadening routine finally wears me down. I like the idea of seasons, but up there it sometimes goes straight from winter to summer, with maybe a week or two of spring and fall to break the monotony. I miss the sun. I miss the surf. I miss my mother and my little sister. Besides, I figure three years at the *Times* paying my dues is all the experience I'll need to nab a plum job on a big paper. Especially after I stumble upon a story that stays above the fold for more than a week. Hanging out at one of the downtown precincts and reading the daily logs finally pays off. What starts as a domestic violence case soon turns into a quadruple-homicide drug case with the victims all being in one family. This eventually leads to an expose of the drug trade in upstate New York, and even though I share a byline with another reporter on the paper, I'm fortunate enough to get top billing since I'm the one who follows the initial lead.

Time to cash in.

My first choice is the *L.A. Times,* but I'm willing to settle for *The New York Times, Boston Globe, Chicago Tribune, Miami Herald*, or the *Philadelphia Enquirer*. I send my resume to all of them and while I wait for an answer, I contemplate freelancing. I've recently broken off a relationship that is going nowhere, so I'm free to do and go wherever I want. Maybe traveling through Central and South America, sending back stories that will be picked up by all the major newspapers and magazines, like *Vanity Fair* and *The New Yorker*. It might sound foolish, conceited even, but I know I'm good enough—I get plenty of compliments on my writing style and even manage to win a few local awards. Besides, why not aim high?

I think I'm prepared for rejection, but when it comes, and it does come, I realize no one ever gets used to having their dreams dashed. Or being told they're not good enough. Friends tell me I'll get used to it, but I know they're wrong. Every rejection stings, no matter where it comes from.

It appears my timing is far from perfect. The Internet is making a splash and news is getting to people quicker through social media than it does through the morning edition of the newspaper. Newspapers are folding right and left, while at the same time there are rumors some papers might be going exclusively online.

I'm about to quit my search and look for a career change when I get an email from the editor of the *Sacramento Bee*, asking me to come in for an interview. Financially, I'm living on the edge, but I've accumulated enough mileage so the trip will cost next to nothing. And killing two birds with one stone, I talk my mother into meeting me in San Francisco for a couple days before I return to Albany.

That invitation to an interview is enough to get me to stupidly walk into my editor's office and tender my resignation. He tries to talk me out of it, but eventually he tells me he isn't surprised. "I'm shocked you lasted this long," he says.

"So am I."

"Got something else lined up?"

"I'm working on it," I say.

He smiles. He knows exactly what that means. Part of me is embarrassed I've acted so irresponsibly while another part of me is thrilled I've taken a risk. Risks, I tell myself, are what life is all about. Nothing ventured, nothing gained becomes my mantra.

"If you need a recommendation or a reference, I'll be glad to write one for you." He smiles. "A glowing one, of course."

"Thanks," I say. "That'd be great," I add, suddenly realizing I probably should have nailed this down before I began to test the market. The next day, I catch him at the water cooler and ask about that letter he's promised to write and he apologizes, explaining he's been swamped. "Why don't you write it, Dakota, and I'll sign it."

So, that's what I do. I think he could write a better letter than I do, but I don't want to add more work to his already busy day. Later, I think I should have written a better letter than I did.

I give two weeks' notice, promise to break in the newbie, and start packing.

Yeah, yeah, I know. I haven't even had the interview yet. But a little voice inside me insists I'm going to get the job, so I don't think of it as much of a gamble. Later, when asked, I always advise others to never, ever, under any circumstances, quit a job before getting a new one. It's advice I probably should have taken myself.

As it turns out, the little voice is right. I'm hired on the spot and two weeks later, when I show up at my new paper, I find myself back on the crime beat. Evidently, my new boss is a strong proponent of "write what you know," which explains the familiar beat. He even mentions that big murder and drug story I'd written. "Nice work," he says, which is about as good a compliment as you'll ever get from a seasoned newspaper editor.

I don't care. I've grown to love crime and, in my own way, criminals. Not because they flaunt the laws of civilized society, or because I approve of their lifestyle, but because crimes almost always result in interesting human-interest stories. That's what I really like writing about. Not so much the whodunit or howdunit, but the whydunit and how the rest of the world is affected by the crime. For me, it's all about human nature. I'm not just interested in the criminals. I'm interested in the victims. I want to see them get justice, even if they're not alive to see it. And I am fascinated by what drives people to commit crimes against property and people. What makes these people tick, and how far from committing crimes are so-called law-abiding people like you and me?

I'm not sure why, but I want, above all, to get deep into the criminal mind. To see how it works. To try to understand how they're different from you and me. Or, *if* they're different from you and me.

I guess that's the part of all this that winds up getting me into trouble.

5

Francis

I know what hell is like up close and personal after hiding out in Jersey the past few months.

Time to shake things up.

As a kid, I had a dream. This dream did not include being one of those penny-ante crooks knocking over parking meters for chump change. In this dream, I'm Cary Grant in *To Catch a Thief*. Like Grant, I want money. I want girls. I want respect. I realize early on I will not get any of those things by knocking old ladies over the head, then stealing their pocketbooks.

Eventually, the day comes when I realize I don't have to listen to the old man anymore. I'm smarter than he is. Stronger. Tougher. Once this sinks in, I take control of my life. I see clearly the path in front of me, and I figure out a way to get where I want to go. I decide once I hit sixteen, I'm out of there.

I know this dream won't come easy. It means hard work. It means making a plan and sticking to it. Once I have that plan, I don't stop there. I make sure I have three other plans in case the first one doesn't work out. I will survive by adapting, by persistence, by changing direction if I have to. I will let nothing or anyone get in my way. In a school science class, one of the few times I'm listening, I learn about the "survival of the fittest." This, I decide, will be me. No one will be fitter than I. No one will survive better than I.

I read somewhere that if you really want to be good at something, you have to put in at least ten-thousand hours of practice. You keep doing it till it's second nature. Till you're not thinking about it. Just doing it. And once you think you've mastered it, you come up with other ways to do it better.

I don't spend hours or days planning a job. I spend weeks, sometimes months. Nothing is spontaneous. I research the job from every angle, then check it inside and out. I read magazines and newspapers. I take open-house tours. By the time I'm ready to strike, not only do I know what's in that house but exactly where it is and what it's worth. No fishing expeditions. I know why I'm there. I don't waste time taking shiny objects without much value. I learn how safes work and how to crack them. I study the latest alarm systems, how they work, why they work and how I can get them to stop working. I learn about motion detectors and surveillance cameras. I know where they're likely to be and how to avoid them.

If I had a motto, it would be: *those who are unprepared get pinched.*

I've been nabbed twice in my life, and that includes all the shit I boosted as a kid. The first time was because I said yes to taking along some piss-ant nephew of one of the mob bosses. I didn't listen to that little voice in my head that kept repeating, *walk the fuck away.* I know it's a mistake the minute I say yes. By then, it is too late. The second time is on me. I let some jealous bitch rat me out. I break a cardinal rule: trust no one. Ever. And then I do something really stupid, something I do just to show-off. It's that damn ashtray that leads to possession charges that land me in court that day. It is hubris, man. Pure and simple. That's what Charlie Floyd calls it as his spic partner, Manny Perez, snaps on the cuffs. I look up the word and, as much as I hate to admit it, he's right.

After I walk away from the courthouse, I spend the next few months lying low. I don't surf couches. I don't live in the fucking forest. I'm smart enough to use some of my dough to set up "safehouses" across the Northeast. One is a studio apartment in Pennsylvania, just outside Wilkes-Barre, a broken-down, shit-hole former coal town that's turned into an industrial wasteland. Another is outside Boston, near the New Hampshire border. A third is in western Connecticut, near the New York border. And this one, in Hoboken, is just across the river from New York City.

None of them is meant to last. I don't spend much time in any of them. When I start to feel itchy, I know it's time for me to walk away.

Now, finally, my time on the run is over.

The best place to lose myself is not some small, hick town in Middle America. Someone like me sticks out like a sore thumb. Wouldn't be long before the questions start and they never stop. Who is he? Where's he from? Why's he here? What's he do for a living? How come he's moved to a place where he doesn't know anybody?

Instead of blending in, I'd be the fucking talk of the town. Suddenly, everybody would have their nose all up in my business.

A big city like New York's the perfect place to get lost, to start a new life. But not for me. I can't walk a block without the risk of bumping into someone I know. There are too many people there who'd sell me out. After the murder of that fence, well, as they like to say in the gangster flicks, the heat is on. Maybe they'll tie me to it. Maybe not. It's not something I'm gonna worry about.

Chicago's okay, but I hate the fucking cold. And the wind. And the deep-dish pizza, which is no more fucking pizza than an English muffin, no matter how much tomato sauce and cheese is on it. Besides, that city's got bad juju, what with Dillinger getting whacked there just for going to the fucking movies. From the day I read about that as a kid, red becomes my most hated color. San Francisco? Maybe if I were a fag.

That leaves L.A., where you can pretty much hide in plain sight behind the wheel of your car. It's a transient city where freaks and strangers are the norm. Pretty much everyone in that town is there to reinvent themselves. I'd just be one more odd-ball blending into the crowd.

So, that's where I eventually land. But only after I make a slow amble across the country. I don't buy a car. I don't rent one, either. I don't hop a train. Or a plane. Instead, *I skip the bother. I skip the fuss, I take the good, old-fashioned Grey-hound bus.* I pay cash for every ticket and every ticket is purchased separately. This way, there's no record of my route. For the first time in my life, I have no plan. I have no itinerary. All I have is a destination.

I take a seat in the back where I keep to myself. If someone tries striking up a conversation, I don't answer. If they don't take the hint, I move seats.

It's like a game of musical chairs. When the music stops, if the mood strikes me, I get off the bus. I walk around some nameless town. I pass dads mowing lawns, moms sitting on the front porch, knitting, kids playing in the front yard, or the streets. It is a glimpse of a life I've never had. A life I'll never have. A life I'd never want.

Occasionally, my mind drifts toward work. Every so often, when I get off the bus and explore the town, I'm tempted to throw in a practice run. Like any other skill, if you don't use it you'll lose it. But it's more than that. *Why do I still have this urge?* The question gnaws at me. At first, I push it aside. But it keeps coming back. It demands an answer. Finally, I confront myself and the answer surprises me. Being a thief is not *what* I am, it's *who* I am. So if I'm not breaking into people's homes and taking what belongs to them, defiling their privacy, who am I?

I realize I've let myself be defined by what I do. Without do-ing my thing, who am I? What am I? Do I even exist? But there's more. By breaking into the homes of strangers and taking what might be their most prized possessions, I inject a dose of the real world into their "perfect" lives. While I'm rewarded with the rush of adrenaline that makes me feel alive, my victims are total-ly unnerved. An uninvited guest, I've invaded their sacred space.

I've shown them that they are never completely safe. Their world is turned upside down in the time it takes for me to violate their home. I show them how vulnerable they really are. I show them how unsafe they are, how fragile their lives are. In the end, it's all about power. I have it and they don't. And in that moment when they realize an uninvited guest was in their home while they slept, they are permanently violated, robbed of something they can never get back.

Once back on the bus, tapping into the hypnotic sound of the wheels rolling over the highway, I stare out the window at the passing flatlands of Kansas or Nebraska or whatever fucking state we're in at the moment. Without the luxury of a map, there's no way to tell the difference, other than occasional signage announcing an upcoming town or village.

Why am I experiencing this unnerving sense of dislocation? Of disorientation? It's not the fear of being caught. I never allow for that possibility. It's not about moving from one place to another, without a home base. I've been in transit my whole life. I'm a rolling stone. I roll too often and too fast to gather any moss. The word "home" is not part of my vocabulary. I've never had a real home. Or maybe it's that I've never felt *at* home. Homes are for other people. Homes are for breaking into.

This is what my old lady used to call a "revelation." It's what she swore she got from going to church every Sunday. "The Lord reveals himself to me, Francis," she'd tell me in the midst of a stupor much like the one my father's in every time he stumbles home from the local tavern. "We don't always know what His plan is. All we know is He has a plan."

They're both addicts. One alcohol, the other hope.

And so, if I am a child of two addicts, the chances are good that I'm also an addict, hooked on the high I experience every time I break into a home. This is my revelation, only it has nothing to do with seeing the Virgin Mary or the Holy Ghost. My mother's religion or anyone else's religion has nothing to do with my revelation. My *divine light* comes from a different source. My revelation tells me that wherever I finally land, I will embrace who I am, as well as what I am. I can change my name. I can alter my appearance. I can modulate the way I talk. The way I walk. The way I sit. The way I stand. But the one thing I can't change, the one thing I don't want to change, is who and what I am.

In the end, this is the *revelation* that sets me free. I don't *have* to re-invent myself. I am who I am and that's who I'll always be. If anything, I will become more like myself. A bigger and better version of Francis Hoyt. All this has absolutely nothing to do with religion or with God. I answer only to me. When and if I talk to God, I find I'm talking to myself. Which means that I am my own God.

It takes me the better part of two weeks to get across the country. When I finally arrive in L.A., a few days before Christmas, I am a new man, ready for my new life. I have purged myself of the bad vibes and bad habits of the past. I have a new name. Billy Sutton. I have the papers to prove it. I have a credit card in his name, though I know I'll use it sparingly. As an added service, Staples, who turns out to not be as much of a fuck-up as I thought, sets up a P.O. Box at one of those private services in mid-town Manhattan. This way the bills, if there are any, will have somewhere to go. He even offers to check it once a month. And other than letting my hair grow out, I still look pretty much like the old Francis Hoyt, rather than the new Billy Sutton.

I won't change who I am, but I will change what I used to be. Cops aren't stupid. They study patterns the same way I do. If I'm going to remain free, unpredictability is the best shield. Unique. I will change how I work. How I live.

As a kid, they claim I have a learning disability. Now they have a name for it: dyslexia. Back then, they call it stupidity. I'm mocked by kids. By teachers. I see words backwards. Upside down. Inside out. Words that convey meaning to everyone else are ancient hieroglyphics to me. Instead of making me feel inferior, which I know I'm not, it means I'm special; I see things different from everyone else.

One day, one of my teachers reads aloud a story called "The Murders in the Rue Morgue," by Edgar Allen Poe. The story speaks to me. The hero, August Dupin, sees the world in a special way. The way I see it. As a dark and dangerous place. When I learn the author's name, I steal a book of his short stories from the library.

Reading is painful for me and yet I don't give in. If I read the words over and over again, they start to come alive. This is how I teach myself to read. One step at a time. Words. Sentences. Pages. Chapters. Books. At first, it's like translating a foreign language, a language I can speak but can't read.

Suddenly, I have power I've never had before. Books, the right books, provide knowledge. And that knowledge can be consolidated and teach me everything I have to know.

Poe's short story, "The Purloined Letter," teaches me a valuable lesson, a lesson I put to good use when I start breaking into houses. I realize that most often, valuable things are left in plain sight. People want to see what's valuable to them. And inside their home, everything they own is safe. Objects of value remind them how *special* they are. People are defined not by what they do or who they are, but rather by what they own. They want other people like me to see what they own so we'll be jealous of what they have. These are things they think someone like me can never own. They hang them on their walls. They openly display them on bookcases and in glass cabinets. They leave them out in the open, like Floyd's silver ashtray. The ashtray that almost sent me to prison. Floyd didn't even smoke, but there it was, sitting on an end table, waiting for someone like me to pick it up, turn it over, see the provenance, then see Floyd as someone special because he owns this object of value. Taking it might have been an act of hubris, but it is the only way I know to show how much better I am than he is.

In the end, Floyd is right. It's all about hubris, man. "Excessive pride in what you own." Taking something of value from someone who doesn't deserve it, makes everything better. The real thrill comes not when I grab something, but later, when I imagine the look on my victims' faces when they realize their prize possessions are gone.

Remember this: Once I'm in your house, what's yours is mine.

The first few weeks on the run were exhilarating, disorienting and frightening. I learn early on you can't truly enjoy freedom unless it's taken from you. Eventually, it becomes frightening. Suddenly, as I move west, toward my ultimate destination, my life feels out of control. I'm reacting instead of acting. I am controlled by the fear of getting caught. I am allowing other people control me. They're renting space in my head. I can't let that happen. I can't let someone else dictate my behavior.

Fear leads to carelessness, which leads to getting caught. It's a cycle I can't let myself fall into.

I know those two guys, Floyd, the retired state investigator, and Perez, the suspended Miami cop, are on my tail. They're not going to forget me. Especially after all the time and trouble they've put into bringing me down.

As I get closer to L.A., the life ahead of me gets clearer. I'm on a mission to stay free. If everyone looking for me fails, I win. I have a new challenge in front of me now and it's more than just breaking into places where I don't belong. Now, in my new life, I have to prove I'm the best at getting lost.

6

Francis

This much I have always known.

In the deepest, darkest recesses of our tiny, black hearts, murder and mayhem lurk. Think I'm full of shit? Okay. Ask yourself this: Why are you so obsessed with crime shows, books, movies, and now, these two-bit crime podcasts? I don't care who you are, you're drawn to the thrill of getting away with murder, larceny or other crimes that cross your mind on any given day. The driver who cuts you off on the highway? Kill the son of a bitch. The armored truck picking up bags of cash from the bank? You're mentally plotting how those bags can be yours. The difference between you and me is that I not only think it, I do it. But you're not me, and so the next best thing to having the experience yourself is watching someone else get away with something. I get that thrill early on, the first time I tuck something under my shirt and walk out of a store without paying. It doesn't take long to learn that it's not about the thing, it's about the feeling. Anyone who tells you crime doesn't pay is a fool. It pays all the fucking time. In all kinds of ways. But the ultimate thrill is not just doing it, it's getting away with it.

I don't grow up wanting to be a thief. I don't go to college to study the art of thievery. I don't read books about it. I don't have some Fagan-like mentor teaching me the ropes. It comes naturally to me. Like breathing. The first time I see something I want that isn't mine, I figure out a way to get it. It doesn't take long for this to become a way of life. If you have something I want, it's my job, my destiny, to take it from you.

The first time I take something that isn't mine I'm eight years old. I'm in the neighborhood *Five and Dime*. Roaming the aisles, I wind up in the toy section. I don't have toys at home. My old lady is too busy trying to stretch a dollar so we can eat, while any dough that happens to find its way into my old man's pockets only stays there long enough to make it to the nearest bar. I'm pissed. Other kids had toys, why not me? It isn't my fault my old man is a good-for-nothing alky who can't hold a job more than a week. What makes those other kids better than me?

One of those Match Box trucks catches my eye. My pockets are empty, just like my father's after an all-night binge, so there's no chance I can pay for it. But I want it. I don't think twice. I grab it and stash it under the waistband of the jeans my mother picks up at the Salvation Army. I beat it out of that store as quick as I can and run all the way home. I run not from fear of being caught but from exhilaration. When I get far enough away and I pull that truck out from its hiding place, I realize it isn't owning it that makes me happy. It's the thrill of taking it. For the first time in my life, I am in total control of something. I don't have to ask anybody for anything. I can just take it. I am the master of my own fate. Rules that apply to others don't apply to me. There are no boundaries. I feel freer and more powerful than I ever have before. I like the feeling. I want it to last forever.

Yesterday, before I grab that truck, I own nothing. Today, I own the world.

By the time I turn eleven, I graduate to stealing anything and everything that moves. Bicycles, wagons, skates, scooters. Anything that gets me away from where I am. I steal my first car at fifteen, unless you count the old man's truck, which I run off the road when I'm fourteen. While he's passed out on the couch, exhausted from the beating he' gives me hours earlier, I lift the keys from his pocket, and take a little joy ride. I've never driven before and have no idea what I'm doing, or where I'm going. But I've watched my old man enough times to figure out how to drive. The thrill of movement is intoxicating. For the first time in my life, I feel free. And when I'm done riding around the neighborhood, I run the truck off the road into a ditch. This is no accident. Finally, I finally find a way for retribution: I've taken my father's most valued possession and destroyed it. Suddenly, and for the first time in my life, I realize that I, too, have power.

It is a life-changing moment. No matter who hurts me, I know I can even the score.

My life changes forever. Wheels are my ticket out of this shithole, away from a life I know will ultimately destroy me.

Stealing becomes second nature. At first, I am surprised how easy it is. The more I do it, the better at it I get. I am a piss-poor student in school. I rarely pay attention. But now I have a goal. I want to learn how to become a better thief. I read everything I can get my hands on about robbers like Dillinger, Bonnie and Clyde, Willie Sutton, Machine Gun Kelly, Alvin Karpas. These are my heroes. These are the people whose lives I want to live.

But I am smart enough to realize there's a problem. All these people either wind up in the joint or on a slab in the morgue. No longer are they on top of the world. They're just another bunch of losers. I don't want to end my life locked in a six-by-eight jail cell. And I don't want to end my life buried in an anonymous grave in some Potter's Field.

This won't happen if I have a plan. It won't happen if I come up with rules of behavior. Early on, I decide there will be no weapons. Not because I'm afraid of hurting someone—I don't much care if I do—and not because I'm afraid of getting hurt—that fear has been beaten out of me a long time ago. Those beatings from my old man give me a superpower: the ability to withstand pain. Carrying a weapon raises the stakes and adds an unnecessary element of risk. Using a weapon means stealing is no longer an art. It becomes a matter of brute strength. I want to be the Picasso of crime. To use a weapon is to cheat. It shows a lack of imagination. To use muscle is brutish, and I am not a brute. I am an artist. I don't need a weapon. All I need is my mind, my body and steely determination. Used properly, they will be all the weapon I'll ever need.

I am always the littlest kid in class. I never grow taller than five-four, which makes me a target. But I am wiry, quick, and surprisingly agile. Team sports never interest me, but when I discover gymnastics, I realize I can use it to train my body to do things that will help me in and out of tight spots. I run track, not because I like it but because I realize it's important to build stamina and breath control. I begin to develop muscles in all the right places. I find that I am surprisingly strong for my size, probably the result of having to pick my old man up off the floor so many times. I even do a little weight training. I don't overdo it, because I need to stay limber. Bulking up will only slow me down. Speed is an important asset.

It doesn't take long for me to establish rules of engagement.

Rule Number One: Most criminals are dumb fucks who wind up spending most of their lives as guests of the Graybar Hotel. Every criminal I meet would have trouble breaking the century mark on an I.Q. test. That's why most of them eventually wind up in stir. Many more than once. I learn from my mistakes. I learn from the mistakes others make. That year in stir I listen to everyone's story. I make note of how they succeed. But more important, I make note of how they fail and why. By the time I'm sprung, I've earned a graduate degree in crime.

Crime is just another word for chaos. Chaos unnerves people. They're frightened by it. They live every day of their pathetic lives doing everything they can to protect themselves against it. They think by locking their doors at night they can keep chaos out. They can't. I provide a public service. I prove to them that nowhere is safe. I grow up in the midst of chaos, why should others expect anything different?

Life is messy. Any order that comes from chaos is only temporary. Questions must have answers. Crimes must be solved. The sun must shine and blue birds must perch on shoulders. When the guilty are punished, order results.

Only it almost never works out that way.

There are no happy endings.

Welcome to my fucking world.

7

Dakota

I begin the podcast a year and a half ago, not long after I lose my job, along with so many others, at the *Bee.* We see it coming. For the past ten years and or so, the newspaper business has undergone a cataclysmic change. Newspapers are biting the dust at an alarming rate. They simply can't keep up with the Internet in terms of breaking stories as they happen. And 24/7 cable news doesn't help. But speed often results in mistakes. A constant barrage of instant news from dozens of different sources makes the situation worse. People read breaking news on their phone as they ride to work in the morning. All this makes the only thing worse than working for a newspaper in terms of job security being a coal miner.

I get an okay buyout, considering I've been at the paper less than five years. Okay meaning I can live on it frugally for a couple months, so long as I'm willing to skip a few meals every week, cancel my premium cable channels, and supplement my measly income with twenty-six weeks of unemployment benefits. Guilt money, I call it. I feel guilty getting it, and the state assuage their guilt by giving it to me. This put both of us in a win-win situation.

When the axe falls, I ask myself the same question everyone else does: What am I going to do with the rest of my life?

My mother, always trying to be helpful, gives me that tired, worn-out line, "When one door closes, another door opens, Honey." I reply, "And then there's the window, Mom, but fortunately I live on the second floor."

She doesn't like that answer so she stops bringing up doors or windows, and for that I'm grateful. But then she does something worse. She puts herself in charge of finding me my next career. Every time I see her, she's either handing me want ads she finds online, or suggesting a new career path. "You could go to law school, Dakota. You know, put that smart mouth of yours to work." Or, "What's this computer science thing? Maybe you should look into that. I mean, everyone's got a computer, don't they?"

The only way to put an end to this barrage of advice is to tell her I've signed up for a course in pole dancing. My mom isn't stupid. She gets the point.

First thing I do is get myself out of Sacramento. Unless you're working for the state government, there's no earthly reason anyone should be here. I know Gertrude Stein was talking about Oakland when she wrote, "There is no there there." But she could just as well have been referring to Sacramento.

I need to be in a big city, because that's where the opportunities are. Not only for jobs, but a social life. And because my mom is getting on in years, I wanted to be closer to her. Not too close, you understand. That would be disastrous. Close enough so I can see her every so often and be there within an hour if, God forbid, she needs me. This means moving to L.A., where I still have a small support system of friends.

And let's be honest, there's no better place to hide out than the sprawling city of Los Angeles. Especially if the one you're hiding from is you.

There is too much noise in my head right then to make any kind of rational decision. As my mother is continually reminds me, I'm pushing forty. Four more years and I'll be over the edge. The question of where I see myself in five years scares the hell out of me. Do I want to settle down and have a family?

Yes, part of that noise in my head is probably the sound of a ticking biological clock. Will I ever get used to not having job security? Probably not. Will I leave the world better than I find it? Unlikely. And what about a life partner? Will I ever find one? Do I even want one?

These are some of the questions that still keep me up at night.

I've never been especially fond of L.A. Even though I learn to drive at fifteen, I've never been a fan of car culture. The other thing is, L.A. is a company town. Everyone who lives here has something to do with the entertainment industry. I know this sounds like an exaggeration, a worn-out joke, but it's truer than not. Almost everyone in this town is a wannabe actor, director, or screenwriter. But I know, at least for now, living in L.A. makes the most sense. What makes it a little easier is that I see my time here not as a period, but a comma.

After finding a relatively inexpensive apartment, I need to find a way to pay for it. Traditional journalism? Forget it. There are no jobs now and there'll be fewer in the future. The thing of it is, I don't really have any marketable skills other than writing, being able to tell a story, along with pretty good interviewing skills. Oh, and I type pretty good, between seventy and eighty words a minute.

The first thing that comes to mind is to write a book, something I've always wanted to do. This set off dreams of a large advance, leading to a best-seller. Trouble is, I can't seem to come up with anything to write about that would justify this imaginary hefty advance.

Sitting home alone isn't the answer, so before I move down to L.A., I visit a job counselor, someone recommended by human resources at the *Bee*—it's actually part of the final package offered by the newspaper, which seems to be saying, "Oh, let us help you find another job that'll be obsolete within a year or two." After a couple of sessions, Sheila, that's her name, is as stumped as I am about my future. After a particularly embarrassing bout of whining—mine not hers—she advises, or rather commands, "Dakota, I want you to get a pad and write down all your skills in one column, your interests in another, and your experience in the third column. After you finish, it should be apparent what you should do next."

I think she's full of shit, but the amazing thing is, she's right. Not that it comes easy, of course. I stare at that blank pad for what seems like hours. I get up and make coffee for myself. I feed Hemingway, my cat. I watch a movie. I even consider taking my imaginary dog for a long walk. And then I think, *why an imaginary dog? Why not the real thing?* For companionship. For protection. I come to my senses before I bring home a rescue. After all, I can hardly take care of myself, much less another mouth to feed.

Finally, as day turns to night, I manage to come up with three columns and, as Sheila predicts, the answer becomes apparent.

My interests and skills meet in a Venn diagram, at the nexus between crime, writing, reporting and public speaking. (Have I mentioned I have a tiny narcissistic streak?)

As I sit trying to put these interests together it comes to me. As a kid, I love lying in bed in the dark, listening to the radio. I close my eyes and imagine I'm in the studio. I even make up my own talk show where I, the host, interview fascinating people and, as a result, became fascinating myself.

With *Serial's* first season focusing on a perhaps innocent young man in prison for killing his girlfriend, true crime podcasts take off. TV shows like *48 Hours* and *Dateline* feed the beast, satisfying the public hunger for true crime. The audience is large and there's never a shortage of content.

I spend most of my days and nights listening to true crime podcasts. I'm hooked after the first one and, even though they sometimes rehash the most horrendous crimes, for some reason listening to them is surprisingly soothing.

I check it out and find the arena already over-saturated with true crime podcasts. For some reason, this doesn't stop me.

(Maybe the reason is desperation.) In fact, it energizes me. All I have to do is come up with a compelling concept that will set me apart from the other podcasts.

Without having the slightest idea what I was doing, I come up with a name for it: *Prime Time Crime with Dakota.* I figured the rhyme would help people remember the podcast. But now I have to distinguish it from all those other true crime podcasts, especially if I wanted to eventually monetize the show.

After couch surfing with friends for a couple of weeks, I find a relatively cheap apartment in Silver Lake. Since it's atop a hill, I have a decent view of Dodger Stadium at night, but only if the atmosphere cooperates. I love sitting on my small balcony, staring out toward the Pacific—I can't see it, but I know it's out there. And when the Dodgers are home and the lights from the stadium illuminate the dark sky, I find myself as soothed as if I've taken a mood-altering drug.

I sign up for an extension class at UCLA on how to create a podcast. The first lesson teaches me how much I don't know. I add a class in communications, focusing on radio and public speaking.

I need to come up with a theme. I don't want to be just another show that does murders, solved or unsolved. And I most certainly want to stay away from serial killers. I hate to say it, but after a while murder is boring and multiple murders even more boring. And the idea of doing a podcast focusing solely on unsolved crimes runs the risk of being unsatisfying—to me and to listeners. People like closure, something we rarely get in life. Do I really want to add to everyone's anxiety?

What does interest most of us is people. Not only those who commit the crimes but those affected by them. Why does someone fall into a life of crime? What kind of person commits a crime? How does it feel to be the victim of a crime? How does crime affect the family and the community? Are we all potential victims or victimizers? These are the kinds of questions I'm interested in answering.

I decide to concentrate on "controllable" impulses, which pretty much leaves out crimes of passion and those driven by insanity. I wanted to try, through my podcast, to understand the criminal mind. What makes a criminal? Can we, as a society, do something to stop criminal behavior before it starts? I'm not out to solve the world's problems. I'm out to understand them better. That leads me to decide I shouldn't do a single-episode podcast, but rather a series of multiple episodes—up to six weeks on one story—so I can delve as deep as I need to.

I realize this will require tons of research, which, after all, is my strength. I look forward to this part. But research takes time and money, and so I know I have to find something, even if it's part-time, to pay the rent. After a week or two of searching, I snare a part-time job as a reporter/editor for a small, weekly neighborhood throwaway. It doesn't pay much, but it's enough to sustain me until the money begins pouring in from advertisers to my podcast.

It doesn't take long to realize I can't do this alone. I learn pretty quick that'll need at least two other people to join me: an editor and a producer. I can't afford to pay anyone yet, so I scour my address book for friends from my journalism days who might work with me for a piece of the action. I find two, one who lives in the Valley and the other, one of my best friends, who lives nearby. I know I'll also need someone to sell ads, but I figure I'll have time to fill that position later, since I don't have an actual product yet. Just an idea.

I write down possible ideas for my first show. An art forger and an embezzler. I run them by my two silent partners and they're impressed, so I move ahead. In the beginning, I over-research, something I learn in journalism school.

"At a certain point, you have to stop, Dakota," a professor warns me. "Because if you don't, you'll spend the rest of your life researching the story and never writing it. You have to know when to abandon researching in order to allow it to breathe."

"But what if I miss something? What if there's more?"

"There's always more. Life is about choices. At a certain point you'll have to let go and no one can tell you when that is." He stops, letting his words sink it. "But I guarantee you'll know it when you see it."

He's right. I don't stop researching because I know everything there is to know, because that would be impossible. I stop because I learn when enough is enough. It's a lesson I wish I could apply to my personal life.

I create a lineup of my first three podcasts. I give myself three months to research the subject, then write the script. For my first season, I focus on white-collar crime, finding someone who's embezzled millions of dollars from clueless investors. I line up interviews with some of his victims.

The show builds slowly through word of mouth. My newspaper connections help. I make sure I get listings in the small neighborhood rag I work for part-time. Through a contact still working at the *Bee,* I get a mention that's picked up by several other newspapers across the country. Eventually, the L.A. *Times* does a story on true crime podcasts and names mine one of the Top 5 Up and Coming. They even quote me, including one unfortunate quote that slips out, referring to myself as a "crime whore." I know, the minute the phrase passes my lips, I know it's a mistake, a mistake that probably will stick to me like seaweed after a swim in the Pacific. I can immediately see it in big, bold black letters as a pull-quote. I worry about it for weeks, thinking it might finish my career. But I'm wrong. Instead, it helps my visibility. People are tuning in, not only to hear the story I'm featuring, but to listen to the *crime whore.*

In the newspaper story, I mention that one of my upcoming shows will focus on a notorious "master burglar." Even though I don't mention his name, this is the story that tips off Francis Hoyt and sends him my way.

8
Dakota

When I make the final decision to become a podcaster, I want to be prepared. That's why I take classes at UCLA and why I listen to scores of podcasts of all shapes and sizes. Once I have a feel for it, I contact some of the better podcasters and ask to interview them. Not knowing whether they will welcome more competition, I tell a little white lie, telling them I'm writing a magazine piece about the rising popularity of true crime podcasts. It's only a white lie, really, because I'm sure at some point I probably will write about my experiences. I suck out all the information I can. I reason that if I know all the potential pitfalls before I begin, I can save myself a lot of time and probably money, too. Bottom line: I need to know how to make my podcast as professional as possible. The last thing I want is to be thought of as some ditzy blonde white chick who runs around with a tiny tape recorder, babbling about crime in front of a microphone to half a dozen listeners.

I'm able to raise close to five thousand dollars in seed money donated by friends who believe in me, even if they don't quite understand why I'm doing this. One of my close friends, Christina, a very successful corporate attorney, my go-to person when I have legal questions, eggs me on and then puts her money where her mouth is by giving my twenty-five hundred bucks. When I start to write out an IOU, she grabs my hand and asks,

"What are you doing?"

"Memorializing your loan."

"This is not a loan, girl, and it's not an investment, either. I don't want the money back. It's a gift, because I believe in you and when you're successful, and you will be successful, I want you to thank me over and over again for believing in you."

I still try to hand the check back to her, but she will have none of that.

"You're making me angry, Dakota. Why don't you just accept it graciously and then spend it wisely. And if you need more, please don't hesitate to come to me."

"But twenty-five hundred..."

She laughs. "We're talking about what, three billable hours, honey? Besides, you're doing me a favor by letting me use the money to do some good, rather than just go out and piss it away on Rodeo Drive and a few shots of Botox."

"Botox? You use Botox?" I ask, staring at her perfect, nearly unlined face, looking for signs.

She doesn't answer, so I let it go. All I can think about is how I won't have to go into debt pursuing a career that has a high probability of flat-lining.

Being a podcaster is not, I discover, a one-person band. First, I need to find an editor, someone who will pore over hours of conversation and narration to make sure it's in the right place at the right time. A good editor, I'm told, will help me shape each episode individually, as well as the entire arc of the series. When I start work on my first story, I conduct interviews, tape my commentary, then show everything to my editor, Marcia, who I meet when she comes to the UCLA class I'm taking to give a presentation on editing podcasts. I like what she has to say and how she says it. After class is over, I ask for her business card. I call her the next day, tell her a little about myself, what I'm trying to do, and ask if she'll sign on for the pittance I'm able to pay her. Turns out, she's a crime junkie, so she happily joins my team. I feel bad about asking her to work for such low pay, so I sweeten the pot with a percentage of the profits. She flashes an enigmatic Mona Lisa smile. Only later do I understand what she's smiling about—the idea of actually making a profit.

After listening to what I have in the can for that first show, a series about that embezzler, Marcia suggests what she calls a "papercut/script." She works with me to develop a narrative voice, which means visualizing who I'm speaking to. This, she explains, will give my podcast voice authenticity that will help me connect with listeners. "If they like you, chances are they'll like the podcast. And if they like you and the podcast, they'll keep coming back for more."

I don't ask her what will happen if they don't like me or the podcast voice, because I don't want to hear the answer. I already have enough negative thoughts.

After some coaching from Marcia, and by *some*, I mean hours and hours, she announces I'm a "natural," that I have a "real knack" for this kind of work. Normally, I would dismiss any hint of praise, but in this case, Marcia seems so sincere and so excited that I actually start to believe she is telling the truth.

I don't get far before I realize I need to add someone else to my "team." I'm used to doing all the legwork myself, researching, setting up interviews, paying bills, but I quickly learn this is not a good use of my time. Besides, I'm not a detail-oriented person, and I need someone who is.

Marcia says I need a producer. "Other than you, your producer is the most important person on your podcast," she explains. The word producer scares me, until she talks me off the ledge by telling me to think of it as a right-hand man (or woman). This should be someone I am compatible with in terms of "vision." Someone I can bounce ideas off. Normally, it wouldn't be easy to find someone like that, but as it happens, I have a producer right under my nose: my friend Mark.

Mark and I go way back. Well, not way back but it certainly feels that way. It's actually only three years, but the way my life has been spinning forward, three years seems like a lifetime. We meet soon after I move to Sacramento and start working at the *Bee.*

I'm not big on the bar scene, so soon after my move I look for other ways to pass my non-working hours. This particular night, I attend a reading at one of the few bookstores in town. Mark is there, pushing his latest novel. I feel really bad for him because there are maybe five people in the audience, and half of them look like they've wandered in by mistake. They have no idea who he is or why he's there. When he finishes reading—a very funny section of his novel about a guy, after the breakup of a long-time relationship, traveling through Latin America—he takes questions from the audience, which has now dwindled down to three, one of whom is the bookstore manager. No one raises their hand to ask a question, so out of guilt about the embarrassing silence, I do. He shoots me a smile of relief and answers my question. I purchase a copy of his book (half guilt, half curiosity) and when I come back to get him to sign it, I realize mine is the only sale he's made. He asks my name and signs the book: *To the one and only Dakota. Thanks so much for being brave enough to buy this book.*

Just as I'm about to leave the store, he comes up behind me and taps me on the shoulder.

"Excuse me, Dakota, but this is my first time in Sacramento and I don't know a soul. They were supposed to have someone here to kind of chaperone me, you know, keep me out of trouble, but she got sick. I guess I could go back to the hotel and have room service send up something, but this small turnout was depressing enough so..."

"Are you asking me to have a drink with you?"

"Actually, I was thinking dinner. But thanks for saving me the trouble. How about it?"

"Are you trying to pick me up?"

"Um. Yeah. I guess. Maybe I am."

"Well then, sure, why not?"

"You say that like you have nothing else to do."

"Ain't that the truth. I've only been in Sacramento a couple months and if you count up the number of people I've had a conversation with, other than ones having to do with work, it would amount to fewer people than were here to hear you read."

"Ouch!" he says, clutching a spot just above his groin, "low blow."

I laugh. But I don't apologize.

"How do you know I'm not some insane serial killer? I mean, so far as I know they still haven't caught the Zodiac."

"I'm taking a chance based on what you just read. Besides," I say, pointing to a camera mounted above the checkout counter, "we're being watched, and," I wave at the camera, "I just made sure we're noticed."

It turns out he's only in Sacramento overnight, leaving the next day to go back to Los Angeles, where he lives. He doesn't strike me as the typical West Coast guy, which, I learn over dinner, is because he's actually a born and bred New Yorker.

What I think will be a quick meal lasts more than two hours. Romantic sparks don't fly, but we have a lot in common and the conversation flows freely. When the evening ends, we promise to keep in touch. You know, like when you say it but you know there's no way on earth it's going to happen. But it does happen. We start a phone and email friendship and we visit each other every few months, either in San Francisco or L.A. He's one of the reasons I move down to L.A., because I know I'll have at least one good friend there.

Mark is in on the podcast thing from the very beginning. I bounce ideas off him. We talk about what kinds of stories I should do. And so, when I realize I need a producer, he is the first one I ask.

"Let me preface this by saying, I will not take no for an answer. And, in fact, if you do say no, our friendship is over."

Turns out, this is right up his alley, because the book he is working on is a crime novel.

We work well together. He gets along with Marcia, and it turns out he's a genius when it comes to structure and pinpointing exactly where the story is. I'm used to newspaper writing. You get in and you get out. He's more into the long form, making sure every base is covered.

So, Mark becomes my field producer. He researches equipment, ultimately choosing multi-directional mics, ideal for on-location interviews. He takes his job seriously enough to learn the ins and outs of audio, including how to mic a subject, which he teaches me. And, in the beginning, he accompanies me on almost all my in-person interviews.

While we're getting the hang of podcasting, we're inseparable. But now that I'm more experienced, he goes back to his own life, which includes teaching a couple of writing classes and working on his latest novel, for which he got a small advance. He never offers to show me his work, and when I ask, he artfully changes the subject. This makes me more curious. But I respect his choice and don't bring it up again, though it's always in the back of my mind. What's he hiding? Is he just insecure? Is he afraid I won't like what he's writing and it'll affect our friendship? I'm much too persistent to let this drop, so I know eventually I'll bring up the subject again. And again.

One of the most important things about creating a podcast, I soon learn, is getting people to tune in. Marcia lays it out for me: "You've got to get the show to the ear of an influencer."

"Influencer? What's that?"

"Someone with followers."

"You mean like Jim Jones?"

She laughs. "Not exactly. Someone who has people who want to wear what they wear, smell like they smell, shop where they shop, vacation where they vacation. Find an influencer who talks about your show, Tweets about it. Puts photos up on Instagram. If you do, I guarantee people will tune in. And if people tune in, your podcast will be attractive to a sponsor and advertisers."

It's a simple formula to understand. Not so simple to put into practice. In part, because it means networking, something I'm not very good at.

Suddenly, now that I'm a podcaster, I have a career direction, something my mom has scolded me over and over again for not having. Personal life, not so much.

I know I should sit down with myself and figure out what I want to do with the rest of my life. But every time I consider making an appointment with me to have that discussion, something comes up that forces me to reschedule.

Finally, I decide the only way I'm ever going to do something about life outside work is to find a good therapist, which is not difficult in L.A. Everyone who's anyone in this town has either a personal trainer or an analyst, and many of them have both.

That's how Sheila and I hooked up. We've got the perfect relationship. I talk, she listens. Occasionally, she gives advice, some of it good, very little of which I take. It's not that I'm oppositional—although if you ask my mom, she'll nod her head enthusiastically and utter one of her favorite laments, "Now you know what I've been up against." It's just that when there's more than one path to take, I usually choose the wrong one. It's gotten to the point where I think maybe I should do the opposite of whatever my instinct tells me to do.

But here's where therapy has helped: It doesn't take me anywhere near as long as it did to realize what's the wrong choice, and when I do, I (almost) always stop, back up, recalculate—as my GPS says—and head in another direction. If I'm lucky, it's the right direction.

Although my personal life is a bit of a mess, Sheila agrees my professional life is going in the right direction. When she tells me so, I beam. I know this not because I'm checking myself out in the mirror, but because these are Sheila's actual words: "Dakota, you're beaming."

I take this as progress. I know I'm not there to please Angela, and yet, when she's pleased, I'm pleased. Maybe that's why when I'm about to embark on something risky—at least I know it's risky (that's progress, right?)—I sometimes conveniently forget to bring it up in one of our sessions. Let's face it, I don't want to disappoint her. Oh, by the way, eventually I do make the connection with my relationship with my mother. Not bad, right?

This explains not mentioning to Sheila anything about Francis Hoyt or my upcoming trip back East to further dig into his life. I don't say anything because I already know what Sheila will say. So, why waste precious therapy time (what is it, like four bucks a minute?) when I already know the answer.

9

Francis

I haven't pulled a job in more than a year and I'm getting itchy. I can feel the rust forming. I know it'll affect my ability to perform up to my standards. I know when I'm not up to my game. And I know inactivity leads to sloppiness and sloppy is what gets you pinched.

When it comes time to scratch the itch, I target the Valley. I choose a house at random, case it for a few days and nights. I read as much as I can about the house, even getting the floor plan. Usually, I strike at night, when everyone's home. But as part of my plan of starting fresh, this time I strike during the day, when no one's home. It doesn't come anywhere near the high I get at night, but eventually that'll come. But the itch needs to be scratched and so, a few days later, I target another house. This time, I strike after midnight, when I know everyone's tucked into bed and the house is dark. The first time, I don't bother taking anything. The second time, I help myself to some silver of middling value.

The itch is scratched.

I turn the stuff over to Vince. I explain I'm just warming up. That he should expect better next time.

"I'm happy to take care of this for you, Mr. Hoyt. But I am wondering when I can expect a more lucrative delivery."

"When I'm good and fucking ready," is my answer and,

87

fortunately for him, he backs off.

It's too early to make a final judgment, but so far, Vince turns out to be a good choice. He's prompt. He doesn't bullshit me. And he gives good return on a buck.

Bigger jobs take time and extra planning. Especially out here where everyone's still freaky since that Manson thing. Even though it was more than fifty years ago, it still resonates. So does the Hillside Strangler and the Night Stalker. Those serial rapist killers were back in the '70s and '80s, but the public has a long memory for these kinds of high-profile, violent crimes. It gives guys like me a bad name.

In L.A., anyone with dough has installed sophisticated anti-burglar paraphernalia, including motion detectors. That just ups the challenge, because I haven't found a system yet I can't beat.

Now

"The distinction between the past, present and future
is only a stubbornly persistent illusion."
—Albert Einstein

1
Dakota

I begin at the edges and work my way in toward the middle.

I have plenty of work to do before I'll feel comfortable and confident interviewing Hoyt, which is why I'm glad he's not pressing me to get the interview done. I need to know as much about him and his life of crime as possible. Without that information, I won't be able to ask intelligent questions, and I won't have a clue as to whether I'm getting honest answers. When you know the facts, it's way easier to trip someone up in a lie. Unless he says something that sends me spinning off in another direction, the chances are he'll be the grand finale of the podcast. This means that, ideally, interviewing him is several weeks away, which would set it a week or two after the July 4th holiday. I know by putting him off, by ignoring him as long as I can, I run the risk of his changing his mind. But I also know I only have one shot at him, and I don't want to waste it.

I've been doing the podcast for more than a year now and though the learning curve is steep, I'm feeling much more confident than when I started. Looking back, I ask myself, *What the heck was I thinking?* And then I realize that's the point. It's one of those things you do *without* thinking, *without* considering the possibility of failure. Otherwise, you might not do it at all.

By the time he accosts me in front of Starbucks, I already know all about this guy. I should have. I've been researching him for weeks. The trouble is, there's not much out there about him. Google him and you'll see what I mean. I've never been able to find a decent photograph of him, other than the old, black-and-white mug shot from when he was jailed that one and only time. And like motor vehicle licenses, no one ever looks remotely like themselves in those things.

Somehow, he manages to fly under the radar, which makes him a bit of a cypher. Law enforcement knows about him but the rest of us, not so much. But by the time he walks out of that courthouse, he's started to get some ink. He's been written up on newspapers like the *Miami Herald* to the *New York Post* to the *Boston Globe*. But each story pretty much regurgitates whatever facts, if there are any, have already been written about him. For instance, there's very little personal information. The only reason I know his age is because of that stint in prison he did in his late-twenties. He's in his mid-forties now, and if you look at a photo of yourself at both those ages, you'll see two different people.

Hoyt makes no bones about being the best in the burglary business. Not one of the best. *The* best. Law enforcement agrees. One article likens him to the Scarlet Pimpernel. In the words of Barness Emmuska Orczy, who wrote the series,
"They seek him, here, they seek him there
Those Frenchies seek him everywhere
Is he in heaven or is he in hell?
That damned elusive Pimpernel."
He gets in and out of spots no one else can. At first, I think these tales of derring-do must be fake, or hyperbole, but it turns out they're true. I know this because I'm able to track down folks, like the chief of police of a New Jersey town, who verify at least one of the tales.

"Is it true you knew Hoyt was in the area and was most likely going to break into a house, so you plastered the neighborhood with cops, thinking there was no way he could show up and not be caught? And that in the morning you found he'd hit not just one but two houses, right in the middle of the sector you were surveilling?"

"Yes," he says. "That's true. I don't know how he did it, but he did."

There's very little known about his past and even less about his private life now, especially since he calmly sashayed away from that courthouse about a year ago. I know that seems contradictory—the man who never gets caught winds up in court—but my listeners, once the podcast goes live, will learn what I mean. If I'm lucky, and the podcast is a good one, I'm hoping to get people to come out of the woodwork, people who know him now, and in the past, to give us a better idea of who he really is and what drives him.

As a former reporter who relishes research, I enjoy digging into people's lives. I love the challenge. Unfortunately, he hasn't left much in the way of footprints. I've narrowed it down to the part of the country where he was brought up: somewhere outside St. Louis. I'm able to track down the St. Louis hospital where he was born, so I get the names of his mother and father on his birth certificate. They weren't married at the time of his birth, but married a couple years later, after the birth of his sister. The trail pretty much runs cold after the family leaves St. Louis.

His father died in 1997 of liver disease, which probably means he was a heavy drinker. I'm pretty sure his sister and mother are still alive, but I haven't been able to track them down yet. As a result, I know nothing about his childhood. I do know he's had several girlfriends over the years, but I don't find any evidence of his ever being married. I'm pretty sure he doesn't have kids. At least none that I've found.

I'm able to track down a few guys who were in prison with him, but none of them will talk to me. I don't know whether it's because of some kind of loyalty code among bad guys, or fear. Despite his small stature, Hoyt has the reputation of being a tough guy, someone not to mess with. There are even rumors he's had people killed, but I'm not sure that isn't just urban legend, because there are no reports of any violence committed during any of his break-ins.

When it comes to law enforcement, I have better luck. I'm able to track down one of the two guys responsible for his latest arrest. Charlie Floyd is a former Connecticut State investigator who's almost as much of a character as Hoyt. He's very chatty and charming and, as the result of a phone conversation, I'm able to persuade him to be interviewed for the show. I'm supposed to head back East to Connecticut in a couple weeks, after he gets back from vacation. Before he hangs up, he says, "Just saying the word 'vacation' seems a little ridiculous. Vacation from what? Doing nothing? This retirement I'm supposed to be in is tough to get used to. I spend most of my time figuring out what to do with myself, so being interviewed for your little podcast is a no-brainer for me."

Little podcast? I almost say something snarky. But I learn from being a reporter when to keep my mouth shut, especially while trying to get someone to open up. *Never insult or get into an argument with a potential source.* I learn this the hard way. Just because I know when to keep my mouth shut doesn't mean I always do. I'm pretty much all in your face when I start out, but eventually I learn to tone it down. But every so often my real self materializes and my mouth gets me into trouble.

2

Francis

Vince texts my burner.

Contact me as soon as possible. Have something you might be interested in.

VC

I'll answer him. But not yet.

I've been in L.A. a few months. I've settled into a small, two-room, one bath, sparsely furnished cottage in Santa Monica, half an acre behind the main residence. The owner, a seventy-ish, rail-thin former bit player who wears way too much makeup and claims that back in the '30s and '40s a bunch of stars stayed in what she refers to as the "guest quarters." She lists a few, but the only name that sticks is Robert Mitchum. As a kid, I watch *Night of the Hunter* a zillion times on TV. While most kids my age want to be Tom Cruise or Bruce Willis, I want to be Mitchum, or more precisely, the character he plays, the Reverend Harry Powell, whose fingers of one hand are tattooed with the word LOVE, the fingers of the other with HATE. I take a magic marker and write those words on my fingers, which doesn't go over so good with my teachers or the vice principal, who suspend me a couple days for being a bad influence on my fellow students. When he pronounces my suspension, I try hard not to laugh in his face, since all he's doing is giving me a free vacation. I use it to roam the streets, looking for real trouble to get into. The kind of trouble Mitchum and Harry Powell would approve of.

It takes close to a week for the letters to finally fade. If it weren't for my old man, who doesn't want me out of school—only because he knows the kind of trouble I can get into—I'd make the ink permanent. He's always threatening me with serious bodily harm if he has to take time out of his precious fucking day to come to school because I've gotten into trouble. What makes his day so fucking precious is beyond me. Unless he means waiting for the bars to open. "I dropped out after ninth grade, so why the hell would I want to go back there now?" he says.

The cottage I rent, only a couple miles from the beach, suits me not just because of the Mitchum connection, but because of the privacy it offers. There are no neighbors within fifty yards sticking their noses into my business. I rarely see my ancient landlady, who lives in the main house and rarely ventures out. I pay three months' cash in advance, which keeps her happy and our interaction at a minimum.

Despite costing me three grand a month, the place is nothing fancy. Two rooms. The living area has a faded, flower-print couch, a couple of chairs, a hutch, a folding table and a twenty-one-inch flat-screen TV. There's a Pullman kitchen with a half-refrigerator, a sink and a hotplate. The bedroom is just large enough to hold a single bed, a dresser and a small nightstand. There's one small closet. If I sit on the edge of the bed, I can practically reach out and touch all four walls. The bathroom has a shower stall, sink, and toilet. It's perfect for me, since I don't own many possessions.

Even though I never learn to swim, I like being near the water. It represents freedom. Growing up in the Midwest made me feel boxed in.

Most afternoons I jog over to the Santa Monica pier, varying the route slightly each day.

I find the same bench on the pier and sit in the same spot on the bench, as close to the ocean as possible. I carefully arrange my backpack next to me, in an attempt to discourage anyone from sitting too close. I'm not looking to make friends. I only want to sit there and read, or stare out onto the Pacific while I ponder my future. The hypnotic sound of gulls swooping across the shoreline gives me the same calm I get from meditation.

Only once does someone come close enough to make me uncomfortable. He's a middle-aged goofball wearing a Polo shirt, plaid Bermuda shorts, black calf-length socks and brand new white Nikes. A blue nylon fanny pack is strapped around his waist and he's carrying an L.A. guidebook.

There are other benches, but for some reason he chooses mine. I glare at him, but either he doesn't see me or he doesn't care. Seemingly oblivious to my existence, he sits there, maybe four feet away from me, thumbing through his guidebook. Occasionally, he looks up, a slightly bewildered look on his face, squints up into the deep blue, cloudless sky, then returns to his book.

I want him gone. I push my backpack closer to him, trying to mark what I think should be the proper distance between us, knowing, of course, the proper distance is that he should be on another planet.

Finally, the inevitable happens.

"Excuse me, sir," he says, dropping the guidebook down in his lap and leaning slightly toward me.

I ignore him.

"Excuse me, sir. Sorry to bother you but…"

His whiny, Midwestern voice reminds me of my father's. Which probably explains why I feel like bashing his fucking brains out.

I keep glaring at him, hoping he'll get the message.

He doesn't.

"Would you happen to be from around here?" he asks.

I say nothing, but he doesn't take the hint. He inches closer and raises his voice, as if he thinks I haven't heard him. "Excuse me, sir, but if you don't mind, I could use a little help."

I want to say, *do I look like the fucking Chamber of Commerce?* But I don't. I just want to get rid of him, so I say, "What's the problem?"

"I just got into town the other day. First time here. Always wanted to visit, but never had the chance. Some place, huh? It really is a little slice of paradise. I mean, is the sun always shining?"

What do I have to do to get this guy to shut the fuck up?

"I was just wondering if you know how far it is from here to Venice Beach. According to the guide," he pats the book, still in his lap, "that's where they have what they call Muscle Beach. I've seen it in so many movies, I want to see for myself what it's like."

What the fuck? This guy looks like he's never lifted a weight in his life and that's what he wants to see?

"I'm new in town. Check your guidebook."

"You're right, of course. I'm sure it's in here somewhere. It's just that I have trouble figuring out distances from these tiny, little maps. Being this is the first time I'm in L-A, I don't have a proper sense of distances. Especially with the traffic you have here. I've never seen anything like it. Is it like walkable from here?"

"This is L-A, pal. Nothing's fucking walkable."

He laughs. "Yes, you've got that right. By the way, my name's Jeffrey." He extends his hand. I ignore it. He shrugs and takes it back.

"I'm usually pretty good with accents but I can't quite figure out where you're from," he says.

"Somewhere else," I say, as I dig into my backpack and pull out a frayed paperback copy of Hammett's Continental Op stories. It's one of the books that got me through my cross-country bus trip. I open it to a page somewhere in the middle, marked with a bus ticket stub.

He laughs. "I guess that's true. Everyone here seems to be from somewhere else. But where exactly are you from?"

"See this," I say, holding up the book.

"Sure…" he says. He bends over to read the cover. "Dashiell Hammett. Don't think I've ever heard of…"

"I come out here so I can get some peace and quiet. I don't want to be rude," I raise my voice just a little, "but I just wanna read my book and be left the fuck alone."

The smile disappears from his face, replaced by a look of fear.

"Um, well, I guess I shouldn't interrupt you."

"I think that's probably a good idea."

He mumbles "asshole" under his breath. He doesn't think I hear him, but I do.

"You think I'm an asshole?"

"I'm uh…"

"You're right. I am an asshole. In fact, I'm the worst kind of asshole. I'm the kind of asshole who can take you out with one fucking punch. That's the kind of asshole I am. A dangerous asshole. So maybe you should get the hell off this bench…"

His face turns red. He's frightened. He doesn't know what to do. Should he apologize? Should he stand up for himself? Should he just get the fuck up and leave?

His mouth opens, but no words come out. Finally, he stuffs his guidebook into his fanny pack and gets up to leave. I watch him as he disappears into the growing afternoon crowd.

I smile and stare back out into the Pacific.

It's been a couple hours since Vince's "urgent" message.

"What's up, Vince?" I say in a voice that's supposed to communicate annoyance at being bothered.

"I'm calling about a business opportunity I think might interest you."

"Do you think someone like me needs help finding work, Vince?"

"Of course not."

"I'll give you the benefit of the doubt, Vince, because I'd expect someone at your supposed level would do his homework. So, let me set you straight. I don't take assignments."

"I understand, Mr. Hoyt, but I think this particular opportunity is something you might be very interested in pursuing. You're perfect for the job. And I guarantee you'll be quite satisfied with the compensation."

Money only interests me as a way of keeping score. What I've socked away is more than enough for several lifetimes. A challenge is much more important than the payoff. But I'll listen to Vince's proposition, because I can tell from his voice that he's excited about it.

"What you got?"

"I think this is something we should discuss in person. I've got two tickets to the Dodger game tomorrow night. They're playing St. Louis. I thought we might mix business with a little pleasure."

"I'm not big on team sports, Vince."

"I suspected as much, seeing the trajectory of your career. But I thought I might persuade you to change your mind. In this town, going to a Dodger game is more about being seen than watching the actual game."

"Give it a try," I say, as he launches into a boring speech about America's pastime and his theories on why understanding baseball helps you better understand life.

Finally, I've had enough.

"Okay."

"Okay, what?"

"I'll meet with you."

"Fantastic. I promise you'll have a good time. I'll pick you up around five."

"I thought games start at seven."

"If you don't want to get stuck in traffic for two hours, you leave early."

"If you can avoid traffic in this town, Vince, you're a fucking magician,"

"You don't avoid it, Mr. Hoyt. You work around it."

I don't want him to pick me up—I don't need his favors and I don't want him to know where I live. I tell him I'll grab a cab and meet at the stadium.

I heed Vince's warning and order a cab early enough to get me there in plenty of time.

I spot Vince standing in front of the gate, wearing a nylon Dodger windbreaker, a Brooklyn Dodger hat and brand new jeans a couple sizes too big.

"You made it," he says.

"I said I'd be here, so here I am."

He sees me staring at his outfit.

"My boys are responsible for my fashion choices. They won't let me out of the house unless I'm wearing Dodger blue. They have no idea the Dodgers were originally from Brooklyn. No sense of history. Mention a player who was in the game ten, twenty years ago, their faces go blank. Wearing this Brooklyn cap," he brings his hand up and with two fingers grabs the brim and tips it forward, "is my way of showing they can't push me around." He laughs. "They can, of course. They're pissed at me for not taking them tonight. I'll make it up to them with an afternoon game next weekend when the Giants are in town. As for the pants," he sticks his thumbs in the waistband and pulls forward, exposing an inch or two of air. "The result of losing twenty-five pounds. Of course, you witnessed the trade-off, which was me smoking again."

I'm not the target audience for his family shit. "What say we get this show on the road, Vince."

"Of course. Come. Follow me."

He knows where we're going, but I'm the one setting the pace. All I want to do is get to the fucking seats, find out what this job is, and get the hell out of here. On the other hand, Vince is treating this like a date, complete with small talk.

"You grow up rooting for a particular team, Mr. Hoyt?"

"Too busy rooting for myself, Vince."

"Did you play sports as a kid?"

"I found other ways to occupy myself."

I don't tell him about the gymnastics or the running. The less Vince knows about me, the better.

It's a Wednesday night, but the crowd is surprisingly large and growing larger.

"Pretty incredible, right? Nothing like Dodger fans, except maybe Laker fans. You'd be surprised how many deals are consummated here."

Vince is right about the seats. He's scored a primo box along the third baseline, only a couple rows back from the field, which is so lit up by the powerful flood lights the grass appears to be glowing.

The crowd is chicly dressed, as if they're on their way to some Hollywood opening. Even though the game hasn't started, between the crowd and the music blaring over the loudspeaker, the noise is deafening. If feels like I'm in the middle of a giant video game.

"If you enjoy seeing Hollywood stars," he says as we weave through the crowd on our way to our seats, "you'll see plenty of them here. Kim Kardashian, Matthew McConaughey, Will Ferrell, Rob Lowe, Danny DeVito, Sharon Stone, even Jackie Chan. They all eat, drink and breathe Dodger blue."

"I'm impressed," I say. Truth is, I couldn't give a shit. I recognize the names of maybe half the stars he's mentioned. Vince and the rest of these assholes, can think of themselves as celebrities, but all I see is a stadium full of potential marks. Halfway through his litany of names I begin to wonder if maybe I should start paying attention. I might wind up adding more celebrities to the list of homes I rip off. What better time than when all these assholes are at the game?

In the end, Vince is right. It's tough not to get caught up in the excitement. As we make the final descent down the aisle to our seats, we're met by an elderly usher who leads us the rest of the way. Once there, he wipes imaginary dust off our seats.

Vince takes a neatly folded twenty out of his pocket and presses it into the old man's hand.

The players are bigger than they should be. Loud rock music blasts from hidden speakers. Every so often the growing crowd cheers as images are projected onto the Jumbotron hovering over the packed stadium. It reminds me of the carnivals that used magically appear every summer, setting up in a large, empty field not far from where we lived. Our old lady takes me and my sister there once. I'm maybe seven or eight, and haven't officially started on my life of crime. After that one time, she seems to lose interest in providing us with entertainment. I guess she figures life will be disappointing enough without believing there's the possibility of fun.

Without money, I find creative ways to sneak in. I scour the grounds for dropped or discarded tickets. Soon I realize there were other ways to cash in. If I played little boy lost, I could con people out of a few tickets. Or I will come up with some sob story that results in someone slipping me a buck or two. The better the story, the more they give.

By the time I'm a teenager, I manage to convince some carny I'm old enough to work a booth. While he slips away looking to find teenage girls to screw, he leaves me in charge. It doesn't take long to figure out how to skim a few bucks. It isn't so much the money, though that'll come in handy; it's the high I get from conning a conman. Soon, I get up the nerve to ask for a piece of the action and when he hesitates, I let slip I know about those underage girls.

A few minutes before the game starts, a vendor appears. He smiles at Vince, giving the impression they know each other. He crouches down so his head is practically in Vince's lap. Vince whispers something in his ear. The vendor nods. Vince pulls out his wallet, and hands the guy a couple twenties.

"How much I owe you, Vince?" I ask.

"This one's on me, Mr. Hoyt." He smiles. "You're a legitimate business expense."

Suddenly, the crowd roars and I look up to see the Dodgers lining up on the first base line. A young girl, maybe twelve or thirteen, emerges from the dugout and skips toward the mound. The crowd, already ramped up, rises. So does Vince. I hesitate, but rather than call attention to myself, I rise, too.

This tiny little black pre-teen, her hair tied back in a pony-tail, belts out "The Star-Spangled Banner" like a pint-sized Aretha Franklin. While she's still holding the last note the crowd roars its approval, and the players start jogging onto the field.

The pitcher, a tall, lanky kid who looks like he just started to shave, throws white pellets that thwack into the catcher's glove. As the announcer runs down the lineup, the vendor, carrying a cardboard tray holding a large, plastic cup of beer, a seltzer, and two sandwiches reappears. The aroma triggers my appetite.

"I know you don't drink and I know you don't eat meat, Mr. Hoyt, so I've taken the liberty of ordering you a vegetarian option. This is L-A. Half the town is vegan and the other half is gluten-free so the alternatives are surprisingly tasty."

I'm impressed. Not about the food, but Vince's knowledge of my eating habits. I've known Artie close to ten years and he still doesn't know better than to order me one of those fucking, fatty pastrami sandwiches every time we meet.

"You've done your homework, Vince," I say, as he hands over a sandwich wrapped in foil.

"It's part of my job to know my clients' likes and dislikes, Francis. You don't mind if I call you Francis, do you?"

I don't answer, which he takes as a yes.

By the beginning of the third inning, the spectacle has worn off and I'm getting antsy. Vince must sense he's losing me, because he leans in and whispers, "I know this isn't your sweet spot, Mr. Hoyt, and I appreciate your indulging me. But I think it's time we get down to business."

"Good idea."

"First off, and I know this isn't something I have to address with someone as experienced as you, but I'd be remiss if I didn't remind you that everything we speak about tonight goes no further than the two of us. Agreed?"

I nod, yes.

"Let me start by saying that this is a very exciting opportunity and I know this is not your usual 'thing,' but I'm convinced you're the right man for the job."

"I'm all ears, Vince."

"Well, for one thing, this is not a home invasion. In fact, it's not a home at all."

"So, what is it?"

He leans in closer. "It's a place known as The Warehouse."

"A warehouse?"

"Not *a* warehouse, Mr. Hoyt. *The* Warehouse. But it's not a warehouse at all. Rather, think of it as a giant bank vault. It's a large room, about the size of a basketball court, with four walls lined cheek-to-jowl with what can best be described as safety deposit boxes, some of them as large as a sports locker."

"You're talking about a bank for bad guys."

"Exactly. You've heard of this?"

"Yeah. There was one up in Providence.

"Yes. People in our line of work, with large amounts of cash, often waiting to be laundered or with goods waiting to be fenced, can't, for obvious reasons, go to their local Wells Fargo or Bank of America and open an account or rent a safety deposit box. And they often require immediate access to the fruits of their labor. Cash, bearer bonds, rare coins, stamps, silver, jewelry, gold, even works of art. In short, Mr. Hoyt, these people require a safe haven, away from prying eyes, with twenty-four-seven access. The *Warehouse* offers the perfect solution. But at the same time, it offers others a unique opportunity."

Vince is interrupted by a roar from the crowd. Some kid named Bellinger launches a rocket into the left-field stands.

"I love that kid," says Vince. His attention jerks back to the field. "He's what, twenty-four? And he's got some career in front of him. He's pulling down twelve mil a year." He shakes his head. "What the hell's a kid like him gonna do with that kind of dough? If my kids didn't have two left feet I'd have 'em on the ball field every day. Unfortunately, they take after me. Brains, but no discernible physical prowess. I'm hoping eventually they'll be able to walk and chew gum at the same time."

"What say we shelve the chit-chat and get back to business, Vince."

"Yes. Of course. Business, not pleasure. In any case, I have a client who's looking for someone to get into The Warehouse and liberate cash and certain other items of value, with as little fuss as possible."

"You're looking for someone to break into a mob bank and steal from them? How long you think that person would continue to exist? Couple hours? A day? A week? If you find someone stupid enough to do it, take out an insurance policy on him. That's about as safe an investment as I can think of."

"Under normal circumstances, that'd be a fair estimation. But these are not ordinary circumstances. I've given you the big picture. Now here are the salient facts. Because it's a mob bank and everyone knows it, security is remarkably lax. Who in his right mind would steal from the mob? Even if they did, it's not like the owner can go to the cops and report the theft. And the owners of the bank can't let it be known that they've been taken down. How would that look? Hence, the only worry would be retaliation at the hands of the owner..."

"That's a damn big worry..."

"Yes. But there's an important factor that mitigates the danger enormously."

"What's that?"

"The bank is owned and operated by someone who shall remain nameless. But this someone is, how about we refer to him as the bank *president*..."

"Wait a minute. Are you saying that it's the owner who wants his own bank taken down?"

Vince's eyes light up. He nods his head slowly up and down.

"Are you fucking kidding me? Why?"

"Even if I knew why, I couldn't tell you. So far as you and I are concerned, it's irrelevant. Think of it, though. It's like getting a combined free pass *and* a Get-Out-of-Jail card. You won't even have to worry about gaining access, because you'll get full co-operation. You won't have to worry about the law, because it'll never be reported. And most important, there'll be no fear of retaliation."

Something happens back out on the field and the crowd roars. Vince stands to join the cheering. I don't. I'm too busy trying to let this sink in. Rolling it around in my mind to see if it's really as good as it sounds.

The cheering settles. The fans sit back down. So does Vince.

"If you want to know the truth, Vince, it sounds too fucking good to be true. But even if it's true, why me? Anyone could waltz in and out of there with the goods. You don't need some-one like me to pull this off. Any fucking flunky off the street could get it done."

"You sell yourself short, Francis. It's important to have this done by a pro, by someone with your talent. The job has to look like the real deal. Only someone with your talent can pull this off."

"You mean there can be no hint of it being an *inside* job."

"Exactly. Even with all the information you'll be provided, you'll have to figure out a believable and plausible plan for getting in and out, without raising suspicions that it is an inside job."

"So, you're telling me that it's my job to make something simple look hard."

He smiles.

"Okay. Okay. Give me a minute," I say, as I drift off into my own head. I've got a thousand questions. I look over at Vince. He's got a big, fat smile on his face. He knows I'm interested, but I'm not about to give him a quick answer. I need to look at this from every angle.

"First off, let me enlighten you, Vince. There's no such thing as an *easy* job. You'll find anyone who thinks it is banging a tin cup on the bars in the joint."

"I know. That's why I thought of you. If you can make an impossible job look easy, then you can make an easy job look impossible. Everything depends on your selling it as an outside job. Some rogue punk with shit for brains who thinks he can play with fire and not get burned. Let's face it, there are plenty of those people out there. There can be absolutely no suspicion of this being an inside job, which means you might have to leave a false trail. You understand, don't you, Francis?"

"Don't insult me, Vince."

"I apologize. I know how well-planned your operations are. That's why I think you're the right man for the job. You'll be provided with enough information to carry out the operation in the most efficient, safest way. I promise you, there will be no surprises."

"There are always surprises, Vince. The goal is to anticipate what they might be and be prepared. Where is this place?"

"Strip-mall not far from the Marina. It shares space with a high-end jewelry store."

"What's that supposed to mean?"

"The jewelry store is on street level. Beneath it, in the basement, is the vault room. But before I get any more specific, I need to know if this is something that interests you."

"Yes. But I'll have to know more before I commit."

"Such as?"

"Who's behind this?"

He smiles. "I'm afraid that's not possible."

"That would be a major impediment."

"I understand, Francis, but it's non-negotiable."

I'm interested, but I can't appear to be too anxious.

"I need to know more about the setup."

"There are two entrances. The front entrance is through the jewelry store. And then there's a back entrance."

"Cameras?"

"Inside and out."

"Alarm system?"

"There's an alarm button behind the counter that's connected to a private security firm. If you take the job, we'll provide you with a very detailed blueprint of the entire building, as well as a detailed rundown of the alarm system, and anything else you might need."

"Guards?"

"It depends."

"On?"

"I don't want to seem like a broken record, Francis, but all these details will be provided only when you agree to take on the job. It's a very big pay day. Is this something that might interest you?"

I'm not ready to show my hand yet. The less anxious I am, the more leverage I have. It's not about the money. It never is. There's got to be something else. In this case, the idea of ripping off guys who make a living ripping off other people is very appealing. Plus, there's the challenge of making it appear to be something it's not. And I don't care what Vince is trying to sell me, there's the very real element of danger, which only adds to the adrenaline high I'm always chasing.

When I was first starting out and pretty much living on the streets, I had more than my fair share of running with junkies. They lived from one day to the next, always chasing that dragon. But here's the sick thing. If word hit the streets that this particular strain of dope was a killer, an actual killer, you'd think junkies would avoid it. But it was just the opposite. If the stuff was dangerous enough to kill, it meant it could also provide the ultimate high.

This is the very same appeal for me. I fuck up, I die. The stakes couldn't be higher.

"I'll think about it."

"I understand. We wouldn't want you to jump in without giving it serious thought. But my people would like to have an answer by the end of the weekend. If you turn us down, we'll have to look elsewhere."

"One more thing."

"Yes?"

"How much are we talking about?"

He smiles. He knows he's got me on the line. Now all he has to do is reel me in.

"I'm not prepared to negotiate the deal at this time, Francis. If your answer is yes, I have to go back to my client and then, if he approves, we can meet again and discuss details and discuss payment. But again, I want to stress that our discussion remains between us."

I lean in closer until I'm only a few inches from his face. Close enough so I can smell the mustard on his breath.

"Francis Hoyt is no snitch."

From the look on his face, I believe he gets the point.

4

Francis

No one plays the game better than I do. Too anxious, my price goes down. Cool, my price goes up. I follow the most important rule of negotiation: be ready to walk away.

This job might be just what I'm looking for. It might seem like an easy score, but nothing is ever as easy as it seems. No matter how Vince pitches it, no matter how fool-proof it might seem, all kinds of things can go wrong. There are plenty of red flags. But that's what makes it especially appealing. Because when something goes wrong, that's when the adrenaline level jumps off the chart.

Three days after our meeting at Dodger Stadium, while sitting on my regular bench on the Santa Monica pier, I give Vince a call.

"Good to hear from you, Francis. When I didn't hear from you, I assumed you weren't interested."

"There's a lesson there for you, Vince."

"I hope the answer's yes."

"Let's say I'm interested."

"How can we close the deal?"

"I need another face-to-face. But not a fucking baseball game. Just you and me, Vince."

"I understand."

"You got an office, right?"

"I do."

"Tomorrow morning. Seven A-M."

"Seven A-M?"

"I'm an early riser."

"It's Saturday. I take my boys to soccer."

"Maybe you ought to get your priorities straight, Vince."

"Would it be possible to make it a little later?"

"No."

He hesitates. "All right."

"What's the address?"

He gives me the address of an office building on Wilshire.

"See you tomorrow, Vince. Seven. Sharp. Don't be late."

5

Francis

At six forty-five the cab drops me off a couple blocks from Vince's office. I stroll by the front entrance of the building, hunched down, cap pulled down to avoid a clear shot of me from any cameras in the area. I enter the underground parking garage and take the elevator up to the seventeenth floor. Alongside Vince's name on the office door is *Danny Schwartz, Accountant*.

I don't like surprises. This is a surprise. This is not an auspicious start.

The door is locked. Vince better be inside, waiting for me. I rap on the door a couple times, until I hear the shuffling of feet heading in my direction.

Vince, dressed casually in a bright green Lacoste polo shirt, khaki pants and brown tasseled loafers, opens the door. His deeply tanned face reeks of after-shave and since the last time I saw him he's had his hair cut. His fingernails are neatly manicured, He's got a gold wedding band on one finger, and on the other hand there's a gold pinkie ring. He looks like he's been dressed by some preppie art director at *GQ*.

Vince greets me with a big smile and throws his arm around my shoulder as if we're old buddies. We're not.

There are two doors in front of us. The one to our right has Vince's name on it, the other, to our left, Schwartz's.

"Who the fuck is Danny Schwartz?"

"An old friend. He needs an office, I've got an extra one. Don't worry, he has no idea what business I'm in. And to be honest, it makes my operation seem more legit."

"Anyone home?" I nod toward Schwartz's office.

"Are you kidding? When he does show up, and that's not often, he doesn't roll in till ten, eleven o'clock. Never weekends. It's just you and me, pal," he says, patting my back.

"You shoulda mentioned it, Vince," I mumble. "I don't like surprises."

"Sorry. Didn't think of it."

I could let it go, but I don't.

"It's the fucking principle, man. If I'd known the setup here, maybe I'd have found someplace else to meet. Let's get something straight from the get-go, Vince. I like everything on the table. All the time. No half-truths. No omissions. No surprises. It's how I roll. When I make decisions, I need to know all the information."

He throws up his hands. "Sorry. Mea culpa. My bad. I didn't mean for us to start off on the wrong foot. What say we try moving past this?"

I glare at him for a moment, but say nothing. If he's paying attention, the look on my face says it all.

"I'm very pleased you've decided to take the gig, Francis," he says, as he leads the way into his office, a circus of chrome and glass. Plush black leather couch, Eames chair, an enormous slab of glass held up by two blindingly white file cabinets. There's a full bar in one corner of the room. On the wall, prints by Calder, Miro, Oldenburg, Salle and Hockney. At least he's got good taste.

"Can I get you anything?"

I shake my head. "Let's get to it."

"I don't know about you, but I need something to wake me up."

He goes over to a bar across from his desk where there's a pot of coffee brewing. While he pours himself a cup, I check out the framed diplomas on the wall. UCLA. University of Southern

California School of Law.

"You never said you were a lawyer."

"Technically, I'm not. I passed the bar, handled a few cases, but I was involuntarily retired."

"What's that supposed to mean?"

He smiles. "Let's just say the state bar and I had a little disagreement about what was acceptable behavior and what wasn't. As it turned out, it was the best thing that could have happened to me."

He sits down at his desk.

"I have to say, my being a lawyer, even for so brief a time, did make the Jewish side of the family *kvell*. My mother's side, not so much. I think they would have been much happier if I'd become a priest." He laughs. "Unfortunately, I never got the calling."

"Before we get started, Vince, let's get something straight. I've got a funny feeling about this job. There's something that doesn't quite make sense. I don't know what it is, but I'll find out. And if you fuck me. I promise you, I will find out and you will live to regret it. And if you don't believe me, or you think you're smarter than I am, well, just ask around."

"I have no reason to fuck you, Francis. I depend on people like you for my livelihood. I know you don't especially like me, but frankly, I don't care. What I do care about is that you trust me. Because if you don't, this thing we have," he waves his hand from me back to him, "this relationship, for want of a better word, will not work. And I very much want it to work. I think working together will be very productive...and rewarding. For both of us. I lead a comfortable life and I've gotten used to it. I have every reason in the world, including a family I love, to stay out of trouble. I need you to understand what's good for you is good for me. If we can agree on that very simple principle, I think we can create a long and lucrative association. Am I making myself clear?"

I don't say anything. I don't have to. He's the one who has to worry if things go wrong. Not me.

"One thing you ought to know about me, Vince, is I do not turn the other cheek."

"I understand. Frankly, one of the reasons we're approaching you is because you work alone, you get the job done with discretion."

"You mean I keep my mouth shut."

"You proved that when you chose jail time over ratting out a partner."

"Ultimately, it wasn't in my best interest. If it had been, who knows what I would have done?"

"Since you're here, I assume you're accepting my proposition."

The idea's to keep people off-balance, so I look him straight in the eye and say, "The door's open."

"What do you need from me to get you to walk through that door, Mr. Hoyt?"

"To fill in some of the blanks, like who's behind this and why?"

He leans back in his black leather chair, his hands knitted behind his head, and sighs. "I wish I could help you out there, Francis, but like I said earlier, I'm afraid I'm not at liberty to divulge that information."

"Why not?"

"It's a delicate situation. And the information isn't all that important anyway. I'm sure you can understand the ramifications to my client if word ever got out."

"This is not the way I usually do business, Vince."

"I understand. And if this is a deal-breaker, I'm sorry…"

"Let's table that for a while and move on. What's my cut?"

"My client is willing to pay you a quarter of a million dollars, plus a handsome bonus after the job's completed."

"How's this supposed to work?"

"I'll provide you with a list of exactly what my client wants, both in terms of cash and non-cash assets. You'll also receive instructions as to which boxes are off-limits."

"Why's that?"

"To be blunt, Francis, you're being hired to perform a specific task. The why shouldn't concern you."

"But it does."

He unknits his hands and leans forward. "I'm afraid this is how the deal is structured. If it bothers you enough to miss out on a golden opportunity you can simply say no, we'll go our separate ways and there'll be no hard feelings."

"Hard feelings are my specialty, Vince. I'm an expert at them. I'm curious. Just how much cash is there in the vault?"

"From what I understand, in excess of several million dollars. But some of that is untouchable."

The payoff is okay, but the challenge of making an inside job look like something else is appealing. And though I'd never admit this to Vince, the element of danger, in the form of getting involved with the mob, is a major turn-on. Not knowing who's behind it is a huge red flag. I know Vince is never gonna give it up, but there are other ways for me to find out.

"Do we have a deal?" he asks, extending his right hand across his desk.

I hesitate. "I think we do."

"Excellent," he says, practically catapulting himself out of his chair. For a split second, he's suspended in mid-air, leaning out over his desk, not quite sure what to do with his outstretched hand, because I don't make a move to match his gesture. Finally, after a few well-timed seconds, I reach my hand out and shake his.

"All righty then. I'll be providing you with blueprints of the building, including the vault room. You'll have the work schedules of everyone on the premises at all times. This includes who's guarding the building, where they are, and what kind of alarm system there is. And, of course, you'll be provided with all the codes to all the locks. Anything else you might need will come from me. I'll be your sole contact."

"Before we get started, you need to know one thing, Vince. I do not, under any circumstances, share plans. With you or any-one else. This includes when I do the job and how it gets done."

"Understood. And as it happens, that benefits all of us. If we don't have that information we can't share it with anyone. I'll be in touch with you in a day or two when I have all the infor-mation, and we'll set up a time and place to hand it over. You'll receive fifty thousand dollars up front and the rest when the job is completed and you hand over what you've liberated. Is that satisfactory?"

I shake my head, no. "Half up front."

"Excuse me?"

"You heard me, Vince. Half and half. I don't negotiate. Tell your boss he can take it or leave it. I'm not doing a job like this for a measly fifty grand. Especially without knowing who I'm working for. No way I'm gonna trust someone for two hundred grand to be paid on the other end. I don't want to have to resort to self-help to get paid."

"That wouldn't be prudent, Francis. My employer has a very biblical sense of justice."

"Then we have that in common. But if you think threats like that are going to keep me in line…"

His face turns red. "Francis, please, you totally misunder-stand me. I'm sorry you're interpreting that as a threat. It's any-thing but…"

"Half now. Half when I turn over the goods. That's the deal. Take it or leave it."

He hesitates a moment.

"I'll communicate that to my employer."

"One more thing."

"Yes?"

"If I have the slightest suspicion I'm being set-up, I'm out and I keep the first payment."

"It won't come to that. I promise. And if for any reason we believe there's been a leak and we believe that leak comes from you, intentional or not, not only is the deal null and void, but we'll go to great lengths to get back our initial payment. My boss is not an understanding or patient man. If the job goes south because of something you do or don't do, I'm afraid there'll be retaliation. This is not a threat. It's simply a fact. So, Francis, we're now partners and we'll all be rooting for your success."

Before I leave, I reach into my back pocket and remove a folded-in-half list printed in block letters, and hand it to him.

"What's this?" he asks.

"Read it."

He reads a couple lines then looks up.

"You knew before you got here you were taking the job, didn't you?"

"I knew it was possible."

He continues reading.

*A detailed layout of the strip mall, the jewelry store, and the vault room downstairs

*Detailed photographs of both the front and back of the store.

*Details about the alarm system, and where all the electrical boxes are.

*A list of who's likely to be in the jewelry shop every minute it's open. How many clerks? When do they arrive? When do they depart?

*The location of inside and outside cameras.

*Are there motion detectors anywhere inside or outside the building?

*The hours the jewelry store is open.

*The number of guards, inside and out. Their schedules, including how often they take breaks.

"Very impressive. "I can see why you're so successful, Francis. You don't leave anything to chance, do you?"

"The best preparation for good work tomorrow is to do good work today."

He looks surprised. "Who said that?"

"Some guy named Elbert Hubbard."

"I don't know who that is."

"It doesn't matter. And to answer your question, Vince, I didn't spend that year in the can jerking off. I read anything and everything I could get my hands on."

"I'm impressed."

"I don't give a fuck about impressing you, Vince. But it's to your benefit, whether it's true or not, to think I'm some dumb, illiterate fuck who reads with his lips moving. Oh, and without the answers to all these questions, the deal is off. And I don't want it in bits and pieces. Wait till you've got it all before you get back to me."

"I'm aware how big a score this is, and that there's a lot riding on the operation, for all of us, and I do respect your thorough approach. But I'm sure my client will periodically ask for progress reports."

"Tell him to go fuck himself. You really think I'm gonna broadcast how I work? It's my way or it's the highway. Understood?"

Vince nods his head slowly, as he jots down something on a notepad.

"One more thing. Make a copy of it now, give me back the original, and then I want you to destroy it as soon as all the information is collected." Suddenly, I reach across the desk and grab his notebook.

"What the...?"

I tear out the page, fold it up and put in my pocket.

"If you can't fucking remember what we're talking about, Vince, I'm not so sure we should be working together."

I can see from the expression on his face he'd fucking like to wring my neck. But I also see a flicker of admiration. He knows the more careful I am the more likely I'll get the job done and the more likely nothing will be tied back to him.

I'm finished, so I get up to leave. Just as I get to the door, I turn and say, "We'll meet in a week. I'll be in touch with the details. But you'd better have my first installment, because I don't lift a finger till I get it. Cash, of course."

"That's a lot of cash."

"I know who I'm dealing with, Vince, so I know it won't be a problem."

6

Francis

I get to the Rose Café ten minutes early. I choose a table in the garden area in a back corner, which offers some privacy and allows me an unobstructed sight-line. As soon as the hostess deposits me at my table, I take off my cap and put it on the plate across from my seat. I head back inside where I find a spot off to the side of the entrance where I can see anyone entering the restaurant.

A few minutes past eleven a small red convertible pulls up front. The valet approaches, Dakota hands him the keys and steps out of the car.

She's wearing a salmon-colored tank top, a white cardigan, faded blue jeans and open-toed sandals. She's got on a wide-brimmed white hat and a large straw bag is slung over her shoulder. She looks like every other thirty-something, good-looking chick in L.A.

She adjusts her hat, leans over, checks her face in the side mirror, then heads into the restaurant. She gives a quick look around and when she doesn't see me, she approaches the hostess, who leads her out to the garden.

I fall in ten or fifteen feet behind. When she arrives at the table and sees it's empty, she turns to the hostess, who's already headed back into the restaurant. But as soon as she notices my cap on a plate, she looks back toward the entrance and sees me.

She flashes a big smile, then takes a seat opposite my hat.

"I thought maybe you'd run out on me," she says.

"No chance of that," I say, taking my seat opposite her.

"Would you mind if we ask the waiter to open up the umbrella? I really shouldn't get too much sun."

"Forget the sunscreen?"

"Never," she says, patting the straw bag she's placed on the empty seat next to her. She takes off her hat, and runs her fingers through her short, blonde hair.

"Do I have hat hair?" she asks. "Be honest."

"You look fine." And she does. She reminds me of those surfer girls on the old Beach Boys album covers. "Surfer?"

"Why do you ask?"

"I figure all you California chicks like to ride the waves."

"I hate to disappoint you, Francis, but no, I don't surf. Tried it once and nearly killed myself. I'm a dry-land chick. When I go, it's not gonna be because I got knocked over the head by a surfboard."

The intimacy of her using my first name excites me. For a moment, I forget why we're here. It's not a first date. It's *business. Just business.*

I see a waiter loitering by the garden entrance and motion for him to come over. He cranks up the umbrella and it's like the sun is obscured by a large, passing cloud. I hand him a tenner. He thanks me, then takes our drink order. Dakota requests a mimosa, me an iced tea with an orange slice.

"You didn't have to do that," says Dakota.

"Do what?"

"Tip him for putting up the umbrella. It's part of his job. You're tipping him at the end of the meal anyway. Are you trying to impress me?"

"Why would I want to impress you?"

She shrugs. "I don't know. Why would you?"

I realize she's probably right. I am trying to impress her. I don't know why. She's just another chick. I don't have to answer her, but I do.

"Is this the way the next hour or so is going down?"

"What do you mean?"

"Like we're two boxers feeling each other out in the first round with jabs to the head."

"You know, I like that metaphor…" she stops.

"You think I don't know what a metaphor is?"

"No. Of course not."

"Let me tell you something about me, Dakota. If I didn't know what it meant, I'd fucking look it up."

"I'm sorry. I didn't mean to be condescending." She smiles. "Because I'm sure you know what that means, too."

This might be more fun than I thought it would be.

"But to get back to the tip…"

"It's important to you to know the answer?"

"I'm just trying to get a handle on you."

"I identify with the common man," I say. "The working stiffs."

"Do you see yourself as some kind of modern-day Robin Hood?"

"Is this the interview? Or are you just trying to see how many insults I'll absorb until I walk out?"

"Nope. Just curiosity."

"I suggest you stop trying to paint me into a corner, Dakota. I am what I am and believe me, Robin Hood I'm not. I steal from the rich. And if the poor have something I want, I take that, too. And I don't give any of it away. To anybody. If you do a service for me, you get well compensated. It's as simple as that."

"Did you ever think maybe you're overdoing it?"

"I know what you're thinking."

"Really? What's that?"

"You think I'm over-compensating for a small dick. You're thinking I use money to get respect."

"That's not what I was thinking. But since you brought it up…?"

"Don't try to psychoanalyze me, Dakota. I promise you, it won't end well."

"Everyone cares what other people think of them. It's nothing to be ashamed of or defensive about."

"You really think I give a fuck what other people think about me?"

"I don't know you well enough to answer that."

"Since we don't know how well you're gonna know me, I'll give you the answer. I don't give a damn what other people think about me. I only care that they respect and fear me. If they don't, that's gonna be a problem. A big problem."

She's squirming in her chair, like she's trying to find a comfortable spot. I'm making her uncomfortable. I don't mean to, but I'm not sorry she is.

Finally, she stops wiggling, straightens up and smiles. "So, here we are," she says. She looks around. "You know, I've never been here before—probably because it's out of my league. But it's quite nice.

"You think I only know about dive bars and shrimp shacks?"

She giggles. Not many women can pull that off without appearing silly or empty-headed. She can.

"What's so funny?" I ask.

"Nothing. I guess you're someone I never would have predicted I'd be breaking bread with."

"Having lunch with an outlaw?"

Two tiny dimples that look like bullet holes from a .22 appear on both cheeks, and there's a very sexy twinkle in her eyes. If she was uncomfortable earlier, she seems to have recovered.

"I don't think of you as an outlaw."

"I'm not exactly a law-abiding citizen."

"No. You're not."

"What then?"

"I'm not sure…"

"Let me help you. Felon. Thief. Miscreant. Law-breaker. Gangster. Crook. Public menace. I'm sure all those words come up on your podcast plenty. You're not exactly dealing with titans of industry, are you?"

She smiles. Her teeth are remarkably straight and white.

"Not exactly."

The idea to introduce myself into this woman's life was, at first, nothing more than an amusement. Something to keep me entertained. I had no idea it would go this far and now, for the first time, I start to wonder why I'm here, sitting across from her, seriously entertaining the possibility of cooperating with her by going on her podcast. I don't know where this is going, but what I do know is that so far, I'm enjoying myself. So long as I'm in charge, everything's okay. But I'm looking for trouble if it gets out of hand. I'm not quite sure what it is yet, but somewhere in the back of my mind, there's this gnawing feeling that I can get something out of this. I'm just not sure yet what it is. But in the meantime, I'm kinda having fun.

The waiter delivers our drinks and takes our food order. Egg white omelet for me. Some kind of California salad, extra avocado, for her. "It's the fish of the vegetable world," she explains. She's waiting for me to ask what that means but I already know. Except for a few exceptions now, I'm still a dedicated vegetarian. I know the value of avocado. I also know they grow in abundance not far south of where we are.

"You look like you dressed up for the occasion," she says.

"What occasion would that be?"

"Brunch. With me."

"You think I dressed this way especially for you?"

"Well, didn't you?"

"I hate to disappoint you, honey, but I've got three basic outfits. This happens to be in today's rotation."

"I don't believe that for a minute. I think everything about you is very carefully calculated. I'm guessing you don't do much without planning it in advance. For instance, this morning, when you were getting ready for this lunch, I'll bet you spent as much time thinking about what you were going to wear as a teenage girl getting ready to go out on her first date."

"If you're trying to get my goat, you'll be disappointed. Others, much better at it than you, have tried. And not to get all shrinky on you, I think maybe that's a bit of projection on your part."

"How do you mean?"

"You're wearing makeup. You've got your hair cut and styled recently. And," I say, nodding down toward her hand, which is holding her mimosa, "a manicure."

"My God, nothing gets past you, does it?"

"Not much."

"I know this is gonna sound really strange, but I think maybe we're more alike than either of us would like to admit."

She's full of shit. We couldn't be more different. But I know exactly what she's doing. She's trying to bond with me. Sure, I feel some kind of connection to her, but I'm not sure yet what it is. The last thing I need now is another chick complicating my life. And yet, here she is, sitting across from me, all dolled up, with those fucking dimples and that fucking twinkle in her eyes.

Our food arrives. Before she starts to eat, she plucks olives out of her salad and carefully lines them up side by side on her butter plate.

"Not a fan of olives, huh?"

"If I'd known they were in the salad I would have asked them to hold them. Would you like them?"

"No thanks. Not a fan either." Two can play her game.

Throughout the meal she tries to engage me in meaningless conversation. Even if I wanted to play along, it's not something I'm good at. At a certain point, no matter how pleasant her voice is, I have to shut her down. It's time to get down to business.

I push the plate away, wipe my mouth with my napkin, lean back and say, "So, what is it you want from me, Dakota?"

She looks up at me, a surprised look on her face.

"What do *I* want? In case it's slipped your mind, you're the one who stalked *me*."

"I didn't stalk you. I sought you out. There's a difference. Don't make it sound like I'm some kind of creepy pervert. I had good reason. You're sticking your nose in my personal business. If anything, you're the one stalking me."

"In case you haven't noticed, Francis, you're a public figure, which makes you fair game."

"How do you figure?"

"Ever Google yourself?"

"Don't need to. I know everything there is to know about Francis Hoyt. I don't need the Internet to muck things up with a bunch of lies, exaggerations, half-truths and myths."

"Oh, I see. Is it an exaggeration that you're considered possibly one of the best burglars of all time?"

"One of?"

"Oh, excuse me. *The* best burglar of all time. Is that better?"

"Much."

"My God, you are so fucking full of yourself."

"Anything wrong with that?"

She smiles. Are we having fun? I think maybe we are.

"And you're so darn humble."

"See? Could you have gotten that information from your research on the Web?"

"Touche. Which brings me to that offer you made the other day."

"What offer is that?"

"To be on my show."

"I didn't say that."

"You didn't say you wouldn't. So, how about it? You and me and a microphone."

"Why should I? What's in it for me?"

"Does there always have to be something in it for you?"

"Yes."

"You really are a jerk, aren't you?"

"Is this the way you intend to get me to do what you want? By insulting me?"

"If you act like an asshole, that's the way you're gonna be treated. So, how about it?"

There's that smile again.

"Tell me why I should. I'm all ears," I say, leaning forward, resting my chin on my right fist.

"I think you'd like the opportunity to tell your own story."

"Why should I care?"

"Because no one wants to be misunderstood."

"Who do you think I am? Some half-wit movie star?"

"You're someone people are interested in."

"Ask me if I give a fuck."

"See? Now how could I possibly impart to my listeners that kind of attitude unless they hear for themselves?"

"So, you want me to go on your little dog and pony show just so your listeners can get a vicarious thrill, hearing from a real, live outlaw?"

"That's offensive."

"What is?"

"Calling it a little dog and pony show."

"That's what it is, isn't it?"

"I'll ignore that, because I think you're just trying to get my goat. How about me interviewing you, just the two of us. Think you'd be up for that?"

"You must think I'm idiot, sister. I do something like that and you can edit the damn thing any way you want. What if by talking to you I give myself away? I'm off the radar now. Why would I want to get back on? Besides, if I do sit for an interview, even if someone doesn't figure out where I am, they'll be all over you?"

"I wouldn't mind that. Or, in your lingo, I can take the heat. Are you afraid I'll make you look bad? Or ridiculous? It can't be you're afraid I'll make you look guilty, because we already know that."

"I'm a fugitive. I've got a price on my head."

"Oooh, I didn't know about that," she says, with a big smile on her face. "How much?"

"Fucking look it up."

"I'm glad you don't clean up your act just because you're talking to a woman. Or is this just another way of trying to impress me," she says, cocking her head to one side and running her hand slowly through her hair. I know that move. I've seen it dozens of times. It doesn't work on me. No way I'm giving up my power to this little bitch.

"I am who I fucking am. It's too much damn trouble to be someone else, someone you or anyone else thinks I ought to be."

"You see? That's exactly my point. I want you to tell my audience who you are, coming directly from you. No fake news. Just news from the horse's mouth."

"Why the fuck should I care about you or your audience, or anyone else for that matter?"

"Because I know people. And I know most people love attention. And they very rarely get it. What's the good of being the best in the world at something if no one else knows it?"

This chick is good. She gets me. Or at least part of me. I'm not one of those pathetic losers who's constantly telling you how great they are. I can prove it. And do I get a kick out of people knowing how good I am? Sure. I've worked hard to get there, taken risks no one should have to take, and I've been handsomely rewarded. But I'm not one of those who counts success in dollars, man. For me, success is doing what by all rights shouldn't be done. Success is being the best. Like being able to steal your wallet while your hand is still in your pocket holding onto it.

But I'm not a fool. And I'm certainly not reckless. Especially when it comes to my own skin.

"You think flattery will get you what you want?"

"I'm willing to try and see if it does."

"Listen, I'm not sitting down in front of a tape recorder and letting you ask me a whole bunch of stupid questions."

She gets quiet, which I think might be a first for this chick.

"Well, I've never actually done a live show, but how about that as a possibility? I mean, that way I couldn't manipulate your answers. Whatever you say is what's heard. How about that?"

"What exactly does that mean?"

"It means you sit across from me with a live mike between us and I ask you questions and you answer them."

"I'm not going to any studio, where I'm trapped, if that's what you're thinking."

She laughs. "You're living in the past, Francis. I don't have to do this thing in a studio. This is the twenty-first century." She waves her hands in the air. "The world is my studio. So, what are you really afraid of? Oh, of course. You're afraid I'm going to contact the cops and they'll be waiting for you. And then I'll have it all on tape."

"I don't think you're that dumb and I sure as hell know I'm not."

"We could do it on your terms. Anywhere, anytime you choose. You name the place and the time. You're not afraid, are you?"

I don't dignify that question with an answer, because it's a fucking joke.

"So, what do you think?"

"I'll think about it."

"Really? You'll consider it?"

"Don't push it, Dakota. I said I'll give it some thought."

"You know, when I was a kid whenever I wanted something and asked my mom for it the answer I'd always get, every single time, was, 'We'll see.' After way too many times getting those 'We'll sees' I realized it was just another way of my mom saying no without actually using the word. You're not stringing me along like my mom did, are you?"

"You're starting to piss me off, Dakota."

"I am?" she says, leaning forward, flashing a killer smile and running her hand through her hair again. "Does that mean I'm getting to you?"

"I gotta go."

"Why? You have a hot date or something?"

"I'm a working man. I got work to do."

"Oh, that's fascinating. Planning another job, are we?"

"If this the kind of questions you're expecting me to answer on your little podcast, you're not helping your case any."

I get up, take out my wallet, toss a C-note on the table.

"What's this," she says, picking up the hundred. "I'm not sure I've ever held one of these."

"It's to pay for lunch. Including tip," I say.

"First off, I was going to pay…"

"No, you're not."

"Well, it's way too much."

"I'm a big tipper. Put that in your damn podcast."

7

Dakota

In the end, Francis doesn't say yes, but he doesn't say no, either. I'm not sure why, but I have this feeling, call it intuition, that he's going to do it.

I know he's not going to make it easy for me. That's a big part of his personality. He enjoys making trouble, causing a stir, making people uncomfortable, keeping people off balance, shaking up lives. He thrives in chaos.

And yet, he still manages to be...well, charming. He's got this aura. Wait. I know. Sounds very Southern California woo-woo, doesn't it? But it's true and maybe it would be easier to understand if I call it charisma. There's something bigger than life about him. And what makes him even more appealing, probably a little *too* appealing, is he doesn't work at it. By that I mean nothing seems calculated. It's just who he is. I'm beginning to see breaking into people's houses isn't the only thing he's very good at.

If he does wind up saying yes and we spend more time together, I'm going to have to be careful because if I look into his eyes for too long, it'll be like getting sucked into a whirlwind. I know it's crazy, but it's like he has some kind of hypnotic power. Like Rasputin, the Russian guy I read about as a kid who put people under a spell and was almost impossible to kill. Or Franz Mesmer who had this theory that involved magnetic forces, which he called animal magnetism. Even though he's a tiny, little thing, he comes off as huge. Like he's a giant. Bigger than life. Several years ago, I was invited to a gathering in D.C. Suddenly, the whole room goes quiet and people freeze in place. I look up and see why. Striding into the room comes none other than President Barack Obama. He looks like he's at least a head taller than everyone else. And there's this aura around him. It's as if his mere presence can stop time. I swear, Hoyt's got that same "thing" going.

I know it's crazy. I know there's no comparison between Obama and Hoyt. But that's the feeling I have, sitting there across from him. The same feeling I had it when we were standing on the sidewalk outside Starbucks that first time.

I'd better be careful. Damn careful. Because I have this sneaking suspicion that if I don't watch out, I'll wind up selling my soul to the devil. And in this case, we all know who the devil is.

Getting him to cooperate is not going to be easy. I'm going to have to keep after him, using any charm I might have. But in the end, if I prevail, it probably won't be charm that'll do it. It'll be persistence. Trouble is, I don't know how to reach him. Not that I don't ask.

"Francis, how can I get in touch with you. Phone? Email? Carrier pigeon? Mental telepathy?"

"I'll contact you."

I smile. "Can't blame a girl for trying. Here's my info," I say, rooting around my bag looking for a pen or, if I've bothered to throw a bunch in, my business card.

"Don't bother."

"Huh?"

"I already have it."

"What?" I say, practically leaping out of my chair.

"Relax. You have contact information on your website."

Whew! That was a close one. I mean, how creepy would it be if he had my cell number or, heaven forbid, my home address. Suddenly, I'm overcome with this creepy feeling that he already knows everything about me. But I'm not gonna go there, because I don't want the answer. All I want is for him to come on the show. I must keep reminding myself that Francis Hoyt is a powder keg that can blow any time and so I have to treat him carefully, like I would any kind of explosive material.

Of course, if I were he, I wouldn't give me any of that contact information. He is, he reminds me, a fugitive, a man on the run. But about that reward? I don't know for sure, but I think maybe he's exaggerating a bit, or lying. It's not something I've come across doing my research so far. But then, I'm really only in the beginning stages. And so, if it turns out I find there's a price on his head when I do a little more digging, that would be kind of cool and it would also explain his super-careful behavior, at least in part. He claims several insurance companies have pooled their money and the reward for information leading to his arrest and subsequent conviction is now up to fifty thousand. That's a tidy sum. More than enough to turn someone into a rat. Not me. But someone.

I make a mental note to ask him the next time I see him, if I see him, how he feels about that number. It seems pretty big to me, but knowing what little I already know about his giant ego, I wouldn't be surprised if he doesn't think it's anywhere near enough.

If there is a next time.

That will be up to him.

8
Dakota

For a week, I hear nothing.

Like a lovesick teenager pining for a message from a crush, I constantly check my email, voicemail and texts. And to be honest, as inappropriate as it sounds, this is a little bit the way it feels. Like I'm waiting for Francis Hoyt, the boy of my dreams, to invite me to the prom.

How far gone is that?

I can't help it. I think about him way too much. At first, I tell myself it's all business. But every once in a while, when I give myself one of my rare reality checks, I realize it's more than that. It's not like I have a crush on him or anything like that. I mean, sure, he's kinda cute in that exciting, heart-stopping bad-boy way, and certainly a lot more interesting than most of the guys I've been out with lately. But he's a criminal. He's spent practically his entire life on the wrong side of the law. There are the things I know he's done and then there are the things I don't know he's done that could be worse. As my mother might say, "he's no choir boy, Dakota."

Suddenly, I'm that sad, pathetic, desperate woman who falls for the guy in prison. I know, I know. The joke is: At least you know where he is every night. But the last thing I want is to become a cliché.

When I take the time to *shrink* myself (it's cheaper than going

136

to Sheila twice a week), I realize it's not like I'm falling for him in that icky, schoolgirl crush way. It's just that he's got this incredible gravitational pull and now that I'm in his orbit, well, it's like I just can't seem to claw my way out. I decide what it is and slap a name on it: unfinished business. What a coup to get him on the show. And if by getting him to cooperate I can nail who he is and what motivates him, then somehow, I'll learn something about myself and everyone else on the planet.

Sounds crazy, right? I mean, after all, what do Francis Hoyt and I have in common? Okay, so maybe it doesn't just sound crazy. Maybe it is. But maybe crazy is only crazy because I don't understand it yet. Once I figure out exactly what's between Francis and me, it won't be crazy anymore. At least, that's what the inner therapist in my head keeps telling the patient outside my head.

Even if he doesn't wind up cooperating, even if I never see him again, he's given me a great story. *I was stalked by Francis Hoyt and lived to tell the tale.* How's that for a show-stopping teaser?

When I finally do hear from him, exactly one week after our brunch at the Rose Café, it's in none of the normal ways.

I come home from work at the paper one evening to find an envelope jammed into my mailbox in the vestibule of my building. On the front, printed in very precise block letters, is "DAKOTA." That's it. No return address. No indication as to who sent it. But I don't have to open it to know who it's from. It's almost like I can *feel* his presence inside that envelope. Like his essence is seeping through the paper and into my fingertips.

Time for a reality check. What the hell is happening to me?

Part of me wants to rip it open right there in the vestibule. But another part me, the part that treats it as a deep, dark secret, like a note from a secret lover, knows I need to read it in the privacy of my apartment. Where the prying eyes of strangers can't see us. Where it's just me and Francis.

As I slip the key into the lock, a chill runs down my spine. I know this sounds like a cliché, and if I'd ever used it in a story, my editor would have demoted me to copygirl for a week, and I would have deserved it. But I swear, that's exactly what happens. And the reason for this sudden chill is that it dawns on me that in order to deliver this message, Francis knows where I live. And if he knows where I live and where I make my usual coffee run on weekend mornings, what else does he know about me?

He's invaded my head and now he's invading my space, violating my privacy. I know what he's doing. He's showing me how powerful he is. How smart he is. How ruthless he is. How omnipotent he is. How omniscient he is. How cunning he is. How powerless I am. And then it hits me: This is how one of the victims of his break-ins must feel! An uninvited "guest" has inserted himself into their life, the same way he has inserted himself into mine. He's violated what is most sanctified, what symbolizes safety and security: my home. Their home. He has taken away any power they might have had.

I'm angry. I'm frustrated. And for the first time since I've met him, I'm even a little frightened.

How much more of this am I going to allow?

As I stand there frozen in time and space, unable even to commit to step into my own apartment, I realize the writer part of me has just been engaged. What I mean is, it's important for me to understand exactly how and what his victims feel. You can use this, Dakota, I tell myself.

As I step into my apartment, I realize this is ridiculous. *Get a hold of yourself, Dakota.* He's not a killer. He's not a rapist. I haven't dug up anything yet that indicates he's prone to violence. And one thing you learn when dealing with criminals is they don't just appear from nowhere. They have a history. Most are from broken homes. Most have been abused when they were young, either physically or sexually. But there is one cardinal rule: if you find someone who has a history of hurting animals, pulling the wings off butterflies, run, don't walk, in the opposite direction.

I haven't found anything like that about Francis Hoyt, so he's probably not as bad as I'm imagining at the moment.

Francis Hoyt is a thief. Pure and simple. He takes things that don't belong to him. And yes, he does invade other people's space. He violates their privacy. But I've seen nothing to show he's ever harmed anyone physically. He gets in and out without his victims ever being aware he's there. I know this doesn't mean he hasn't hurt someone along the way. And it doesn't mean he's not capable of violence. But this incident is a necessary reminder that I have to avoid being reckless. What that means is I cannot, under any circumstances, trust him. He's a narcissist and he'll do whatever suits him best. So long as there's benefit to both of us, I'm fine. But the minute I see that it's a question of benefit to either me or him, I know he's always going to choose himself.

Ours will never be a *normal* relationship. It is a relationship of mutual benefits. And when that runs its course, our relationship will be over.

Without opening it, I toss the envelope on my dining room table. I go to the refrigerator and take out a half-full (I'm not a half-empty kinda girl) bottle of Chablis. I pour myself a glass. I sit down at the dining room table and stare at the envelope, face up, my name on the front of it, sitting there where a dinner plate should be. I'm about to take a sip of wine when Hemingway suddenly bolts out of nowhere and leaps onto my lap. It's something he does when he either misses me or has gotten into some kind of mischief and is trying to bond with me before I discover it. The last time was when I left a drawer open (I doubt he has the cat super-power of opening the drawer herself) and he got into it and played havoc with my underwear, shredding a couple of pairs of my underwear beyond repair.

I know he's glad to see me. I also know he's hungry. I'm not sure which drives him most, but I'd like to believe it's that he misses having me around. Since his needs always come before mine, I leave my glass of wine untouched while I prepare his dinner. He's very fussy, like most cats, so unless I want to try to get into a power struggle with him, I give him wet food, rather than dry. I learn that power thing a long time ago, when I first bring him home from the shelter.

Friends say to train him, I should keep a spray bottle of water handy and when he misbehaves, squirt him. I knew I don't have the heart to do that, so I never bother to buy one. But the first night I have him, about four-thirty in the morning, he begins to meow. And he just won't stop. I assume it'd because he wants to be fed. But then I remember I've left out a whole bowl of dry food, so how can it possibly be that? Using human logic, I figure I'll just let him meow for a while and when he realizes I'm not going to jump up and give him fresh food, he'll learn his lesson, and I can just go back to sleep while he waits until a decent hour to be fed.

Big mistake. He meows for almost an hour. Unrelentingly. While I lie in bed, a pillow pressed tightly over my ears, hoping he'll finally get the message and I can go back to sleep.

No dice. Eventually, I'm the one who cracks. I think to myself, *I'm in a battle of wits with a cat. There's no way I can win. He'll keep meowing until he gets what he wants.* And so I do what I now do every single morning. I get up and prepare a fresh bowl of wet food. Hemingway is happy. I'm happy. So yes, you're absolutely right: he has successfully trained me.

Once Hemingway is taken care of, I sit back down at the kitchen table and take a couple of sips of wine. I'm starting to calm down. Finally, I'm fortified enough to see what's in the envelope.

I'm right, of course. It is from Francis Hoyt, and in very precise, thick block letters, written with a magic marker, it is as close to a ransom note as I'll probably ever get:

RULES FOR DOING YOUR LITTLE PODCAST
- THE SHOW IS LIVE
- MY VOICE IS DISGUISED

- NO ONE IS TO KNOW BEFOREHAND THAT I'M GOING TO BE ON YOUR SHOW. THIS MEANS NO PUBLICITY!!!!
- THE SHOW IS TAPED FROM A LOCATION CHOSEN BY ME AND YOU WON'T GET THAT LOCATION UNTIL SEVERAL HOURS BEFORE AIRTIME
- I SEE THE QUESTIONS BEFOREHAND

THESE TERMS ARE NON-NEGOTIABLE.
IF YOU AGREE WE CAN MOVE FORWARD. YOU MAY TEXT YES OR NO TO THIS NUMBER 315-555-5555. THIS IS A BURNER PHONE AND AS SOON AS I RECEIVE AN ANSWER FROM YOU, THE PHONE WILL BE DESTROYED.

He doesn't bother to sign it.

At first, I think maybe he's just forgotten, but then I realize he's always so careful. I'm sure he doesn't want any trace of himself on the note. Not his handwriting. Not his prints. Not, I'm sure, his DNA.

I smile. It's another story I can tell about him.

I take another sip of wine. There's no doubt I'm going to agree with all his rules, but that doesn't mean I'm not going to try to stretch them, whenever possible.

Suddenly, it strikes me. It looks like I'm actually going to have the legendary Francis Hoyt on "my little podcast show."

9

Francis

We're walking down Melrose Thursday afternoon. Vince, carry-ing a briefcase and wearing a light-weight seersucker suit, is ready to hand over the information I requested and this is where we agree to meet. It's as private a public place as I can think of and it gives us the opportunity to keep moving. If anyone's fol-lowing us, I'll spot him.

After a few minutes of meaningless small chatter, Vince finally dips into the inside breast pocket of his jacket, pulls out a thick manila envelope that's been folded in half and hands it to me.

"I think you'll find everything you need in here," he says. "I've included specs for the lockers and I've provided you the codes for the lockers you'll need to access. If you let me know exactly what kinds of tools you'll need, drills and such, I can arrange for them to be hidden somewhere on-site, so you won't have to carry them in. Will that be satisfactory?"

"I'm used to working with a little more subtlety, Vince, but I'm not averse to getting my hands dirty if necessary. After I check out what's in here," I say, patting the envelope, "I'll be in touch to let you know if I need anything else."

"Excellent. And if you have any questions, or require any other information, please let me know and you'll have it."

"How about the name of this mysterious boss man?"

He smiles. "Nice try, Francis. I'm sorry, but we've been down that road before."

I tuck the envelope into the pocket of my windbreaker. We pass a bench at a bus stop and Vince motions for us to take a seat.

"You don't mind, do you? I've got a four o'clock meeting and I don't want to show up with sweat stains on my shirt, smelling like I just got back from the gym."

I look around. What few pedestrians aren't paying any attention to us, so I see no reason not to sit. It'll give me an opportunity to scan the area to make sure we're not being watched.

Vince takes off his jacket, folds it in half, and drapes it over the back of the bench. He sets the briefcase down between us.

"Ever taken a bus in this town, Francis?"

"Never even seen one."

He laughs. "It's one of L-A's most guarded secrets. How else would the maids and nannies get to work?"

He pushes the briefcase toward me.

"*This* is a lot of money, Mr. Hoyt." He pats the top of the briefcase, then turns it on its side. He spins a little dial on the top of the briefcase. I hear the click.

"I know how much it is, Vince."

"What I mean is, you should be very careful with it."

"I've handled money before. And I'm always careful. About everything."

"I'm sure you are. But I wouldn't be doing my job if I didn't say my little piece. How you spend it, where you put it, is none of my business. But what is my business is to make sure you don't call attention to yourself."

"If you're afraid I'm suddenly gonna buy drinks for everyone at the fucking Beverly Hills Hotel Bar…"

"I know that's not happening."

"Then we're good."

"Yes. We're good."

He turns the briefcase toward me and pops it open. He lifts the top a few inches, just enough so I can see the stacks of bills—packages of C-notes, neatly stacked next to one another.

Quick as he opens it, he slams it shut.

"You'll find it's all here, Half the agreed upon price."

We sit in silence for a moment or two. Our business is over, yet he makes no move to leave.

"Anything else on your mind, Vince?"

"Well, yes. There is. I know about your rules, Francis, but regardless, my client would like to know what kind of timeline he can expect."

"We've already been through this. I don't do timelines or timetables. It takes what it takes. Let me explain something, Vince. The reason I don't get caught is not only because I'm the best at what I do, it's also because I know the most important thing is the plan. And until I sign off on it, until I think it's as good as it's going to get, which means going over it again and again, I don't make a move. Keeping everything to myself not only protects me, but it protects your client, too. What he doesn't know can't get either of us in dutch."

"I understand. But in this case, perhaps you can bend your rules a little." He taps the top of the briefcase. "My client is paying an awful lot of money and asking very little in return, other than that the job be completed. I understand you haven't worked out details yet, but perhaps maybe a little something when you get a little further along. Even something like, 'By the end of the month,' would suffice."

"It gets done when it gets done. But tell you what. Let's trade. You tell me who I'm working for and I'll give you a timeline."

He laughs. "Nice try."

I'll never get the answer from Vince, but that doesn't mean I won't get it somewhere else. Before I fully commit to the job, I have to understand it. Not only who's behind it, but why. Something's fishy. Why would someone knock over their own bank and risk the wrath of a bunch of dangerous sociopaths?

Our business is completed. Vince gets up, grabs his jacket, folds it over his arm. "I'm not parked far from here. Can I give you a lift somewhere?"

"No thanks. I'm good. I'm sure there'll be a bus coming along any minute."

10

Dakota

Several days after I receive Francis's disturbing note, I'm still making sure my door is double-locked and my windows safely fastened shut. At night, when I shut my eyes and wait for sleep to come, I hear strange, threatening noises I'm not sure are really there.

This morning, I finally come to my senses and put an end to my bizarre behavior. *Dakota,* I say to myself, *if he wanted to get in while you're here, he'd have done it already. He just wanted to show you he could do it, that's all.*

Mind games. He loves playing mind games. But just because he's playing them doesn't mean I have to play along with him.

The weekend is over. At seven-thirty, just as I'm about to head out to the gym for my usual Monday morning workout, my phone, which sits on the kitchen table, begins to vibrate. I pull my *Late Night* sweatshirt over my tank top, and stare at the phone as it slowly jigs its way toward the edge of the table. I make absolutely no effort to pick it up, answer the call, or even admit its existence. For some reason I can't quite articulate, I don't want to make contact with the outside world yet. Until I walk out that door into the mysteries the day holds, I want it to be just me and Hemingway.

I'm pretty sure I know who it is. My mother, checking to see how I'm doing. She worries about me. She thinks I'm drifting.

She thinks I'm directionless. She thinks, well, that I'm a huge, hot mess. I've given up trying to convince her otherwise. After all, how successful could I possibly be since the undeniable truth is I'm single and barely eking out a living? To be honest, there have been times when I have to agree with her, though oddly enough, this wouldn't be one of them. As of last night, I'm feeling pretty good about myself, now that I've gotten over the fear that Hoyt will break into my apartment, rape and murder me. Especially now that I've proclaimed it a new day, a new week, a new me. I don't know how long this new me will last, but I intend to enjoy myself while it does.

Even if my mother is right, her call certainly isn't going to change anything. Sure, it makes her feel better. There's that. She can play the role of concerned mother, which she didn't do much of when we were growing up. But I get it. I believe in redemption—to a point—and if these calls assuage some of her guilt (the result, by the way, of her two years in Al-Anon after my father skipped town and she decided she was an enabler and partially to blame) that's okay by me.

But I've made one thing perfectly clear to her. Time and time again.

"Don't even think about it, Mom. Read my lips. I am not coming home and moving into my old bedroom."

I've said it enough times over the past few years that it's become one of those Abbott and Costello "Who's on First" exchanges. We're both saying the exact same thing, and we're saying it over and over again, and yet it's like both of us are hearing it for the first time. What is that? A ritual, right? A weird, annoying family tradition? Whatever it is, it seems to get us through the day, week or month. But that doesn't make it any less crazy.

Mom knows the best time to catch me is before I leave for my part-time job writing and editing at *The Hood*). It still provides the only regular stream of money coming in, along with a little freelance magazine writing or editing work I pick up every now and then. Mom knows I don't answer my phone during the day, at least that's what she thinks because that's what I tell her. Of course, I answer the phone. I just don't answer if it's her. I claim she's interrupting work and tell her to limit the number of calls she's tempted to make. Since my youngest brother got married and moved to Texas for a job opportunity, my mom has very little to keep her occupied, which is why, unlike when I was a child and she pretty much ignored me, I've suddenly become her pet project. And so, I try to be patient and not be short or cross with her when she does manage to break through my wall of silence.

When I tell her about my daytime phone rule, she does not take it well.

"What if it's an emergency?" she whines.

"First off, I'm pretty sure we're not on the same page as to what constitutes an emergency, Mom. Like if the cat is up on the roof, that does not qualify as an emergency."

"Very funny, Dakota. I'll remember that if I ever get a cat. Then what, may I ask, *does* constitute an emergency?"

"It's like Chief Justice Potter Stewart said about pornography, Mom. 'I know it when I see it.' But let me put it this way: If there's blood involved, and it's more than a tablespoon and it's yours, then it qualifies as an emergency. Okay?"

Still, mother or not, when it keeps ringing (my mailbox is full) I'm drawn toward the phone. I reach it only seconds before it's about to jitterbug off the kitchen counter, and it doesn't announce MOM, but rather, "Unknown Caller." Most likely it's one of those horrid robocalls and I'm about to ignore it. But a little voice in my head tells me this is not what it is, so I swipe my finger across the phone and offer a tentative, "Yes?" fully expecting to be answered by silence or one of those annoying recorded messages, trying to sell me something I don't want or need.

"Hope I didn't disturb you, Dakota, but I figured you for an early riser."

Holy shit! It's Francis Hoyt.

At first, I'm disoriented and the unexpected words that escape from my mouth are, "As a matter of fact, you are disturbing me, Francis."

Truth is, I'm happy to hear from him, but I'm not about to let him know that. This is so damn creepy. This is not good. Not good at all. The man is in my head, getting me to do things I don't want to do. Like answering the phone this early in the morning.

"Excuse me?" he says in a voice dripping with insincere innocence, which only heightens my anger.

"That fucking stunt you pulled the other day. Leaving that note in my mailbox. Not cool. Not cool at all." As soon as the words tumble out of my mouth, I feel myself starting to calm down. And yet, like I'm possessed by some evil spirit, I don't stop. "And if I'm not mistaken, I never gave you this number. But obviously, you have it. Also, not cool. I gotta say, Francis, you're starting to freak me out a little."

"Enough so you don't want me to cooperate with your little podcast thing?"

I can't see him, but I can imagine a big fat smile on his face. This guy loves stirring the pot. He loves keeping people off-balance. He loves fucking with minds. It's something I might admire from a distance, if it didn't affect me. But it is affecting me and I'm pissed. And I know—despite the fact it might queer any deal that has him cooperating with me and my show—it's better for me not to hold back.

Hoyt is perceptive enough to know when someone's lying. When they're telling the truth. And when they're holding back. I only know him from the couple meetings we've had, but I already respect his ability to read people. It's a skill many writers have, which is probably why I have it to an extent. We're able to pick up on the whole package. Put pieces together to get the whole shebang. It's not a conscious thing. It's not only about what people say or don't say. It's also about their body language. Or the look on their face. It's why I always try to do in-person interviews, unless it's purely for informational purposes.

It's a double-edged sword, and so with some people I make it a point not to look them in the eye because I'm afraid I might not like what I see. Francis Hoyt is one of those people you need to be particularly careful with. It's like staring into the sun. I remember this quote by Francois de la Rochefoucauld from my two years of high school French and two more years in college, *"Ni le soleil ni la mort ne peuvent se regarder fixement."* Which translates as *Neither the sun nor death can stare at each other.*

"And there's something else. Would you please, please, please stop referring to it as my 'little podcast.' It's fucking demeaning. And you know it. My so-called 'little podcast' has a couple hundred thousand listeners every week, and that's world-wide. I wouldn't call that 'little,' would you?"

Okay, so I'm exaggerating a little. But it's probably close to that number if you add up the entire audience for any one series. And the truth is, my audience is climbing as a result of the newspaper story naming it one of the Top 10 Best Crime Podcasts in the country.

He clucks his tongue.

"Looks like someone got up on the wrong side of the bed this morning."

"Fuck you!" I shout into the phone so loud I scare myself. Why do I let him get under my skin like that? It reminds me of how my little brother could do the same thing. Eventually, I'd explode and my mom would come in and, of course, I'd be blamed. And then, when I complained, she'd say, "Just ignore him, Dakota. Just ignore him." As if that's so easy to do.

Get hold of yourself, Dakota. Calm down. Don't give him the satisfaction of knowing he can get to you.

I take a deep breath and sit down at the dining-room table because I'm thinking this might not be a quick call. Sure enough, as soon as I get comfortable, Hemingway leaps into my lap. This time, it's not food he wants. It's attention. Which, at this moment, I cannot give him.

"How about we start over?" he says, his soothing voice in stark contrast to mine. My anger is genuine but I realize it might be a constructive tool of manipulation. It makes me think of the time I ask my mom, "Mom, what was I like as a kid? Did I have a temper?"

She thinks for a moment, as if she's relegated my childhood so far back in her mind she can't access it immediately. For someone who likes to be the center of attention, this is not a good thing. I like to think she can remember every single moment of my childhood, simply because I was so darn fascinating and lovable.

"No," she says, as she slices her hand through the air. "You were like this: I never knew what you were thinking." My initial thought is, *maybe I shouldn't have asked*. But instead, I keep pushing, "What about Montana, did he have a temper?" (Yes, we were all named after states—my other brother is Rhodes. I still don't know why, despite asking my mom who answer, "Ask your father. He's the one who came up with the names." Only I couldn't ask him, because by that time he'd left the family, never to return).

"Oh, yes," she says. "Montana would throw tantrums. He'd hold his breath until he got what he wanted."

Since Monte (short for Montana) is still alive and well and living in Texas, I have to assume he always did get what he wanted.

Maybe it's because I'm a girl, but growing up I was always discouraged from showing anger. During this conversation with my mom, I realized if I ever did start to show signs of anger, I'd be told to go to my room. The lesson? Anger is best kept locked up in your room, rarely, if ever, to be displayed to outsiders.

But now it seems my anger, which is genuine, has put me in a better, stronger position. Francis Hoyt is not unlike most men in that two of the things they don't want to see from a woman is anger or tears. They can't handle it. They don't know our dirty, little secret: that anger and tears can be weaponized, which is what I aim to do now. And it seems to be working. My anger has hit a nerve. I put this potent weapon in my back pocket and promise myself I'll use it sparingly. Not because I'm ashamed of using tactics to manipulate a man, but because I'm afraid if I use it indiscriminately, it will lose potency.

"So, I assume you're up for being interviewed, otherwise you wouldn't be calling," I say, trying to project as much nonchalance as possible, while inside there's a mini-me jumping up and down.

"Yeah. I'm in. But there are rules."

"Funny thing about rules and me. I see a rule, I want to break it."

"Without rules, society is in chaos. And without rules, Dakota doesn't get Francis to sit for an interview for her little podcast thing. You got the note. You know what they are."

How odd! Here I am pontificating on breaking rules and here's Francis Hoyt, a man who's probably broken more rules that I know exist, arguing for law and order. Me, in favor of chaos. Him, in favor of the rule of law. Will wonders never cease?

"So, in or out?"

Oh, I get it. He's trying to get a rise out of me. Sorry, buddy, no such luck.

"I'm a journalist. I'm not crazy about the idea of 'conditions.' Conditions translates into prior restraint."

"Call it what you like, girlie, but this isn't happening unless I set the rules and you follow them."

"Like I said, I'm not good with rules."

"Get good, or it's off."

"Before we get into an argument about it…"

"Too late. We're already there. You got my rules. Yes or no? Simple as that."

"Can you refresh my memory, please?"

"First, and most important, there is absolutely no mention of or hint of where I am. Not even something general like the West Coast or Southern California. We do the interview outside L-A, at a site of my choice and you won't find out where that choice is until we actually get there."

"Sounds like the rendezvous for a kidnapping exchange."

"Think of it any way you want. I'm not gonna tell you what you can or cannot ask me, but if I don't like a series of questions and you persist, I'm walking."

I stay mum. Why open that can of worms now? I know from experience once I get someone talking it's hard to get them to shut up. Besides, I know there's nothing more dramatic than the subject of an interview taking a hike.

"And trying to find my family to talk to them is totally out of bounds. Same goes for any past associates of mine you're able to dig up."

I wonder if he means that literally.

"And this interview is for you and you only. I don't want to see it popping up all over the fucking Internet. Or in print. You understand what I'm saying?"

"I can't stop people from quoting from the interview, Francis."

"Find a way. Copyright it, or some such shit. I don't want any-fucking-body making dough off my name. Understand? And I don't want any of these so-called amateur crime sleuths trying to follow leads they think they can get from the interview. Which leads me to the next rule."

"I can't wait to hear it."

"The interview stays up for one week and one week only. After that, you take it down. And this is very important. You do not announce beforehand that you're going to do that. I don't want any assholes taping it because they know it's only up for a limited time."

"But Francis, I can't just leave a big fat hole in the series."

"Fill it with whatever the fuck you want. I just want my voice taken down. Paraphrase what I've said, but I don't want some asshole actor reading my words. Understood?"

I want to argue. I want to ask, *What happens if I don't listen to you?* But I don't because I don't want to hear the answer.

What's the point? If I keep it up there, what's he gonna do, sue me? I'll cross that bridge when I come to it. For now, I'll say yes to everything.

"Is that it?"

"One more thing. You are not to ask me details of jobs I've pulled, unless I bring it up. And no asking what I'm working on now."

"So, you are working on something?"

"That's exactly what I fucking mean, Dakota."

"Oh, lighten up, will ya? I'm just playing with you, Francis. Don't take everything so damn serious. Any other of your so-called 'rules?'"

"For now, no. But that doesn't mean I won't come up with something. I don't underestimate you, Dakota, so please don't underestimate me."

"When are you going to be available?"

"Not sure yet. I've got previous engagements."

"A new job?"

He laughs. "Fucking playing with me again, Dakota?"

"Yeah. I do that sometimes. I can't help myself. You shouldn't take me all that seriously. So, how will I know when you're ready?"

Truthfully, I'm in no rush. Despite what he tells me and what I say back to him, I have a lot of research I want to do, a lot more I want to know, before I actually get him in front of my microphone. I haven't even started writing the first episode.

"Oh, and since we're talking rules, I have some of my own. No more creepy stuff, understand? No notes stuffed in my mailbox. No sneaking up on me while I'm shopping for toilet paper. Can you just act like a normal human being for once?"

"That's asking a lot."

One beat. Two beats. Three beats.

"But okay. Now that I have your phone number, I'll just give you a call."

"Or you could email me..."

"Nice try. You'd like my email address, wouldn't you?"

"Oh, gee. You know, I never even thought of that. My bad."

11

Dakota

Mark knows what our next project is, Master Burglar Francis Hoyt. But I haven't told him about actually meeting Hoyt. I'm not sure why. Is it to protect Mark? Or maybe myself? Or is it to protect Francis and, if so, why?

But Mark's my producer and eventually he'll find out. And even if he doesn't, at some point, I'll have to tell him. But for now, I file it under "need to know" and keep my mouth shut.

When I tell Mark I have to go to Connecticut to interview Charlie Floyd, and perhaps a couple others, he jumps at the chance to tag along. I don't ask, but I'm thrilled to have his company and his expertise. Often, he sees things I don't. I think it's his novelist's eye. He says it's because I don't always pay attention as much as I should. That my mind is going in all different directions instead of keeping focused. We argue about that until I realize he's right. I'm the kind of driver who likes to watch the scenery pass by when I ought to be paying attention to what's in front and back of me.

I'm on top of everything when it comes to work, but not so much when it comes to my personal life, which at this particular moment is pretty much a mess. That's another good reason to have Mark come with me.

"I've got friends and family there, so I can kill two birds with one stone by staying with them. And don't worry about it, I'll pay my own way."

"I was actually going to buy your ticket."

"No way. I've got plenty of miles. I can even ask around and see if there's an empty apartment we can use. How's that sound?"

I don't have to say anything because my smile tells him everything he needs to know. Suddenly, it feels like we're ready to embark on a once-in-a-lifetime expedition. Except, instead of sailing down the Amazon filled with man-eating piranhas, we're headed for the Big Apple where there's a whole other species of man-eaters.

12

Francis

Once Vince hands over the briefcase, my work officially begins.

He provides me with a precise, minute-by-minute schedule of everyone who works in the jewelry and the two adjacent stores. It's a two-story building with three separate offices on the second floor, one of which is empty. The other two are a real estate agency and a dental office, and Vince includes a detailed work schedule for both. In addition, he provides the rundown of the vault area, including a blueprint of the large room, schematics of the alarm system, codes, and photographs of the various lockers.

Vince also gives me a map of all the camera positions. At night, which is when I plan to do the job, there's only one guard on duty inside the jewelry store because the entrance to the downstairs is behind the counter. There are also a series of photographs of the front of the store, the inside, and the back of the building. I'm most interested in the back of the building, since that's where I'll enter. There's only one camera to beat and I have the coded keypunch number.

With the cash Vince has given me, I purchase several money orders from different banks across the city, which I deposit in several off-shore accounts. I send ten grand each to my mother and sister, instructing them to find good hiding places for it around their houses, which I paid for, by the way. I tell them to take half the money to use whatever way they want. They see this as generosity. I see it as insurance.

Later, with what's left of this payment and the second installment, I'll turn the cash into collectibles and precious metals, which I will stow in my safe houses and various safe deposit boxes across the country, taking advantage of the very kind of security I'm being paid to liberate. After committing everything to memory, I destroy all Vince's notes, using it as fuel in the small barbecue behind the cottage. Everything I've touched will eventually go up in flames.

I go to Google Earth to check out the area around the strip mall, which helps create a mental picture of how I'll do the job. I come up with at least three different scenarios. I write each one of them down, step by step, from the smallest detail to the largest. Next to each step I jot down how I'm going to accomplish that task. Next, I make a list of everything and anything that can possibly go wrong. I create at least one possible solution as to how I can avoid that pitfall. As soon as I've committed all this to memory, I destroy the written list, watching it burn in the kitchen sink, the simmering ashes of blackened yellow paper swirling down the drain in a torrent of water.

The plan now resides only in my head, waiting to be activated.

Once I've chosen the best scenario, it becomes a perpetual film loop in my head. I roll it backward and forward dozens of times, looking for anything that doesn't seem to fit. By the time this part of the process has ended, it's almost as if I've actually completed the job.

When I'm finally satisfied, I'll visit Ground Zero. Geography is organic. It can change overnight. I have to stay on top of these changes. I'll take my final trip to the area the day before I'm ready to pull the trigger.

I pore over maps of the area. I figure out the best escape route. I choose the best place to park the car, not too close to the strip mall but not so far that I can't jog the distance. I note where I can pick up public transportation, or a likely place to have a cab pick me up.

Before I enter the final phase of the job, I have one more thing to take care of. Finding out who am I working for and why this bizarre heist.

I know for sure this scheme has to do with an organized gang. Before I can figure out which of the many possible L.A. gangs is behind this, I need to understand the hierarchy of the L.A. mob scene.

I put in a call to a freelance reporter friend who's worked for several of the New York tabloids. Alex is an expert on organized crime in the northeast. Over the years, I've provided him with plenty of background information on several big heists, and now he can return the favor.

It's late back east, close to midnight, but Alex is nocturnal, so there's little chance I'll be waking him. He picks up on the second ring.

"Francis. Good to hear from you, man. By the way, that was some disappearing act you pulled off last year. No wonder they call you the Houdini of crime."

"I think you were the one to stick that one on me, Alex. Never did like it. Makes it look like what I do is magic and not hard work and smarts."

"Hope you don't hold it against me. I'm not gonna waste time asking where you are or what you're doing. I'm guessing you're either looking for a favor or you got some information you'd like me to spread around. Which is it?"

"I need you to get me all you can about the mob structure in Southern California, specifically the Los Angeles area."

"Jeez, you're not getting back involved with any of those guys, are you? I mean, I thought you'd learned your lesson. What's the deal?"

"I'm working on something and I need to know who I might be getting involved with."

"Okay, but you gotta be more specific. Years ago, we'd be talking the five families, Cosa Nostra, Mafia, whatever they hell they want to call it. Now, it's a free-for-all. Everyone wants a piece of the action. The Russian mob. The Albanians. Local street gangs like the Bloods and the Crips. Latin gangs like MS-13, Mexicans. Even the Angels are still in the picture."

"This feels more traditional to me. Most likely, I'm dealing with the Wops. But I gotta be sure."

"Exactly what are you looking for?"

"I want to know who the top guys are and maybe a short rundown on the pies they got their fingers in."

"That's a tall order, my friend. If you were talking about here in New York, Jersey, no problem. But I'm not as familiar with the Midwest or West Coast mobs. A lot of them are loosely connected, except for the Albanian mob, well, they pretty much do their own thing. And let me give you a word of advice, Francis. If it is the Albanians, turn around and run in the other direction fast as you can. You got a time frame on this?"

"Yesterday."

He laughs. "Good thing I'm semi-retired and got nothing but time on my hands. Don't do it, Francis."

"Do what?"

"Retire, man. It sucks, man. I don't know what the hell to do with myself. My wife's got me on a strict routine. She says she'll throw me out on the street if I don't have a project. As tempting as that might be, the truth is I love the witch and I still haven't learned how to feed myself. So, I'm writing a novel. But what the fuck do I know about writing a novel? So, you might have saved my life since this gives me a good excuse not to have to work on that novel. Would you believe, she does a friggin' page check at the end of every day. I don't have at least two pages, she won't let me have my nightly cocktail. You do not want to see me after six without some alcohol in me, Francis. This is a chance to keep some skin in the game. I can't promise anything, but I'll do what I can. I'll get back to you quick as I can."

Not one to put all my eggs in one basket, I call Eddie, a guy I did time with. He's a contract killer who worked for a couple New York families, as well as the Russians, based in Brighton

Beach. He got nabbed, flipped, and landed in the Witness Protection program. Only the asshole got bored so he worked a
couple cons, passed a few bad checks. They threw him out.
Now, like me, he's on the run. I know one of his former mis-
tresses, Nadine. They got a couple kids together, so she's likely
to know how to reach him. I give her one of my burner num-
bers and finish the conversation by tossing around a nice number he'll get if he comes through for me.

I put out the word with a couple guys I know down in Miami—but not Artie. I don't want to risk word getting back to
Capowitz, and Artie has a problem keeping his mouth shut.

Until I hear back from any of these guys, I'll just sit tight.

13
Charlie

Whatever genius called golf a "good walk spoiled," knew what they were talking about.

So why am I on the links, the eighth hole to be exact?

Simple.

For some unknown reason, my ex-wife Sara believes she's still responsible for my health and welfare. She claims if I don't find something to do with myself other than sit on the back porch, staring into the woods behind my house, feet up on a table, my dog, Hoover—named for the vacuum cleaner, not the FBI guru or the president or the Hoovervilles that popped up during the great Depression, because he eats everything in sight and even things that aren't—at my feet, chewing on one of those fake bones, she'd be visiting me in the nuthouse. Only she says I shouldn't count on that. Her exact words: "Charlie, honey, don't depend on me visiting you too often. I'm sure I'll have plenty of other better things to do with myself."

When I can't come up with any pastimes or hobbies that interest me, other than watching a Red Sox or Patriots game with a cooler of Dos Equis close by, her face brightens and she says, "How about golf?"

"You mean the most boring sport ever created by man?"

"How would you know? You don't even watch it on T-V."

"There's a good reason for that. The only thing more boring

163

than playing golf is watching grass grow, which, now that I think of it, might even be more exciting. But I have to admit, I do like the way they keep the grounds. Almost inspires me to pull the electric mower out of the garage and take care of the property. Or hire someone else to do it."

"Much more likely," she mumbles under her breath. "We both know that's never gonna happen, so why not Just give it a try? You might like it. It's not like you've never been wrong about anything."

"I suppose I must've been wrong about something once upon a time, it's just that at the moment it escapes me as to what it was."

"Very funny," she says, punching me on the arm just a little too much on the wrong side of playful.

"I know there's no way I'd get you to join one of those fancy country clubs…"

"Hell, there's no way they'd have me. Case closed."

"Not so fast, honeybun."

Oh, do I hate when she calls me that and she knows it. Which pretty much sums up why we're not together anymore.

"Probably true. But there's a public course not far from you. I'm pretty sure they'd even let the likes of you play there. So long as you don't show up wearing one of those Speedos. Why don't you give it a try?"

"That Speedo was a gag gift from the boys at the office and I don't even know where it is."

I wasn't a state investigator for more than twenty years not to pick up on the fact that this is not a spur-of-the-moment suggestion. Sara's done her homework. She knows exactly how close I live to the public course. I'm surprised she hasn't already signed me up for a tee time. Still, I'm not ready to give up. Not without a fight, at least, which is something we did often enough when we were married, especially near the end. I gotta admit, and this is not something I'm proud of, part of me is curious as to whether she's still in fighting shape. But I quickly realize I'm the one who's probably way out of practice. Still, I'm not ready to give up without a little pushback. I mean, I have a reputation to uphold.

"I don't know the first thing about golf, and besides, I don't have clubs."

"You can use some of that money you've saved on all the alimony you haven't had to pay since I got remarried, to buy yourself a set. Or, if you're too cheap for that, I'm sure you can buy a previously owned set. That's what they call used cars, isn't it?"

After all these years, she still knows how to push my buttons. I'm not miserly, but I am careful with money. Probably the result of my parents growing up at the tail end of the Great Depression. But no, they did not reside in Hooverville.

"What if I don't like it?"

"Charlie, honey, I know you're not going to *like* it. That's not the point. From what I've heard, it's addictive. And that's what I'm hoping for. I want you to have a good reason to get the heck out of that house every once in a while. And a little exercise wouldn't hurt, either." She shakes her head back and forth then flashes one of her killer frowns. I realize this is something I do not miss. But she's not finished yet.

"This is just downright depressing, watching you fritter away what's left of your life. You're not even sixty-five yet. I mean, come on, Charlie, it's over two years since you put in your retirement papers. Time to get a life, don't you think?"

"I've been thinking about going private."

"Private?"

"Yeah. Like in private investigator. You have to admit, it's something I know how to do pretty damn well."

"You were the best," she says and this time I know she's not mocking me. She knows how good I was and she knows that's the one thing I'm proudest of. "No one worked harder and was more diligent than you. But why on earth would you want to do that again? For God's sake, Charlie, try something new for a change. Maybe, God forbid, you'll even make some new friends."

This has always been a bone of contention between us. I didn't have time for friends. I was much too busy working. And on the rare occasion when I wasn't I was doing my best to hang out with my family. That didn't leave much time for friends. Making them or keeping them.

"I'm not so crazy about the ones I already have."

"Neither am I. They're all people you met working for the state. How about branching out? There are plenty of interesting people out there." She waves her arms out wide. "Just think, more people for you to piss off and be pissed off by. You'd like that, wouldn't you?"

She knows me way too well.

"Very fucking funny."

In the end, just to get her off my back, I go out and buy an overpriced set of clubs (did I do it subconsciously to prove I'm not a skinflint?). I figure if I use them once and don't like it, which I'm sure I won't, I can probably sell them to some other duffer who has a wife or ex-wife who doesn't understand the phrase, "Not interested."

To make sure I actually carry through on my promise to buy clubs, Sara decides to accompany me to the sporting goods store, where I lay out way more than I imagine to purchase a set with Tiger Woods's name on each club. I'm guessing the lie it's supposed to foster is that by using them I'll play like Tiger.

Thing is, I'll probably be pretty good. Growing up, I was a natural athlete. I played centerfield on the high school team, also lettering in tennis and basketball. And before the kids were born, I used to play softball every week with the office team, and when they were a little older, I'd play in a pickup, half-court hoops game every Saturday morning. But from what I understand, these skills don't necessarily translate to golf. What my ex-wife doesn't take into consideration is that if I can't excel in something, the chances are I'm gonna walk away. It's not a trait I'm proud of. It's just the way it is.

Having those clubs collecting dust in the garage doesn't mean

I'm actually going to play. But just to make sure, for my birthday Sara sends me a gift certificate for six golf lessons with the local pro who works out of the public course.

Knowing full well this will give her an excuse to call me two or three times a week to see if I've used the certificate, I figure, what the hell? So, I take the lessons. I'm right about liking the game. I don't. But I'm also so fucking competitive that I promise myself I won't quit until I master this most frustrating of sports. I'm not sure what I mean by mastering, since this seems impossible. But so long as I'm taking the lessons, why not actually play a few rounds?

I'm paired up with three other guys and twice a week, Tuesdays and Thursdays, to avoid the weekend logjam, we meet up at the public course. We have a standing tee time for ten a.m. I wouldn't mind if they'd make it earlier, since I'm an early riser and wouldn't mind getting it out of the way early, but the others demur. "Seems too much like having an actual job, Charlie," says Keith, a retired accountant. "Yeah," agrees Eric, who retired a couple years ago from some insurance company. "It's been almost two years and I'm still getting used to getting up at a decent hour without hearing that damn reveille." Dave, a former cop, the one I have the most in common with, agrees. As for me, I don't particularly like the feeling of being on a permanent vacation for the rest of my life.

Turns out Sara is right about one thing. The damn game is addictive. Not addictive in the sense that I enjoy it, like drinking and smoking. Addictive in the sense that it brings out that competitive streak in me, the side that always has to win. That's the way I was as an investigator and that's the way I am now.

To make it interesting, we have a small wager each time we play. The first few times, they clean my clock. But after a few weeks I've improved enough to make it a fair fight. I tell myself that as soon as I can beat them regularly, I'll start to look for new partners. But deep down I know that's a lie. That would take the kind of heightened social effort I am not capable of.

And to tell the truth, I'm looking forward to the winter months when it'll be too cold to play.

This explains why I'm on the links when my phone does a little dance in my pocket. It's from a Los Angeles area code, a number I don't recognize.

"Sorry, boys. Gotta take this," I say.

"I thought we had a rule about phones on the golf course, Floyd," says Keith.

"It's my ex-wife," I lie. "It might be something about one of the kids. You guys play through and I'll catch up with you."

Truth is, I'm not playing so hot today. Actually, it's a disastrous front nine. And so, it won't be the end of the world if I skip a couple holes. This call gives me the perfect out, much better than having to fake a heart attack. I can see from their faces my boys aren't happy about the interruption, but what choice do they have?

Whoever's calling is persistent because it rings at least half a dozen times before I pick up. If I knew how the hell to set it up, I might have let it go to voicemail. That's another thing I keep promising myself I'll get around to one day. Or rather get around to having one of my old cronies in my old office set it up for me.

"Hello," I say, half hoping it's one of those robocalls where I can just hang up, then take my sweet time catching up to the boys.

"Hello, would this happen to be Mr. Charlie Floyd?"

It's a woman's voice.

"It is. Who's this?"

"Oh, my God, I didn't expect to get through to you so easily. I was hoping I had the right number. My name's Dakota Richards."

"I'm pretty sure I don't know anyone named Dakota Richards. Nice name, though. Nice state, too. That the one with Mount Rushmore?"

"Nope. That's the other one."

"So, what can I do for you?"

"I'm a journalist and I have a regular podcast—you know what a podcast is, right?"

"I'm old, but not that old," I say. Truth is, the only reason I know about them is because my daughter's always suggesting I listen to one or another of them.

"Mine's called *Prime Time Crime*. It's a true crime podcast. I used to be a crime reporter for the *Albany Times* and most recently the *Sacramento Bee,* so I figured I'd put my training to good use."

"You actually make a living at that?"

"Boy, you don't mind diving right in, do you? That's kind of private and in some circles a question like that would be considered pretty rude."

"Those aren't the circles I frequent, Ms. Richards. So, what can I do for you?"

"Please, call me Dakota. And to answer your question, I have another job to supplement what I make from the podcast. Which isn't much. Yet."

"You didn't have to answer."

But the fact she does, endears her to me.

"You asked a question, a legitimate question, even if it is rude, so I answered it."

"And now, I suppose, you have some questions you'd like to ask me, Ms. Richards."

"Dakota. Please."

"What can I do for you, Dakota."

"I'm not one of those podcasters who does shows on serial killers, murderers, missing people, or even unsolved crimes, though occasionally I'll hit on one that's particularly interesting. And I'm not a fan of murders. I'm more interested in the more off-beat crimes, the crimes that affect more of us than murders do. I mean, how many people actually know someone who's been murdered?"

"Depends where you are. Up here around New Haven, I'd guess plenty of people are familiar with murder. Especially folks like me who made a living working all kinds of crimes. People like reading and hearing about murders, don't they?"

"They do. But like I said, I'm much more interested in the so-called lesser crimes, especially the people who commit them, and the people affected by them. Sometimes they're career criminals. Sometimes they're first-timers."

"So, where do I come in?"

"I'm planning on doing an upcoming podcast series about someone you're very familiar with. Francis Hoyt. I don't think any story about him and his criminal career would be complete unless I speak to you. From what I gather, there isn't anyone around who knows more about him than you do."

"A dubious distinction. But yeah, that's probably true. Except for maybe a cop down in Miami."

"You mean Manny Perez."

"Geez, you really have done your homework, haven't you? I hope you're not gonna tell me you're looking for Floyd and you'd like my help. Because, been there, done that. If the law can't hold onto him, that's their problem. And in case you're getting ready to ask, no, I don't have any idea where he is."

"No," she says. "I'm not interested in finding him. I just want to learn all I can about him, about his career. You don't know me, Mr. Floyd, but I'm like a dog with a bone. So, even if you turn me down now, I promise you haven't heard the last of me."

I laugh. I'm getting fond of this woman I've never met.

"What'd you say your name was again?" I ask. I know what her name is. I just want to hear it from her again. Let her think I'm a little spacy, a little addled from age.

"Dakota Richards. Would you like me to spell it?"

"Now, why would I want you to do that?"

"Because I know darn well you're probably already typing my name into Google, or maybe emailing friends of yours still working in law enforcement to check on me and see if I'm legit."

"You really are that dog, aren't you?"

"When you get to know me, Mr. Floyd, you'll know I don't

fool around. And I can save you a lot of time by sending you my resume and recommendations, if you like. Or, you can look me up on the Internet. If you know how."

"Ouch!"

"Sorry."

"No need to apologize. I deserve it."

"But seriously, I can send you links to my work..."

"Honey, I'm not hiring you for anything, so why would I need that kinda information?"

"Because you're Charlie Floyd. And if you don't think I've done a pretty thorough check on you, you'd be mistaken. So, what about it? Will you cooperate?"

"I don't know. Just what does 'cooperate' entail?"

"It means me coming to see you with my tape recorder and you sitting down with me and answering a bunch of questions."

"Seems like a whole lotta time, trouble and expense when we can just speak on the phone."

"I prefer not to work that way. I like to do my interviews in person, if I can. I'm sure you understand all about that. Besides, there are a couple other people I'm trying to arrange talking to while I'm there."

"Assuming I say yes, how long would something like this take?"

"Depends on how much you have to say. And while I'm there, I wouldn't mind hearing a little about that John Hartman case you were involved with a while ago."

"That's ancient history, Dakota. I don't think I have any-thing more to say about that other than it was not a time I look back on fondly. So, if I say yes, when would you want to do this thing?"

"How's sometime near the end of next week?"

"I think I might be able to pry open a window of time."

"Great. Why don't I check the plane schedules and get back to you? Would that be all right?"

"I guess," I say.

After we finish the call, my spirits are a lot higher than before

I spoke to Ms. Dakota Richards. No surprise, since talking with her promises to be a lot more interesting than another frustrating round of golf with the boys.

14

Dakota

I'm surprised how easily Charlie Floyd agrees to an interview. Now, not only will I have the one and only Francis Hoyt on the show—fingers crossed—I'll also have his arch nemesis, Charlie Floyd. And from what I've learned so far, no one in law enforcement knows more about Francis Hoyt than Charlie Floyd.

If Charlie Floyd is my white whale, Manny Perez, the Cuban-born, Miami police detective is Santiago's elusive marlin.

I'm not content to quit while I'm ahead. Instead, I look at it as being on a roll, and so as soon as I get off the phone with Floyd, I dial a number I've obtained for Manny Perez. This is not the first time I try to reach Perez. I leave him half a dozen messages at his office, send a couple emails, and I even mail an actual letter. But all I hear back is crickets. Now, with Charlie Floyd agreeing to sit for an interview, perhaps Perez will agree to do the same.

Miraculously, as if the gods are suddenly smiling on me, this time Detective Perez actually answers his phone. I tell him who I am and what I'm doing, and as casually as possible, I drop Charlie Floyd's name. It's even possible I tell Detective Perez that Floyd sends his regards—an outright fib, though I tell myself if I'd mentioned I was trying to get in touch with Perez, Floyd's old partner, Floyd would have, indeed, sent his regards. So, I file it under *creative nonfiction,* a term I could never quite understand.

As it turns out, the gods are not with me that day. Though extremely polite, Perez turns me down.

"I am very sorry, Miss Richards, but at this time I am afraid I am unable to accept your kind invitation to be a guest on your podcast. But I wish you the best of all luck."

Yes, that's the way he speaks, with a slight Cuban accent, articulating every single word, as if each one were so precious it must be heard. In some cases, this might be obnoxious, but with Detective Perez, it's actually endearing and shows his love for the English language, where each word is sacred.

When I persist, asking why not, he claims his superiors won't allow him to give any interviews, especially concerning an open case, which technically this is, because Hoyt is a fugitive. I'm not sure I believe him, but I'm not about to make a trip all the way down to Miami Beach on the off-chance I can get him to sit down and talk to me.

Anyone who knows me knows I don't give up easily. Like I tell Charlie Floyd, I'm a dog with a bone. Maybe, after I finish talking to Floyd, Perez will change his mind. I even have the fantasy that if Floyd and I hit it off, he'll act as intermediary and persuade his old pal to talk to me, even if it's off the record. I'm not quite sure I believe his excuse of not getting clearance from the upper echelon of the Miami police force. I mean, it is true that whenever you deal with cops, you have to get clearance from the public communications division, and I suppose technically it is an open case, but I find it hard to believe that Perez doesn't have the clout to make this happen.

I take this defeat surprisingly well, better than I usually do. Probably because I'm much too excited about the opportunity to talk with Charlie Floyd. I'm so revved up I have this urge to get in touch with Hoyt and brag about my coup. But not to worry. There's no way I'll do anything that stupid. I can only imagine what his reaction would be if he knew I was consorting with "the enemy."

No, this is the time to keep secrets, something I am getting surprisingly good at.

15

Francis

A week has passed since my meeting with Capowitz. To prepare mentally, I take long walks in Griffith Park or on the Santa Monica beach. There is no destination. Like baseball, there is no time limit. It's over when it's over. I walk until I can "see" the entire operation unfold in my mind, like a movie playing in a never-ending loop. I run through it again and again, looking at it from every angle, searching for possible flaws, holes, stumbling blocks. By the time I'm done, I've synthesized all the information into the best possible plan. Even then, it's not over. I'll continue revisiting it, again and again, looking to see if I can make improvements, looking to see if there's even the slightest flaw.

Till now, I've made it in L.A. without a car. I enjoy the freedom driving gives me. And yet, it's a potential source of danger. Owning a car means registering it, getting plates, buying insurance. All of which puts me firmly on the grid. Renting doesn't change that. Both leave a paper trail, even if it is under my newly adopted name of Billy Sutton. Using an alias is still a risk. Being stopped by some over-zealous L.A. cop, even for a minor infraction, can wind up having serious consequences.

But I can't continue using cabs and car services. I need to have the flexibility of having a car because now that things are heating up, I need the privacy of coming and going as I please.

Hot-wiring is a skill I learn when I'm fourteen. I cut my teeth

176

stealing my old man's pickup truck that time. At first, it's the thrill, but soon I find I can make a few bucks stealing a car and delivering it to a chop shop.

Back then it was a piece of cake heisting a car. Today, everything's computerized, which leads to learning a new skill: overriding automobile computer-generated anti-theft devices. But I haven't done that in years. Now if I need wheels and don't want to risk being traced, I'll use my head and imagination.

I scour Craig's List till I find several ads that suit my purpose. I settle on one and offer to meet the owner of a used, twelve-year-old Honda Accord, explaining before purchasing it I'll need to take it for a road test. We text back and forth. At first, he hesitates, but eventually his need to sell the vehicle trumps any fear he might have of someone stealing or messing up his precious car.

When I arrive at his house in mid-Wilshire, I've got on a baseball cap, pulled down low, sunglasses and several days' stubble. I'm wearing blue jeans, and a loud Hawaiian shirt several sizes too big. The Hawaiian shirt is not a fashion statement. It's a ploy designed to make sure the shirt is the first thing anyone uses to describe me. At the end of the day, I'll destroy it.

He's in his driveway, tinkering under the hood of the car. He introduces himself as Cal. He's in his early to mid-forties and he's wearing ripped jeans and a grease-stained, white wife-beater. As soon as he spots me walking down his driveway, he slams down the hood, wipes his hands on the sides of his jeans, and saunters toward me. He pulls a red bandana from his back pocket and wipes his forehead.

"You Eddie Felson?" he asks, using the name I've given when we exchange texts yesterday.

"That's right. Car looks good."

"Should be. I take good care of it." He smiles and I see a couple missing teeth. A sure sign of being a tweaker. Probably crystal meth. "It's my wife's car. Well, used to be. She split a month ago and she don't want it no more. I offered to sell it and split the dough with her. Now, she can go fuck herself. With all the work I put into it, it's cherry."

"Just like that little old lady from Pasadena."

"S'cuse me?"

"Never mind. So, your odometer doesn't lie?" I ask, lifting the hood and peering under it, as if I know what I'm doing.

He raises his hand. "As God is my witness."

I slam down the hood.

"What do you say? We got a deal or not?" I'm anxious to get this over as quickly as possible. The longer I linger, the more chance he'll change his mind.

"You said cash, right? Three grand?"

"I did. But like I said, I need to test drive it. A couple hours. I been burned too many times."

"Gee, I don't know." He shakes his head. "I feel like in that case I oughta ask for all the dough upfront. You know, as security. It ain't that I don't trust you. But I just met you. You look like an honest guy, but who knows, right?"

"You don't know. But no test, no sale."

"Yeah, yeah, I get it. But I don't know you from Adam, so how do I know you're gonna come back with the car?"

"I guess you don't."

"Well, I don't know." He wipes the sweat off his forehead with his grease-stained bandana. "Maybe I should find out something about you first? You from around here?"

"Back East."

"How long you been in L-A?"

"Few weeks."

"Jeez. How the hell did you last here effin' weeks without a car?"

"I was borrowing a buddy's while he was away on a business trip. He's back now. Needs his wheels."

"What kinda work you do?"

"Independent contractor."

He looks baffled, but he doesn't want to show his ignorance.

No one does. So, he lets it go.

"Married man?"

"Used to be," I say, with a wink. "Like you. We split up recently."

He smiles. "Guess we got that in common, right? But you're a good-looking guy. A little on the small side, but some chicks dig that. And now you'll have a nice set of wheels. You'll have chicks comin' out of the woodwork."

"Ya think?"

"Ab-so-fucking-lutely, man. One thing this town has is plenty of pussy. And this car," he jerks a thumb back in the direction of his heap, "is like a chick magnet. I swear. You oughta hear the engine purr, man."

I'm way past standing here in the hot sun having meaningless conversation with this asshole. I need to end this as quick as I can. Time to pull the trigger.

"Look. How about this? I'm only gonna be in town another week, ten days, and then I'm going back East. So, now that I think about it, there's no real reason I need to own a car. What say I just rent it from you for a week or two?"

"Huh? I don't get it. Why not just go to Hertz or something like that?"

"Good question," I say, leaning forward, like I'm about to impart the ultimate secret of life. "I'm sure someone like you, someone in your position, can understand. Truth is, I'm not even supposed to be in L-A. I got myself in this little financial mess and I've got some assets here in L-A I have to take care of before my creditors...well, you don't want to hear about that shit. You got your own problems, right? But I don't want my wife to know I'm here and since we have the same credit card, she'd..."

"Say no more, man. I see where you're headed."

"So, what if I rent your car for, let's say, five hundred a week? And if I need it longer, even if it's only a few days, I pay for another week? Then, I bring it back and you can sell it. Whaddya think?"

His forehead crinkles, a sign he's considering my proposition. "Well. Maybe. But I don't know. Maybe I'm missing something..."

"You're not missing anything."

He gets quiet.

Finally, the light bulb flashes.

"Okay. I get it. You're hiding assets."

"You got me. And the last thing I need is for the people I owe money to or my wife to know I'm out here. I figure I cash in the assets, stash the cash, then declare bankruptcy. And she gets what she deserves." I make a zero with two fingers. "But it's all gotta be on the Q-T. As is, I wouldn't be surprised if my wife hasn't hired a team of private dicks to follow me."

His head swivels in all directions, like he's looking for someone lurking in the shadows. I have a hard time keeping a straight face.

"Anyway, now you know why I don't want a record of my being here. If I rent, I'd have to give them my credit card, and she'd know right away..."

"Gotcha." He nods his head vigorously. Suddenly, we're co-conspirators. He's victim of a greedy, underhanded spouse. I'm a victim of the system *and* a greedy, underhanded spouse.

"So, what say we do each other a favor. Here's an easy way for you to make a grand, just by renting me your car for a week. I stay under the radar, get done what I have to get done, bring the car back. Easy money for you and then, when you get it back, you just put it up for sale again. It's like selling the car twice. That'd really stick it to the bitch, right? Guys like us gotta stick together against the bitches of the world. Whaddya you say?"

He likes that. He nods his head slowly up and down like one of those bobble-head dolls on a car dashboard. "Yeah. Yeah. Sounds great, man."

"Right on, baby," I say, offering a high-five.

He hands over the keys and shows me the registration in the glove compartment.

"Here's the two-weeks' rent in advance," I say. I open my wallet and peel off ten C-notes, as I watch his eyes bulge out of his head.

I almost feel sorry for this schmuck. He's got no fucking idea how this is going to play out. He can kiss this baby goodbye, because it's gonna be the last time he ever sees his pride and joy.

Now, for a week or as long as I need it, I have a car on the up and up that's registered to this bozo, and there's no way it can be traced back to me.

16

Francis

For the first time in more than a year I wake up with a bounce in my step. I feel more alive than I have in months. It's like a giant boulder has been lifted not only from my shoulders but every other inch of my body. Fuck the bounce, man. I feel like I'm floating on air. No shit, it feels like the first day of a new life. And I know why.

Up till now, my only aim in life is to stay out of the grasp of John Law. Most of my time is spent covering my tracks while I create my new identity. But let's face it, I miss the old one. I miss the adrenaline rush I get when I'm in the midst of a job. Researching it. Planning it. And then there's the best part, the part that pumps blood through my body, blasts a heavy shot of adrenaline through my veins, heading straight for my brain, like I'm some kind of hopped-up junkie shooting H. And then there's the ultimate high: Doing the job. Proving to the goddamn world again that there's never been anyone like me. And then the final jolt: getting away with it.

The only thing left is to make a couple dry runs. I visit the scene three times and each time I snap a mental picture. I follow the three escape routes I've marked off, making sure I'm familiar with each one, as if I've used it dozens of times.

In the meantime, I make good use of my new wheels. I deactivate the GPS, which keeps a record of my movements, and drive through various neighborhoods adjacent to the strip mall. I spend hours driving around, trying my best to get lost, not hard in L.A. Then, using an old Thomas Guide I pick up at a used bookstore, I try to find myself. This helps to familiarize myself with the area and will come in handy in case someone might follow me.

By the time I finish my last rehearsal run, I've gone through an entire tank of gas. I find a parking spot about a half mile away from the cottage, then walk the rest of the way home. By now, it's early evening and after dining on a couple fish tacos I pick up at the local Mex joint, all I can do is collapse on the bed, where I quickly fall asleep.

I don't want to hold onto the car for more than a week or so, which is when the asshole owner will realize it's never coming back. He'll report it stolen, but by then I'll have either torched it or run it off a cliff. Either way, that poor, dumb sucker will be shit out of luck.

Meanwhile, I wait for a callback from Alex and my other source. It's only been a couple days, but I'm getting antsy. If I don't get answers soon, I'll abort and wait another week or two. This isn't something I want to do. Besides losing my edge, I'll have to find another set of wheels. But without knowing exactly who I'm dealing with, I'm not about to risk my life.

Finally, the wait is over. Alex texts the burner number I give him and asks for a good time to call. I text back one word. "NOW."

"What you got, Alex?"

"Chances are you're dealing with the *paisanos*, Francis. I know you're a details guy, so I'll tell you everything I found out, then you can decide what's important and what isn't."

"Shoot."

"Let's start with a little history lesson."

"I haven't got all day, Alex. How about we skip the creation story?"

"Come on, Francis. Let me have some fun."

I humor him, which means I'll have to sit through a shitload of useless information till he gets to his point.

"You got all these other gangs out there. The Crips. The Bloods. The Mexicans. The Chinese. The Vietnamese. You name it, they got a gang. But they're much more hit-and-run and far more violent and unpredictable. Having a bank like the one you described just isn't their style. They don't have years of organization behind them. The Mafia does."

"Makes sense."

"Let me tell ya a little about the West Coast mob. First off, it's not the mob of Bugsy Siegel, Mickey Cohen and Meyer Lansky, the boys who pretty much breathed life into the Vegas we know and love today. The L-A family's nowhere near as powerful as the five families back here in New York. Back in the '80s, Pete Milano was the boss and his little brother Carmen was underboss. They were heavily involved in drugs, pornography, gambling, and loan-sharking. Milano breathed life into the mob when he inducted new members like Stephen "Steve the Whale" Cino, and the shylock brothers, Lawrence and Anthony "The Animal" Fiato. The law finally caught up to them, but when Milano was paroled back in '91, he took back control of the family. Since then, the L-A mob, along with the Buffalo crime family, has made moves into Vegas. By the end of the '90s, the L-A crime family had maybe twenty members."

"They're still active, right?"

"You bet. They've become the old guard, the establishment. There are no strong figures like in the past. But I'm guessing they still generate plenty of dough, even with all the competition, and they've got their fingers in many pots."

"Who's in charge?"

"Guy by the name of Vinnie Ferrera. He's serving time now. They got him on RICO. I'm guessing he anointed some capo to run things till he gets out."

"What about that mob bank thing?'"

"It's real and it's nothing new. I know one in particular, up in Providence, that got hit a while back."

"Got details?"

"Francis, my friend, you're not talking to some amateur here. It was hit by a bunch of tough guys, but eventually they got caught. Couple didn't make it out alive. It's just a rumor, and it sounds crazy, but word on the street was Raymond Patriarca, head of the New England family, was behind it. The crazy thing is, he was in the joint at the time. Story goes he wasn't happy with the tribute he was getting while was he was in Walpole. Thought he was being cheated and disrespected. Feeling unloved and under-appreciated, he resorted to self-help."

I hang up knowing a whole lot more than I did. Seems to me this is Providence all over again. Which means there's a good chance Ferrara is behind it. And Alex's explanation about Patriarca sounds like it could be in play here.

I'm not happy. Getting in bed with the mob means waking up with bedbugs. The kind that can kill you. It's not my first rodeo. You don't do 'business' in New York, New Jersey, Connecticut, and Miami without crossing paths with them. The one time I do them a favor by taking one of their guys along with me on a job winds up getting me a year in stir. I keep my mouth shut, which earns me respect. As a result, they let me do business without asking for tribute.

Knowing who I'm dealing with doesn't make things any easier. Or safer. Despite what people think, there is no honor among thieves. These are not the kind of people you want to be in business with. Among their own, they got that honor thing going. But for someone like me, well, I'm a fucking outsider and they don't give a rat's ass about what happens to me. If it ever gets out that one of their own is behind it, it'll get very messy for me. I'm expendable, just a loose end who can royally fuck things up if I shoot my mouth off. That's all a guy like Ferrara needs, word out that he's behind the heist.

Knowing what I know now, most people would run from a deal like this as fast as their mother-fuckin' legs will take them.

But I'm not most people. Crazy as it seems, this makes the job even more desirable, because it adds that extra level of danger. It's not gonna end when I hand over the swag. The end will come when I'm either found floating in the L.A. River, which isn't a river at all, or as a sack of bleached bones out on the Mojave.

Knowing what the score is means either I return the dough and give up on it or I come up with a damn good escape hatch for after the job is done.

17
Dakota

I offer to pay for Mark's ticket as well as mine, but he absolutely refuses. He says he's got plenty of miles. And then, with a Cheshire cat grin, he adds, "I didn't tell you this yet, honey, but you know that novel that came out five or six years ago? Well, some moron producer just optioned it for, as they say, 'a major Hollywood movie.'"

"You're kidding!"

He shakes his head, his face bursting into a huge smile. I couldn't be happier for him. Mark lives very frugally, so a big payday like this will take financial pressures of him for a long while. I know him well enough to know he's not about to go out and blow it on a yacht or a beach house.

"How does it work?" I ask.

"First off, the chances of it ever getting made are pretty slim. But they paid a nice chunk of dough for the rights to the book. And if by some chance it actually does appear at your local theater, I'm due another chunk of do-re-mi. So, this trip is on me, paid for by Hollywood bucks. I love America!"

I give him a big hug. Not because he's being paid Hollywood dough. Not because more people will probably read his book. But because he works so hard and he's such a good friend. Which only proves that sometimes good is rewarded.

The plan is to fly into JFK then head into Manhattan. Mark

has arranged for us to stay in the apartment of an old friend of his, who happens to be in the Hamptons for the week. "Turns out we'll be doing her a favor—feeding her cat, watering her plants. We can manage that, right?"

As we fly in the dead of night across the continent, neither of us can sleep. So, we pull out notebooks and begin to discussing strategy. We even make a list of areas we'd like Floyd to address.

While I'm in Connecticut getting Charlie Floyd on the record, Mark will be in Jersey interviewing the police chief of that small town where Hoyt pulled off an incredible feat. I want Mark to check out that story about Hoyt breaking into houses right under the noses of the cops, making sure it's not just another myth that's grown up around Hoyt. I want him to get details. He'll be recording, so we'll have the Chief's voice as part of the podcast. Plus, Mark is going to see if there's anyone else of interest to get on the record.

There's another rumor I need to run down. A high-profile fence was murdered a couple years ago and rumor has it that Hoyt might have had something to do with it. I can't find any other hint of violent acts committed by him, so I'm anxious for Mark to see what he can uncover.

After landing, we take a cab to his friend's apartment on the Upper West Side, where I'll drop my things, including Mark, then head up to Connecticut. Later, we'll meet up for dinner and share the information we've gathered. Our flight back isn't until tomorrow evening, which gives us most of tomorrow to follow up any other leads we stumble across.

Even though I've had very little sleep, I'm so pumped I feel like the Energizer Bunny. After a quick stop at the apartment, I head straight to Grand Central to catch the eleven-ten train up to Stamford. Floyd instructs me to text him when I'm on the train. He'll pick me up, then we'll head over to the Ferguson Library where we'll do the interview. "They know me there and they'll let us use the conference room upstairs for however long we need."

188

"How will I recognize you?"

He laughs. "Don't worry, that won't be a problem."

I can't wait to see what he means.

I do not travel light. After leaving a small suitcase at the apartment, I'm left with my extra-large J. Crew backpack, stuffed with half a dozen notebooks; recording equipment; half a dozen pens, each a different color ink; a fold-up umbrella (as a reporter I learn to be ready for all kinds of weather); baseball cap; sweater; half a dozen double-A batteries; a box of sugar-free cookies; an extra pair of socks (don't ask me why, it's just something I obsess about—wearing clean socks every day); my Kindle—I'm alternating between *In Cold Blood* and *The Executioner's Song*; my mini-iPad; a copy of today's *New York Times*; and the two of the latest issues of *The New Yorker*.

It's twelve-thirty when I arrive in Stamford. I hit the bathroom then exit the station. Walking toward me is a tall, slim man, six-one or six-two, wearing cowboy boots, faded blue jeans, a pale blue shirt, and a black sport jacket, and the pièce de résistance, an ecru colored cowboy hat. The only thing missing are spurs and chaps. I smile to myself, wondering if I've magically arrived in Dallas, Texas, not Stamford, Connecticut.

I've told him to be on the lookout for a slim, blonde who could easily pass as a Delta flight attendant. As soon as he spots me, he flashes a big smile and stops in his tracks, waiting for me to come to him.

"You must be Charlie Floyd."

"The one and only," he says, tipping his hat and bowing slightly.

"I sure hope you're not going to call me ma'am."

"Wouldn't think of it, Miz Dakota," he says, stressing the *Ms.*

"Whew! For a minute there, I thought you wanted me to kiss your hand, not shake it."

"Not a chance, especially in this me-too environment. Here, gimme that heavy-looking backpack you're carrying."

Two hours ago, I hardly felt the weight on my back, but now, all of a sudden, it feels like I'm carrying a bag loaded with rocks. I'm tempted to let him, but a little voice in my head says, *no way, I'm gonna let him think I'm the weaker sex.*

"No thanks. I'm good."

"Suit yourself. Car's over there," he says, pointing to a very cool looking electric blue convertible.

"You were right," I say, as I try to keep up with him as we head to his car parked across the street. His stride is twice the size of mine and I think he's unaware that I'm having trouble keeping up. But there's no way I'm going to ask him to slow down. I just pick up my pace to the point where I'm almost out of breath.

"About?"

"Recognizing you."

"I've been told there's something about me that tends to stand out a little."

"A little?"

Without breaking stride, he turns and says, "Looks like this is going to be a lot more fun than I thought it'd be."

"Why's that?"

"You've got a little sass. I like women with sass."

I feel my face turn red. I know he's playing me, but dammit, it's working.

"Good thing you didn't say ass. Then we really would have a problem."

He shakes his head. "See what I mean?"

When we reach his little blue, two-seater, he gallantly opens the door for me. When he goes around the other side of the car, I can't help wondering how he'll be able to fold himself into such a small space. Surprisingly, he does it easily, all in one fluid motion.

"We're not going far," he says as he buckles up. I do the same. "It's walkable, but heck, to be honest I just love riding around in this baby. My ex calls it my Midlife-Crisis-Mobile. I tell her, only if I'm gonna live to a hundred and twenty. To be honest, it's the kind of car I've wanted my whole life. But with a wife and kids, well, something like this just wasn't in the cards till now."

He parks around the corner from the library, a large, stately looking building that looks like something you'd see in the state capital. Inside, there's a bookstore to the left and straight ahead there's a stairway leading up to the main reading areas.

Floyd tips his hat to a middle-aged woman who sits at the information desk and we shoot past her toward a bank of elevators.

"She knows you?"

"Everyone does, Dakota. All right to call you Dakota, right?"

"Of course."

"I'd take the stairs. Good exercise. But we're up a few floors and since you won't let me help with that thing on your back, I thought we'd take the easy way out."

"Fine by me," I say. My legs, which are in pretty good shape from running, feel rubbery and heavy, like they've got ten-pound weights strapped to them.

We enter a small, glass-enclosed conference room, directly across from the elevators. There's a round glass table, surrounded by six chairs. Floyd waits until I choose one, then sits down opposite me.

Just as we're about to begin, an attractive woman in her mid-to-late fifties opens the glass door and pops her head in.

"Everything okay, Charlie?"

"Better than okay, Barbara. And I really appreciate your letting us use your conference room."

"Oh, please, any time. I'll have my assistant bring in a couple water bottles for you guys. Is there anything else I can get you?"

Charlie looks at me. "No thanks. I think we're good. Much appreciated though."

"Where's my head? Barbara, I'd like you to meet Dakota Richards. She's come all the way out from Los Angeles to interview me for her podcast. She's gonna make me famous. Dakota, this is Barbara. She runs the whole shebang here."

I stand and reach my hand across the table.

"Please don't get up, dear. I'll just get out of your way now, so you two can make Charlie more famous than he already is."

As soon as she disappears down the hall, Charlie says, "Terrific woman. And this is some operation she runs."

"It's a huge library."

"They offer terrific programs for the community. Let's get started. I'm sure you've got plenty of questions for me."

"Sure do," I say as I pull out my notebooks, pens, and two tape recorders, and line them up on the table in front of me. I move the microphone closer to him, open up one of the notebooks, flip on the recorder and we begin.

18

Francis

I work alone.

But rules are sometimes made to be broken.

After learning who's most likely behind this heist, I realize I need insurance. In this case, insurance would be in the form of a patsy.

A patsy, also known as a fall guy, is there to create chaos and confusion. A patsy doesn't have to be stupid or witless. All he has to do is be easily manipulated and be in the right place at the wrong time.

Lee Harvey Oswald was the perfect patsy. The guy takes the fall for offing Kennedy. And whoever did, walks off into the sunset, scot-free. You don't get much patsier than that.

I don't know anyone in L.A. other than Vince and Dakota and neither of them is patsy material. But I know where to find someone.

There are standards. No punks or street thugs. Someone who follows orders without questioning them. Someone with half a brain in their head, but no more than that. Someone with enough ambition to know that working with me might be a gateway to bigger and better things. Someone so fucking full of himself he thinks he's someone he's not and never will be. This description pretty much describes Kenny Staples. Too bad he's on the other side of the country.

There is no club for patsies, but they aren't hard to find. An hour or so on Yelp and I tag the perfect nesting spot for the kind of person I'm looking for. It's a hotel lounge in downtown L.A., a gathering place for the hip, wannabe hipsters, a place where everyone there is on the make.

That evening, around seven-thirty, just before the sun is about to make its nightly descent into the Pacific, I hop in the Honda and head directly into the heart of the beast. It feels good to be on the road. Good having my destiny in my own hands for a change.

The hotel is on South Broadway, between the flower district and the Staples Center. I find a parking spot and walk a couple blocks till I see an older building with a huge *Jesus Saves* sign on the roof.

The floor of the lobby is a giant chess board of black and white squares angled in such an odd direction that it makes you feel tipsy. I take the elevator up to the roof-top bar, which is filled with a couple dozen glass tables surrounded by plush, white fabric chairs. It's still a little early, so maybe only half the tables are occupied. I pick one in the corner, where I have a good view. I order a non-alcoholic beer from the cute waitress, and wait for the show to begin.

It doesn't take long to see I'm in the right place. Everyone in the joint is either under thirty or over sixty. And they're all there for the same reason: they're all on the make.

Finally, after an hour or so, I spot him. Late-thirties. Deep tan. Slicked back, bottle-black hair. Armani sport jacket. Jeans. Deep blue shirt. Loafers. No socks. No tie. The closer he gets, the surer I am of who and what he is.

He's a wannabe predator. Greased up and ready to pounce. When it's obvious he's getting nowhere at one table, he moves to another, looking for someone, anyone, who'll buy what he's selling. I know the type. I've been dealing with guys like him my whole life. Dudes who think they're hot shit. Dudes who think they're smarter, better looking, slicker than everyone else in the room.

This, my friends, is prime patsy material.

I keep my eye on him while he continues to work the room. Finally, after he strikes out with a table of three middle-aged women, all big-haired blondes who look like they've just come from raiding the makeup department at Bloomingdale's, he takes a break. He's heading toward the john and his path takes him close to my table. I see the defeated look on his face and the slump in his shoulders He reminds me of a balloon that's slowly deflating. I can see defeat on his face, and smell the distinct scent of desperation as he passes by.

Here's the chance I'm waiting for. When he's at his most vulnerable. When his fly is open and his dick is in his hand.

I follow a discreet distance behind, holding back a second or two before I trail him into the john. He's standing in front of one of the half dozen urinals lined up on the far wall. As soon as I see him unzip, I approach an empty urinal, keeping one as a buffer between us.

"Some crowd tonight, huh?" I say.

He's startled. No guy expects conversation while pissing. I'm breaking men's room protocol, but that's the point.

He turns his head slightly in my direction, while I keep my eyes fixed straight ahead. I don't want him to get the wrong idea.

He doesn't say anything, but I persist.

"What is this, a loser's convention tonight?" I say.

This gets his attention.

"Excuse me?"

"The crowd. It sucks tonight."

He shakes his dick, tucks it back into his pants, zips up and starts to turn toward the row of sinks. "My first time here. How's about you?"

He stops. Turns around. He's weighing whether or not to engage. From the look on his face, I know he will.

"I been here before," he says.

"Seen better turnouts, I hope."

He's still hesitant. He's thinking. Should he engage? Should he ignore me? He should. But he won't.

"Yeah. I guess I seen better."

I zip up and make my way over to the row of sinks, where he's now standing, punching the liquid soap dispenser. I take the one next to his. He reeks of that deadly combination of cheap cologne and flop sweat.

"Name's Eddie. Yours?"

He hesitates a moment. "Derek."

"Nice to meet you, Derek. I guess, under the circumstances, we should skip the handshake."

He smiles, as he lathers up his hands.

"You from around here?" I ask.

He shakes his head no. He doesn't know quite what to make of me yet. Am I some kind of pervert? A sad, pathetic loser? Or just an overly friendly guy?

"Where from?"

"Chicago. You?"

We both reach for the towel dispenser at the same time. I pull my hand away and say, "be my guest."

He smiles, pulls down a couple sheets and dries his hands.

"Cincinnati," I say. "We're practically neighbors."

I finish up and take a step back. He does the same.

His face is a question mark. He doesn't quite know what to do. Just walk away? Keep the conversation going?

I make up his mind for him. It's the least I can do.

"A few nice-looking chicks here tonight, right?"

He measures me warily.

"I guess," he says.

"Cold as ice, right?"

"Whaddya mean?"

"Looks like they don't wanna give guys like us the time of day."

His body language changes. Suddenly, he's more relaxed. We've bonded. We are compadres lined up against a common enemy.

He shrugs. "Maybe it's just not my night."

"Guy like you shouldn't have to beg, man. Every night should be your night."

"I don't get you, friend," he says, as he turns toward the exit.

"No offense, man. I'm just tellin' it like I see it."

"What's that supposed to mean?"

"I can sniff guys like you a mile away. I used to be one of them."

"Listen, buddy…"

"Eddie. Remember?"

His body stiffens as he takes an aggressive stance. I've seen this cock-of-the-walk shit plenty of times in the joint. Usually, it's the guys who don't have shit to back it up with. The ones you gotta watch are the ones who don't give warning. They just pounce. You'll never see them coming.

"Listen, I don't know what your game is…"

"Easy, pal," I say, crushing the used paper towel into a ball and shooting it, like a basketball, into the circular receptacle only a couple feet to his right. "No game. I get guys like you." The crumpled paper towel hits the rim and bounces in.

"What's that supposed to mean? Guys like me?"

"How long you in the joint?"

"What makes you…?"

I don't have to guess. It's written all over him. The way he holds himself. The way he walks. The way his eyes dart back and forth.

"It's written all over you, man."

He takes half a step back. He doesn't know my real name, but he knows who I am. He's seen guys like me all his life. The guys that make it. The winners who shove the losers like him around. That's fear I see in his eyes.

"Relax, man," I say, leaning back, a signal he's safe with me. For now.

"What do you want from me?"

"It's not what I want from you, my friend. It's what I can do for you."

"For me? What the hell are you talking about? I have no fucking idea who the fuck you are and you're gonna do something for me? How the fuck dumb do you think I am?"

I'm getting under his skin. It was so easy, I'm almost ashamed of myself.

"Maybe I'm gonna find out how smart you are."

Suddenly, the muscles in his face relax. The reptilian part of his brain that acts without thinking is starting to realize I'm not an immediate threat to him. In a flash, he's moved from fear to confusion to curiosity.

He's hooked. But I'm in no rush to reel him in. I need to play him a while. But it's just a matter of time before he's mine.

"Let me buy you a drink, Derek" I say. "But not here. Too damn noisy."

"Why the fuck should I have a drink with you?"

"Because you're smarter than you look." I tap my right temple with my forefinger. "Wanna prove me wrong?"

He can't hide that *what's-in-it-for-me,* look.

Before he can answer, I add, "I have a proposition that will benefit both of us."

Boom! He's hooked.

We walk a block or two till we end up at a dimly lit bar a block or so away from the hotel. I keep my mouth shut because I want him to run all kinds of scenarios through his head. By the time we sit down at a small table near the back, I want him to be so hyped up he can't think straight.

We sit there in the back of the half-empty bar, nursing a couple drinks, as he waits for me to get to the point. I'm in no hurry.

Finally, he can't take it anymore.

"You gonna tell me what's on your mind, friend, or what?"

"Let me ask you something, Derek. What made you follow me all the way out of the hotel and to this place? You don't know me. You don't even know my fucking name."

"Sure, I do. It's Eddie."

"That's what I told you. But how can you be sure that's really my name?"

He hesitates a moment. I don't wait. I dive in. "I'll tell you why. Because something up here," I reach across the table and tap the side of his head, "is telling you this is opportunity knocking."

"Yeah? Keep talking."

"I watch you five, ten minutes, I know exactly who you are. I've seen dozens of guys like you. Outside. Inside. Guys on the make. Guys looking to score. Whether it's a chick or a job. It don't matter. You got a hunger. I'm the guy who can feed you."

He starts to open his mouth, but no words come out.

"I watch you and I see something more than just a small-time, penny-ante creep trying to hustle women."

He opens his mouth, but before he can say anything, I raise one finger and put it to my lips. "You know what that is, Derek?"

"I ain't got no fucking idea."

"I see possibilities. That's what I see. I see, under the right circumstances, you're a guy that's better than the guy I just met in the bathroom. The guy who was striking out all night. Let's be honest here, Derek. I haven't seen that many strikeouts since Randy Johnson. But I see your future can be, Derek, and it damn well doesn't include trolling for rich women in fucking upscale bars. Unless, of course, that's what you want to be doing the rest of your life."

"I don't know what the fuck you're talking about," he says. But he knows exactly what I'm talking about. And his tone isn't one of anger. It's one of, *tell me more.*

"I think deep down in here, Derek," I tap my heart, "you know exactly what I'm talking about. It just hasn't made the trip up here yet." I tap the side of my head. "But if you're willing to listen, you might learn a lot about yourself. Tonight, Derek, I'm your fucking guardian angel. I'm here to change your life, Derek. I'm here to put you on the road to success. But only if that's what you want. Is that what you want, Derek? Because if it isn't, I'll just pay for the drinks and move on."

He glares at me. Part of him wants to get the hell out of there. But I know he's not going to do that. Because the other part of him sees the possibility of a life that doesn't start and end with hanging out in pick-up joints looking for his next score.

Time to reel him in.

19

Charlie

It's obvious Dakota has worked with cops before. After five minutes with this little dynamo, I'm sure she had them pissing all over themselves trying to help her out. I feel kinda sorry for her male competitors. With this woman on the job, they never stood a chance.

First, she asks if I'm comfortable. Right away, this establishes she's empathetic and knows how important it is to bond with her subject.

Funny thing is, when I was on the job I hated talking to journalists. For the most part, they just got in the way. Most asked dumb questions and if that wasn't bad enough, they asked the same ones over and over again. On the other hand, I learned to play nice with them because I knew they could sometimes be useful. It's always a delicate balance, but fortunately I was able to carry it off. I think if you ask the Connecticut press about me most would say I was a hard-ass. Cooperative up to the point where it was part of my job to keep information from them they wanted, but respectful of the job they had to do. I learned early on that staying on the right side of the working press could benefit me, especially when I wanted or needed to get information out to the general public. Bottom line: I knew how to work them well enough so they thought they were working me instead of for me. And early on I realized that if I was a little flamboyant, the story would most likely be about me and my cowboy hat and boots, deflecting from the story they thought they wanted.

Dakota knows how to play the game. Every so often, she stops and asks, "are you okay?" It's sweet, until it starts to get a little annoying. "Dakota, honey, I appreciate your concern, but you don't have to check with me every five minutes to see if I'm okay. I was once in an interrogation room for seven hours straight and I only had to leave to pee once. And I probably could have held that in, too, if I'd had to. Of course, that's when I was much younger and could, you'll excuse the expression, hold my water."

She laughs. Even her laugh is cute. It's also sincere. I can tell. I can spot insincerity a mile off. It's one of the things that made me an excellent investigator. My friends in the department used to call me The Human Truth Machine. And without bragging, I have to admit I'm a heck of a lot better than the best polygraph machine. After so many years in the biz, I've learned a lot. I can read people. I know what they're thinking and I know why they're thinking it. Everyone comes in with a story, their story. It's my job to break that story and get the truth.

We're twenty minutes into our conversation, background she calls it, with me trying to run through my entire career in less than half an hour, before she finally gets to Francis Hoyt.

"When was the first time you became aware of Francis Hoyt?"

"To be honest, I don't remember exactly—you start to lose track after a while. I could check my journals. But off the top of my head, I'd say it was five, six years ago."

"Do you remember the circumstances?"

"It wasn't anything earth-shattering. I believe we were at a staff meeting, going over some of the cases we were involved in or about to get involved in, when George Hancock, we call him Georgie Porgy—the man just loves his pies, cherry, apple, Boston cream, doesn't matter, Georgie's all over it—one of my junior investigators brought up a series of break-ins in several of the toniest neighborhoods in Southern Connecticut. Greenwich, Westport, New Canaan. They all had a similar M-O. 'Looks like there's 'a new face in town,' was the way he put it. 'Guy's like Spiderman. Climbs up the sides of houses. Breaks through the most sophisticated alarm systems. Days. Nights. It doesn't matter. No prints. No D-N-A. No footprints. Nada.' That was more than enough to get my attention."

"What did that tell you?"

"That we were up against a real pro. Right away, I recalled reading about a series of burglaries in New Jersey, Westchester and Long Island, all in high-end neighborhoods, and they all had pretty much the same M-O. Someone breaks in, not only while people are in the house but while they're downstairs having dinner. The person—or persons—are so slick, so good, the folks never even realize anything's missing till they start looking for something the next day and it isn't there. And then, no one seems to know why, suddenly, the M-O changes. No more dinnertime break-ins. Now, it's either late at night when everyone's asleep, or during the day when no one's home. And all the guy takes is silver."

"How did you know it was the same guy?"

"By how he got in and out, what he took, and how well-prepared he was. In the past, it was pretty much anything of value, anything he could carry out. Now, it was all about silver. Not just any silver. He only took silver that was pure, or had a provenance."

"Meaning?"

"It was valuable not only for the silver content itself, but for who made it and the workmanship involved. Up here, we've got a lot of pieces that were made by Paul Revere. Yup. That one. 'The British are coming' Paul Revere. So, it was valuable for the silver, but also for the artistic and historical value of the piece. To me, that meant we weren't dealing with just some run-of-the-mill thief. We were dealing with someone who knew what he was doing. Someone with smarts. He never bothered with the inferior stuff."

"So, Hoyt was pretty well known by this time?"

"By the time I got involved, he was pretty well known by law enforcement. Part of that's because of the only time he got collared. And it wasn't because he was caught in the act. He's much too smart for that. This time, and no one knows for sure why, he went in with a partner, some low-level mob guy. Turns out the guy screws things up in the house, pulls out a weapon, something Hoyt never has anything to do with, at least so far as we know, and the homeowner got shot. They take off and eventually the other guy gets pinched. He rolls over on Hoyt—fortunately, the guy was only superficially wounded—who winds up getting a deuce. It was his first conviction and he was sprung after a year for good behavior. I might be wrong, but seems to me when he got out, that's when he started to change his approach."

"Meaning?"

"He always works alone."

"What about the code? You know, honor amongst thieves?"

I smile. "Dakota, honey, crooks don't have a 'code.' And they don't know the meaning of the word 'honor.' That's for T-V and the movies. Nine times outta ten it's every guy for himself. Besides, Hoyt is an outsider. He isn't one of the boys. I don't know what he is, but he sure as hell isn't Italian. So, even if there was some kind of code it wouldn't apply to him."

"Whatever happened to that partner?"

"Got off with a suspended sentence and a few months in lockup for cooperating. After that he vanished into thin air."

"You mean he was killed?"

"We can't be sure, 'cause there was never a body. But you don't need much imagination to figure out what happened."

"Do you think Hoyt had something to do with that?"

"He was up in Otisville at the time, but that doesn't mean he didn't have something to do with the 'disappearance.'"

At the mention of the missing partner, Dakota gets this odd

look on her face. Like this is something she's hearing for the first time. I'm not here to preach, but I think it's important she understand who she's dealing with. I'm a bit of a history buff and it's like with Jesse James. Everyone believed the P.R. — which he spread, by the way—that he was stealing from the banks and railroads and distributing it to the "little guy." No such thing. He was a stone-cold killer, a punk who murdered innocent people whose money he was stealing from banks.

"Let me tell you something. A lot of people who don't know the way things are romanticize guys like Francis Hoyt. You know, the Cary Grant *To Catch a Thief* thing. They see burglary simply as a crime against property. But that's not true. There's always an element of danger for the crook and the victim. There's a very slim line between taking things that don't belong to you and violence. Hoyt has never been pegged as being a violent felon. But that doesn't mean he isn't or hasn't been. It just means we haven't heard about it, or caught him at it. Trust me, anyone who gets involved with Francis Hoyt is at risk."

I can tell she's hearing me. But what I can't tell is whether she totally understands what I'm trying to warn her about. She doesn't follow up, and I hope it's not because what I've just told her doesn't fit into the story she wants to tell. But I'm not her Daddy, so I let it go.

Once we establish how I first learn of Hoyt, we spend the next couple hours talking about him, including the run-in Manny and I had with him up here, which eventually lands him in that frustrating, disappointing, heartbreaking fuck-up in the courthouse.

"If he's so good, how did you finally nab him?"

"Hubris, honey. Pure and simple. Hubris."

"What do you mean?"

I hesitate a moment, wondering how much I should tell her. I don't see much harm, though I'm certainly going to leave out some of the details.

"I'm telling you something I've, we've, me and Manny, haven't told anyone before, but here goes. Manny had his own run-ins with Hoyt down in Miami. Hoyt was responsible for Manny's suspension from the force, which ultimately led him up here to team up with me to find Hoyt."

"Why did Detective Perez get in touch with you?"

"To answer this one, Dakota, honey, I'm gonna have to dispense with the *aw-shucks, I'm just a simple hick cop* rap. Truth is, Manny and I go back ten, twelve years ago, when I was hunting a killer named John Hartman."

Her face lights up. "He's the guy who murdered his wife, mother, their three teenage kids and the family dog, then disappeared, right?"

"That's him. I guess I was kinda obsessed with finding Hartman and I tracked him to Miami. I always inform the local gendarmes when I'm working in another jurisdiction. That's how I met Manny. Years later, when he called for help, I answered it."

"How did he know Hoyt was headed here?"

"We know how Hoyt operates. He's like one of those Snowbirds..."

She looks confused.

"Sorry. You West Coasters probably don't know what a Snowbird is. It's someone who lives up North, New York, Connecticut, Massachusetts, New Jersey, even Canada, during the warmer months but as soon as it turns cold, they head down South. Lots of 'em wind up in the Miami-Palm Beach-Fort Lauderdale area. And many of them are folks of means. Lots of it. Hoyt follows the money. It was mid-May, so Manny figured he'd be headed back up here."

"Was he?"

"You bet. We didn't know exactly where he'd hit next, but knew it'd be in the area. So, we did what cops do. We hit the jackpot when we found a couple of his girlfriends. We wanted to flush him out, so we made a lot of noise so he knew we were on his tail, hoping to flush him out. It worked. He's also got the biggest damn ego I've ever seen—if you don't count mine, of course. So, one day there's a knock on my door..."

"Your office?"

"Nope. My home. By this time, I'd retired, so I had no office."

As I'm telling her this, I notice a weird look on Dakota's face. It's kinda like a half-smile, and her eyes look like they've grown to twice their size. I'm familiar with that look. We get it when we're close to something big.

"He actually showed up at your home? How did he find you?"

Her breathing speeds up. I can't see or hear her heart beating faster, but I can sense it. At the time, I chalk it up to her excitement about getting a good story. Later, when I think about it, I'm not so sure.

"Basically, this guy's a punk. But he's smart. Not only smart but clever. He's also manipulative and competitive. Once he finds out we're looking for him he takes it as a personal challenge. He wants to show us he's better than we are. Smarter than we are. So, he starts taunting us, daring us to catch him. These days, it's not hard to find anyone's address. And he's not just anyone."

"So, he just shows up at your door? Wasn't he afraid of being arrested?"

"What for? Knocking on my door? We hadn't caught him doing anything yet. It would be like me arresting you for some crime you haven't committed yet. You're not planning anything, are you? Because if you are, I'd look pretty damn foolish giving you this interview."

She smiles. "Not yet. What happened?"

"We sit in my living room like we're three heavyweight boxers testing one another. After maybe twenty, thirty minutes, I guess he got what he came for, he just ups and leaves."

"This is incredible," she says, her eyes nearly popping out of her head. "So, what happened next? How did you finally get him?"

"It was his fucking—pardon my French—giant ego. I don't

know exactly what was running through his head, but just before he leaves, he steals a pretty valuable silver ashtray I inherited from my grandmother."

"Wait a minute! He comes to your house and he steals something right under your eyes?"

"Embarrassing, huh? And hey, not only my eyes, but Manny's, too. I didn't realize it till after he left. But that infantile, reckless, stupid act is what eventually gave us a reason to charge him for possession of stolen goods. First time I was ever a complainant."

"And then you found him."

"We did. But I can't go into details how, especially with Hoyt still on the run. We wound up getting some invaluable information from someone close to him. We planted seeds of doubt in her mind, let it marinate and eventually she gave up information that brought us to an apartment where he was staying. He invites us in—and it's a good thing he did because we don't have a search warrant, couldn't get one even if we'd wanted to since I'm retired and Manny's way out of his jurisdiction *and* since he was suspended. Anyway, just as we're about to leave, I glance over and there, right in front of our eyes, what do we see but..."

"The ashtray!"

"See, you'd make a pretty good cop. Anyway, now we have a charge we can make stick. So, we arrest him on the spot."

"What a story."

"What makes it even better is that, as smart as he is, as smart as he thinks he is, he was the one responsible for his own arrest."

20

Dakota

The first thing Charlie says when I switch on the recorder is, "How much tape you got in that thing?"

"It's digital. You could talk for a week."

He laughs. "Don't tempt me. Folks who know me would say that's not enough. But don't worry, I promise to rein it in."

"Oh, please, don't do that!"

Any journalist will admit they've conducted good interviews and godawful ones. Sometimes, the bad ones are our fault. We haven't prepared adequately. We've been up till dawn after partying all night (though I haven't "partied" since senior year in college). We have little or no interest in the subject or the person, resulting in a wandering mind. Bad breakup. Call from Mom. Sometimes, our subject is a complete dud. No matter what you ask, the answer comes back in two or three monosyllabic words. Then there are the interviews you ace, because you've prepared good questions; the subject matter actually interests you; the subject knows how to give a good interview, is naturally entertaining and truly wants to provide you with as much information as he or she can.

Occasionally, someone says to me, "Oh, Dakota, it must be really tough to get people to talk to you." The answer is, just the opposite. Often, it's tough to get them to shut up. The reason is simple: people are dying for someone to talk to. I mean, come on, how many people in your life actually listen to what you have to say? Your parents? Forget it. Your spouse? You've got to be kidding. Your kids? I can hear you laughing before the question mark appears at the end of that sentence. But now, not only is someone listening to you, they're taping you and taking careful notes, hanging on every word, every nuance, every possible meaning of what you say.

Which brings me to Charlie Floyd, who is, hands down, the best interview I've ever done. And I don't think I'm going out on a limb to say he'll probably be the best I'll ever do. And it's not about me. It's him.

First, he has close to total recall. You ask him to paint a scene, and it's as if you're there with him. Second, he's articulate. He's one of the best storytellers I've ever met. He tells them with a beginning, middle and end. And he's got tons of stories. Third, he doesn't mind explaining things in detail. And finally, he oozes charm. Not the edgy kind of charm, like Francis Hoyt, who's compelling for a lot of other reasons; Charlie exudes genuine, light-up-the-room charm.

As I'm sitting there, in awe, listening to him ease from one tale to another, the thought occurs to me to do a podcast series just on his life. Or, how about that book I've always wanted to write?

I don't know if I've ever liked someone as quick as I like Charlie Floyd. I only hope this isn't going to be a problem. That it won't get in the way of the story I'm trying to tell. I have to keep reminding myself I'm not here to make a new friend. I'm here to get the scoop on Francis Hoyt. But I'm so in love with this guy I sometimes forget I'm conducting an interview instead of just chatting with a fascinating friend.

Charlie loves being the center of attention. He truly enjoys holding court, talking about his experiences. I don't mean this in a mean or critical way. He's not high on the malignant narcissist scale. This is who Charlie Floyd is. Sitting here listening to him, I can't help comparing him to Francis Hoyt. There are similarities, but if you look closer, you'll realize they're opposite sides of the same coin.

The longer we talk, the more I realize the man sitting across from me might know Francis Hoyt better than anyone else in the world. From what research Mark and I have done, I still haven't found any of Hoyt's friends. Either he doesn't have any, or he's buried them, and I don't mean this literally. His family, or what he has left of one, is presumably living somewhere in the Midwest. Maybe Missouri or Oklahoma or Kansas. I believe he has a sister, and there may also be a brother. His father, with whom Francis did not get along, and who had a record as long as your arm for petty crimes, mostly having to do with alcohol and barroom brawls, is dead. I actually found a small newspaper clip about his body being found in an alley. An autopsy found his blood alcohol was well above the 0.08 percent legally drunk level. The police marked it a homicide, probably a mugging, but so far as I can find, no one was ever arrested for the crime. I find no death certificate for his mother, so I assume she's still alive.

At one point, I ask Floyd point blank what he knows about Hoyt's private life. He flashes an enigmatic smile, which signals he knows something but isn't going to share it with me.

I try to bluff. "I understand Hoyt was born and raised somewhere outside St. Louis. Is that true?"

"It's possible," he says.

"Does that mean he was?"

Floyd shrugs. "Google him. Maybe you'll find what you're looking for."

"Oh, come on. You know there's very little about him on the Internet. It's not like he's some movie star."

"You know, Dakota, I don't underestimate you so you probably shouldn't underestimate me."

"Meaning?"

"I know you've done your homework, honey. You probably know everything there is to know about Hoyt that's out there," he waves, "in cyberspace. That's not much, because Hoyt care-fully manages everything and everyone around him. I'm not gonna shine you on. There's stuff I know about him I'm not about to tell you. And you can guess why."

"You've checked up on me, haven't you?"

"You think I'd be sitting here talking to you if I hadn't done my homework? Once an investigator always an investigator. The reason I said yes is because of who you are and what you've done. I'm an admirer of your work."

I feel myself turning red. "That's a compliment, right?"

"It surely is."

"What harm would it be to tell me everything you know? I mean, it's not like you're actively looking for him. Or that you have a stake in protecting his reputation."

"True. But even though I'm on the shelf, if you don't think I'd be out the door in a second and a half if I knew where I could find him now, well, you'd be wrong."

"Why?"

"Why what?"

"Why do you care about finding him now?"

"Because I'm me and he's him."

"Meaning?"

"I don't like losing and neither does Hoyt. As much as I hate to admit it, we have that in common."

"But *you* didn't lose. You won. You not only found him but you were able to charge him with a crime. It wasn't your fault he got away."

"No. It wasn't. And it was a damn shame. But that doesn't mean if I have an opportunity to right that wrong I wouldn't. I should have been there, because if I had been…"

His voice trails off, and suddenly it hits me. What if Charlie Floyd suspects that not I've not only made contact with Hoyt, but that I pretty much know where he is? At least what city he's in. I wonder if I've said anything he picked up on that might give him that idea. I mean, this guy is no dope. I'm sure he's sat in rooms just like this with people who have much more to hide than I do, and he's nailed them. Am I being paranoid? Has having been immersed in the sordid world of crime so long warped my sense of reality?

My mouth is dry. When I try to speak, my lips stick to my teeth. I once read somewhere that Miss America contestants spread Vaseline on their teeth. Now, I know why. I reach for the water bottle. *Relax,* Dakota, I say to myself. There's no way he can know you've been in touch with Hoyt. And even if he did, don't you think he'd bring it up?

I glance up at the clock on the wall. It's a few minutes past three. I haven't slept in a day and a half. We've been at this for almost three hours. No wonder I'm starting to fade. But not Charlie Floyd. He looks fresher than he did hours ago. *He thrives on this, Dakota,* I tell myself. He looks like he could easily go another three hours. More. Me, not so much. I feel drained, though I blame it on being sleep-deprived.

Floyd must pick up on my fatigue because suddenly he leans in and says, "How's about we take a little break? I don't know about you, but I could use a trip to the john."

I know he's just being kind, and I appreciate it. I think, what a good cop he must have been. He's so darn good at reading people.

"That'd be nice," I say.

"You know, Dakota, we don't have to polish off everything today. I don't know what your schedule is, or when you're flying back, but if it's easier for you, we can call it a day and pick up the interview tomorrow morning. How's that sound?"

"Sounds great, actually. I'm traveling with my friend and producer, Mark. We're supposed to meet for dinner tonight and I am starting to fade a little. I could come back up in the morning, if that's okay?"

"Tell you what. Why don't I make it easier on you? How's about I come down to the city and we finish there? I've got a few things I can take care of after we're done. What do you say?"

"That'd be great, Charlie."

"Cool. Let's say around ten, ten-thirty. We can do it right there in Grand Central. Why don't you pow-wow with Mark, that's his name, right? Then get back to me. In the meantime, I'll check the train schedule."

I nod, okay.

"I have no problem if he joins us. I'll drive you back to the station, but before I do, I'd like to turn the table and ask you a question."

"Hmm. Interviewee becomes interviewer. I guess that's fair. What is it?"

"Why are you doing this thing?"

"You mean why did I choose Francis Hoyt?"

"No. I understand the fascination with him. But why the interest in crime...?"

"You're not going to say, 'What's a nice girl like you writing and broadcasting about crime?'—are you?"

"I wasn't going to say the 'nice girl' part. Although, from what I've seen, you probably are a very nice girl. But my ex-wife and daughter are constantly correcting me about using the word 'girl.'"

I smile. I like jousting with Charlie. He's fun and serious at the same time. He's also sharp as a tack. And, dare I say, cool? I kinda like that he's not afraid to do a little harmless flirting with me. It takes the edge off and I think it's fun for both of us.

"Girl. Woman. Whatever. Believe me, I've been called a lot worse."

"So, what's the answer?

"It's a very good question..."

"You're stalling."

"Man, you're good. Okay. But honestly, it's a question I ask myself all the time, especially before I decided to enter a 'life of crime,'" I use air quotes. "I guess it's because I'm interested in human behavior. Why people do what they do. What it says about the human condition. It reflects moments in time when people are at their worst and most vulnerable. I'm interested in how crime affects all of us, especially the people close to the crime itself, be it victim or bystander. So, I guess it eventually comes down to trying to understand myself."

"Good answer. And let me pontificate for a moment. Crime is inherited."

"You mean it's in our D-N-A?"

"No. What I mean is crime doesn't only affect the criminal and the victim. It's passed on through generations. Crime, especially violent crime, doesn't stop with the crime itself. Or the punishment. I don't think crime is part of our D-N-A, but I know it's still passed on from generation to generation. I've seen it. Think of an abusive husband-slash-father. He beats his kids. That violence is embedded in those kids. It can either make them an abuser or, it can have exactly the opposite effect. And when those kids have kids, the way those kids are raised is a result of what happened to their parents. You get what I'm saying?"

"Yes," I say. "I do."

"One last thing, Dakota. If you don't mind…"

I don't mind, at all. In fact, sitting here with Charlie Floyd is like getting a master class not only in crime but in human behavior. "What are you, Columbo?" I say.

He smiles. "I wish. Look, I'm sure I'm not telling you something you don't already know, but criminals like Francis Hoyt lie. They lie all the time. They lie to everyone, especially themselves. So, I'm just warning you not to take anything at face value. Gangsters like Hoyt are a living lie. And, Dakota…" he stops and nails me with his eyes. "that's why you have to be especially careful around them. Because, not only will they steal your soul, but they'll break your heart in the process."

21
Francis

His name's Derek. And he's my patsy. I own him. Though he's too stupid to know it. That's the thing about patsies. They're not the brightest bulbs on the circuit.

I reel him in slow and easy. Once I see where he's coming from—and where he wants to go—the rest is easy. He's no virgin when it comes to the law. It's tattooed all over him. Just not in ink. It's the way he holds himself. Aggressive, to keep you away. Passive, to hide in plain sight. He's got a history, but it's penny-ante stuff. A couple B and E's. Passing bad checks. Low-level drug dealing. So, what's he doing now?

"Looking for some rich bitch to sugar mama me," he says, with a smile so greasy it practically slides off his face. That's why he was at the hotel roof lounge tonight.

"What do you have to offer them?" I ask.

He grins and reaches down to his crotch. "Once they get a little of this, the Big D, they always wanna come back for more."

Can I pick 'em? This guy thinks he's God's gift. A regular Brad Pitt. Time to knock him down a peg or two.

"So how is it you're here with me, and you're the one paying for drinks?"

"Huh?"

"You think I'm picking up the tab?"

He gets all flustered. "No. No way, man. I'm not gonna let

MAN ON THE RUN

no dude buy me drinks. You asked me to have a drink with you, so..."

"The way I see it, Derek, I just saved you from a rough, humiliating night. I watched you flit from table to table like a fucking *maricon*. You weren't hooking up with anyone tonight. Except me."

"You calling me a fag?" he says, thrusting his chin forward.

"Just wondering if you got balls."

"I got balls, man. I got plenty fucking balls. Big balls."

"So how come you're here with me and not some sweet sugar mama?"

He shrugs. "Slim pickings tonight. That's why," he says. He talks tough, but I see he's so deflated, I can almost hear the fucking air hissing out of him.

"You got something else going for you now, Derek?"

"Uh..."

"So, the answer's no."

"Didn't say that, man. I'm waiting for the right opportunity."

"Well, Derek, my friend, your luck might be changing 'cause that sound you'll hear if you listen closely is opportunity knocking."

"Who the hell are you, man?"

"I told you. Eddie Felsen."

"I don't mean your name. I mean, who the hell *are* you?"

"I'm the man who's gonna change your sad, pathetic life, Derek."

There's a little more back and forth, but it doesn't mean anything. I got him where I want him. By the time I finish with him, he thinks hooking his wagon to my star is a fucking rocket ride to success. I tell him I'm looking for someone to help me with a big job. I can't tell him what it is.

"Like how?" he asks.

"I need you to pick up a few things for me."

"I'm no errand boy. Do it yourself," he says defiantly, again thrusting his chin forward.

"How's that 'do-it-yourself' thing working for you so far, Derek?"

This shuts his mouth.

"I need you to do a few things for me. If that works out, there'll be more."

"Like what kind of things?"

"You'll see."

"How much?"

"Five bills a week. Then maybe, if things work out, a small cut of the score."

"What score?"

I don't answer. He gets the point.

"When do I get paid?"

"Half now, half when you finish. Let's see how good you follow orders."

He makes it look like he's thinking about it. I don't know why he bothers. We both know he's gonna do it. What choice does he have?

"Okay," he says. "You got yourself a deal."

I take out my wallet. I peel off a couple Benjamins and a Grant. I snap 'em in front of Derek's face and the sound makes heads turn our way. I slide them across the table.

"This could be the start of a beautiful friendship," I say. "Oh, and the drinks are on me."

22

Charlie

This kid knows her stuff. I've had plenty of run-ins with journalists over the years, some good, some bad. The bad ones can't
get out of their own way. The good ones usually get the quotes
right. But this one's something special. She knows how to ask
the right questions and she listens to the answers, which then
leads her to good follow-up questions.

"You know, Dakota, if I were back in the game, I'd hire you
to do interrogations."

"Really?"

"Yes ma'am. You've got all the necessary qualities."

"Which are?"

"You're smart. You know how to phrase questions. You actually listen to the answers. Your follow-up questions are spot-
on. And you've got that seductive thing down pat."

Her face turns red.

"Excuse me? You think I'm flirting with you?"

She's smiling when she says this, so I know I haven't stepped
over that imaginary line. It takes me years to see that line—
thank goodness it was well before the recent #MeToo movement. It's not that I'm some kind of Neanderthal—I like to
think I treat everyone equally—bad or good. It's more like I'm
just—what does my ex-wife call it? Oh, yeah, clueless. She tries
explaining it to me once.

"Charlie, honey, it's not that you're insensitive or condescending to women. It's that you're condescending to everyone."

"That sounds about right," I say.

"You're the proverbial bull in the China shop. I know you, so I know it's nothing personal. You know what you want and you don't think about social norms when it comes to getting it—when it comes to your job, I mean. You've got the keenest sense of justice of anyone I've ever met, and you haven't got a prejudicial bone in your body. But…"

"There's always a but, isn't there?"

"Not always. But in this case, yes. I think you'd do even better if you'd played the game sometimes. By *the* rules. Not *your* rules, honey. I'm talking about polite societal rules. For a starter, you should be more sensitive to women's feelings."

"So, you're saying I have to treat them different from the way I'd treat men."

"Well, in a sense, yes. But in another sense, no."

"Now you've confused the hell out of me."

She smiles, like she's swallowed not only the cat but all the kittens, the scratching post and the kitty litter.

"You're not gonna give me that 'you'll catch more flies with honey than with vinegar' routine, are you?"

"It wouldn't hurt to keep that in mind sometimes. You're a good man, Charlie. You've got two daughters and I see the way you deal with them and you're great. Better than great. And you don't do that mansplaining thing…too often."

"I'm not even sure what that is."

"Good. Just be happy you don't do it. Much. You really do treat people the same. But there should be exceptions to that rule. And I know you don't have the time or the inclination to explain things to anyone sometimes."

"And that's a good thing?"

"Not always. But in this case, it turns out to be a good thing."

Dakota can't erase that huge grin from her face, so I know

she isn't pissed at me. I wouldn't want to hurt her feelings.

"You know exactly what I mean by being seductive, don't you?" I say.

Dakota nods. "Yes, I do. I learned early on that an interview is like a first date. It's a mutual seduction. I'm trying to get answers to questions and the other person is often lying or at least not telling all the truth. In that case, it's always good if the person being interviewed likes me. I'm not always so likable, but I'm working on it."

"Exactly," I say. "You've got a feel for it. That's what I mean."

Finally, after three hours I can see she's tiring, so I suggest a short break, which is good because my kidneys are about to burst. It's not like the old days, when I was like a camel.

When I look closer at Dakota, I see the fatigue in her face. And so, I suggest we break for the day and pick it up tomorrow morning. I even offer to come into the city, to make it easier for her. She jumps at the offer.

It's not all altruistic. I need a timeout because there's something that concerns me.

I'm not sure where it's coming from, but I have this sneaking suspicion Dakota isn't telling me everything. Maybe it's nothing. But maybe it's important. Whatever it is, it's bothering me enough to make me itchy. I may have retired, but my instincts haven't.

When we get back to the table, while Dakota is packing up her equipment, I say, "What got you interested in Hoyt?"

She looks up, putting a hold on loading up her backpack.

"Excuse me?"

"What got you started on Francis Hoyt? He's not exactly a household name."

She hesitates a moment. "I think I read about his escape, one of those little A-P filler items. It piqued my interest, so I read up on him, found him kind of fascinating and thought he'd make a good subject for the podcast."

I'm a human lie detector. When you've dealt with liars and conmen (and women) as long as I have you pick up a seventh sense. It's never one thing. Sometimes, it's because they don't look you in the eye. Sometimes it's the eyes themselves. They bounce back and forth like one of those pellets in a pinball machine. The face turns red. They literally start to sweat. Sometimes, it's what they do with their arms. Or their voice rises slightly. I'm not infallible, but I'm damn good.

I'm not saying Dakota's lying, but I'm pretty sure she's holding back. I can't swear to it, but it's something I tuck in the back of my mind. It could be something innocent, something inconsequential. Like maybe she had some personal connection to him or one of his victims, way back when. It's probably nothing, so I let it go. Well, I let it go as much as I can let anything go.

She pulls a train schedule out of her bag and looks at it, then her watch.

"I think I can make a four-ten," she says. "Are you sure it's okay about tomorrow? You coming all the way down to the city, I mean."

"I'm sure. And I look forward to meeting your partner."

She blushes. "He's not really my partner. He's my producer...and friend."

"Whatever," I say, using a word that annoys the hell out of me when one of my daughters uses it. I don't know why it comes out with Dakota. It just does.

23

Francis

I text my boy Derek and tell him to meet me at the Griffith Park Merry-Go-Round, by the picnic tables, this afternoon at four. By then the park will be flooded with screaming kids and no one will be paying attention to us.

I arrive early and position myself behind a tree, with an unobstructed view of the merry-go-round. A few minutes before four I spot him sauntering toward me, like he doesn't have a fucking care in the world. He's wearing baggy jeans, a black T-shirt, a brown leather jacket and hiking boots. I step out from behind the tree and sit down at one of the picnic tables.

"Hey, boss, what's happening?" he asks, sliding onto the bench opposite me. "Never been here before. Didn't even know it existed. Had to look it up. Ever been on one of those merry-go-round things?" he asks. He doesn't wait for an answer. "There's a shit-load of good-looking mothers and nannies. I might have to spend me a little more time in the park."

"Finished?" I can't wait to be done with this asshole.

"Yeah, yeah. Sorry. Got carried away. So, what's up?"

"I need you to go to this address," I pull a small, folded piece of paper out of my pocket and hand it to him. He takes it, unfolds it, reads it, then starts to put it in his pocket. I reach across the table and grab him by the wrist.

"Hey!" he says.

"I want you to memorize what's written on it, then give it back to me. Now."

"Okay. Okay. Why didn't you say so?"

He stares at the paper a minute or two. I can see his lips moving as he reads. He lifts his head and stares into the sky, like he's projecting the message onto the clouds. Finally, he nods his head, then slides the paper back across the table. I pick it up, tear it into tiny pieces and toss them in the air where the wind blows them in all directions.

"I guess you ain't worried about gettin' pinched for littering, huh, Boss?"

I ignore him, even though I know that's not going to make him go away.

"So, what's at that address?"

"A jewelry store. I want you to check it out."

"Check it out? Like how?"

"It's in a strip mall. Drive over there, park your car as close as you can to the store, and then I want you to sit there and watch the place for a couple hours. Take notes on who goes in and out. How many, how often. Exact times. When the first hour's up, go into the store, browse around, then ask to see merchandise."

"Anything in particular?"

"Whatever the fuck you want. Make sure they let you hold it. Smile, like it's something you like, then hand it back to the clerk. Make like you know there are cameras but you're trying to avoid them. You know, like keep your head down. Shit like that. But don't make it obvious, D. Tell the clerk you want to think about it a while, and you'll be back. Make up any fucking story you want. Ad-lib, baby. Use that undeniable charm of yours, Derek."

"Sounds easy. Then what?"

"Go back to the car, sit in it for another hour. You keep your fucking eyes on that store. Anything out of the ordinary, you write it down. Anything ordinary, you write it down."

"That's it?"

"That's it."

He looks at me with a big, fat grin on his face. "You gonna hit the place and I'm doin' the casing for you, right?"

"Let's get something straight from the get-go, Derek. I don't answer questions."

"I was just curious…"

"You know what happens to cats when they're curious, right?"

"Yeah. They wind up in cat heaven."

"Exactly. I don't care what the hell you think, whatever it is you keep it to your fucking self. Got it?"

"Okay. Okay. So, when do you want me to do this?"

"Tomorrow morning."

"Okay. No problem. Anything else?"

"Not for now. You got what I asked you to bring?"

"Oh, yeah. Sure," he sticks his hand into his leather jacket and pulls out a cellophane baggie. In it, there are a couple skeleton keys. He slides the baggie across the bench. I line it up next to my phone.

"Wasn't so easy to get these," he says. "Had to call in a couple favors. So, you gonna tell me what this is all about?"

"No."

"Come on, man. You can trust me. I'm a fuckin' accessory already."

"You'll know when I'm ready to tell you."

He shrugs.

"Okay. We're done."

"When am I gonna hear from you again?"

"I'll let you know."

I step back behind the tree and watch him as he walks back toward the merry-go-round. When he gets there, he stops, looks around, approaches one of the benches and starts chatting up some chick.

I take a latex glove from my pocket, slip it on, pull an envelope

225

out of another pocket, slide the piece of paper and set of keys into it. I lick it closed. I get up, turn away from the merry-go-round and walk away.

When I look back over my shoulder, Derek is still sitting on the bench, his arm around one of the nannies. Guy hits on the fucking help.

Can I pick 'em, or what?

24
Dakota

I meet Mark for dinner around eight at Maison Pickle, a trendy Upper-West-Side joint not far from where we're staying. When he gives me a choice of several restaurants, I settle on this one because of the quirky name. All the way up from Grand Central on the subway, I keep imagining a menu of all different kinds of pickled choices combined with entrees like Coq au Vin. In fact, there's nothing even remotely French about the menu, which is pretty much solid American with a Southern flair. But yes, they do serve pickles.

Mark's at the bar, which is surprising since he's not much of a drinker. He kids that the only drinks he likes are the ones that come with little umbrellas. He refers to them as "girly" drinks.

"They wouldn't seat me until you got here," he says, grabbing my elbow and leading me toward the host's station. "I'm starved. How about you?"

I haven't really thought about food, but now that he's asked, I realize I'm hungry. Now that the interview with Charlie Floyd is over—well, not over, half-over—my stomach has finally unclenched. I still get nervous before every interview. I think it's a remnant of my younger days when I worry that I won't get the story I'm after. Mark insists it's a good thing. "When you get too complacent about that stuff, you'll know you're not doing a good job."

Mark requests a quiet table but we soon realize there's no such thing. The closest we get is a table at the back of the restaurant, toward the rear exit. I sit on a banquette, under glass shelves of neon-backlit liquor bottles. Mark sits facing me. If we lean forward and turn up the decibels, we can actually hear each other.

Mark can't get over the menu. "Look," he says in childlike glee, "chicken and waffles! What the heck is that all about?"

"It's a Southern dish."

"For people who can't decide whether they're eating breakfast or dinner?"

This is one of the reasons I like Mark. He's funny and charming. I'm sure that's what attracted me to him back when we first met. I even consider dating him at the time, but decide against it because I realize it's more important for me to have a long-term friend than a short-time lover. I don't say anything to him about that until we've known each other a year, and then only because he brings it up.

"There's something I've been wanting to tell you for a long time," he says.

"You're not a serial killer, are you?"

"Oh, my God, all this time I was worried and you knew?"

I punch him lightly on the arm. "Very funny."

"Seriously, I've always wanted to tell you when we met in that bookstore, I had a little 'thing' for you."

"A 'thing?' Why didn't you say something? Better yet, do something about it?"

"Because…well, I'm not sure. Maybe it was because I didn't sense the same vibe from you."

"Well, buster, maybe you didn't look close enough…"

"Damn!" He punches a fist into the other palm. "Well, it's not the first opportunity I've blown and it won't be the last."

"Why are you telling me this now?"

"I was thinking about it lately and about what our relationship has become and how important it is to me, and I didn't want you to think that I didn't find you, you know, attractive. I still do. But it's not the same as it was in the beginning. Now, I'm just happy to have you in my life the way things are. You know, friends and working together. I'm not sure it would have worked out that way if I'd let my penis get in the way."

I laugh. "I don't have a penis, at least I didn't the last time I looked, but I feel the same. It's like we're meant to be in each other's lives, but not romantically, as lovers. You know, Mark, I'm happy you told me this. I think what we have is very special, like we're kindred spirits or even soul mates. Without all the messy complications."

I think about this conversation every so often, but I'm still not sure what to make of it.

After we place our order Mark leans forward and says, "I don't know how your interview went, Dakota, but man, let me tell you, this Francis Hoyt is some piece of work."

"Why do you think I chose him for the show? Find out anything juicy?"

Mark spends the next hour spinning stories about Hoyt's exploits. Like the time he burgled three houses under the noses of the cops. Or the time he broke into a famous person's house and stole a bunch of antique silver, including pieces designed by Paul Revere. Or the bar fight he instigated just to give himself an alibi. All good things to hit Francis with if I ever do wind up interviewing him.

The one thing I don't tell Mark is how I think Charlie Floyd might suspect I have a real-life connection to Francis. I can't discuss this with him because he knows nothing about my meeting with Hoyt and his promise to let me interview him. At the time, when I could have told Mark, it didn't seem right. It's still something I think I should keep to myself, and I'm not even sure why.

But this secret is burning a hole in my psyche and so, while we're waiting for the check, I consider spilling the beans, telling Mark about Hoyt's stalking me. But once again a little voice in my head says, *don't do it*. I convince myself that by not telling

Mark I'm protecting him. From what, I'm not sure. The thing of it is, and it hasn't really sunk in, if I'm afraid to tell Mark because it might put him in danger, then what about me?

When I do tell Mark he can tag along to our meeting with Floyd in the morning, his face lights up. "I was hoping for a chance to meet this guy," he says.

By the time we get back to the apartment it's ten-thirty and I'm so tired I can hardly stand. But, as tired as I am, I can't seem to fall asleep. Things are starting to come together and for the first time I feel really good about the show. All my ducks are getting in line. But the most important duck, Francis Hoyt, is still a question mark. I need to pin him down. And I know that won't be easy. And what with all I've heard about him, I'm starting to wonder why he's even considering it. What's in it for him?

And so, with Hoyt on my mind, in the wee hours of the morning I text to ask him if we can finally schedule our interview. In the past, he's taken hours, sometimes a day or more to answer me. So, I don't expect to hear from him right away. After I send it, I lie back down and, within a matter of seconds, I'm fast asleep.

25
Dakota

The next morning, I wake at 7:30 to find Mark still asleep on the couch. Our appointment with Charlie isn't till ten-thirty, so I see no reason to wake him.

I go into the kitchen and make coffee. While I wait for it to brew, I check my phone to see if Francis has returned my text. Nothing.

At nine-thirty, we grab a cab to Grand Central. He suggests meeting at the information kiosk with the big clock in the middle of the main floor. Mark and I decide to get there early to find a good spot and discuss strategy before Floyd gets there. By the time we arrive, the crowd of commuters emptying from trains is pretty thin and we find a place to sit downstairs. Then, over genuine New York bagels and more coffee, we plot how we're going to proceed.

"What is it you're looking for you didn't get yesterday?" Mark asks.

"More personal stuff about Hoyt."

"Such as?"

"Girlfriends. Family. People he knows. People he's dealt with, like his fences. Boy, would I love to talk to someone like that."

"You didn't have time to get to any of this yesterday?"

"He's a real talker, and a great storyteller, but it is hard to get

231

him to talk about things he doesn't want to talk about. He's a seasoned investigator. He knows all the tricks. What to say. What not to say, which, of course, is exactly what I want. It's very frustrating. He's really sweet, but to be honest, in his own way non-aggressive way, he can be manipulative."

"What do you mean?"

"He knows how to steer the conversation away from topics he doesn't want to talk about. I know he has strong personal feelings about Hoyt, but I can't get it out of him. Ditto on the details of how he and Perez tracked Hoyt down."

"So, how do I fit in? Not the usual eye candy, I hope."

I laugh. "I think he might tell you things he wouldn't tell me."

"How's that?"

I shrug. "I don't know. There's just a different vibe between guys. So, if you see an opening to pick up on a subject or a question, please jump right in. You're bound to ask something I've missed. And you might even get a truthful answer."

"I can't imagine your missing anything, D," he says. I don't bother to contradict him.

A few minutes before ten, Mark and I head upstairs to the information kiosk, and wait for Floyd to arrive.

"What's this dude look like?" Mark asks.

I smile and give Mark the same answer Charlie gave me. "You'll know him when you see him."

As if on cue, I spot Floyd, wearing his signature cowboy hat, boots, blue jeans, blue sport jacket and button-down shirt, heading our way. I nudge Mark, cocking my head in the direction Floyd is coming from. "See what I mean?"

He smiles and nods.

The rush hour is over and the station has emptied out. We have no trouble finding an empty table at a Starbucks downstairs. While I set up the equipment, Mark takes our coffee orders.

"No milk, a couple sugars," says Floyd. "And nothing fancy, Mark. Just plain, old American joe is good enough for me."

Mark smiles and gives a thumbs up. I can see he likes Floyd

and he's only known him three minutes. I know how Mark thinks. It's the way I imagine all writers think. Anything and everything is potential fodder for their writing. Fine by me. I want Mark to get something out of this other than just helping me out.

"Thanks again for coming all the way down here, Charlie," I say.

"My pleasure. It's good for me to get out of Connecticut every once in a while. Gives me a much-needed dose of what the real world is like."

"If you don't mind, I'll wait till Mark gets back before we start."

Charlie nods, takes out his phone and places it on the table.

"Hope you don't mind if I tape this," he says. "Old habits die hard."

I'm a little surprised. Why would he need to tape us this morning when he didn't yesterday? Or maybe he did and I just didn't see it? And then I stop myself. Am I really getting this cynical? Maybe I am.

"Sure. What's good for the goose…" I say. But before I can finish the sentence, Mark arrives balancing a cardboard tray holding three coffees, three bottles of water, and an assortment of sweeteners.

I flip the switch on the recorder and we're ready to go.

26
Francis

Sunday night. The end of the July Fourth weekend. Most people will be pigging out at backyard barbecues, or drinking heavily while watching fireworks. There's a big deal over at Marina Del Rey, where boatowners spend the day tailgating from their docked boats, waiting for the fireworks to light up the sky. Some, sober enough to risk the trip, take their boats out to sea and watch the fireworks from there.

All this action will inevitably lead to confusion, meaning the cops will have their hands full that night. There's less chance being stopped for some stupid traffic violation, or some nosy citizen calling 9-1-1 to report someone loitering around the strip mall.

In the five days left, I have plenty to do. I'm in the midst of tying up a few loose ends when, after not hearing from her for days, Dakota texts that she's ready to schedule our interview.

I'm in no particular rush to answer, so it isn't till the next morning that I text back.

Not yet.

But she's a persistent little bitch. Minutes after my text she calls. I want to ignore it, but if I do I know she won't give up.

As soon as I pick up, she says in a phony, cheery voice, "Hey, long time no see."

"I'm busy."

"Busy? Oh, my. Busy with what? I mean, what's so important you can't carve out a couple hours to talk to me, your favorite California surfer girl? You're not planning something naughty, are you?"

Does she really think cute works with me? I want to get her off the line quick, but she's not having any of it.

"Seriously, Francis. I'm pretty much finished with all my research, and I'm in the middle of putting together the first episode of four, which means I'd like to get you in the next couple weeks. That means I'd like to get you sometime the week of the eleventh. What do you say we put something on the calendar?"

"We're gonna work on my schedule, not yours."

"Oh, come on, Francis. Why don't we just get this over with."

"Keep pushing, Dakota, and there might not be a show."

"I don't think you understand, Francis, there's a show, with you or without you. I just think maybe you'd like to tell your side of the story. But if I'm wrong..."

She's trying the hardball approach. But she's right. I do want to get it over with. But the timing has to suit me and it doesn't yet. Besides, I don't like ultimatums. Especially from women. My first inclination is to say, "Fuck you," and hang up the fucking phone. But I don't. I can't let the bitch know how much I want to get this thing done, because then she holds the power. That never works out well.

"Tell me again how much time you need?" I say.

"A couple hours. Maybe a little more. But we can always make two sessions out of it. I can be flexible, Francis. Anything that works for you works for me."

Suddenly, her voice fades and there's noise in the background. The honking of horns. A siren. The sound of moving traffic. These are not the sounds of L.A. More like New York or Chicago.

"Where the fuck are you?"

"Excuse me?"

"I said, where the fuck are you? I can hardly hear you with

all the fucking noise."

"Where do you think I am?" she says in a little girl, sing-songy voice.

"I'm in no mood for games, Dakota. I can tell you're not in L-A. So, where the fuck are you?"

"Jesus, Francis, do you really think I'm going to let you keep tabs on me? Do I have to check in with you before I do any-thing or go anywhere? I am where I am. And where that is, frankly, isn't any of your business."

I don't like being talked to that way. The last chick who did paid for it. You give an inch they take a mile. But I'm not about to push the point on the phone.

"Call me when you get the fuck back in town," I say, and hang up.

I'm not sure why I'm so pissed, but I am. I don't like the idea she's out of town, because it's obvious she's doing research on me. Maybe I should have pulled the plug on this a while ago.

I can't let it go. I'm so angry I throw the fucking burner against the wall as hard as I can. It seems to hang there on the wall a split second, as if deciding whether to defy gravity, then drops to the floor, smashing into half a dozen pieces.

Okay. Now that I got that out of my system, I feel better.

As for the phone, no problem. I've got half a dozen more.

27

Francis

I park a mile and a quarter away. Before locking up, I make sure I've left nothing that might incriminate me. The glove compartment is empty. There's nothing in the backseat. Nothing in the trunk. Nothing on or under the front seat. I hide the key under the wheel casing, making it stick with a small chunk of yellow putty.

It's a warm, overcast night. A black watchcap is pulled down to just above my eyes. I'm wearing a black, tight-fitting, long-sleeved T-shirt, and black, close-fitting cotton sweatpants. I've retro-fitted the pants, adding two small zippered hip pockets, one on each side, one more in back, providing me with plenty of room for anything I need to carry with me. In the dark of night, I will be close to invisible. A black blur. Blink once and I'll be gone.

I have precisely one-point-two miles before reaching my destination. It's eight minutes past midnight. I set the timer on my watch. Not because it's necessary, but because I'm always competing with myself. Even tonight the goal is to beat an eight-minute mile without being out of breath when I finish.

I take several deep breaths, then begin to jog the route I've chosen only a few hours earlier, using dark side streets whenever possible.

It's a quiet, residential section of L.A. and street traffic this time of night is light and there is no pedestrian traffic. The chance of being spotted is remote.

I arrive at my destination. I check my watch and see I've beaten my goal by sixteen seconds. I inhale deeply, shake my legs out, stretch my arms above my head as far as I can, then bounce up and down, landing softly on the balls of my feet. It's something I picked up from Muhammad Ali, my version of the rope-a-dope.

I check my watch again. Exactly seven minutes and thirty-seven seconds, and I'm not out of breath. *Haven't lost it, Francis,* I mutter to myself.

I'm standing in front of a half-block-long two-story building, which looks like a motel. Everything in L.A. is either very old or very new. This building, an exception, thereby proving the rule, is somewhere in-between, probably erected in the mid-'70s or early '80. In front of the building there's a fenced-in swimming pool with several chaise lounge chairs lined up neatly on each side. The pool is illuminated by a blue tinted light that casts eerie shadows onto the side of the building, making me feel like I'm in the midst of a waking dream. Between me and the pool, there's a large expanse of well-manicured lawn. A sign sunk deep into the lawn says,

Apartments for Rent
See On-Site Manager for Information.

I've been here before, but it's different in the dark. Everything is. More sinister. Less inviting. That's fine. Tonight, I am an uninvited guest.

I check to make sure no one's around, then slowly make my way toward the front entrance, which splits the building in half. There, I find a long corridor, which gives access to the back of the building.

I walk through the dimly-lit corridor. On my left, there's a wall of mailboxes. Next to them is a door marked LAUNDRY

ROOM. Opposite that, a door marked OFFICE. I will be going through neither door tonight.

When I emerge from the shadows of the corridor, I'm facing a parking area, large enough to accommodate a couple dozen cars. Each spot has a number painted on the curb, from 100 to 108, and 200-208, corresponding to the apartment number of each tenant. Sixteen numbered spots equal sixteen apartments. There are eight additional parking spots designated GUEST. Tonight, the only spot without a vehicle is one-oh-eight.

I look up, left and right. Every apartment is dark. I listen for noise. The barking of a dog. The sound from a TV. The raised voices of an arguing couple. A car pulling into the parking area. The slam of a car door. Now, for the moment, it's silent. I'm ready to do what I'm here for.

At each end of the building there's a staircase leading up to the second floor. There are eight apartments on the ground floor, eight on the second, where there's a safety railing that runs the length of the building.

I stand motionless, back pressed up against the wall of the building, listening, trying to pick up any sound that might indicate someone is walking the grounds. Nothing. I turn left and keep walking until I reach apartment one-oh-eight.

I unzip one of my side pockets and remove a thin, metal strip, which I wedge into the slim opening where the door meets the jamb. I find where there's resistance then wiggle it a couple times. There's a click.

I'm in.

I gently close the door behind me, listening for the tell-tale click that will tell me I'm safe inside. From the back of the one-bedroom apartment, I hear the faint sound of music. It's the poor man's idea of how to keep people like me out by offering the illusion someone's home.

I unzip my back pocket and remove a small LED flashlight, the size and width of a credit card. I press down, and like magic, a beam of light suddenly appears. I shine it around the apartment, holding it low, so the light won't be visible from beyond the windows. I'm in a typical apartment of a young, single woman.

I hear a purring sound. I look up to see a cat, staring at me from the doorway of the bedroom, its eyes glowing from the beam of my flashlight. It's *her* cat.

I move to the kitchen. Open the refrigerator. A soft light fills the room. Staring at me from the front shelf are a bottle of green liquid; a couple apples; three bananas; a half-dozen oranges; a couple of containers of Chinese or Thai food; half-dozen plastic bottles of water; half-loaf of sliced wheat bread; a couple bottles of Dos Equis; and a box of Godiva chocolates. A gift from an admirer, maybe? In front of the freezer are two empty ice cube trays; a pint of Ben & Jerry's Moo-phoria Light Ice Cream; a pint of Half Baked FroYo; and a pint of Cherry Garcia. I open each one and find all are half- to a quarter-full.

I take a large spoon from a drawer next to the oven, twist off the Cherry Garcia top, dig the spoon in as far as I can, and scoop out a large hunk of the ice cream. I flick the spoonful into the sink, turn on the water and watch as the melting ice cream disappears down the drain.

I go back to the refrigerator and remove the box of chocolates. Open it. See only a half dozen or so left in the box. I pop one in my mouth. Not because I crave one. In fact, I rarely eat sweets. I eat it only because it's hers.

I bypass the living room and head into the bedroom. I swing my flat, credit-card-size light around the room. A queen-sized bed, covered by a multi-colored quilt. A bedside table on which there's a cordless phone in its cradle, a jar of cold cream, and a small clock radio.

I open the closet to find several dresses and a few pairs of jeans, all neatly hung. On the shelf above are a half dozen neatly folded sweaters. Several hats hanging from hook are on the inside back of the door.

At the back of the floor of the closet there are four shoeboxes. I open each one. Each holds a pair of shoes. Some people stash papers, or photos, or embarrassing material in simple shoeboxes. But if she has secrets, she does not keep them here, in this closet, in one of these shoeboxes.

I move to the dresser. On top there are several framed photographs. One is her as a child, riding a pony. She's smiling, one arm raised triumphantly over her head. There's a picture of a young boy in a bathing suit, on the edge of a pool, his arms outstretched as if he's ready to dive in. There's a photo of a pretty woman, in her forties, kneeling in front of a flower garden, as if caught in the act of planting. She's wearing a large, floppy hat to protect her from the sun. She has a familiar-looking face. Suddenly, for no apparent reason, a wave of anger engulfs me. I feel like smashing the photos against the wall. The feeling passes. I take each one and place it face down on the dresser.

One by one, I open each drawer. The top one is filled with underwear, socks, stockings, tights, bras. I slide my hand under them and feel something hard and square. I pull it out, a jewelry box. I open it and find a couple cheap necklaces, a few silver rings, and a pearl necklace that looks like it might be the real thing. There's a vintage man's gold pocket-watch. It's the kind of thing that would be handed down generation to generation. Other than the pearls, it's the only thing of possible value. If this were a work visit, which it's not, I'd be disappointed.

I slide the box back into its position beneath the underwear, but in a different location. I continue my search until I reach the bottom drawer. I feel under sweaters and T-shirts. Under workout clothes. I'm still looking for secrets. A diary, perhaps. But there are no secrets here. Everything is as it appears to be.

I move to the bathroom where I'm met by the sweet fragrance of soap, shampoo and perfume. I open the medicine cabinet. A few containers of prescription drugs. Aspirin. Tylenol. Ambien— she has trouble sleeping. Diazepam. A package of birth control pills. On a shelf below the medicine cabinet, several bottles of perfume are neatly lined up, like little soldiers waiting to get their marching orders. The rest of the shelf holds makeup, powders, all the usual tools of womanhood. I move a few of the bottles and jars around.

I leave the same way I come in.

Moments later, I've disappeared into the dark.

No bitch will ever call the shots. She'll dance to my tune, or no tune at all.

28
Dakota

I give it my best, but no matter how hard I try I can't seem to break Charlie Floyd.

Floyd doesn't mind talking about Francis Hoyt. In fact, he seems to relish it. He's so enthusiastic, spinning one tale after another, all concerning Francis Hoyt, he doesn't touch the coffee Mark brings him. But there are some things he just will not talk about.

He tells us what an arrogant son of a bitch Hoyt is. Nothing I don't already know. He talks about the crimes Hoyt has committed and how he committed them, a lot of which is new to me. He explains how careful Hoyt is not to leave any trace behind. How cops never find even a whisper of him at the scene of the crimes. No fingerprints. No DNA. Not a single thread of clothing. No mud or grass dragged into the house on the bottom of a shoe. No shoe print outside the window or door he uses to enter. No errant piece of paper with an address on it perhaps. No matchbook cover with the name and address of, say, a strip club. All these, Floyd explains, are things the average criminal often leaves behind. When it comes to Francis Hoyt, there is not one, single piece of physical evidence. Ever.

"You have to understand how unusual this is, Dakota. Most bad guys are just plain dumb," he explains. "Let's face it, we're not dealing with candidates for MENSA. That Hollywood conception of the evil genius, well, it just doesn't exist. They almost always give themselves away. Sometimes it's because they can't keep their mouths shut. Or because they do something incredibly stupid before, during or after. One guy even brought his dog with him when he broke into a home, tying the animal out front on the porch. Neighbors knew the owner didn't have a dog so…"

"That's why most crimes are eventually solved. I once had a reporter ask me, 'Why are so many crimes solved as the result of wiretaps. Don't these guys know they're being recorded?' Of course, they do. But they're stupid, so they forget. They'll start off saying something like, 'You know that guy from downtown, right?' Eventually, they forget they might be being taped, so the other guy might slip and say, 'Yeah, Freddie's really an asshole, isn't he?' But with Hoyt, he never seems to let his guard down. He learns from his mistakes. Not everyone does. I don't know where he'd score on an I-Q test, but I can tell you this, he's a genius at what he does. But even geniuses make mistakes. He made one, and I'm sure he'll make another."

I ask how it's possible that Hoyt can be such a ghost.

Charlie smiles. "Because, as much as I hate to admit it, I've never come across anyone as good as Hoyt. Burglary is a craft, but he's turned it into an art. He leaves nothing to chance. I can only speculate, since I've never seen him in action, but I'm pretty sure he shaves off all exposed body hair; wears gloves; covers himself from head to toe, probably in something like those Spandex, skin-tight outfits runners and ice skaters wear. The other thing is, he leaves absolutely no signs of a break-in. No broken windows. No scratches on locks. And he's incredibly athletic. It's like he's frigging Spiderman. He usually enters on the second floor, which means he shimmies up something, like a drainpipe. You'd have to be one of those circus acrobats to do what he does. He's obviously an expert on disarming alarms, no matter how sophisticated, because I don't know of a single instance where an alarm has gone off. And some of these multi-million-dollar homes use state-of-the-art equipment."

"You're making him sound superhuman," says Mark.

"Not quite. We proved that when we caught him. And everyone, I don't care who it is, eventually makes a mistake. But it's up to us to find it. He made a big mistake with us, but you better believe he'll never make a mistake like that again. He has an amazing ability to adapt. That's what makes him so slippery and so dangerous. He learns from his successes but more important, he learns from his failures. But he does have his kryptonite."

"What's that?" I ask.

"His ego. Mark my words. It was his downfall once, it'll be his downfall again."

"So, he's always prepared?" says Mark.

"He does his homework. Once inside, he doesn't waste time looking around for stuff to steal. He knows exactly where to go for what he wants. I believe he knows the layout of every house he's ever entered. He does not leave anything to chance."

"How does he do that?"

"I know for a fact he's taken those charity guided house tours. And a lot of these homes get written up in magazines—we found a bunch of them in the apartment we caught him in. Some of them have even shown off their homes on those cable shows that show how the rich live. The only people who come close to Hoyt in terms of ego are the wealthy who can't help themselves from showing off."

I'm furiously taking notes, even though I know I'm catching all this on tape. It's all gold and I'm getting more and more excited about the project. Floyd is providing us with not only valuable information but great quotes. And, even more important, insight. I look over at Mark and he's absolutely entranced. I can practically see him soaking up every word coming out of Charlie's mouth.

Charlie continues.

"One of his strengths is his willingness to improvise. As careful and well-prepared as he is, he's still capable of changing up things at the last moment, if he has to. I hope you don't use all this on your podcast, because I'd hate to give him the satisfaction he craves. But it's true. And here's what I think." He stops for a moment, probably considering what he's going to say before he says it for posterity. "I don't think at this point it's about the money. I'm not even sure what he steals matters to him. It's more that he *can* steal it and that no one, at least no one so far, has been able to stop him. He's all about the challenge. About proving he's smarter than everyone else in the room. And much as I hate to admit it, up till now, he's right."

"Hard to believe he's never, ever screwed up," says Mark.

"The only mistake he's made so far as I know, Mark, other than partnering up with an asshole, is boosting that silver ashtray from my house. I'm sure it wasn't planned. It was a spur-of-the-moment thing. He wanted to show how good he is. How fearless. How he could steal something right out from under the eyes of two of the guys dedicated to bringing him in. And get away with it."

"But he didn't," I say.

"Sure, he did. His mistake was holding onto it. He should have tossed it in the Housatonic. We were lucky to track down one of his girlfriends and turn her against him. If we'd never found her, and if we hadn't been able to piss her off enough to turn on him, well, it would have been a very different story. As much as I hate to admit it, the fact he got away means in the end he won."

This is the opening I've been waiting for.

"Tell me about this girlfriend of his."

Charlie smiles. "You don't expect me to tell you who she is, do you? Or any of the women we know he's been involved with over the years?"

"There've been a lot?"

"Enough. Though God knows what they see in him."

I freeze up. I could probably list some of the reasons. But I won't.

"I'd love to speak to one or two of them. I could do it anonymously. No one would have to know who they are. I don't want to know where they are or who they are. I only want to talk to them, even if it's off the record. What do you say?"

Charlie grows uncharacteristically silent. Finally, he says, "I'll think about it."

From childhood, we all know what this means. But I'm not about to let up. I'm ready to pursue it right there and then, but fortunately Mark pipes up, stopping me from embarrassing myself.

"What is it about him that gets under your skin?"

He shrugs. "I guess it's just because of who I am."

"Who's that?" I ask.

"More stubborn than a mule. Capable of becoming obsessed to the point of blindness. Someone as arrogant, just as competitive as he is. Someone who hates to admit defeat. Someone who thinks of himself as the best of the best..."

"Sounds a lot like Hoyt," says Mark.

"You got it, my friend. And that's exactly why I gave up the chase. Because, if I hadn't, I'd be no better than he is. And I am better, which is why I said enough is enough. Of course, I'm not sure how long I'll keep saying it."

"So, if you had a chance to catch him again...? I mean, what if someone called you up with a tip where he was?" I say.

"To be honest, Dakota, honey, I'm not one hundred percent sure. I'd like to think I'd be strong enough to pull a Nancy Reagan and just say no. Maybe I need one of those twelve-step programs. You know, like how to get unhooked from Francis Hoyt."

"Have you ever known him to be violent?" Mark asks.

This is a question I've been waiting to get into. I lean forward to hear the answer.

"If you're asking do I know of any cases where he was physically violent, I'd have to say only one immediately comes to mind. A bar fight over in Hoboken was captured on tape, which is how we know about it. He started it, but we're not sure why. Knowing Hoyt as I do, I think it was planned."

"How so?" I ask.

"I think he wanted us to see him. Maybe for alibi purposes.

Maybe just another way to taunt us. But very little if anything Hoyt does isn't well thought out. But to get back to your question, I have no doubt, no doubt at all, he's capable of violence. There were a few dustups when he was in the penitentiary. But that's to be expected because of his size. He had to send a message. Make no mistake about it. He is a very dangerous man. He's the worst kind of dangerous because he doesn't come at you straight ahead. It's your back you have to watch."

"Anything more serious?" Mark persists. I'm not sure why he's not letting go of this topic, but knowing Mark I think he's trying to get as full a picture of Hoyt as possible, trying to get into the man's head.

"There are a few unexplained deaths that might be connected to him."

"Like what?" I ask.

"There was this fence over in the Diamond District. Not far from here, in fact."

"What happened?" Mark asks.

"Murdered. In his office. Looked like a typical mob hit, but you never know."

"What do you mean?" I ask.

"The place was full of valuable stuff. Jewelry. Watches. Gold. Nothing was taken. Haven't found the killer yet."

"Hoyt is a suspect?"

"We know he didn't do it himself, because we've got video of the guy who did. We can't I-D him, though, because he kept his face hidden from the cameras. But his body type was nothing like Hoyt's."

"I'm confused," I say. "Then why would you think Hoyt had anything to do with it?"

"Part hunch, part word picked up on the street. The official version is one of his clients thought he was ripping them off. Or maybe he knew something he wasn't supposed to know.

"He was a long-time associate of Hoyt's. He knew about Hoyt's connection to the mob, and it's possible he knew more than he should about Hoyt's personal life. Life is cheap to these guys. You'd be surprised how little it takes for someone go get erased."

"But you know from the video he wasn't the actual killer?"

"Yeah. But that doesn't mean he wasn't behind the murder. He's a master of manipulation. It's possible someone owed him a favor and Hoyt, for whatever reason, called in the chit. Or he could have paid someone. Just because you don't commit an act of violence yourself doesn't mean you're not responsible for it."

"Why would the mob owe him a favor?" asks Mark.

"Remember that job Hoyt was forced to take and the guy with him screws up, shoots someone, and Hoyt winds up going down when they track the other guy down? Hoyt was a good little boy. He did his time. Kept his mouth shut. He's marked as a stand-up guy and because of that the mob owes him."

My head is spinning. I want to believe Hoyt isn't capable of murder, but I know he might be. If Hoyt is behind this fence's death, what else might he be responsible for? I don't have to wait long to find out when Mark, God bless him, picks up the ball again and runs with it.

"Has he been linked to any other violent crimes?"

"Nothing I'm aware of. But that doesn't mean he isn't capable of violence if it suits his purpose. While we were on his tail, Manny's wife was threatened by some guy who accosted her in the supermarket."

"You sure Hoyt was behind that?" I ask. I really, really want the list to end there. I can't quite articulate why to myself, especially since these added details are going to make it an even better story. The thing of it is, I can't talk to Mark about it after our interview has ended, unless I decide to fill him in on my connection to Hoyt.

"Who else would it be, Dakota? I don't believe in coincidences and it was right in the middle of our investigation."

It's getting toward three in the afternoon. Mark and I have a nine o'clock flight back to L.A. We have to go back to the apartment to pick up our stuff, and then get out to JFK. I have to wrap it up, but not without giving it another shot to try to get the names of the women who have been associated with Hoyt.

But Floyd is having none of it. When I ask, he shakes his head back and forth slowly. I know it's a bad sign, since he's readily answered every other question we've put to him.

"You know, I might have finally met someone more stubborn than I," I say.

I give him my Linda Ronstadt poor, pitiful me look. Sometimes it works. Sometimes it doesn't.

"If I can find them, and I can't promise I can, I'll see what they think. Naturally, they're scared to death of Hoyt, afraid of what he'll do to them, and I don't blame them."

"I understand. But I'd really appreciate it if you'd just ask them. Would you do that for me? Please."

"I don't make promises I can't keep. So, I'm not gonna promise anything. I'll think about it. How's that?"

"I guess it'll have to do."

I'm disappointed, because I'm dying to talk to some of the women in Hoyt's life. I know if I can sit down with them, I can get some juicy stuff for the show. But it's more than that. I'm not sure why, but Hoyt fascinates me. I can't seem to get a handle on who he is or what he is. I recognize what's happening, but I can't really help myself. I'm getting obsessed. I keep telling myself that it's all professional, not personal. But I'm not so sure that's true. I do know what my therapist would say. That there's something about him that reflects something about me. I know I'd brush it off. But I also know she might be right.

We finish up. I thank Charlie and tell him what a pleasure it is to make his acquaintance. He gives me a hug and says I shouldn't hesitate to get in touch with him if I have any more questions.

Before I start to pack up, I check my phone and see there's a message from Francis. He's asking me to call him. Mark is off to hunt for a bathroom. I tell him to meet me outside, in front of the station on the 42nd Street side.

It's only when I get out there, without Mark hovering over me, that I put in the call to Francis.

29
Charlie

After finishing up with Dakota and Mark, I'm too amped to hop on the next train back to Stamford.

I need to do something to burn myself out.

Usually, I try not to think about my former life much. Occasionally, something comes up, like this interview, that makes it impossible not to revisit the 'old days.' Sometimes, it's a meandering trip down Memory Lane I don't mind making. Other times, it revs me up, makes me want to get back into the game, especially when I'm reminded of a case that hasn't been resolved. It's a bell unrung. It's like there's this loose thread on a sweater, and because I am who I am, I can't help pulling at it.

Hoyt is a loose thread. As tempted as I might be, I have to keep telling myself to let someone else do the pulling.

Talking with Dakota and Mark makes me realize how much I miss what I used to do. I've joked plenty of times with my ex about going private, but that's what it was: a joke. Now, I'm thinking maybe there's nothing funny about it.

As long as I'm down here, I decide to visit a museum. Maybe soaking myself in some culture will dissipate the urge to get back into the game. It's not yet four, which means there's plenty of daylight left. I take a stroll uptown, toward Central Park. By the time I reach MOMA, the urge has passed, and, after grabbing a quick bite to eat, I return to Grand Central and make the seven-twenty-eight train back to Stamford.

But I can't stop my mind from wandering back to Francis Hoyt. I start to wonder where he is now. What's he doing? Wouldn't it be ironic if we find ourselves in the same position: both "retired," me by choice, him by circumstance? Both thinking about what we're gonna do with the rest of our lives?

Meanwhile, something keeps gnawing at me. It's not something I can put my finger on. But it's there, floating around in the ethers of my mind. Finally, as the train pulls out of the 125th Street station, I find the words to form a sentence, then a thought. *Dakota is holding back.* This little voice in my head, a voice I've learned to listen to, tells me she knows more about Hoyt than she's willing to say. At first, this feeling is just that. A feeling. But the more I think about it, the sharper the feeling gets.

This is nothing new. Every cop I've ever worked with eventually develops a sixth sense. I can spend ten minutes, sometimes fewer, with a suspect and know if they're innocent or guilty. It's not one thing that gives them away. It's a bunch of things. An almost imperceptible hesitation before answering a question. The way their eyes float toward the ceiling before they answer. They don't look you in the eye. Where they place their hands. A slight twitch. A quickening of eye blinks. And if you leave them alone, within minutes they will cradle their heads in their arms, leaning on the table, and fall asleep. With others, it's easier. The old joke about Lyndon Johnson applies: If their lips are moving, they're lying.

I can't help myself—there are some things you can't just turn on or off. It isn't long before I pick up on Dakota's *tells*. The way she knits her fingers together while she's listening to an answer. The way she subtly leans back in her chair, as if there's something she doesn't want to hear. The way she nervously taps her foot when I talk about the dangers of being in Francis Hoyt's path when he wants something. Something's eating at her. I just don't know what it is.

I've never had to take notes during an interrogation. It breaks the flow of conversation. And that's how I learned to think of it—as a conversation, not an interrogation. Years of experience results in an almost uncanny memory for the spoken word. I can repeat entire conversations, verbatim, days after they've occurred. And during those days, subconsciously, my mind is analyzing the words. Shifting them around. Sifting through them word by word. Trying to figure out what's behind them.

Now, several hours away from our encounter, images of Dakota and Francis Hoyt are fresh in my head. With Mark I see only what's there. But with Dakota, there's something else. Something I think there's a good chance she's even keeping from Mark.

What is she hiding?

I close my eyes and my mind settles into the rhythm of the rails. It's hypnotic, putting me into a weird altered state. I try to keep my mind blank, hoping a thought, an idea, an epiphany, will suddenly fill that empty space.

Finally, it hits me. Her secret. Somehow, some way, she's been in touch with Francis Hoyt. And if this feeling is true then she may well know where he is now. And if she knows where he is, it's possible she also knows what he's up to. Because knowing Francis Hoyt, I can guarantee you he's not sitting around twiddling his thumbs. This is a man with an ego that has to be stroked.

Wherever he is, he's up to something.

The question is, if I'm right, what, if anything, do I do about it?

30
Francis

I learn early on I don't need much sleep. Good thing, too, because I never know when my old man will stumble into the bedroom I share with my sister and kick me the hell out of bed. Then, depending on how shit-faced he is, he'll either beat the crap out of me just for being me, for doing something or not doing something, or for something he thought I might do in the fucking future. This is his primary form of exercise. Or, as the fucking prison shrink once told me, "He beat the hell out of you because he hated himself so much."

Fucking shrink mumbo-jumbo. He beat the hell out of me because he could. And when he couldn't anymore, because I fucking stood up to him, he turned on my mother, then my sister.

I function remarkably well, even after getting only five, six hours' sleep. Most times, I don't even need that much. The prison shrink claimed it had something to do with my "sleep metabolism." I don't even know what the fuck that is.

On the day of a job, after weeks of preparation and total focus, my body seems to collapse, and I wind up sleeping eight, ten hours a night. It's like I've been on overload and suddenly my brain and body shut down. But when I finally wake up, I'm fully charged, ready to go.

The day of the job, I kick back. I go over the plan in my head a few more times, even though by then there's no need. I know exactly what I have to do—it's deeply engrained in my brain—and how I'm going to do it.

31
Dakota

By the time we're settled in our seats, exhaustion strikes. Until this moment, I am running on fumes. Now, all I want to do is lean back, close my eyes and sleep until we land at LAX.

But Mark seems particularly amped, his nervous energy resulting in a whole set of physical tics I never noticed before. He doesn't seem to be able to get comfortable. His seat goes back, then forward, then back again. He brings down his tray, leans his elbows on it, then takes his elbows off and closes it. He fiddles with the video controls, checking out the available movies, TV shows, news channels. Then, without making a choice, he shuts the whole thing down.

With all this going on I can't sleep. In fact, I can't even think. Finally, I can't take it anymore.

"You wanna tell me what's wrong?"

He looks at me, startled. "Huh?"

"You're like a six-year-old who's had way too much sugar."

"Huh?"

I tap his forehead with my fingers. "Calling Mark. Mark, are you in there?"

He smiles. I think I've got him back, but I can't be sure.

"So, what's going on?"

"I don't know. I was just thinking about our interview with Charlie Floyd."

"What about him?"

"It's not him, it's you."

"Me? What about me?"

"I don't know, Dakota. Maybe that's why I'm so jumpy. I keep getting this strange feeling about you. You're different. I can't put my finger on it, which is probably why I'm driving you...and me, a little crazy. I'm just picking up this strange vibe."

"Too much excitement."

"Wanna put me in a timeout?"

"It's a thought," I say, wishing he'd just put his seat back down, close his eyes and fall asleep. It's not only because I want to get my sleep. It's because I have a feeling what's bothering him, and it's the last thing I want to talk about. Not with him. Not with myself.

He's silent for a moment or two. He's thinking about something and I'm not sure I want to know what it is. Finally, he can't hold it in any longer.

"This is going to sound very strange, Dakota, but by any chance have you had contact with Francis Hoyt?"

Oh, no. The moment I've been dreading. I knew it would come, but I haven't rehearsed what I'm going to say when it does. I've known all along there would come a point where I'd have to tell Mark about my association with Hoyt and that not only have I met with him, but I've booked him to do the podcast. I've always known it would be a touchy subject, that he'd give me shit about not telling him right away. How irresponsible I've been. How I'm playing with fire. How much do I tell him? That not only have we had physical contact, but he knows where I live?

I'm already struggling with some of the information Floyd has told us about Hoyt. This only complicates everything. Especially since Mark now knows how dangerous associating with Hoyt can be.

I can't put it off any longer. I have to decide whether to come clean. Do I tell Mark something, anything, everything? Mark is forcing my hand before I'm ready to show it. But I know, as much as I'd like to, I can't just shove his questions aside. I have to say something.

In that split second, I make a decision that comes not from careful analysis but rather from self-preservation. I will tell him everything I know because to hold back anything, to manipulate the story, is more than I can possibly manage in my sleep-deprived state.

"Okay, Mark. I know this is going to piss you off and you have every right to be upset. I probably should have told you this before, but..."

"You're stalling, Dakota. Just spit it out, will you?"

And so, I admit that yes, there is something, but I need time to sort it out. But I promise I'll tell him everything. Later. Right now, all I need is to sleep.

32
Francis

I'm waiting at the door of the Santa Monica Library when it opens Tuesday morning. I'm there to find an open computer, log onto the Internet and create a fake email account. I'll use it sparingly and as soon as the job is over, it will disappear into cyberspace.

The first person I write to is Derek.

We need to meet. Go to the Hollywood Reservoir. Get there a few minutes before 8 a.m. Park your car, then start walking the path around the reservoir. I'll find you.

Early Thursday morning I head over to the reservoir, also known as Lake Hollywood, located in the Santa Monica Mountains north of the Hollywood neighborhood of Los Angeles. It's a popular spot for weekend hikers and fitness nuts who like to think they're killing two birds with one stone: exercising while communing with nature.

It's overcast and the humidity hangs heavy in the air. It's early enough so there are fewer people on the trail than there will be later in the day. A few hours from now, the L.A. fitness crew will swarm the area, trying to jog or walk themselves into shape. But now, with the exception of a hiker or two, I'm pretty much alone on the trail.

Several hundred yards in, I find a place just off the dirt trail that snakes around the reservoir. Hidden by heavy vegetation, I have the perfect vantage point to see Derek before he sees me.

A few minutes past 8, I see him ambling slowly toward me, as if he doesn't have a care in the world. He's got on a set of earphones, snapping his fingers, his hips swaying back and forth. Every so often, he looks to his right, to his left, then behind. When he's no more than ten, fifteen feet from where I'm hidden, I casually step out from my hidey-hole.

Only a couple feet from me he stops dead in his tracks. He pulls the earphones from his ears, and slides them down his chest, till they rest on his shoulders.

"Jesus, you scared the shit out of me, man," he says.

"Maybe you ought to pay more attention."

"I follow instructions good, right?" He looks at his watch and taps it to make a point. He's looking for my approval. Like I'm his daddy. He'll get plenty of things from me or because of me, but approval won't be one of them.

"You're the best, Derek. Let's walk."

There's an outside chance he's wired, but to pat him down shows weakness so instead, I'm just careful as to what I say and how I say it.

Instead of leading him back to the parking lot, I keep us moving forward. I know precisely how long it'll take to make the full loop, enough time to do what needs to be done.

We're just getting started when my phone vibrates in my pocket. It's a text. From Dakota. Without reading it, I jam the phone back into my pocket and continue walking, picking up the pace.

"You wanna take that?" says Derek.

"It'll wait."

"So, Boss, what's up?"

I know he wants me to confide in him, but that's not gonna happen. Instead, I'll pump him for information while at the same time making him think he's part of the plan.

I ask him to tell me everything he saw at the jewelry store.

His answers flow freely. Derek aims to please. He sees a future in our relationship.

Derek tells me nothing I don't already know. But that's not why I sent him there. He describes the inside of the store, the people who work there, where the security cameras are. From what he reports, Vince has provided me with accurate information. He tells me about his interactions with the people who work in the shop. By the time he's finished, I know for sure any cameras in the place have grabbed good images of him, and that the people who work there won't have any problem identifying him if asked to.

As we're about to complete the loop in sight of the parking area, Derek suddenly gets quiet. I can tell something's bugging him. I know I'll find out what it is without asking, so I don't.

Finally, as we're walking toward our cars, he can't hold it in any longer.

"So, boss, how about letting me in on what's going on—I mean, I ain't stupid. I know you're about to hit the jewelry store. I'm nobody's flunky. If I'm gonna work with you, I want in."

I don't say anything because I'm trying to figure the best way to handle this. But Derek takes my silence as my being angry enough to cut him loose and starts to backtrack.

"Don't get me wrong. I totally get the need for secrecy. I mean, it's not like you can trust anyone, right? I mean, I could be a snitch…" He quickly adds, "I'm not. I swear. But I could be. So, I understand why you don't want to talk about anything. I mean, what could I snitch about? I don't really know who you are and I certainly don't know when you're gonna do what you're gonna do. I just, well, I just have a real good feeling about you and I want to be part of the operation. I mean, whatever this is. Or maybe if not this then maybe something in the future. I get it. Why should you trust me now? Let's just see how this goes and then, if everything comes off A-O-K, then I'm sure we can move up to the next step…" He stops abruptly, like he knows how fucking ridiculous he sounds. He's lucky I don't give a shit. He's lucky I've got everything I want from him.

"It's okay, Derek. You did good." I pull out my wallet and peel off three Benjamins and hand them to him. "But you're right. I can't let you in on what's happening. But it's not because I don't trust you."

"Then why?"

"Look, I'm not in this thing alone. I got people to answer to. So, I can't be springing strangers on them. They don't like that. You see what I'm saying?"

He breaks into a smile. "Yeah. Yeah. I do. I definitely do. And you know what, I'm good with it." He folds the bills in half and makes to shove them into the back pocket of his jeans. But before he does, he waves them in my face. "And I really appreciate this. It's a show of good faith. You're an A-number-one gentleman, and I really want you to know I look forward to working with you again."

I extend my hand. He takes it. "Yes, this could be the start of a beautiful friendship," I say, surprising myself at how sincere I make it sound.

33
Dakota

The minute I step into my apartment I sense something's wrong.

The energy is different. Someone's been in my apartment besides my neighbor Carl, who sticks his head in every day to feed Hemingway and change the litter box whenever I'm gone.

Now, it feels like the scene of a crime.

It's nothing concrete. It's more like I can "sense" a foreign, malignant presence. I don't believe in ghosts or spirits or communicating with the dead, so I it's not that. It's something human. Something real.

The first thought that shoots through my mind, the result of way too many fairy tales when I was a child, has to do with "the three little bears." But this intruder is no bear.

I immediately turn on all the lights and Hemingway bolts out of the bedroom like he's been shot out of a cannon and makes a beeline for me. Just before he reaches me, he stops short and hisses. Like he's possessed by an evil spirit. He continues hissing for a few seconds, then turns tail and charges back into the bedroom.

He's pissed. He gets that way whenever I leave him alone for more than a day. At first, it pisses me off that I piss him off, but then I realize it's because he misses me. And since no one else seems to, I consider it, whether it is or isn't, his way of showing how much he loves and misses me when I'm gone.

But this is different. I've never seen behavior like this. He's not just punishing me for leaving him alone. He's punishing me for not protecting him.

I walk slowly around the apartment, checking to see if anything's missing. I walk into the kitchen and open the refrigerator door. I'm ready to close it when I realize something's out of place. An almost spoiled half-filled container of milk that's always on the top shelf, up front, is now on a shelf on the refrigerator door. Could I have absently put it there? I don't think so. But I suppose in a rush it's possible I put it in the wrong place. But there are a few other things...

It's not till I reach the bedroom that I'm convinced someone who doesn't belong in my apartment has been there. I see things moved from their normal spot in a few of my dresser drawers. In the closet, clothing has been moved around. One shoe box, always next to another, is now stacked on top of another.

And then there's the radio. I always leave it on when I leave the apartment. It's off. Could it have shut down during a blackout? I check. No. It's been turned off manually.

A shiver jolts my body. Suddenly, it occurs to me. Could someone still be in the apartment? Hiding behind the bathroom curtain, perhaps? Under the bed. Is that why Hemingway is so freaked? Or am I just being paranoid?

I'm frozen in place. Like I'm glued to the floor. I don't know whether to stay in the apartment and look around or get the heck out of there.

I know what I should do. I should leave and call the cops. But I can't possibly leave Hemingway there alone, so I do the opposite. I turn the radio back on, full blast. I pick up a sharp knife from the kitchen and, like an explorer in a new land, I slowly stalk through the apartment, holding the knife at the ready in front of me, turning on every light as I go. Hemingway has filed in behind me, as if I'm his protective shield.

My heart is beating so fast it feels like it's going to burst through my chest. I swear I can hear it, even over the radio blasting from the bedroom.

Finally, I make it through the entire apartment. It's just me and Hemingway. But I'm certain someone's been here, and although I'm pretty sure nothing's been taken, I'm just as sure that someone wanted me to know they were here. I know this because when I open my medicine cabinet, I can see things have been shuffled around.

It doesn't take a genius to figure out who it was.

Francis Hoyt.

That rotten, evil bastard. It's not enough he's in my head. Now he's in my home.

I've never been so freaked out in my life. Or so frightened. I sit down on my bed and start to shake. And then the tears come. Things are so bad Hemingway, who usually holds a grudge, jumps up on the bed and wiggles himself onto my lap. What's going on? What have I got myself into? Should I call the cops? Should I move out?

But before doing anything, I suddenly realize this is exactly what Hoyt wants. He doesn't want to hurt me. He just wants me off balance. He wants to get into my head so he can manipulate me.

I'm furious, and my anger only builds. I debate with myself for hours, all through the night. What should I do? Should I call him on it? Should I make believe this never happened? Should I let him know, casually, that I know he's been in my apartment, and that if he thinks that's going to scare me or intimidate me or let his little mind games manipulate me, he's wrong?

The sun is coming up and I'm still wide awake. And worse, I still haven't figured out what I'm going to do.

34
Charlie

I've never had trouble sleeping. Even in the depths of despair while I searched for the mass murderer John Hartman—which preoccupied my life for years before it finally came to an unexpected end—I could still lay my head down on the pillow every night and fall asleep.

My ex-wife Sara claims I have a particular knack for falling asleep in the most unlikely places. She kids me that I've never seen a movie in a theater all the way through with my eyes open. "The lights go out, Charlie, and so do you."

I chalk it up to my ability to focus on the task at hand, whatever it is. What made me an excellent investigator made an excellent sleeper. What else are you supposed to do when the lights go out and you're lying prone on a comfortable mattress with your eyes closed?

But sleeping and going to sleep are two completely different things. When something is gnawing at me, like this Francis Hoyt podcast deal, there's no way I'm going to lie down and fall asleep. The little voice in my head is not about to let that happen. I'm gonna stay wide awake until I figure things out.

The day after finishing my two interviews with Dakota, I'm back in Connecticut, sitting on my porch, rocking back and forth, watching the sprinklers spray the lawn with undulating waves of water, bending this way and that as they change direction. I'm thinking. Well, not exactly thinking as much as trying to put a puzzle together in my head.

So, what's the problem? I do my thing to help the young woman out and now I should be out of it. But it's not as simple as that. The thing of it is, I'm pretty sure Dakota is holding back. I know she's here to get interviews for her show, but I have this sneaking suspicion, a strong feeling, really, that she's somehow more involved with Francis Hoyt than she's willing to say. Specifically? I think she's been in touch with him.

Why do I think this? Well, therein lies a dilemma. I can't put my finger on anything specific. It's nothing she says. It's more like a look in her eyes and her body language. It comes whenever I say something, anything, about Hoyt's darker side, the side sometimes obscured by this American obsession with outlaws, which dates all the way back to folks like Jesse James, John Dillinger, Al Capone, Bonnie and Clyde, and more recently, John Gotti and Whitey Bulger. Why we make heroes out of these people when they're nothing more than violent, amoral, psychopathic punks is beyond me. Sometimes, it's the Robin Hood syndrome. The idea of stealing from the rich and giving to the poor. Let me set you straight. *There is no such thing.* It's a figment of the imagination, a figment often fostered by the press, looking to make a story that will catch the imagination of the public. Back in the days of the outlaws, it was reporters like Ned Buntline, who made up fantastic tales that titillated the imagination of folks back East who'd never get closer to the frontier than the Appalachians. Even murderous punks like Jesse James knew the benefits of good press, and Jesse was not averse to sending letters to the editors of various newspapers, extolling his good intentions.

The truth behind these outlaws is that more often than not, they're brutal, amoral narcissists who prey upon the weak and vulnerable. Hoyt fits that profile to a T. And I've taken it upon myself at every opportunity to point this out. Which is one of the reasons I said yes to participating in Dakota's interview. I want folks to know the truth. In this case, the truth is that Francis Hoyt may be many things, but folk hero is not one of them. He destroys everything he touches and he never, ever looks back. He's amoral and cruel. For him, it's more than simply stealing your possessions. This man is out to steal your soul. He's miserable, so he wants everyone else to be just as miserable. He embodies the old saw of misery loves company.

If he weren't such a despicable human being, who shows absolutely no remorse, I might feel sorry for him. Who knows what goes into the mix to create a monster like Hoyt. And make no mistake, he is a monster. Not the Buffalo Bill, Hannibal Lector, John Wayne Gacy, Ted Bundy kind of monster. But in some ways, just as evil. He cares about no one but himself, and if Dakota is in some way involved with him, I worry for her.

Of course, I can't prove Dakota has had any connection to Hoyt. But even if she hasn't, I worry how he'll react once he finds out he's the subject of a podcast. He's not the type to sit back and let it happen. I'm not sure what he'll do, but I know he'll do something. He needs to control the message and he'll do whatever he can to make sure he does.

No matter how hard I try, I can't stop thinking about this. I worry about Dakota. I worry about what Hoyt, who's been under the radar for well over a year now, is doing and where he is. I know him, maybe better than anyone else in the world, and I know he's not the type to take his loot and kick back on some Caribbean island. He has a constant need to prove to himself and to the world that he's the best at what he does. People like Francis Hoyt don't retire. The only way to pry them out of the spotlight, which is like oxygen to him, is to physically grab him and drag him off the stage. We almost did that. But, in the end, we failed. And that failure, even though it wasn't really mine or Manny's, sticks in my craw. I know it's not up to me to do something about it now, but I'm not sure I can control myself. That's what I'm struggling with now.

Francis Hoyt is who he is and Charlie Floyd is who I am.
I have to do something. I just don't know what it is yet.

35

Francis

I don't hear from Capowitz for a couple weeks. This is a good thing. But all good things come to an end.

It's late afternoon on an uncharacteristic rainy afternoon. Me, I don't mind the rain. It often fits my mood. Especially since I don't like the fucking sun shining all the fucking time. To be honest, I miss seasons. Out here, they got three seasons: summer, windy and gloomy.

I'm sitting in my little cottage apartment. It's four days before what I've taken to calling "the operation." I'm lying on the couch trying to nap, but the details of "the operation" keep making an uninvited intrusion, making it impossible to clear my mind enough to sleep. There's something wrong, but I can't quite put my finger on it. Finally, I decide the only way I'll be able to figure out what's out of whack is to keep picturing the scenario in my mind, over and over and over again. This way, I'm sure I'll pick up the piece of the puzzle that doesn't quite fit.

Suddenly, the buzzing of one of three phones I have tucked firmly between me and the inside edge of the couch, makes that impossible. I grab the offending burner and see it's the one dedicated to Vince. I'm not happy. Either something's wrong, something's changed, or he's calling to check up on me. None of those options pleases me.

"Yeah," I answer gruffly. He's interrupted me when I don't

want to be interrupted and I have no reason to let him think I'm happy about this call.

"Francis. Vince Capowitz here."

"I know who you are, Vince. What I don't know is why the fuck you're calling me."

"I'm sorry. Did I interrupt something important?"

I can answer "every fucking thing is important when it comes to me," but I catch myself before the words tumble from my mouth. I realize maybe I should tone it down a little. After all, I'm still owed half my fee. Besides, if things work out this might be the start of a fruitful business relationship, and although I need Vince to know exactly where he stands, there's no reason to drive an unnecessary wedge between us. And so, I tone it down. At least until I find out why the fuck he's bothering me.

"It's okay. What's up?"

"Just checking in. It's been a while and my client is wondering when we can expect results."

This pisses me off. No one backs Francis Hoyt into a corner. I come and go as I please. I do what I want when I want.

"I'm pretty sure I mentioned early on in our relationship, I don't appreciate being checked up on."

"I'm sorry if it comes off that way. My client is putting a little pressure on me so I figured maybe I can get back to him with a progress report."

"I don't do progress reports, unless your *client*"—the word drips out of my mouth coated with sarcasm thick as honey—"is willing to tell me who the fuck he is. Otherwise, I can't imagine a reason to hear from you unless you've got new information for me."

He's silent for a moment. I know exactly what he's doing. He's trying to come up with something to justify this call. To assuage me. To calm me down. To put the tiger back in his cage. If he says something like, *we're all on the same team here,* then I swear I'll throw this fucking burner against the fucking wall.

"Let's pretend this call never happened," he says.

"Too fucking late for that, Vince. But now that you're in my fucking ear, I need to know exactly what the procedure is once the job is done."

"Excuse me?"

"You know what the fuck I mean. My money?"

"Oh, that. Of course. My client will get the cash to me within twenty-four hours and we can set up a rendezvous spot where you and I can exchange the goods."

I don't like the sound of this. Does he really think I'm going to sit around twiddling my thumbs for twenty-four hours? Does he think I'm stupid enough to arrive at a spot naked, just me and the loot? People have gotten ripped off for a lot less.

"I do the job, I make the rules. I don't fucking want to meet you or anyone else. I want the funds transferred to an off-shore account."

"Does this mean you're getting close to fulfilling our contract?"

I ignore him. "The offshore account?"

"I'm sure it can be arranged."

"I know it can. I want it done by nine A-M Sunday morning."

"That's July Fourth."

"Where I'm having you transfer the dough they couldn't care less about fucking Independence Day."

"Will the job be done by then?"

"It doesn't matter. That's when I want my money."

"May I remind you the deal was for the second payment to be delivered *after* the job has been completed."

"I know what the fucking deal is, Vince. I'll let you know when the job is done."

"So, you want me to tell my client that he's to pay before the job has been completed?"

"Tell him whatever the fuck you want."

"I don't know, Francis. My client is not really the trusting type."

"Neither am I. But have him take a look at my history, Vince.

I've dealt with plenty of guys like him and not one of them ever complained. That should tell him something. If this bothers him, we can call the whole thing off. But if we do, remember, he can kiss that first payment goodbye."

"I'm not authorized to make any promises, but I will contact him and see if that's satisfactory."

"Do that. And since I don't want to be bothered again, I'm gonna text you the account number. If I don't see that money there by noon Sunday, all bets are off. Capiche?"

"I'll try to get back to you within the hour."

"No. You won't get back to me. We're to have no further contact till the job is done and you'll know that when I tell you. I'll know if it's a deal when I check my account Saturday night."

"And how will we arrange the delivery of our goods?"

"I'll call you right after the job is done and we'll set up a time and place."

"It would be advantageous and a show of good will if you could let us have that information now, Francis."

"I'm not known for good will, Vince," I say.

And then I terminate the call.

36
Francis

I see things. Sometimes I see things that are there. Sometimes I see things that aren't. But I know the difference.

It's Wednesday and today's task is to make a dry run to the strip mall. I want to time it and I want to try two or three different routes. One of them will wind up being the one I take Sunday night. But I won't know which one till that morning.

As soon as I get into the car, I have a feeling I'm being watched. I start up the car, but I just sit there for a minute or two, looking around. Looking to see if there's anything out of the ordinary. Any unexplained movement. Nothing. But still. I have this feeling.

I pull out and drive slowly at first, trying to see if anyone is on my tail. No. Yet. Maybe I'm wrong? Maybe it's just a case of jitters before a big job. Maybe not. I head in the direction of the strip mall, using one of the three routes I mapped out last night. I drive slowly. But not slow enough to attract attention. Just slow enough so I can pick up a tail, if there is one.

I get to the mall, circle it, then drive back in the direction of the cottage. I check the rear-view mirror and for the first time I notice a black Toyota, about twenty, twenty-five feet behind me. I speed up. It speeds up. I make a left. It makes a left. Maybe I'm seeing things that are there. Maybe not.

I try a few maneuvers in an attempt to lose my tail, but

whoever it is, he's good. He sticks with me. But it's got to be obvious to him now that he's made and so, when I stop for a light, he's two cars behind me. When the car directly between us turns off, it's just me and him.

Since it's obvious I know what he's doing, his cover blown, he steps on it and breezes past me on my left. I only get a brief glance at the driver. There's something about him that looks familiar. I'm not sure what.

I've seen him somewhere before, but I can't place him.

It isn't till I'm back in the cottage, the rest of the day aborted, that I realize who it is.

It's that goofball from the Santa Monica Pier. The one who wouldn't leave me the fuck alone.

What the fuck is going on?

37
Dakota

If Hoyt's goal is to shake me up, mission accomplished.

I've never felt so creeped out in my life.

I'm not about to call the cops and I'm certainly not about to stay in the apartment. So, I call Mark. He's not the first person I think of, but he is the first person it makes sense to call. I know, of course, as soon as I walk into his apartment, I'm beholden to tell him everything, something I've been putting off since our trip to New York. It's not something I'm looking forward to, but it's something I know I have to do.

In the meantime, what to do about Francis Hoyt? Do I confront him? Do I ghost him? Do I make as if nothing's happened? I guess these are questions I can't answer until I decide how important this podcast is to me. Which really boils down to how important is he to a successful podcast? Before we met, it never crosses my mind to look Francis up, to ask him to sit for an interview. But things have changed big-time since he accosts me on the sidewalk that morning.

There's something else. Something that surprisingly hadn't occurred to me until my interview with Charlie Floyd. Maybe it's a tunnel-vision thing. It comes to me because of something Charlie says near the end of our last interview:

"What I worry about most, Dakota, is what Hoyt has up his sleeve now."

I don't know why that question never occurred to me. The truth is, looking back, I realize I've never asked myself the real reason Francis sought me out. I realize it's a question I never ask. Charlie is right. Hoyt never does anything unless there's something in it for him. At first, I think he's trying to get me to chuck the broadcast. But he never asks for that. In fact, in his own perverse way, he's been supportive. Why? Is it just another ploy to get attention? Is it all about ego? Or is there something else?

When Charlie asks me that question about why I'd selected Francis Hoyt for the podcast, I tell him the first thing that pops into my head:

"What do you think?"

"I'm retired, Dakota. Remember? But I do know this much. It's been more than a year now and not a peep out of him. That's not going to hold."

"Have you heard anything? You know, like from your sources?"

"No. But remember I'm on the bench. I'm banned from talking to anyone from the office by my ex-wife and kids. But if something were in the air, I'm pretty sure I'd have heard from Manny or someone I worked with. As much as I want to bring that son of a bitch down, Manny wants it even more. With him, it's personal."

"Why's that?"

Floyd smiles. "That's Manny's story to tell."

"But I'm here and Manny's not. And he won't talk to me. I've tried several times, and when I finally reached him, he said absolutely not."

"Well, I can't tell you what Hoyt is doing now, but I can tell you what he's not doing."

"What's that?"

"He's not sitting on his ass, popping bonbons into his mouth and drinking margaritas on some beach. Francis Hoyt exists only to be Francis Hoyt. If he's not doing something to make sure he's relevant, then he's not Francis Hoyt anymore. You get what I mean?"

At the time, I hadn't given what he told me much thought. But now, well, now it's pretty much all I can think about. What Floyd was telling me is that people like Francis Hoyt don't retire. They don't suddenly step out of the limelight and take up a hobby, like making model airplanes. What Floyd was saying, and what I should have already known myself, is there's a strong likelihood Hoyt is in the middle of something. Either he's planning a job or he's actively involved in one. It's so obvious, but for some reason—well, I actually know the reason—I've been too darn occupied with myself and what I'm doing.

But this break-in, this intrusion into my "personal space," is like someone throwing a bucket of water over my head. It's a wake-up call. Francis Hoyt, no matter how charming or how fascinating he might appear, is still a severely damaged, hardened criminal. He's someone who's continually probing, checking for weak spots. Looking for an advantage. Looking to keep his opponent, which means everyone but him, off balance.

Francis Hoyt did not break into my apartment as a prank. Or did he do it as some existential exercise to let me know how good he is. It's like the old story about the scorpion and the frog, both of whom are on one side of a river, both wanting to get to the other side. The scorpion suggests he hitch a ride on the frog's back. The frog, aware of the possible danger, says, "But what if you sting me?"

"Why would I do that?" answers the scorpion. "If I did, we'd both sink and I'd drown."

So, the frog tells the scorpion to hop aboard, but half-way across the river, the scorpion stings the frog, dooming them both.

"Why did you do that?" asks the frog. "Now we'll both die."

The scorpion answers, "Sorry, I couldn't help it. It's my nature."

Francis Hoyt is the scorpion.

I do not want to be the frog.

38
Francis

Friday. Three days left. I get another text from Dakota.

I'm back, Francis. Please call so we can schedule the interview. I apologize if you think I was putting too much pressure on you.

Fuck you, bitch. That's what I want to text back. But I don't. I've cooled down since our last conversation. I'm getting into that special *zone* right before a job and I can't afford to let anything break my concentration. Besides, I'm not quite finished with Dakota Richards yet.

The text breaks my concentration. Before it, I'm in the zone. Afterward, I'm not. Like any top athlete just before the big game, I try to get back in that zone by forcing Dakota out of my mind. I'll deal with her soon enough.

Meanwhile, I get back to putting the all-important pre-game elements into place.

There are three distinct phases.

The Butterfly Stage, when I'm just starting to emerge from my cocoon, ready to turn from caterpillar to butterfly. In this stage, I am anxious, antsy, wondering if I've done all I can to make the job work. I lose track of time. I miss meals. I sleep in fits and starts. I obsess over details. I run through the plan again and again and again in a form of self-hypnosis.

When a little voice in my head tells me I'm ready, I slip into phase two, Euphoria. I'm on top of the world. I am invincible. No one can touch me. I'm on the most potent drug in the world. Time means nothing. Time is nothing. My mind jumps rapidly from one thing to another. I'm super-aware of everything I see, hear and smell. Food tastes better. Flowers smell sweeter. Colors are more vibrant. I am incredibly sensitive to sound. Everything I hear is amped up, as if it's being broadcast from huge, unseen speakers. I can't sit still. I fidget constantly. I need to be on the move. I walk. I run.

Phase Three arrives when I come back down to earth. My focus is razor sharp. I think only of the job. Once I'm firmly planted in Phase Three, I'm ready to go.

Timing is all-important. I have to hit Phase Three, peak-performance level, only hours before I'm ready to pull the job. If I peak too early, then I'm flat when the time comes. If I peak too late, well, you can imagine what happens then.

When I get Dakota's message Friday night, I am nearing the end of Phase Two, ready to move into that final phase in time for Sunday morning's score.

I don't want to talk to her. I can't let anything interrupt my flow. But I know this bitch well enough to know that she's gonna be all over my ass until she gets an answer. And so, against my better judgment, I text her, hoping to put her off.

Out of town. Back next week. Will get in touch then.

I don't know where she's been, but I'm sure it has something to do with me. That's what she's working on now and that's what she'd be secretive about. My guess is she went back east, New York or Miami. She's probably looking to hook up with Manny Perez down in Miami or Charlie Floyd up in Connecticut. She's looking to talk to cops throughout New England, and the New York area. I'm sure she's trying to find some of the women I've been with. I wouldn't be surprised if she tracks down Artie in Miami. But if she tries getting to his counterpart in New York, she'll find he's permanently indisposed.

It's possible she's tracked me down to the St. Louis area,

looking for my old lady and my sister. They'll be hard to find, since they've changed their last names and I've moved them away from where they used to live. Even if she's able to find them, they know better than to talk to her. If they do the money faucet will suddenly dry up.

As soon as this job is over, I'll turn my attention to Dakota. Until then, she doesn't exist.

39

Francis

Time is important. I don't waste it and I don't let it waste me.

I own dozens of watches, from the cheapest, a Timex that does, in fact, keep on ticking, to the most expensive, a Patek Philippe, which ran me close to forty grand. I carry half a dozen or so with me. The rest are stashed in various places across the continent. Every morning, I choose the watch that best fits my mood for the day.

Today, I'm a little jumpy. It's a good sign. A sign the job has passed from the planning stage to the performance stage. To-night, at midnight, it'll be time to get the show on the road.

As soon as I wake up, I immediately launch into my job-day routine. It's not about superstition, it's about tried-and-true methods.

First, I take the first of three or four showers. I shave. Not only my face, but my entire body hair, from my chest down to my ankles. I clip my nails. I lay out my uniform for that even-ing. Everything I choose is brand new and unwashed. Tight black T-shirt. Black stretch pants. Black watch cap. Black Con-verse high-tops. Taken together, I am a shadow. I cut off all the labels. I make sure I have at least three pairs of latex gloves. For this job, I won't need my usual tools, but I carry my handy Swiss Army Knife. Even though I have the passcodes, I have to hide the fact that it's an inside job, so I'll be leaving signs on the doors that indicate I've broken in, not waltzed in with the help of inside information.

I eat only one meal the day of the job. Breakfast. I make sure I'm well-hydrated.

I clear out every inch of the car. The smallest piece of trash is eliminated. I wipe clean every surface I might have touched. I check the trunk, which holds only a spare tire and a quart-size plastic container of gasoline. Hidden under the floor of the trunk is a pack of matches.

By now, it's close to noon and I'll make a final trip to the strip mall to make sure there aren't any substantial changes I ought to be aware of. Once, when I make the same check on a house I'm visiting that night, I find that they've begun construction on a porch. Needless to say, I postponed that job for the two weeks it took them to complete the job.

I hop in the heap, making sure the tank is filled, then take one last trip over to the strip mall. I park the car within view of the jewelry shop, turn on the radio while I keep an eye peeled for anything out of the ordinary.

While I'm sitting there my mind shifts quickly from one thing to another. An image of Dakota flashes through my mind. It's been almost a week since I've heard from her. I know she's back in L.A., because one evening a couple days ago I drive by her apartment and see lights on.

I haven't heard a word from her since I broke into her apartment. I don't know if she's angry with me or if her silence is just a game she's playing.

Time to shake the tree and see what falls out.

40
Charlie

"You must be crazy."

"Not the first time I've been called that, and I'm pretty sure it won't be the last."

I'm in my old office in downtown Hartford, a place I haven't visited for almost a year. During my first several months of retirement, with little to do with myself, I visited the office two, three time a week. Finally, my boss, the attorney general, put his foot down and unofficially "banned" me from showing up. Like every other rule I face, I have no trouble breaking it.

"What part of the word 'retired' don't you get, Charlie?" he asks in a voice filled not with anger but frustration. "It's been almost six months now and I think I see you more than I did my first six years in office. Here's three words for you. Get. A. Life."

"Where have I heard that before?"

"I'm pretty sure you've heard it plenty of times from Sara and the kids."

"No wonder it sounds familiar."

"Seriously, Charlie. What's up? You can't possibly miss us that much."

"Not you, Dick, but yeah. It's more like I miss the work than I miss some of the obnoxious, self-righteous assholes in the department."

He knows me well enough not to take it personally or be offended. Though maybe he should be.

"You're keeping my people from getting their work done."

"How's that happening?"

"Okay, let me put this in a way you might understand, a way
that doesn't result in your having to buy a new cowboy hat because your damn head has swelled up two sizes. When you're
here, you intimidate people. You don't mean to, but you do.
You were so good at what you did, and everyone knows it, that
when you show up it's like the smartest man in the world is
here. People come to you for information. For advice. For con-
firmation. That gums up the works."

"Gotcha. How's this? I promise to limit visits to once a
month."

"Once a year."

"You gotta be kidding!"

"For the annual Christmas party. But only if you promise to
dress up like Santa."

In the end, we reach a compromise. I will only show up for an
official reason. Like old cases. But absolutely no casual "drop-
ins." I wonder how long it'll take me to break that rule?

This time, though, I have good reason to be here. I need the
office to communicate with law enforcement in L.A. Dick's out
of town, but his second-in-command, Laura Schlesinger, agrees
to see me. With her in charge, I'm on better footing. Laura and I
always got along. She's in her late forties, always impeccably
dressed—we used to call her the official representative of Anne
Taylor—very handsome, hard-working and, most of all, a brilliant attorney. There's no doubt in anyone's mind that sooner,
rather than later, she'll be numero uno, and I'm pretty sure the
State will be better for it.

When I rap on the open door of her office—in all the years
she's been with the AG, I've never seen her office door closed—
she looks up, sees it's me, and smiles. A good start.

"Charlie! Long time no see." She catches herself. "Wait, it's not Christmas already, is it?"

"Not unless they moved it to July," I say, as I stand hovering in the doorway. "Mind if I come in? Promise, it won't take long."

"Of course."

"So, since I haven't heard that your office ban has been lifted, I'm guessing this is more of an official visit than a 'how-de-doo, Ms. Laura' visit."

"You always were the smartest one in the whole, damn office."

"I never heard you say that."

"Musta been behind your back."

She motions me to sit in the chair in front of her desk.

I sit, take my hat off, and place it on my lap.

"So, what can I do you for, handsome?"

"I need a favor and seeing I'm not with the A-G's office anymore, it's kind of a big one."

"Anything short of murder, Charlie, and I'm inclined to say yes. What is it?"

"I'd like to go out to California to follow a lead. A hunch, really."

"Okay?"

"It has to do with Francis Hoyt."

She moves her head back and forth slowly, like she's getting ready to give me a lecture.

"May I remind you it's not your problem anymore?"

"Well, yes and no."

"What's that supposed to mean?"

"It's a loose end, Laura. And you know me and loose ends."

"Unfortunately, I do. So, you think he's out there?"

"Might be."

"And you're willing to go out there on a 'might be?'"

"Yup."

"Well, you're a private citizen now, so I can't stop you. Why come to me? You don't want me to deputize you or anything as dramatic as that, do you?"

"No, ma'am, though now that you mention it, one of those cool deputy sheriff badges might be nice."

"Then what?"

"I want you to contact the authorities out there in L-A, maybe even up in Sacramento, and alert them that I'm gonna be out there."

"To what end?"

"If I do find him, I want to be able to coordinate with the authorities so they can pick him up and hold him while we, I mean you, draw up the paperwork to extradite him."

"Is that all? I thought you were going to ask for the moon and here you are willing to settle for a handful of Connecticut soil. That shouldn't be a problem. I'd like to, at least consider running this by the boss..."

"You're a lot easier to talk to but I don't mind your telling the Big Kahuna, honey...oops, I don't think I'm supposed to use that word..."

She laughs. "You know, Charlie, you are the only man left in the world I'll let get away with that 'Honey' crap. I don't even let my husband get away with it. And who'd have thought the day would come when Charlie Floyd would be 'woke.'"

"I'm trying. Just don't tell Sara. She and the kids have been trying to drag me from the nineteenth century into the twenty-first."

"When are you planning to head out there?"

"Don't have to plan. Already got the ticket. First thing tomorrow morning."

"I should've known. Now get the hell out of my office so I can get some work done."

I take my hat out of my lap, slip it on my head, give it a little tip, and stand up to leave.

"Any chance you'd turn me in for sexual harassment if I give you a little hug? You know, for old times' sake?"

She smiles, gets up and takes a step toward me. "What's that they say about an old dog and tricks," she says, as she wraps her arms around me, much tighter than I would have expected.

Halfway out of her office I hear her say, "I'll take care of everything, Charlie. And if you need anything in writing, just let me know."

Sometimes it pays to have friends in high places.

41
Dakota

"Are you kidding me?"

I'm upset, and with good reason. But I try not to let my anger leach into my words. The last thing I want to do is give Francis the satisfaction.

He calls while I'm still at Mark's place, still too nervous to be back in my apartment alone. We're sitting at the dining-room table, papers spread out in front of us, alongside the detritus of our pizza lunch. We're working on scripts for the show when he calls. I guess I should excuse myself and go into the master bedroom Mark has so graciously loaned me, while he sleeps in the much smaller guest bedroom that he uses as his office. But I stay right where I am. I know this sounds crazy, but I don't want to be alone in a room with Hoyt, even if it is on the phone.

No matter how cool I play it, Mark knows me too well not to see I'm upset. He doesn't say anything, but he doesn't move from his spot. He knows if I want privacy, I'll tell him.

I've been hiding out at Mark's several days now, returning to my apartment only once to pick up a few things, including Hemingway's litter box. Mark goes well beyond the duty of friendship by not only taking me in, but Hemingway, too. Especially, since Mark's slightly allergic. I offer to board Hemingway, or foist him off on another friend—I wouldn't dare leave him back in the apartment alone, asking my neighbor Carl to take care of him—but Mark will have none of that.

"I think you need him now as much as he needs you," he explains.

Mark knows all about Hoyt now. I couldn't just show up at his doorstep with my luggage and cat carrier without an explanation. When I tell him, he doesn't take it very well. And to be fair, if I were in his shoes, I wouldn't have, either.

"Are you crazy?" he asks, as we sit across from each other at his kitchen table. I'm sipping Chamomile tea, while Mark nurses a bottle of the latest micro-brew he's discovered.

"Of course, I am. But you've known that for a while."

He shakes his head. "I don't think you should be making jokes about this, Dakota. This guy is dangerous. You never should have let yourself get involved with him. And when you did, you should have told me. You did tell someone, right?"

I shake my head no.

"Jesus, you really are loco in the cabeza." He spins his index finger next to his right temple.

"Excellent, Mark. I see those Spanish lessons are paying off."

I get him to smile and now that we're pretty much past the anger stage, for the next hour or so I endure his well-meaning lecture. Only then does he listen to my lame explanation. Finally, we move on to figuring out what might be our next move. We even talk about what happens if Francis gets back in touch with me, which is exactly what's happening now. Still, I can't say I'm totally prepared.

I utter a few more choice words until Francis cuts me off.

"Relax, Dakota," he says.

"Don't you dare tell me to relax," I say, following a script Mark and I write that first night. Now, several days later, I'm playing out my grievous, angry, betrayed woman role to see where it gets me. "You fucking broke into my home, Francis! That's crossing a line. A very big line. Why in hell did you do that?"

"Self-defense."

"What? You really are certifiably crazy, aren't you?"

"I don't know about the certifiable part. But just calm down for a minute and listen."

I don't say anything. And in a strange, irritating way, his calm tone is successfully defusing my angry, get-the-hell-off-my-lawn persona.

"Good. Are you alone?"

"Of course, I'm alone. Why wouldn't I be?"

"Because you're not in your apartment."

"Dammit! That's exactly what I mean. What gives you the right to spy on me? Who do you think you are?"

"If you'll just cut the histrionics and righteous indignation for a minute, maybe you'll understand my position. In case you've forgotten, Dakota, I'm on the run. I'm a fugitive. That means people are looking for me. Because of that, I have to take precautions."

"How is breaking into my apartment part of your precautions?"

"I had to make sure you weren't cooperating with the law."

"Whatever gave you the idea I'd be talking to the cops? And besides, I don't know your comings and goings. I don't know where you live. I don't even know how to get in touch with you. How could I possibly help them?"

"Please, do not play dumb, Dakota. Respect my intelligence the same way I respect yours. Look at it from my point of view. What's the biggest damn story you could have for your podcast?"

I don't say anything.

"I'll answer that. You help catch the infamous Francis Hoyt, that's what. Your ratings would go through the roof. You'd be on every goddamned talk show in the goddamn world, not to mention the front page of every newspaper."

"Boy, you really do think a lot of yourself, don't you? You think your capture will be worldwide news?"

He ignores the crack. And somehow, he manages to maintain that calm tone. Like he's the one in charge. Like he's the one who's been wronged.

"I went there to make sure I didn't find any signs of your co-operation. That's what I call self-defense."

I don't necessarily believe him, but he does make a point. It doesn't excuse his action, but maybe, if he's telling me the truth, and I'm finding out that's a rare commodity when it comes to Francis Hoyt, this passes as a believable explanation.

"Did you find what you were looking for?"

"I wouldn't be calling you if I had."

Which makes me wonder what he'd do if he had found signs of cooperation. I have a sneaking suspicion he wouldn't just chalk it up to a bad experience and walk away. That's not how he's wired.

Mark is indicating by twirling an index finger in the air that I should wrap up the call. I put up my hand, palm facing him, to slow him down. I've got the feeling I can actually use this to my advantage. Maybe now's the time to press for that sit-down with him. I grab a pad and quickly scribble down, *"I think I'm getting somewhere...patience,"* and slide it over to Mark.

"You do understand why I'm so upset, don't you, Francis?"

He hesitates a moment. "I guess."

What a dick!

"So, why are you calling? Would you like a rundown on what I plan to do with myself for the next few days?"

"You think sarcasm's gonna get what you want from me?"

"Let's get this straight. I don't want *anything* from you. I'm doing the series with or without your help. But you might consider this. Without you, I can pretty much say anything I want about you. But if you do the interview, you can at least get your side out..."

"What do you think my *side* is?"

"I don't know. Which is exactly why it's in your best interest to tell me. And the world."

He laughs. "The *world*? And you think I'm arrogant... What universe are you living in, sister?"

"It's figurative, not literal," I say, suddenly on the defensive when there's nothing to be defensive about. I realize how careful I have to be when dealing with this man, who'll take the slightest, slimmest opening as a weakness to be exploited.

"So, are you calling to tell me you're finally ready to set a date."

"Sure. Might as well get this thing over with."

I need to be more aggressive with him, try to take back any power I can, and so I say, "I'm pretty busy right now. I've got a bunch of editing to do and I'm starting to put together the hourly scripts. So, I need at least a week or so. Certainly not till after the holiday."

"That's fine. I'm sure you've got plenty to do after coming back from your trip."

Damn him. By bringing that up, he's planted a seed in my head, a seed that keeps asking exactly how much he knows. Does he know I've spoken with Charlie Floyd? Does he know we've interviewed Jersey cops? I don't know how he could possibly know all that. I mean, it's not like we've publicized what we've done and who we've seen. He couldn't even know that I've been in New York and Connecticut. He's just fishing, I tell myself. *Be cool, Dakota,* I tell myself. *Don't give him all the power.* But it's too late.

"July tenth," I say, as firmly as I can. "Place to be determined."

"No can do. How's the eleventh?"

Fuck! I know exactly what he's doing. He's always got to be in charge. But okay. So long as I've got a firm date, that's fine. Even if he is the one calling the shots.

"That's a Sunday. Won't you be in church?"

"Very funny."

"You got something else going on the tenth, Francis? Work, maybe?"

"I'll see you get a copy of my calendar for the month, Dakota. In the meantime, let's just say the morning of the eleventh. And I'll come up with a place."

"Make sure it's someplace very private, so we can have a nice chat, with no ambient noise to screw up the sound."

"Remember, just you and me. And if you can't handle that, I guess we'll have to call the whole thing off."

"Just so you know, Francis, threats don't cut it with me. Neither does intimidation. The worst-case scenario for me is I do this without you. If that happens, you'll have to live with whatever I say about you. If you're okay with that, so am I."

The conversation pretty much ends there. I can't quite remember who hangs up first, but I'd like to think it was me.

42

Francis

After watching snippets of the Macy's fireworks on the Hudson, I'm ready to set off fireworks of my own.

It's coming up on midnight and although the official July Fourth celebration is supposed to be over, I still hear the intermittent sounds of firecrackers (or gunshots) going off, punctuating the still night air as I make the forty-five-minute drive to the strip mall.

The five-day heatwave has broken and the temperature is hovering in the low 70s. Still hot for almost everyone except Angelinos who break out the heat lamps when the temperature drops to 70. It rained earlier in the day, but now the atmosphere has wrung itself out and the sky is partly cloudy. Perfect night for a little jog.

I take a couple loops around the area, keeping an eye out for cop cars, while I make sure there's nothing out of the ordinary going on. I find a spot to park on a quiet, tree-lined street about a mile from the strip mall.

I make sure I've got everything I need stashed in my pockets. I stretch for a couple minutes, take a few deep breaths, then begin my jog. I follow the route I've mapped out, which, avoiding any of the major avenues, takes me through a series of nondescript, suburban streets. It's a few minutes past two a.m., and all the houses on the route are dark. The only sound I hear is the occasional barking of a dog.

I don't have a watch on, but I know I've made good time. Probably arriving across from the mall in less than ten minutes from when I started. I stop across the street and stare at my target, now less than fifty yards across the avenue from me.

I'm wearing my black watch cap, black form-fitted sweatpants and a black hoodie, which I pull over my head before crossing the street. I crouch low and make my way through the parking area and to the back of the strip mall. I know exactly where the cameras are, so I avoid them.

I stop across from the back door to the jewelry shop, slip on my latex gloves, and finish off the half-pint bottle of water. I carefully wipe the bottle clean, from top to bottom, then toss it into a dumpster behind me.

There's not supposed to be anyone on guard duty after sunset, but I'm still careful. Once I'm sure I'm alone, I locate the keypad by the back door of the jewelry shop. I have the code, but instead of using it I pull out my smart phone, and using the information I've been provided, I interfere with the electronic signal and disable the lock. I take out my Swiss Army Knife to use to make several scratch marks on the keypad to make it look as if someone has tampered with the plate in order to get in. But before I can make my marks, I notice that the plate already shows a number of scratches. It seems a little odd, but it's possible they've come from normal wear and tear over time. Nevertheless, I add fresh scratches to the plate.

Once inside, I find myself in a small vestibule area. In front of me, there's a door I know leads to the staircase that'll take me down one floor to the vault room. It should be locked, but when I turn the handle, I find it's not secure. I wonder if it's the result of carelessness or maybe the door has purposely been left open in anticipation of my visit.

The stairs are unlit. I remove my small credit-card-sized LED flashlight and squeeze a spot on the bottom that turns it on. At the bottom of the stairs, there's the final obstacle, another door with a keypad. I punch in the code, push on the door, and it swings open. I flick off my flashlight and step inside the darkened vault room.

There's a light-switch on the wall to my left, and another one at the other end of the room, by the entrance to another stairway that leads directly to the jewelry shop above.

Before I flick on the lights, I reach under my shirt and remove a large nylon duffle bag that I've wrapped tightly around my body.

I flick on the light. It takes a split second for my eyes to adjust to the light. The huge room, thirty by forty feet, according to the blueprints, is suddenly bathed in light.

I'm shocked by what I see.

43
Dakota

It's a familiar voice on the other end. It takes me a second or two to realize who it is.

"Charlie? Charlie Floyd?"

"That's right."

I don't know quite what to say, so I say the obvious.

"What a surprise. What's up? Wait, that sounds incredibly rude. I mean, is there something you remembered you want to tell me?"

"More like something I think you forgot to tell me."

"Excuse me?"

"I think this is something we should discuss in person, Dakota."

"In person? But you're in Connecticut and I'm here."

"Well, as it turns out, we're in the same place. And since you're not in Connecticut, I must be in L-A."

"Oh, my God! You're kidding, right? I mean, this must be some kind of joke."

"No joke."

"Where exactly are you?"

"The Mondrian. You know it?"

"Of course. What...what are you doing out here?"

"Came to see you, Dakota."

"But..."

Mark hears me talking and comes out of his bedroom to join me in the living room. I'm sitting on the couch, so he takes a seat across from me in his favorite chair, a ratty, old upholstered rocker that used to be owned by his grandmother. It's a chair he refuses to give up, no matter how much I plead with him to do it. I even offer to buy a new chair for him, but no dice. I even fantasize about getting rid of it when he's out one day and replacing it with something that doesn't look like it was dragged in from the dump. Of course, I'd never do that. But it is fun thinking about it.

"Whatcha doing tomorrow morning?" Before I can answer, he says, "How's about breakfast? I'm buying."

I'm still in shock. I need time to think. "Will you please hold on a sec? I'll be right back."

"Sure thing, honey. I'm not going anywhere."

I mute the phone.

"Who is it?" Mark asks.

"Charlie Floyd."

"What's he want?"

"He's here. In L-A. He wants to talk to me. What should I do?"

"You're kidding. Ask him about what."

"I should ask?"

"Of course, you should. How else you gonna know?"

"What could he want?"

"The only way to find out is to ask."

"He wants to have breakfast with me."

"So, have breakfast with him, D. Maybe he's got a scoop on Hoyt he wants to share with you. Maybe that's why he's out here."

"He could have just told me on the phone, if that was it. He certainly wouldn't come all the way out to L-A."

Mark laughs. "You know, D, it's possible the world doesn't revolve around you. Could be he's out here to see family. Or friends. Or some other business."

I know Mark is talking, but I can't make sense out of any of the words. I'm way too distracted by my stomach, which is doing Olympic-style flip-flops.

"Jesus, Mark! No one makes a three-thousand-mile trip just to make a local call."

"Just ask him, Dakota. He's waiting on the line, isn't he?"

"Oh, yeah." I click back to him. "Sorry about that, Charlie. What was it you wanted to do?"

"Breakfast. Tomorrow. Eight A-M, Mondrian Hotel."

"Oh, yeah. Is it okay if I bring Mark?"

"I'd prefer you didn't. I need to talk to you alone."

"Ooohhh, you make this sound serious."

"Relax. I promise, nothing bad's gonna happen. Now remember..."

"Eight o'clock, Mondrian Hotel. Don't worry, I'm not senile. Yet."

As soon as I end the call, Mark is all over me.

"What's going on, Dakota?"

"I don't know. He wants to meet with me tomorrow morning."

"He didn't give a hint as to why?"

"Nope."

Mark gets up and begins pacing back and forth. Suddenly, Hemingway jumps into my lap. Normally, I'm glad to give him a little loving, but this is not the time. I grab him under his belly and gently place him on the floor.

"There's only one reason he's here."

"What's that?"

"He knows you've been in contact with Hoyt."

"How could he possibly know that?"

Mark sits back down. "D, he's been an investigator more than thirty years. I've never been a cop, but sitting there watching you, I knew something was up, didn't I?"

"I guess."

"No guessing about it. He's a fucking professional. He's probably grilled hundreds of people. Guys like him are skilled at reading suspects. I watched him. Even though we were doing the questioning, he was laser-focused on both of us. I think he figured out that at the very least you've been in touch with Hoyt…"

"Do you think there's any chance he knows we've met?"

"I don't know how he could know that. But it doesn't matter. My guess is that's what he wants to talk to you about."

"What should I do?"

"Keep the appointment. And if that's what it's about, tell him everything. And then, let him figure out where to go from there. But if you do tell everything, don't forget to include that you'll be interviewing Hoyt face to face. And then listen to what he has to say."

"What if he wants to ambush Francis?"

"I'd be surprised if he doesn't. It's up to you how you handle it, but I highly recommend you know what your endgame is."

This sounds like good advice. Trouble is, I have no idea what my endgame is. I know Mark's right. This is officially out of control now. I've been counting on that face-to-face interview for more than a month now. Only now Charlie and Mark are dragging me back into the real world. I have to start thinking about consequences. That's not something I'm good at.

I know I'll have trouble sleeping tonight. Mark had his doctor prescribe a small amount of Ambien in case he couldn't sleep on our trip east. I ask if he has any left.

He does.

The next thing I know, it's seven o'clock in the morning and Mark is gently shaking me awake.

44

Francis

What. The. Fuck.

The goddamn room looks like it's been hit by a fucking tornado. Vault doors are wide open. Papers are strewn all over the floor. It looks like someone took a pickaxe to the lockers. Chunks of the metal doors litter the room, along with torn money wrappers. Holes have been drilled into all the six-foot lockers, and locks have been virtually torn out.

What. The. Fuck.

I make a quick pass around the room and find there's absolutely nothing of valuable left to take. It's one, big, fat fucking mess, and it doesn't take a fucking genius to figure out I've been had. And the longer I stick around, the worse it's gonna be.

I'm inside no more than five minutes, tops. Even that's too much. But I can't help it. I'm frozen in place while my mind is racing.

This is not something I ever imagined, so I have no idea what to do. I know one thing for sure: Sticking around here is definitely not good for my health.

At first, this seems random and illogical, since no one but me knows tonight's the night I planned to get it done. And then I realize it's very possible Vince, or whoever's behind this stunt, could probably pick up cues from what I've said or done that might have indicated this is the weekend I planned to do the job, using the holiday as a perfect cover. And then I remember that time, a few days ago, when I thought someone was watching me. That I was being followed. I should have fucking listened to that little voice in my head, dammit!

The job isn't very subtle, but it doesn't have to be. This is no coincidence. The tables have been turned on me and now I'm the fucking patsy.

My head is spinning. I need to settle down. I need to find someplace safe where I can think this out. I've got some time, but not much. This mess won't be discovered for at least five or six hours, which is when the jewelry store will reopen. So, I've got till then to figure out my next step.

Right now, I have to get the hell out of here.

When I get outside it's eerily quiet, just the opposite of all the noise banging around in my head. I press my body against the building, as if that's going to make me disappear into the concrete, and take several deep breaths. I need to get back to the car, as soon as possible. I scan the area to see if anyone's around. If they followed me before, there's no reason they aren't doing it again. But I don't see anything out of the ordinary. The parking area is still empty, and road traffic is pretty much non-existent.

I start to jog. I'm hoping this will settle the noise in my head. But it doesn't. It gets louder. And louder. I need it to stop and so I concentrate on the sound of my feet striking the road, the beating of my heart. Suddenly, I remember the chant I learn a few years back when I decide to attend a few Buddhism classes. *Aum mani padme hum.* I repeat it over and over again and soon, it aligns with the beating of my heart and the sound of my footfalls until they all merge and become one.

By the time I reach the car, the racket in my head has quieted down and I'm able to think more clearly. Suddenly, that guy from the pier makes sense. It's likely he's on someone's payroll, hired to keep an eye on me. It should have been a red flag. I should've pulled out right then and there. But I didn't. The milk is already spilled. Now all I can do is try to clean it up.

I know one thing for sure: I'm the patsy. But the question is, whose patsy am I?

Is Vince behind this? Ferrera, who gives orders from behind bars? Someone else? Someone I don't even know?

I realize I don't have to sort this out now. What I do have to do is figure out what I do next. Where do I go?

Other than whoever's behind this, no one knows I've been there. Unless…Unless there were cameras, I wasn't aware of. I try to keep my face covered at all times, but it's still possible that from some angle parts of my face were visible. Right now, I'm not going to think about that. I'm going on the assumption that I'm just an anonymous figure.

I realize there's no reason for me to deviate from my original after-plan.

This early in the morning, it's a few minutes short of two-thirty a.m., and there aren't many vehicles on the road. I hop into the car and head toward El Segundo, between the airport and Playa del Rey, just south of Santa Monica, specifically to the Ballona Wetlands Ecological Reserve. I stop when I reach the intersection of Jefferson and Lincoln. To the west is a barren area known as the Ballona Creek. To the north are the wetlands, bordered by Ballona Creek. No houses, no strip malls, no car dealerships. Only grassland leading to the Pacific.

I pull the car onto the grasslands, get out, open the trunk, remove the container of gas, douse the car in it, take a few steps back, light a match, then flick it onto a small pool of gasoline a couple feet from the car.

Varoom! The fumes from the gasoline light up the night sky and the flame travels rapidly snake toward the car. Within seconds the Honda, engulfed in flames, is nothing more than a giant bonfire.

I watch for a moment or two, hypnotized by the flames shooting toward the sky.

When I'm finally able to disengage, I start jogging toward

East Jefferson, where I'll call a cab and head back to my place. It's there that I'll try to figure out my next move.

45

Dakota

When I arrive at the Mondrian, Charlie's already at a table, his face hidden by a copy of *The New York Times*.

I check my watch. Dammit! I'm ten minutes late.

"I'm so, so sorry. I got a late start," I say, as I pull out a chair and sit facing him. "I'm a mess," I add, running my hand through my hair. Since I keep it short for a reason, less maintenance, I know this is simply a nervous tic. And I am nervous, that's for sure.

"Never complain, never explain," Charlie says, with a bright smile on his face. "It's okay, Honey. My time clock's totally out of whack, so I've been up for hours. Besides, I've got nothing better to do."

"Oh, I'm sure you have plenty. Like what brings you out here, for instance."

Damn! Why couldn't I just let him ease into it? I'm trying to come off as nonchalant and clueless as I can. But as soon as the words come out of my mouth, I know that's not working very well.

"You," he says, as he folds up the newspaper and lays it on the chair next to him so it leans up against his cream-colored cowboy hat. "What's your pleasure?"

"Excuse me?"

"Food. Breakfast. Remember, it's on me. What'll you have?"

I feel like such an idiot. Of course, that's what he meant. *Nervous much, Dakota? Calm down, before you give yourself an anxiety attack,* something I haven't had since those early days back on the Albany paper.

"I'm not really that hungry."

"My grandma always use to say, breakfast is the most important meal of the day. You're not gonna make a liar out of my grandma, are you? 'Cause if you are, I gotta warn ya, there's a good chance she'll jump right outta her grave and get all over you. She was a lovely woman, but tough as a barrel of nails."

I can't help smiling, which makes me realize that this is why he's so good at what he does. He knows how to put the other person at ease.

I give in and order coffee and an English muffin. But before the waitress can leave, he jumps in. "Let's add a plate of scrambled eggs with a side of bacon. This young woman needs as much protein as she can get."

Once she leaves, I can no longer contain myself.

"So, how long are you going to keep me in suspense?"

"I'm guessing you've figured out my being out here isn't a coincidence."

I nod my head, yes.

He takes a sip of coffee, leaving me stranded with my thoughts. Man, he's good. He's going to make me break the silence. Well, I'm here. No use not playing along.

"It's about Francis Hoyt, right?"

His eyebrows rise, his forehead wrinkles. But his mouth remains shut.

"How long are you going to torture me?"

He smiles. "As long as it takes."

"Okay, okay." I throw up my hands in a gesture of giving up or giving in. "Uncle. Uncle. That's the word you use when you give up, right?"

A quick image of one of my brothers pinning me to the floor, while yelling, "Say it! Say Uncle." And only when I do does he slap the floor three times with his open hand, officially counting me out and then leaping up, hands high in the air, doing a little victory dance.

"You're a very smart woman, Dakota."

"Well, thanks. This is the softening me up part, right?"

"My wife taught me that."

"What?"

"The woman thing. Not calling you a girl."

"Well, thank you for that, too."

"And because you're a smart woman you know that I know you're holding something back."

"Like?"

"You tell me."

The waitress arrives with my order. She sets down a plate of scrambled eggs, English muffin, and a side order of bacon. The only thing she brings to Charlie is a fresh cup of coffee.

The sight of the food starts to turn my stomach, but despite this, I put on a happy face.

"Hey, I thought you said breakfast is the most important meal. I think I've been hoodwinked!"

"I didn't lie. It is. With the time change, I just don't know what meal I'm supposed to be eating."

I pick up one half of the English muffin, spread butter on it, then way too much jelly. Without tasting them, I sprinkle salt and pepper on my eggs.

I look up to see Charlie smiling.

"What are you smiling about?"

"Just wondering how long you're gonna put this off."

"Oh, jeez. All right. Yes, I've been in touch with Francis Hoyt. Or rather, he's been in touch with me. Is that what you want to hear?"

And so, I'm off and running. I tell him everything, holding nothing back. Every detail. Even the promise Hoyt's given me for an interview. Charlie does not interrupt once. I ramble on for what's probably ten minutes, but it seems much longer. By the time I finish, he knows everything and oddly enough, I feel better. It's like I've been to confession and I'm not even Catholic. I wonder if that's how Catholics feel after confessing their sins? Not that anything I've done is a sin, of course.

Finally, when I'm done, I have this strange out-of-body experience. It's as if I'm on the ceiling, looking down on us. I'm lightheaded and I feel like any moment I'm going to fall and crash into the table, making a spectacle of myself for the entire restaurant.

"Well, aren't you going to say anything?"

"What would you like me to say?"

"You didn't come all the way out here to hear my confession. You're good enough to have gotten it over the phone…"

"Probably. But it woulda taken me a lot longer. And would've been a lot less fun. Besides, I'm not here just to get a confession."

"Then why else?"

"To make sure you're okay. This isn't a game, Dakota. You know what they say about playing with fire."

I don't know what to say, so I say nothing. Neither does he. I move the eggs around my plate with my fork, separating them into two mounds. Finally, I break the awkward silence.

"So, what do you want me to do?"

"You know darn well what I want you to do. I want you to help me catch Francis Hoyt."

"How do you expect me to do that?"

"Not sure yet. But I think if the two of us put our heads together, we can figure something out."

46
Francis

Crazy scenarios are colliding in my head. In the end, they all lead to one conclusion. I've been had. And had good.

This is no coincidence. It's a well-planned hit on the vault that will now result in laying the blame on me. That's probably why Capowitz kept pressing me for the timing of the job. But it also explains that tail I spotted.

In the end, it doesn't take a fucking genius to figure out a good time to go would be the July Fourth weekend. And it doesn't matter if it's Friday, Saturday or Sunday. Everything's shut down for the holiday weekend, which means no one will see there's a break-in till later this morning. Meanwhile, I need to get off by myself to figure things out and decide what my next step will be.

By the time the cab drops me off a couple blocks from my cottage, it's closing in on five a.m. Even if I want to sleep, and I don't, there's no way that's happening. I'm much too amped. And I don't have the luxury of time. By noon, word will be out that the vault's been hit and Francis Hoyt is the one who pulled off the job. That means every two-bit crook and wannabe bad guy in town'll be on the lookout for me. Not only will they be looking for the loot, but I'm sure there's already a price on my head.

First thing I have to get past is blaming myself. There's no way I could have seen this coming. Or if I could have, I certainly can't think of it now. The questions running through my head are a waste of time right now—questions like, why didn't I see this coming? What did I miss? Why the fuck did I say yes in the first place?

Still, I can't help replaying every meeting with Capowitz, trying to see if I missed any red flags. Had I ignored any voices in my head that were warning me not to do it? The answer keeps coming up, "No." Was Capowitz really that good? Was he part of the scam? Or was he also a mark, as much a victim as I am?

In the end, it doesn't matter. As far as I'm concerned, he's the one taking the fall. All I want is to find that fucking son of a bitch and rip his fucking heart out. I know that won't fix anything. I know now's not the time. But I promise you, the time will come. Right now, self-preservation is at the top of my list.

First thing, I need to get the hell out of L.A. Now that I'm running from the mob *and* the cops, I have to get lost.

I call up a map of California on my phone and search for possible destinations. I don't want to be too far from L.A., because I'll need to take care of business here. But far enough away that I feel safe. Eventually, I focus on Santa Barbara, a town less than a hundred miles up the coast.

Once the decision is made, I pack up everything that fits comfortably into a backpack and the same nylon duffle bag that was going to hold the loot from the heist.

I do a last-minute cleanup of the apartment, erasing any sign that I've ever been there. I bleach and wipe down every surface, especially the bathroom and what passes for a kitchen. Anything I'm not taking with me, gets trashed. And then I bid adios to what has been my home for several months. I call a cab to take me to the bus depot, where I'll catch a ride to Santa Barbara.

47

Charlie

I know Hoyt has an angle in agreeing to cooperate with Dakota's podcast—this man does nothing without a plan—I'm just not sure what it is.

One thing I do know is that he's a world-class narcissist. But he's also smart as hell and he does nothing unless it benefits him. It's not about making himself more famous. He doesn't give a shit about the general public knowing who he is. He doesn't want his name splashed across the front pages of every tabloid in the country. What he does want is the respect and admiration of his peers and people like me who are trying to catch him and put him away. He wants to beat us. He *needs* to prove he's smarter and better than we are. With him, it's all about winning. And, if he's not winning, he becomes a very dangerous man.

But all winning streaks eventually come to an end. We almost got him last time. And now, thanks to Dakota Richards and her podcast, I've got another shot at him. It's a shot I don't want to screw up.

"You've got a date to meet with him, right?" I ask, finishing off what must be my fourth cup of coffee.

"Sort of. I mean, he's perfectly capable of changing it at the last minute. Or even calling it off."

"That's okay. As of now, we'll assume he's going to keep it.

Once you establish the place, we're all set."

I know what's coming because I can see her squirming in her seat. Her cute, freckled face is tighter than a drum. I can ask her what's wrong, but I already know what it is.

"You know, Charlie, to tell you the truth, I have to say I feel a little strange about this."

Here it comes.

"The Judas thing?"

She looks up, surprised.

"Look, Dakota, I pegged you right away as smart and talented. That was easy. But I also pegged you as a good person, someone with a conscience. Someone who wants to do the right thing. That's a good thing. In my world, it's a rare thing. But sometimes, in the real world, it gets in the way."

"I think maybe it has," she says softly.

"I hope you don't mind my giving you a little lecture."

I don't bother waiting for her permission."

"When you've had as much experience as I've had with bad guys, it can warp your ability to distinguishing good from evil. If you don't check yourself, you can easily wind up thinking everyone's bad. That everyone has an angle and is trying to get over on the rest of us. In my line of work, most people I come across do just that. And to be honest, it's not always that much different for the guys on my side of the law. Pretty much everyone starts out wanting to do the right thing, the good thing, but after a while you start to make deals with yourself. You compromise your conscience, your value system. And when it gets to that point, you start making excuses. After a while, you get good at rationalizing some questionable decisions. And if you don't think lawmen...and women"—she smiles when I add her gender—"don't sometimes cross the line, you'd be dead wrong. I'm not talking about crooked cops. That's a whole other thing. I'm talking about the good guys who will do anything and everything they can to bring whoever they're after to justice. Sometimes, that means bending the rules, even breaking them. I'd be lying if I didn't admit to doing that occasionally. It's not something I'm proud of. But it's the God's honest truth. And when you do, you somehow convince yourself it's for the larger good. The longer you're in the game, the better at it you get."

"What does this have to do with me?"

"Being around that kind of thing most of my adult life makes me sensitive to people's motives, and what's here," I tap my heart. "You, Dakota, whether you know it or not, and I suspect you do, are one of the good ones. And the good ones don't cross that line easily. You feel guilty. Even though the person you'd be betraying is someone who doesn't deserve your loyalty. But if you think Francis Hoyt would think twice about screwing you over, throwing you to the wolves, or using you for his own selfish gains, you'd be sadly mistaken."

I see tears at the corners of her eyes.

"See? This is exactly what I mean," I say, handing her an unused napkin.

"What?"

"You're starting to tear up. And I know it's not about Hoyt. You know who he is. You know what he's done. It's about you. You don't want to think of yourself as someone who could betray another person, no matter how bad they are."

"How do you know it's not just because I'm afraid?"

"Because I know the difference between fear and conscience."

48
Dakota

I am now, perhaps for the first time in my life, part of the solution, not the problem.

Charlie Floyd makes a persuasive case for me to cooperate to bring down Francis Hoyt. At first, I'm reluctant. Before I figure out why that is, Charlie gives me an easy out. He says I don't want to betray a "source." He's right, of course. But he's also right when he talks me down from the ledge. I don't owe Hoyt anything and he isn't worth my loyalty. Look at the way he's treated me. Breaking into my apartment like he did is a form of terrorism. And who knows what else he might have in mind for me? Why should I worry about betraying a man capable of doing something as horrible as that?

So, we make a deal. As soon as the arrangements are made as to where and when I'll be interviewing Hoyt, I'll tell Charlie and he'll make sure the authorities are there to make the arrest.

"He's really, really smart, Charlie," I say. "If he has the slightest suspicion..."

Charlie smiles and I realize how ridiculous I sound. Like I'm telling him something he doesn't already know.

He reaches across the table and gently pats my hand. At many times of my life, I would consider that to be a patronizing gesture, but at this particular moment, it's welcome. It calms me. It reassures me. It makes me feel protected. And the funny thing is, I think it's something he does without even thinking about it. It's just who he is.

We plot the best way to approach this without making Hoyt suspicious.

"The most important thing is that you don't appear overanxious. The best advice I can give you," he says, "is to make believe we never had this conversation. Treat him the way you would have treated him last week. If you can do that, you'll do fine, because it'll appear natural. You may doubt you can do it, but I don't."

"Are you saying I'm a good liar?"

He laughs. "I'd have to ask your boyfriend about that."

"At the moment, that would be impossible, since I don't have one."

"Then asking Mark will do," he says, and I think I see him wink. "Speaking of Mark, the fewer people who know about this plan of ours, the better."

"You want me to lie to Mark?"

"No. I want you to not mention it to Mark."

"Withholding information is just another form of lying, you know."

"We can sit here and split hairs, Dakota, but if we're going to pull this off, no one but us has to know. In the long run, it'll be easier on you because you won't have to remember who knows and who doesn't. All I'm asking is for you to pretend this conversation never took place. You were anxious to have this interview before we talked, so you'll be anxious now. But for a different reason."

"Mark knows I'm here with you."

"I'm sure you can concoct what we spoke about. Here's a tip. Make it as close to what we're actually talking about as you can. Just leave out the important part. The part about snagging Hoyt."

By the time we part, I'm in a pretty good place. With Charlie on my side, I'm feeling confident I can pull it off.

I've already established the date of our interview; now all I need is the time and place. I figure as it gets closer—it's five days away at this point, a few days after the holiday weekend—there's no reason why I can't text the cell number Hoyt has given me and try to pin him down. Like Charlie, Hoyt seems to be a human lie detector—they've got that much in common. So, dealing with him by text, where he can't pick up anything in my voice, should make it easier.

When I get back to Mark's, he's in his office writing. I knock on the half-open door, just to let him know I'm back.

"How'd it go?" he asks, swiveling around in his chair.

"Great."

"Anything I should know?"

I shake my head. "Nope."

"Why's he in L-A?"

"Visiting one of his daughters." Oh, my. Look how easy it is for me to lie.

"So, why did he want to see you?"

"Because I'm irresistible, of course."

He laughs, "True," he says, turning back to his computer. "I'm kinda on a roll here," he says.

"Then I'll leave you be. I think I'll take a short run and then hit the gym for a bit." I pat my belly. "You're much too good a cook and I think I've put on a pound or two since I moved in."

He laughs. "Yeah, right. So, I'll see you when I see you."

Mark is great. He never pushes. And for this, I'm so grateful.

Later that afternoon, as I'm leaving the gym, which does help to relieve a little stress, I text Francis.

Hey, just wondering if you've come up with a time and place for our interview later next week. I need to get my shit together. You can just text me.

I know he won't do that. He'll call, because he won't want to have a written record of the information he's going to give me.

Now, all I have to do is wait.

As if that's going to be easy.

49

Francis

Word travels quickly.

I'm not in Santa Barbara proper, but a place called Carpinteria, about fifteen miles south of Santa Barbara. I've checked into the Sandpiper Lodge, paying for a week in advance. After that, we'll see. I don't have a car, so the first thing I do after I settle in is buy a bicycle off Craig's List. For the moment, it'll have to do. It's portable, and I won't be calling attention to myself.

I haven't even had time to unpack, which consists of my emptying the contents of my duffle bag and sticking my clothing into drawers, when I get a call on a burner I use for a number of professional business contacts. It's Artie.

"What the fuck did you do, Francis?"

"Jesus Christ! What the fuck? Is it on the fucking six o'clock news?"

"Might as well be. Although you know as good as me that if news like this ever does get picked up by the media... Well, I don't have to tell you about that. You're in deep enough shit, as is."

"So, what's the deal? How bad is it?"

"Fucking bad. I mean, who goes out and fucks over the mob? What. The. Fuck. I mean, to tell the truth, nothing you do would surprise me, Francis. Except for this. Did you have some kind of fucking brain stroke?"

"Not that it matters, but it wasn't me."

"Guys like these don't make mistakes, Francis. The truth is, it don't matter if it was you or not. They *think* it's you and that's more than enough to get you iced."

"I know. I know." My mind is racing a mile a minute. I know I'm in deep shit. Artie doesn't have to tell me that. The question is, how'm I gonna get out of it? And the bigger question on my mind right now is, can Artie be of any help?

"Listen, Artie. I did a stupid thing, but not the stupid thing you think I did. But that's water under the bridge. I just have to figure out how to take care of this."

"I hope you've dug yourself a giant hole and you're hiding in it now, because you've got every two-bit hitman on the West Coast looking for you. But you should be more afraid of the fucking amateurs. That bounty they're offering appeals to every asshole in the country. And it won't be long before there'll be more mob guys coming out there than there are wetbacks swimming across the Rio Grande. And what makes it even worse is that they don't want you hit. They want you brought back alive, so they can get back whatever you took. And then you don't have to use your imagination to figure out what's next."

"I told you. I didn't take a damn thing. When I got there the place had already been cleaned out."

"But you were there?"

"Yeah. I was there. I was the one who was supposed to do the job."

"And someone beat you to it?"

"I'm guessing the people who hired me are the ones who did it. And guess what, Artie?"

"What?"

"The guy who set me up, the one who got me involved in the first place, is none of than your fucking friend, Vince Capowitz."

"Vince? Vince is the guy who hired you? And by the way, just to set the record straight, he's not a friend. He's an acquaintance. I don't got friends like that. But how do you know he's the one behind this?"

Was Vince set up by someone else? Or was it all his idea? Eventually, I'll find out. One way or another. Right now, it doesn't matter who was behind it. What matters is that I get myself the fuck out of it. The question is, how? I need a plan. And I need it quick.

"I don't know if he's the brains, or just the frontman. Right now, that's not at the top of my to-do list. Look, Artie, I want you to do me a favor."

"What kind of favor?"

"I want you to put out the word that I've been set up. That I didn't do it, but that I'm gonna find out who did."

This is a lie. I'm not gonna waste my time playing Sherlock Holmes. Eventually, I'll figure it out and take care of it. Right now, my priority is to get myself off the hook. To give myself breathing room. Artie putting out the word is a good first step. If nothing else, it'll put some doubt in the mind of whoever's looking for me.

"I don't know, Francis…It's not the best time to be associated with you. In fact, it's probably not a good idea I should even be talking to you now."

"You fucking owe me, Artie. And if you don't help me out, so help me God, you're gonna regret it. You know me, Artie. You know what the fuck I'm capable of. And you know there's no such thing as forgetting when it comes to Francis Hoyt."

There's a moment of silence. Then, "Yes, Francis. I know. And you're right. We go way back. And if you say you didn't do it, then you didn't do it. I mean, in all these years I've never known you not to take credit for something you did. I also know there's no way you're dumb enough to try something like this."

"I gotta go, Artie. But I want you to start working the phones. Now!"

"I'll do my best, Francis."

"I don't want to hear about your best, Artie. Just do it, Man. Just. Fucking. Do. It."

After I get off with Artie, I need to take a walk, because

that's when I do my best thinking.

I'm unfamiliar with the area, having been by here only once, years ago, when I took the train from San Francisco to San Diego. It's a scenic ride down the Pacific, and Santa Barbara is one of the wealthier enclaves in Southern California. At least it was, until Silicon Valley made millionaires of kids who had only a few years earlier relied upon Mom and Pop for their allowance.

I walk aimlessly, with no particular destination in mind, other than eventually winding up back at the Sandpiper. Every so often, I plug my iPod into my ears, hoping Motown or a little Nirvana will prime the pump and ideas will flow out.

After logging in a few miles, just as I'm ready to turn around and head back, it comes to me. It's a longshot, but if it works, maybe it'll take the heat off. At least for a while, until I can come back to L.A. and shake some answers from Vince Capowitz, who more and more is looking like he's the key to cleaning up this mess.

50
Dakota

It's a tossup as to who's more jittery, me or Hemingway. Both of us are out of our usual environment and neither of us can do much about it. Between the two of us, I'd have to say he's handling it better than I am. But then he can take refuge in a closet while I have to remain in plain sight.

What adds to my stress level is I have to keep Mark totally in the dark. I can't even look him in the eye because I'm sure that if I do, he'll see right through me. Every time I say more than a few words, I'm sure he's picking up in my voice that something's wrong.

So, I try to avoid him as much as I can, which isn't easy in a two-bedroom apartment of about twelve-hundred square feet. Remarkably, Mark doesn't seem to notice any difference. Or, if he does, he isn't saying anything about it. I chalk it up to all the work he's doing. Not only is he helping put together our first couple of episodes, but he's also trying to meet a deadline for his next novel.

He's very sweet. He knows I'm stressed and so every so often he emerges from his lair, finds me wherever I'm nesting, puts his hand on my shoulder and asks if everything's okay. Do I need anything? At first, this makes me feel good, that someone cares. But then it starts to backfire a little when I start to hate myself for suddenly being so needy.

The plan Charlie Floyd and I, mostly Charlie, work out is simple. I'm to text Francis and push him for the time and location of our interview, which is now only a couple days away. The trick is, I can't appear to be too anxious. But how the heck can you show nonchalance in a text?

My nerves are building. We're supposed to meet tomorrow and I still haven't heard from Francis. It's now late in the afternoon and so far, I've successfully put off texting him by making lame bargains with myself. It reminds me of a story Mark once told me. He said that when he was in his early twenties, back before email was a thing and he wanted to call a girl for a date, he had a ritual.

"I'm embarrassed to admit it, Dakota, but I was so shy and so scared of rejection, I'd pace back and forth literally for hours before I'd make the call. I'd rehearse what I was going to say, over and over again."

"You're kidding."

"God's honest truth. I couldn't trust what might come out of my mouth and my biggest fear was I'd sound like such a dork. So, I'd pace the little apartment I had in Hell's Kitchen and I'd promise myself, *Okay, I'll call at three P-M*. Three P-M would arrive and I'd say to myself, *what a stupid time to call. I'll just wait another hour. Maybe two...* And then that time would come and I'd say, *It's dinnertime. No one wants to get in a call in the middle of dinner*. Anyway, you get the point."

I didn't then, but I sure do now. Especially since I find myself setting similar deadlines that come and go.

This time I swear I'm just about to do it when my phone starts vibrating in my hand. No caller I.D. tips me off that it's Francis because he uses a series of burner phones. But as soon as I read the text, I know it's him.

We're still on for tomorrow.

Oh, my God. Deus ex machina. The hand of the gods! He's the one pressing for the interview. I text right back.

You bet.

Two simple words. You and bet. He can't possibly read anything into that, can he? I mean, he doesn't have the superpower of reading minds, does he?

I sit there, staring at the phone, waiting for his next text. My stomach is doing flip-flops. I try to tell myself to calm down, but it's not working. I take deep breaths. I'm just hoping Mark stays in his office, writing. I know if he comes out now and sees me in this condition, he'll know something's up.

Finally, after what seems like forever but is really more like three or four minutes, Francis texts back.

Let's talk. Half hour.

His message might as well be *You've won the lottery for ten million dollars! We'll be delivering it to your door within the hour.*

I make myself wait a couple minutes before I text back. *Sure!* I stare at it several seconds before pressing send and before I do I go back and delete the exclamation point, because I don't want to seem overanxious.

I take the phone into the spare bathroom and close the door. I punch in Charlie Floyd's number. I know it's stupid, but I don't want to take the chance Mark will walk into the room and overhear my conversation.

"He's gonna call in the next half hour," I say, my voice cracking slightly.

"Great. You okay?"

"No."

"Good. You're not supposed to be. Just do it the way we rehearsed, Dakota," he says in a soothing voice that works. "Let him take the lead. Let him set everything up. But don't just accept it without some kind of push back."

"You want me to, like, negotiate?"

"If you accept it too readily, he'll know something's up."

"How should I do that?"

He laughs. "Dakota, Honey, you're a smart, capable woman. I don't have to lay out how to play it. I have enough confidence in you to know that you'll be fine. Remember, we're gonna make it so we're not already there when you start. We'll have eyes on you, but we'll wait until you're finished before we pounce."

"Oh, God, you make it sound so...so F-B-I-ish."

"J. Edgar's busy, so it'll just me and the local authorities. But you're in good hands. It's not like we've never done this before. Just be yourself, do your job, and we'll take care of the rest. Now get the heck off the line! The last thing we want him to find is when he calls you that you're on already on the phone."

"Why did he wait till the last minute to call?"

"Because he wants to give you as little time as possible to set him up. And let me warn you. I wouldn't be surprised if you get a last-minute text with a change in plans."

"Oh, my. What do I do if that happens?"

"You don't have to do anything. We're putting a tracker on your car. We'll know exactly where you are all the time."

"Do you think he suspects anything?"

"I'm sure he spends his life suspecting everything and everyone, Dakota. But at some point, he either has to trust you or cut bait. For some reason, this interview is as important to him as it is to you. So, I wouldn't worry about that too much."

"Okay. Okay. I'll get back to you when it's over," I say.

But I know it won't be over. It's just the beginning.

51
Dakota

"Where are you?"

His question puts me off-balance, and I hesitate a fraction of a second before answering.

"What difference does that make?"

"You're not in your apartment," he says, an accusation more than a mere statement of fact.

"That's right. And you know why. Because of you! That was a horrible thing to do." I'm trying to remain calm, but I can feel the anger building in my voice. "I'm not sure if I can ever go back there."

"Toughen up, Girlie."

My first reaction is, *Fuck you!* But I hear the imaginary voice of Charlie Floyd in my head, telling me to stay cool. That's certainly how he'd handle this. Unlike him, I haven't had years of experience to fall back on. And so, I decide the only way to handle this is to be stern yet not defensive.

"Are you purposely trying to be as obnoxious as you can? Or does it come naturally?"

"We can turn this conversation into a brawl, or we can get down to business. Up to you," he says. And suddenly I realize how similar Francis and Charlie are. Not only are they great at what they do, but they've learned how control themselves. It's like those yogis who can control their breathing to such an extent that it appears as if they've passed over to another world.

I take a deep breath, then exhale slowly.

"Have you chosen a place yet for our interview?"

"Hope you don't mind traveling."

"I have a car, if that's what you're asking."

"Santa Barbara. Ever been there?"

"Sure. Is that where you are now?"

"It doesn't matter where I am now, it's where I'm going to be tomorrow afternoon. Two o'clock. You know where Shoreline Park is?"

"I can find it. What then?"

"You'll find out when you get close."

"Why can't you tell me now?"

"You ask too many damn questions. You want to queer the whole deal?"

"No."

"Then just do what I tell you. Do you remember the rules?"

"I do."

"Repeat them, please."

I feel like I'm back in grade school, asked by my math teacher to "show" my work. "Come alone. Bring only your recording equipment."

"Good. Wear shorts and a T-shirt."

"That's a new one. What if it gets cold by the water? Can I bring a sweater?"

"You can bring one, but remember, I'll be checking you and everything you have with you. And get one of those kids' transparent backpacks. If you break the rules, it's over. If you try to pull a fast one, it's over. If I see anything out of the ordinary, it's over. Understand?"

"Yes. I understand."

"You'll have exactly one hour, so if I were you, I'd be prepared."

"I'm always prepared," I snap. "But I'll need more than an hour. What if we meet an hour earlier?"

"Two o'clock. Sharp. You're even five minutes late, I'm out of there."

"Why can't we meet closer to L-A? With traffic, it might take me as much as two hours, maybe more, to get up there."

"Then I'd plan to leave a little earlier."

"You're not making this easy for me."

"It's not supposed to be easy. Look, I'm doing you a favor. Oh, and one more thing."

"Yes?"

"Relax. This is gonna be fun."

"I doubt it. And before you hang up, do you really think I'm going to mess things up by turning you in?"

"Do you really think I got where I am today by trusting people?"

52
Charlie

"Good work."

Dakota is on the line. She's reporting how her call went with Hoyt. She's nervous, I'm excited. Suddenly, after more than a year, I'm only one degree away from him. And this time, if things go according to plan, he won't get away.

"Thanks. I can't tell you how nervous I was. I was afraid I was going to blow it."

"But you didn't."

"What's next?"

"Just follow his instructions."

"What are you going to do? How's it going to work?"

"Trust me, Dakota, the less you know the better. Anything you know will wind up betraying you and if I tell you what the plan is, you'll be even more nervous. You'll look for things. You'll anticipate things. Somehow, you'll give it away. I want you to go into this as if we'd never spoken. Act exactly as you would without me in the picture. If you do it my way, you won't be looking over your shoulder. Because if you do that, he's going to pick up on it and we're done."

"What do you think he'll do?"

"If you're asking me if I think you're in any danger, I don't. Francis Hoyt's a lot of things, a lot of bad things, but he's not violent without reason. There's just no reason for violence aimed at you, unless you give him a reason. He's not about to screw everything up by being vindictive. Or looking for physical retribution. This doesn't mean he's a man who likes to keep score, a man who at the very least likes to even the score, but not with someone like you. Francis Hoyt always has an angle. He's not giving you this interview out of the goodness of his heart. There's a reason. We just don't know what it is. But for our purposes, it doesn't matter. Just follow his instructions and don't worry about anything else."

I hope I'm as good at convincing myself as I am at convincing Dakota. I don't know of a plan yet that hasn't, at least in some small way, gone awry. But telling her that will only make things worse.

"Sounds like good advice."

"It is good advice," I assure her, and I can tell by her voice, which has lost the slight tremor it had earlier, that she really is calming down.

"Anything else? I mean, do you want me to contact you somehow if he changes anything? He's capable of that, right?"

"He is. But we're in the twenty-first century, Honey. We'll have eyes on him and you."

"You mean, like drones?"

I smile. "Possibly. Remember, no details."

"I'm still nervous."

"Difference is, now you've got it under control. Besides, if you didn't, that's when I'd start to worry. Good luck."

"Gee, I hope I don't need it."

"It never hurts."

Once I get off the phone with Dakota, I contact the L.A. sheriff's office and they contact the Santa Barbara police. A few minutes later, I get a call from a Santa Barbara detective named Kenny O'Brian. I catch him up on what's happening, giving him all the information Dakota has given me. I tell him I'll be driving up there later this afternoon and that we can meet then and make a plan. I can tell he's excited, but I can also tell by the questions he asks that he's someone I can trust.

I grab lunch at the hotel coffee shop, then hop in my little yellow rental and head up the coast to Santa Barbara. I try to take my own advice and just enjoy the scenery as I cruise up the Pacific Highway.

If things go according to plan, I'll be on the redeye back to JFK tomorrow evening.

53

Francis

I haven't ridden a bike since the last time I stole one as a teenager, so I take it out for a practice spin. Turns out it's true. Riding a bicycle is one of those skills you never forget.

Using my newfound form of transportation, I take an early morning ride through Santa Barbara, making sure I include Montecito, which is only four miles outside the city. It's here that the wealthiest people in the area live, like Oprah, who spent fifty million dollars on her home.

When all this blows over, this might not be a bad place to settle for a while, I tell myself.

During my tour of the area, I stumble upon Shoreline Park. Turns out to be a perfect spot to meet with Dakota. It's wide open, so I'll have a good view of anything coming and going. And, with our backs to the ocean, anyone who comes at us will have to come from the east, making them an easy target to spot. As I pedal through the neighborhood, a plan starts to form.

I know how bad she wants this interview, but I take nothing for granted. If, in fact, she has been in touch with Floyd, there's a good chance he's talked her into cooperating. I'm not stupid. I know the only thing better than having me on her show is luring me into a trap. An even better ending for her stupid podcast series.

One-thirty, from a park bench, I call Dakota.

"Are you close?"

"A few miles away. There's more traffic than I figured, but I'll be there by two."

"I'll call again."

She starts to say something, but I hang up before she can get the words out.

At eleven-fifty, I call again. She picks up immediately.

"According to Miranda, that's what I call my G-P-S, I'm about seven minutes away."

"I'll call again in exactly three minutes."

"Francis, this is getting ridiculous..."

"Just do what the fuck I say."

"All right."

In three minutes, I call again.

"Now what?" she says. I can hear the irritation in her voice. She's off-balance. I'm getting under her skin.

"Where are you?"

"A block or two from the park."

"Good. Now, I want you to find San Rafael Avenue and park your car.

"How will I communicate with you?"

"Don't worry about that." I wait a few seconds. "Are you there yet?"

"I'm just pulling onto San Rafael."

"Do you see a spot to park?"

"Um, yes."

"Park the car."

"Okay."

"And don't hang up till I tell you to."

Half a minute later, she says, "Okay. I'm parked. Now what?"

"As soon as this conversation is over, I want you to shut down the phone. Take the battery out and leave the phone and the battery on the front seat of the car. Then, get out of the car and start walking west, toward the ocean, in the direction of the park. Do you understand?"

"Yes."

"Understand this, Dakota. If you use your phone to call anyone before you shut it down, I'll know it."

"I'm not going to call anyone, Francis."

"Make sure you don't. When you get to the park, veer right and walk toward the playground."

"Then what?"

"You'll find out."

"I don't like the idea of my not having a phone with me. What if something goes wrong and I need it?"

"I'll make sure nothing goes wrong, Dakota. Now, start walking."

54
Dakota

I'm a bundle of nerves. Without my phone I feel completely naked and vulnerable. I consider calling Charlie before I deconstruct my phone, to ask him what to do, find out where he is. But I'm afraid Francis is watching me, and if he sees me do that, he'll know something's wrong.

So, I follow his instructions. I shut down the phone and I take out the battery. I place both on the passenger seat. I can pretty much guess what Francis is probably doing. He's calling me to see if my phone is off. He's smart. Probably smarter than I am. So, I'm going to do just what he asks me to do.

I get out of the car and, with all my equipment stuffed in my backpack, start walking west, toward the park. I can't help wondering if I'm being watched. By Francis? By Charlie? By the cops? By everyone in the fucking world? Suddenly, it feels like I'm in a movie I can't get out of. I have this sick feeling deep in the pit of my stomach. I wish I were anywhere else but here.

To calm myself, I count my steps. One. Two. Three. Four…

I cross the avenue and I enter the park. I see the playground area in front of me, but it's empty. My mind goes just where it shouldn't. How was Francis able to arrange that no one would be around? Or was it Charlie and the cops? I begin to wonder if I'm in the right place, as if there could possibly be two playgrounds in this park.

I catch myself being ridiculous, but I can't help it.

I reach an empty bench. I look around. Still, no one in sight. I sit down. I put my backpack beside me. I cross my legs and wait. Knowing Francis, I'm sure he's being super careful, watching to see if anyone's watching me before he shows himself. I take a quick glance up toward the sky, looking for a drone. Trouble is, I don't even know what to look for, since I've never seen one before. Besides, there's a fifty-fifty chance Charlie was just playing with me. After all, I'm the one who mentioned a drone, not him. And so, when I see nothing other than a few seagulls swooping down, then back up again, patrolling the shore, I wonder if one of them could be the drone.

It's ten past two. Then twenty past. *This is not happening.* I'm starting to get angry. Like I've been stood-up by a treacherous lover. *I'll give it till two-thirty. Then I'm out of here.*

Two-thirty arrives. It's just me and the darn seagulls, who seem to have called for reinforcements. Time to pack it in.

I get up and start the long walk back to my car. I feel like a failure. Charlie Floyd has put his faith in me and I've failed. All I want to do is go home and pull the covers over my head. But now, thanks to Francis Hoyt, I can't even do that. Because, if home means safe haven, I'm not even sure I have one.

I'm back at the avenue, waiting for the light to change so I can cross the street to where my car is parked and then head back to L.A. A man walking a bicycle suddenly appears beside me. He's wearing shorts and a sweatshirt. He's got a baseball cap pulled down low and he's wearing sunglasses.

It takes a moment before I realize who it is.

It's Francis!

"Don't look around. Don't react," he hisses. "When the light changes, I'm gonna take off and I want you to cross the street and head back to your car. When you get there, I want you to read this," he says, and he stuffs a crumpled paper in my hand.

"I don't understand. What about the interview?"

"No interview today."

"But...you promised, Francis," I whine. "If not today, when?"

"How'd you feel when they told you there's no Santa Claus or the Tooth Fairy?"

"Excuse me?"

"Pretty shitty, right? But you got over it. You'll get over this, too. Read the fucking note and you'll understand everything."

The light changes. Francis hops on his bicycle and heads south. If I had my phone, I could call Charlie and alert him. But I don't. But they, whoever's watching out for me, must see what's going on from the drone, right?

When I get back to the car, before I reassemble my phone, I read Francis's note.

Dakota, sorry about the change of plans. But things haven't quite worked out the way I thought they would. I've gotten myself in a bit of a mess and I have to straighten things out before I can consider helping you out with your "little podcast thing." Just kidding. When you get back to L.A., check your mailbox. You'll find a long letter from me explaining everything. Trust me, it'll make a great story for your podcast. Get one of those L.A. actors to read the letter aloud on your show. I promise you'll have quite the scoop. And I swear every single word of it is true. You're gonna be famous, Dakota, and it's all because of me.

I'm sure our paths will eventually cross again. And I'll be listening to your show, just to make sure you get everything right.

Hasta la vista, Baby!

55
Dakota

The letter arrives the next day. And it is just what Francis said it would be. A bombshell. He gives a detailed account of a crazy job he was involved with. It's so crazy, it's gotta be true. It's about a mob vault he was hired to rob, but it didn't quite turn out that way. In the letter, he names names.

Charlie, a very disappointed man, leaves L.A. the next day. By then, I've read the letter to him and I offer to drive him to the airport so I can tell him all about it. He accepts.

The first thing I ask him is why the authorities didn't descend on Francis when they had the chance.

"We screwed up, Dakota. We were there, in a manner of speaking. We really did have a drone on you when you were in the park. But when he didn't show, we figured it was aborted so we just brought the drone home. It wasn't my call. I would have stuck with you. But the cops there, who weren't as invested as I am, got fed up, thought they were on a wild goose chase. So, they bagged it. There's no one more disappointed than I am. We'll get him. I'm sure of that. It's just that yesterday wasn't the day."

I hand him the letter and have him read it while I continue on to the airport.

When I see he's finished, I ask, "So, what do you think?"

"Some story."

"Do you believe it?"

He nods. "Yeah, I do. Maybe."

"Maybe? Do you believe it or not?"

"Francis Hoyt is a liar. He lies to himself. He lies to everyone else. But you know what they say. Even a stopped clock is right twice a day."

"So, what do you think I should do?"

"I think you should do just what he says. Read it on your podcast."

"But it takes him off the hook for the robbery. And maybe it's just a ploy. Maybe he was the one who ripped them off and he's just creating a smoke screen for himself."

"It's not something I'd put past him, but I think he's telling the truth here. Part of me is tempted to tell you not to read it on the show. Just tear it up into little pieces and flush it down the toilet. Let him twist in the wind. Don't let him use you and your show to clean up his mess. But that would be vindictive. It would drag me down to his level. And I'm not quite there yet. Besides, you know what?"

I glance over at him in the passenger's seat and he's smiling. "No, what?"

"Truth is, you couldn't ask for a better story for your podcast. He must really like you."

"You think?"

"I do. Of course, this is totally self-serving. It's a way of announcing to the world, and especially to the mob, that he wasn't involved at all. And it's also a way of getting back at whomever he thinks is involved. He could have just sent this letter to the L.A. *Times* or some other paper. They'd print it. But he gave it to you."

I'm looking straight ahead, making it appear as if I'm keeping my eyes on the road. But I'm doing more than that. I'm thinking about Francis Hoyt. I'm thinking what a conniving son of a bitch he is. But the thing of it is, while I'm thinking that, I've got the biggest darn smile on my face.

ACKNOWLEDGMENTS

It might take a village to raise a child, but it also takes that same village to produce a novel. On one level, writing is a solitary pleasure (or curse), but any writer worth his or her salt will be quick to acknowledge that many hands go into the finished product. So, here goes my thanks to some of those hands.

One of the best things that came out of the pandemic was what I like to call the Monday Night Zoom Boys. Five crime writers who for almost two years met every single Monday evening. We talked about everything under the sun, even writing occasionally, and I think that connection benefited all of us. For me, it helped me focus on my writing, almost like a weekly check-in since one of the questions was always, "How's work going?" So, many, many thanks to my friends forever: Reed Farrel Coleman, Michael Wiley, Matt Goldman and Tom Straw.

Once again, I'd like to thank Eric Campbell for giving life to my novels, and Lance Wright, who answers every question thrown at him with good humor, and who does most if not all of the heavy lifting. I'd like to thank Cynthia Bushmann and Sharon Gurwitz whose eagle eyes pick up errors that would easily elude me. And many thanks to Margo Nauert for the cover.

Thanks to my long-time West Coast friend Janet Kirby Stoegerer, who offered geographical suggestions in and around L.A. Many thanks to Lauren Bright Pacheco who taught me everything I had to know about podcasters and podcasting.

And finally, I'd like to thank Christina Chiu, Dawn Raffel, Elise Zealand, Helen Zelon and Sally Koslow for helping me keep my nose to the grindstone.

CHARLES SALZBERG is a freelance writer who has lived in New York City his whole life. He is a former magazine journalist who's written for *New York* magazine, *Esquire, The New York Times, The New York Times Book Review, Redbook* and other periodicals. He is the author of more than two dozen nonfiction books. His first novel, *Swann's Last Song,* was nominated for a Shamus Award. In addition to the Swann series, he is author of *Devil in the Hole,* named one of the best crime novels of 2013 by *Suspense* magazine, *Second Story Man,* winner of the Beverly Hills Book Award and nominated for a Shamus Award and the David Award, and he has novellas in the collections *Triple Shot, Three Strikes* and *Third Degree.* He teaches writing at the New York Writers Workshop, where he is a Founding Member, and is on the Board of MWA-NY.

On the following pages are a few
more great titles from the
Down & Out Books publishing family.

For a complete list of books and to
sign up for our newsletter,
go to DownAndOutBooks.com.

Right Between the Eyes
Scott Loring Sanders

Down & Out Books
February 2023
978-1-64396-300-6

When a young girl is abducted in an historic New England town in 1981, a family seeks full and total revenge.

Decades later, when two boys skip school to go fishing at Thoreau's iconic Walden Pond, instead of catching a trophy bass, they reel in a human skull which once again brings to the forefront a litany of wicked lies and murderous betrayal.

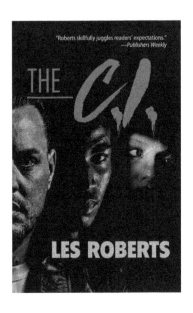

The C.I.
Les Roberts

Down & Out Books
March 2023
978-1-64396-303-7

Laird Janiver, a retired former marine major, is called on to help Jericho Paich, his live-in lover's young son, accused of high-level drug peddling and forced to turn non-paid squealer for the cops, especially the vicious Detective Keenan Mayo. The young man's girlfriend, Jill, has disappeared, too. Reluctantly, Janiver agrees, though the two men are of different races and dislike each other.

Hired hit men after Jerry and a brutal albino drug lord get in the way of Janiver's dangerous investigation, along with a beautiful woman with a questionable past.

Drums, Guns 'n' Money
A Lou Crasher Thriller
Jonathan J. Brown

Down & Out Books
March 2023
978-1-64396-305-1

Rock drummer turned amateur P.I. Lou Crasher has just found his good friend Trix Rockland murdered. Forming an odd partnership with attractive detective Tanaka, the two launch go at the list of suspects. The case begins at L.A.'s rock scene and moves into illegal incarceration, and possibly the for-profit prison system.

"*Drums, Guns 'n' Money* is a jazzy up tempo mystery that kicks like a snare roll. Jonathan Brown brings his musicality to this down and dirty crime story. Loved it!"
—SA Cosby, bestselling author of *Razorblade Tears*

More Groovy Gumshoes
Private Eyes in the Psychedelic Sixties
Michael Bracken, Editor

Down & Out Books
April 2023
978-1-64396-306-8

The Sixties were a time of great cultural upheaval, when long-established social norms were challenged and everything changed: from music to fashion to social mores. And the *Leave It to Beaver* households in Middle America didn't know what to make of it all.

From old-school private eyes with their flat-tops, off-the-rack suits, and well-worn brogues to the new breed of private eyes with their shoulder-length hair, bell-bottoms, and hemp sandals, the shamuses in *More Groovy Gumshoes*—a follow-up to the far-out original *Groovy Gumshoes*—take readers on another rollicking romp through the Sixties.

Printed in the USA
CPSIA information can be obtained
at www.ICGtesting.com
LVHW091802161023
761251LV00001B/107